Champion
A *Just Cause Universe* Novel

Ian Thomas Healy

Local Hero Press Edition

Champion: A Just Cause Universe Novel
Published by Local Hero Press

1st Printing
Local Hero Press: trade paperback, November 1, 2014
Printed in the United States of America

ISBN-13: 9781971445069

Cover art by Irshad Karim
Book design by Ian Thomas Healy

Books by Local Hero Press

The *Just Cause Universe*

Just Cause
The Archmage
Day of the Destroyer
Deep Six
Jackrabbit
Champion
Castles
The Lion and the Five Deadly Serpents
Tusks
The Neighborhood Watch
Jackrabbit: Big In Japan
Arena
Hero Academy
The Path
Cinco de Mayo
Search and Rescue
Rooftops
Plague
Soldiers of Fortune
Just Cause Universe Compendium
Destroyer of Earth
Flint and Steel
The Club
Jackrabbit: Rinse and Repeat
Posse
Extinction Event
Rain Must Fall

Pariah of Verigo

Pariah's Moon
Pariah's War

Three Flavors of Tacos

The Guitarist
Making the Cut
The Scene Stealers

Collections

Airship Lies
High Contrast
The Good Fight
The Good Fight 3: Sidekicks
The Good Fight 4: Homefront
The Good Fight 5: The Golden Age
Muddy Creek Tales
Caped

Other Novels

Assassin
Blood on the Ice
Funeral Games
Hope and Undead Elvis
Horde
The Murder Squad (2026)
Roast Wyvern (and Other Recipes)
Starf*cker
Strings
The Oilman's Daughter
Troubleshooters

Nonfiction

Action! Writing Better Action Using Cinematic Techniques

Acknowledgements

It's been awhile since I visited Mustang Sally's story, and I'm thrilled to be back telling tales about the character that launched the Just Cause Universe. I am indebted to the crack team that helps me bring every new JCU book to completion. Great thanks go to my beta readers, Ben, Karmyn, and Becky. Their feedback helped bring the story to the next level. I'm so happy to have newcomer to the JCU Irshad Karim providing a phenomenal cover. Special thanks to Frank Byrns for his introduction and for giving me my very first break in publishing. A big hearty thank-you to my fellow conspirators at the Pen & Cape Society. I couldn't have done it without the love and support of my two closest friends Shewanda and Allison. And to my family, for putting up with all my writerly foibles, I have nothing but gratitude.

Introduction

A familiar story, at least around my house:

I get an opportunity of some kind to present one of my stories in some way to a new audience. An invitation to contribute to an anthology. A chance to read one of my stories to an audience. An audio adaptation. Something like that.

So, invariably, I go to my wife. My first reader, my harshest critic, my champion. "Hey," I say, "What story do you think I should pick for this one?"

"Oh, I don't know . . ." she stalls.

"You know, something really representative of my work, something that would really show people what my stuff is all about."

"Hey," she says, warming to the task. "How about that one about the girl, you know, the one trying to break the land speed record."

I shake my head. I've heard this before. "I didn't write that one," I say.

"No, no," she says. "I'm talking about the one that takes place in the salt flats in Utah, and mom is there, and she used to be a superhero, too—"

"Yeah, I know the story," I say. "The girl is Mustang Sally—it's called 'Graceful Blur.'"

"Yeah, that one—pick that one."

"I didn't write that."

"Huh. You're sure?"

"Yeah, pretty sure."

"Well, you should have," she says. "That's a good one."

* * *

"Graceful Blur" *is* a good one. And even if I didn't write it, I can put a small claim on it: I published it. The Mustang Sally story was my second exposure to an unknown (to me, at least) author named Ian Thomas Healy. We published his story "Scent of Rose Petals" in the tenth issue of *A Thousand Faces, the Quarterly Journal of Superhuman Fiction*, then followed that one up with "Graceful Blur" in #11. I introduced it like this in that particular issue:

> *Now, if you're like me, I know you've been dying to read a superhero story set in the Bonneville Salt Flats that has no costumes (not exactly), no super-villains, and no violence. Trust me, you have. Check out Ian Thomas Healy's "Graceful Blur", then tell me I'm wrong.*

Ian's subsequent novels in his Just Cause Universe have checked off all of the boxes I mentioned many times over: Costumes, Supervillains, and Violence galore. All the things the discerning reader of superhero fiction has come to love and expect. And I don't want to give too much away regarding the novel you're about to read, but I've read it, and it definitely won't disappoint.

Best of all (for me, anyway)? It's a Mustang Sally novel. This book brings the Just Cause universe full circle for me, back to where it all really began. The hero of the story that I should have written myself.

I haven't told my wife yet. When she finds out I have a full-length Mustang Sally adventure in my hands, she just might snatch it right out of—

Frank Byrns
July 2014

Chapter One

"When you go out into the world, don't be afraid to try new things. You may have talents as yet unrealized which are unrelated to your powers. Don't be blinded simply by the fact that you are parahumans. First and foremost, you're humans."

—Sunstorm, Hero Academy commencement, May 25, 1998

December, 2006
Denver, Colorado

Sally had broken another treadmill, and the people from Ford Motor Company were pissed about it.

She blamed the weather, of course. It had been a chilly winter, and an Arizona girl like her was miserable anytime the thermometer dropped below freezing. When she couldn't run outdoors, as was her preference, she had a treadmill built especially for her by Ford engineers in return for her agreeing to appear in a commercial shown during the Super Bowl. They assured her it would be sturdy and operational up to speeds of three hundred miles per hour. That was less than half of her top speed, and honestly, nobody could keep in any kind of shape just trotting.

She was a speedster and a superhero and she was going to push herself, because someday she was going to break the speed of sound . . . on foot.

The treadmill had let her slowly ratchet up her speed past three hundred and approach four hundred miles per hour. Then the special low-friction carrier rollers started smoking as her feet blurred across the monofilament belt. The fumes reached her nose and she leaped off the machine just as the belt snapped and blasted a crater into the wall of the underground training facility for Just Cause, the greatest superhero team in the world.

Jack told her it had measured on the Richter scale, but she figured he was full of shit.

She'd been fortunate not to have been hurt; although her reflexes were fast enough to let her twist in the air like a cat and stop on a dime when needed, if she tripped or fell at those kind of speeds, well, there wasn't a word for the kind of road rash she could suffer.

Nevertheless, she was out a treadmill, and Juice had made her call Ford and explain what happened.

Now she had to run outdoors in the ridiculous Arctic conditions that Denver called winter.

"Hey, babe, what's up?" Jason walked into the room holding a coffee pot swirling with cream and sugar in one hand. "You look like you're expecting a blizzard."

"I'm going to go run out in the frozen tundra," said Sally. "It sucks."

"Babe, it's like forty degrees out there right now." Jason eyed her slender form with amusement. She was wrapped up in a layer of thermals, sweatshirt, and topped it all off with a *Mustang Sally*-logo stocking cap a fan had made for her. "You're going to roast once you start running."

"Some of us aren't as hot-blooded as you." She pulled on two pairs of socks.

Jason grinned. "Oh, I don't know. You were pretty hot-blooded last night."

A year ago, she might have blushed at such blatant flirting from him, but she and Jason had become comfortable with each other in all the months they'd been living together in Just Cause headquarters. Paparazzi and celebrity websites delighted in posting pictures of the young superhero couple, "the Heirs Apparent to the throne of parahuman power," as one local reporter had named them. Girls swooned over Jason's towering height, thick muscles, and easygoing grin. His shoulder-length blond hair flopped in his face and his chin was perpetually unshaven, and Sally felt incredibly lucky to have been the one to win his heart. She had her own share of admirers who appreciated her slim form and lithe grace, but they were probably all perverts. At least, that's what she told Sondra.

Sally envied the long, ebony hair and flawless skin of her best friend, the winged Desert Eagle. Sondra kept reminding her she could always dye Sally's blonde braids, but Sally never got up the nerve to make that drastic a change to her appearance. Even though conventional wisdom was for speedsters to keep their hair short, Sally broke out in nervous sweats anytime someone suggested a haircut to her. She was proud of the tresses which hung to the small of her back.

Right now, she had those tresses coiled up into a pair of braids which she tucked up into her knit cap. She shivered and reached for Jason's coffee pot. "Is this still hot?"

"Hot and fresh. You know that's how I like it." Jason gave her that grin which always made her want to jump him.

"You really should cut back." She poured some into her favorite Happy Puppies mug, and then sipped it and made a face. "It needs more sugar."

"Hey, I'm bigger than most folks. It takes this much coffee just to get me going." He flexed an arm; Sally could almost hear the muscles creaking.

"Stop it, I have to go run." She held up her hands in feeble protest and spoke with a vehemence she absolutely did not feel.

He flopped onto the couch. "Suit yourself. I'll be here when you get back."

"Right there on the couch?"

"Maybe." He paused, considering. "Or maybe I'll be in bed."

She kissed the tip of his nose. "It's eight in the morning, loverboy."

"You have anywhere to be? It's our day off."

"I have Christmas shopping to do, doofus!"

"Christmas? But that's like a week away."

"What, do you wait until the last minute?"

"Of course not. Most of the stores are closed by then."

"All right, wise guy, I'm going to go run. Then when I come back I'm going to take a shower." She winked. "You're welcome to join me." She kissed him once more and headed for the door.

"Sally?"

She stopped. "Yeah, baby?"

"I love you."

She smiled. He'd been practicing. It sounded so nonchalant and natural now, compared to the struggle it had been for him to say it the first time. "I love you too. I'll be back soon."

In the dormitory hall, Sally bumped into Jack, Sondra's longtime beau. It reminded her that she hadn't picked out anything for them yet. She was leaning toward a spa weekend for the two of them. It was a little pricey, but Sally didn't have much to spend her salary on when room and board was covered by Just Cause. The amount in her savings account was embarrassing and she kept thinking she should talk to somebody about investing it or something.

"Hi, darlin'," said Jack. "Glad I ran into you. Listen, what do you want to do for the talent show?"

"Talent show?"

"At the Christmas party. Jason suggested we have a talent show and I think that's a great idea."

Sally blinked. "*Jason* suggested a talent show? *My* Jason? Is this an alternate universe?"

Jack grinned. "Yeah. Damnedest thing, isn't it? Anyway, we all have to do something."

"Like what? I don't really have any special talents. I can't play guitar or dance or anything." Sally felt her knees go a little watery as stage fright got a tenuous grip on her.

"I'm sure you'll think of something." Jack patted her shoulder and headed on up the hall.

"But all I do is super speed," called Sally after him. "I don't have any hidden talents!"

He didn't look back.

"Shit," she muttered. Any residual interest in running had vanished with Jack's revelation. She pulled out her phone to check the duty roster. Sondra was off, but she'd worked the night shift and might be sleeping since Jack wasn't with her. Sally decided a text message would be less intrusive if Sondra was already asleep.

R U awake?

A reply came momentarily. *Yes. What's up?*

Where R U?

Children's Hospital.

Can I meet U there?

Sure.

Like professional athletes did, Just Cause heroes made an effort to be involved in the community and especially charitable organizations. Sally visited a local center for disadvantaged kids regularly with Jason. They'd gone there on their first date and now she was very popular with the kids there. Sondra spent a lot of time visiting kids in the hospital and giving out extra feathers as special gifts. She was, as she said, always growing new ones.

Regulations required Sally to wear her costume any time she was using her powers off-base, so she stopped by the locker room in the training bunker to change. She gave a wide berth to the workmen who were repairing the damage she'd done to the wall with the ruined treadmill. A selection of four different versions of her red-and-yellow bodysuit waited in her locker. She bypassed the others in favor of the one with thermal lining and electric warmers in the gloves and boots. She called in to the Command Center to report she was leaving.

"Okay, Sally," said Octane. He was still a rookie in spite of being called into emergency service three summers ago when the Archmage threatened the world. He wasn't as fast as Sally, but the viscous fluid that formed his shiny black body allowed him to move much faster than anyone else on the team could fly or run. He didn't so much walk as *flow* from place to place. She liked him in a big sister kind of way, and had kind of taken him under her wing the way Sondra had with Sally. "Maybe we could spar later?"

"Sure, I'd like that." Sparring with Octane would be a good way to distract herself from her apparent lack of all other talents. The combination of his semi-liquid body and his speed made him a tricky and unpredictable opponent.

"Cool. Oh hey, what are you going to do for the talent show?"

"Um, it's a surprise." Sally winced at how bad her lie sounded, but Octane seemed to buy it.

"Okay then. Command Center out."

Sally took to the streets.

She was supposed to keep her speed under a hundred miles per hour on main roads. Most Denverites had grown accustomed to seeing brightly-attired parahumans racing through or over town, but there was always someone who wasn't paying attention and got surprised. In fact, she slowed down long enough to rap on the window of a teenage girl more interested in texting than driving. The girl jumped and the car wavered. Sally made a very clear set-aside-the-phone gesture with her thumb and pinkie. The girl nodded wide-eyed and set her phone down.

Sally knew she'd probably pick it back up the moment Sally moved on.

Sondra was circling lazily over the Children's Hospital like her namesake as Sally ran into the parking lot. With a great fluttering, the winged woman dropped down to the pavement and wrapped her strong arms around Sally. "Hey there."

"Hi," said Sally. "I'm half frozen. Can we go inside and get a hot chocolate?"

"Sure, long as you'll stop in and visit a few of my special friends here."

"I'll be happy to, just so long as I can warm up. Aren't you cold?"

Sondra's costume was mostly form-fitting white leather with turquoise and silver decorations in keeping with her Navajo heritage. Sally couldn't imagine it was very warm, especially a few hundred feet up in the air.

"I'm fine. Cold doesn't really bother me until it gets below zero."

"I'm surrounded by Eskimos." Sally walked through the rotating door.

Sondra followed, careful to fold her great brown and white wings in tight against her broad shoulders to keep them from getting pinched. "Well, we know who to call first if we ever start a third Just Cause team somewhere warm."

"Yes, please. Just Cause San Diego has a lovely ring to it."

"I might sign up for that one myself," said Sondra.

They bought hot chocolates from the barista cart outside the gift shop and then sat beside the indoor wishing fountain. Before Sally could speak her mind, they had to give attention and hugs to a few of the young patients passing through the lobby.

Finally Sondra turned to Sally. "Okay, kiddo, what's on your mind?"

"You know this talent show thing?"

"Sure." Sondra fixed her piercing gaze upon Sally. They were dark and ringed with gold like those of the bird whose name she'd chosen.

"Well, what are you doing for it?"

"Jack and I are singing a duet."

Sally gaped. "You sing?"

"Badly, but I can sort of carry a tune. Jack's much better. We're going to do the cheesiest song ever and bring down the house."

Sally chuckled at the thought of her two best friends singing a love song together. "Maybe I'll see if Jason will do something like that. I can sort of sing, too."

"Sweetie, I've *heard* you sing. Probably not a talent you want to share with anyone if you want to keep them as friends."

"Nice. Do you know what Jason's going to do?"

"I think he said he's going to do magic."

"Magic?" Sally's thoughts immediately flew to the Archmage they'd battled only the year before.

"Stage magic."

"Oh."

"Maybe he'll need an assistant."

"The party's in three days. He hasn't asked me. I think I'm supposed to do something myself." Sally sighed. "Sondra, I don't know how to do anything except be a superhero. I can't sing, I can't dance. I don't have any talents!"

"Sure you do. You just haven't explored outside of the world of superheroes enough yet."

"Who has time for that?" Sally sipped at her hot chocolate. It was too sweet, but she didn't mind because it was warming her.

"Sally, you're going to burn yourself out if you don't branch out. Nobody can be a full-time superhero. You've got to have down time. Hobbies. And I don't just mean humping Jason." Sondra winked.

Sally laughed. "It is one of my favorite pastimes. But yes, I'll try to find something else to do. I still don't know what I'm going to do for the talent show, though."

A commotion made them both look up. A clown was strolling through the lobby, followed by a gaggle of laughing and shouting kids. He was yukking it up as he kept a trio of bowling pins circling around from hand to hand. Sally sped up her perceptions to watch the pins on their path, how each one dropped perfectly into the clown's outstretched hand. The kids shrieked in delight and she knew how they felt as they watched the juggler.

To Sally's super-speed perceptions, it didn't look that hard at all.

"Hello, Earth to Sally," said Sondra.

She snapped back to normal perception. "Sorry, I just had an idea. I need to go to the store. You think there's a Juggling for Dummies book?"

Sondra smiled. "I wouldn't be surprised."

Over the next three days, Sally spent every spare minute learning to juggle. The first thing she learned was that it was a whole lot harder than it looked, even with super-speed and accelerated perceptions. If she threw inaccurately, all a clumsy super-speed lunge to save the ball would do is send it rocketing away. The same thing happened if she moved her hands too quickly—she'd bounce the balls off the ceiling. After accidentally breaking an overhead fluorescent in the team's conference room, Juice banished her to the Combat Training Facility, where she'd have to work to do any damage to the walls. She spent half the time chasing after stray balls under the high overhead sodium arc lights, but slowly started to make progress. The CTF techs were amused by her juggling efforts, but none of them teased her and they applauded when she managed to put together a reasonable series of exchanges. Sally didn't mind; she needed to get over her stage fright enough to stand up in front of her teammates and try to juggle for them.

The Just Cause Christmas party happened to fall upon the same day as Sally's twenty-first birthday, so the party included a cake, champagne, and a rousing, off-key chorus of "Happy Birthday" to embarrass her. She tried to downplay the birthday, because it was the Christmas party and she didn't want it to just be about her. The champagne tickled her nose and she had two glasses, but stopped when she felt herself getting a little loopy. One more might have laid her out, and then she wouldn't have been able to walk, never mind juggle. She hoped a second slice of the chocolate cake would soak up some of the residual alcohol. Jason was working on his sixth, so she didn't feel like she was overeating.

The cafeteria had been redecorated with festive streamers and balloons. A large Douglas Fir stood in the middle, blazing with multicolored lights and tinsel. Younger siblings of team members, as well as Juice's daughters, ran around gleefully, shouting and laughing and eating candy canes. Many of the younger heroes' parents had attended, as well as a few of the retired heroes like John Stone and Sunstorm.

The food was delicious as always, prepared by the house executive chef who everyone whispered was precognitive in his ability to know exactly what people wanted to eat. When her mother wasn't looking, Sally took a taste of the thick, dark beer that Jason was enjoying and pronounced it incredibly nasty. The good spirits and cheer of her teammates made her feel brave, and she found she was actually looking forward to showing off her new talent of juggling.

"It's a lovely party, Sally," said Faith Thompson, Sally's mother who had once been the speedster called Pony Girl. "Thanks for inviting me." She'd come up from Phoenix at Sally's insistence, and was spending most of the party talking with Jason's parents who'd flown in from Atlanta.

"Of course, Mom. I'm glad you came."

Eventually Jack stepped up onto the makeshift stage and took hold of a microphone. "Hello, everyone," he said. "Welcome to my honored teammates, families, and friends, to the first annual Let's Embarrass Ourselves Just Cause talent show!"

The rest of the people at the party applauded. "We'll kick things right off with our fearless leaders, James 'Juice' Forsythe and Stacey 'Doublecharge' Martin."

Looking like they were dressed as presenters for the Academy Awards, Juice in his tuxedo and Doublecharge in a sparkling white gown met on stage and delivered a hilarious sketch full of inside jokes about Just Cause and parahumans in general. Sally laughed as loud as anyone; Doublecharge had a dour personality and wasn't known even to smile very often, but she delivered her straight lines with great aplomb.

The rookies Carver and Snowball had an ice-sculpture race; Carver used his vibrational powers to cut apart a large chunk of ice while Snowball manufactured her sculpture from the ground up. When they finished, Carver was soaked from head to toe and proudly displayed what he called a tribute to Mustang Sally, the birthday girl. Sally thought it looked like a shapeless blob with arms hanging off it but she was effusive with her praise. Snowball, who was not quite three feet tall, showed off a piece of ultramodern art sculpture that she named Living in a Tall World.

Ment, the young psi, didn't have any talents to share, but instead he regaled them all with a tale about his father, who had been a pathetic bottom-feeder of a super-villain in the '70s. His final humiliation at the hands of Just Cause came in, of all things, a poker game. Ment told the tale in an animated style, with lots of gesturing and moving about the stage, applying the talent and timing of a stand-up comedian.

After that, Jack and Sondra sang a rendition of Kenny Rogers' and Dolly Parton's *Islands in the Stream* that was both funny and horrifying at the same time, mainly because Jack wore a fake grey beard and wig and stuffed a pillow in his shirt, while Sondra had shoved two inflated balloons inside her own top and put on a bleach-blonde wig.

Octane came out with some surprisingly good and funny impressions of the other members of the team. When he did Jason, he shaped his hands to look like a big sandwich and proceeded to 'eat' them all the way past the wrists, which had Sally and the others howling with laughter. The running joke amongst his teammates was that being too close to Jason while he was eating meant risking one's limbs to his prodigious appetite.

"Next up . . . Sally." Jack wiped away tears of laughter as he introduced her.

"Uh, hi everyone," said Sally as she stepped onto the stage. "I just learned how to juggle, sort of. Anyway, I hope I don't screw this up."

She picked up three tubes of tennis balls and started working them in cycles. The plastic tubes gleamed in the bright lights, and the weight of the fuzzy green balls made them spin like they were traditional bowling clubs. She was concentrating so hard that she didn't have time to remember her stage fright.

"A lot of people who juggle try to tell jokes while they're doing it." She tried to move her hands mechanically as she spoke. "I'm not very good at telling jokes, though. Whoops!" A canister got away from her and she had to lunge at super-speed to save it. "I bet you thought I was going to drop it."

The audience laughed.

"Anyway, um, here's my joke. I promise it's not as dirty as it sounds, parents. What do you do with an elephant with three balls on him?" She started flinging the canisters higher. "Jack, be quiet. I know you know this one."

"I don't know, what?" shouted Carver from his table.

"You walk him and pitch to the rhino." Sally changed from a crossing to a circular pattern. She was ready for her big finish.

As the audience either burst out laughing or groaned, Sally switched into her high-speed perceptions. She caught a tube, pulled the top off, and dropped out the three balls. She tossed the empty tube away and sequenced the three tennis balls into the pattern. Then she repeated the same thing with the other two tubes. In a moment she went from juggling three tubes to nine balls.

The onlookers cheered and whistled, applauding her. She grinned. "Thanks, you guys! I just wish I knew how to stop."

They laughed as she bowed her head, held out her hands, and let nine tennis balls rain down upon her.

"That was awesome," said Sondra.

"Thanks. Where's Jason?"

Sondra's eyes sparkled. "He's next."

Jack stepped up to the microphone. "Thanks, Sally. That was impressive. I think we'll wrap up the evening with Jason the Magician and his lovely assistant Minerva." A twinge of jealousy shot through Sally's heart.

Like Sally, Minerva was the granddaughter of an original Just Cause member, only her powers had skipped a generation between Lady Athena and her. Of all parahumans Sally had ever met or even heard of, Minerva's were the least defined or understood. She had exhibited such a startling diversity of abilities that Sally wasn't sure there was anything Minerva couldn't do if she chose. Why had Jason chosen her to be his assistant? It had to be something with her powers, Sally thought. That must have been it.

She stood quietly to one side of Jason as he fumbled his way through some sleight of hand and card tricks. Sally made herself not speed up her perceptions at all, to give his sleight-of-hand at least a chance to impress her.

"Uh, for my last, uh, trick I'll need a volunteer."

A dozen hands shot up, but Minerva stepped down lightly from the stage, her velvety robe whispering, to take Sally's hand. Blushing, Sally followed Minerva back up to stand next to Jason.

"Now, uh, I understand that you did something naughty the other day. Not with me," he said quickly, blushing, "but you broke your treadmill, right?"

"Yes." Sally couldn't imagine where he was going with this. Surely he wasn't just going to embarrass her on stage.

He reached up and brushed her hair with his fingers. "This is a lump of coal." Sally was impressed; she hadn't seen him palm it at all. "Naughty children get coal for Christmas. But through the ancient, uh, art of alchemy, I'm going to transform this coal into something else."

He closed his fist around the coal. Sally could see the muscles in his forearm bulging out against his custom-tailored suit jacket as he squeezed. "It's just a matter of pressure and temperature and proper incantations." He grunted with the effort. His hand started to glow and everyone heard a hissing noise.

Steam or smoke leaked out from the cracks between his fingers. "Abracadabra, hocus pocus." He waved his other hand over his clenched fist.

With a bright flash and a wash of heat across Sally's face, Jason opened his hand. Something sparkly rolled around amid his blackened palm.

"No way," said Sally. He couldn't have really just made a diamond.

"You're right, babe," said Jason. "It's not finished yet." He closed his hand once more and waved his free hand over it. When his fingers uncurled once more, his hand was clean, and a small velvet box nestled in his palm.

Sally's heart skipped a beat. Maybe it skipped several, but it was hammering so fast that she wouldn't have noticed. Her throat seemed to constrict around a large lump.

Jason lowered himself to one knee and raised the box toward her. "Sally, you're the most important person in the world to me. I love you, and I don't want to be apart from you. When you're gone, I miss you like crazy." He smiled up at her. "I hardly even eat."

He paused for a moment. Sally heard a few muted sniffles around the room.

"You told me once that we should live for the moment because nobody knows what the future might bring. I guess what I'm trying to say in front of all these people is . . . Sally Thompson, will you marry me?" He opened the box. Inside she saw a diamond solitaire. It blurred into a thousand sparkles as tears spilled down her cheeks.

She'd never been so happy in all her life. "Yes, Jase, I will."

Everyone applauded and cheered as Jason slipped the ring onto Sally's finger. As she held it up, the diamond in it sparkled and she realized she was crying. Then Sondra and her mom were both hugging her. Sondra's feathers tickled her nose and she laughed.

The party changed tone after that. Everyone came up to congratulate her and Jason, who was beaming like a fool and blushing like a sunburned lobster.

"You doofus!" She punched him gently in the arm. "How did you ever keep that a secret?"

"I had Ment put a psionic block in my brain to prevent me from talking about it." He laughed. "You know I can't keep secrets from you."

She kissed him.

Her phone buzzed. So did Jason's. Everyone on the team pulled phones from their belts or out of their pockets to look at them. Even at the Christmas party, they were always on call.

It was an alert from MetalBlade, commander of the Just Cause Second Team, in Richmond, Virginia: *Orb collapsed in his lab an hour ago. Paramedics were unable to revive him.*

Chapter Two

"An individual, in promoting his own interest, may injure the public interest; a nation, in promoting the general welfare, may check the interest of a part of its members."

—Friedrich List

December, 2006
Denver, Colorado

Sally hugged her knees in the lounge at the end of the hallway in the heroes' dormitory. She perched on a couch while Jason softly stroked her hair. Minerva, Ment, and Snowball sat with them, lending silent support.

"I can't believe he's gone," said Sally. "He was only twenty-one, same as me." She sniffled. "He was in my class at the Academy."

She remembered Orb well. He had an affinity with technology that hadn't been seen among parahumans before. He was a soft-spoken young man with sparkling eyes and a bright smile. He built fantastic floating spheres the size of softballs, each with its own unique abilities that only he could control. They'd reminded Sally of the special effects balls from the *Phantasm* movies, except none of them ever drilled a hole in anybody's skull. Wherever he went, the spheres circled around Orb like planets around a sun.

He'd been Sally's friend, and now he was gone.

Octane flowed into the room. "Hey, guys, turn on CNN, quick!"

"Dude, show a little respect, would you?" Ment shook his head.

Octane extruded a tentacle, snagged the remote, and turned on the television. "Sorry," he said. "But you need to see this."

"—rescued eleven people from a burning tenement building in Brooklyn," said the pert and perky reporter. The crawl beneath her read NEW MASKED HERO SAVES LIVES. "Here is the amateur video shot by one of the rescued people."

The screen shifted to a shaky, grainy video of a man in a garish yellow bodysuit with orange trim, a full-face mask, and a cape.

"Oh my God," said Ment. "Who wears a cape? The Fifties called. They want their costume back."

"Shush," said Minerva, whose flowing robes were as much like a cape as Ment's large black overcoat.

"Who are you?" asked an off-camera voice.

"Champion." It was impossible to tell if the man in the suit spoke; his mask covered even his mouth. The voice conveyed power and strength. He raised his arms and a glow surrounded him, even visible in the daylight, and he flew away. People clapped and cheered and then the video cut off.

The scene cut back to the reporter. "Champion has so far not been identified. Although he is technically breaking the law by hiding his face, his actions today have already garnered support from many New Yorkers."

The scene cut again to a streetside interview. "I think it's ridiculous that the law says he can't be masked," said a man in a business suit as people behind him mugged at the camera. "He's just protecting his loved ones from the media and supervillains, isn't he?"

Another cut showed a couple of young women on the same street. "We love Champion!" they said in unison that had probably been rehearsed.

"Whatever his story," said the reporter as the camera showed her again, "it appears New York has a new hero in residence. In other news . . ."

Octane shut off the television. "Pretty cool, huh?"

"Why do you suppose he's masked?" asked Sally.

"Like the guy said, probably to protect his family. Maybe he's already famous or something," said Ment. "Doublecharge wears a mask."

"So does Jason, but their identities are public record," said Sally. "They wear the masks as a tribute to the time when parahumans were allowed to operate anonymously."

Ment shrugged. "I don't see it's that big a deal."

"People, especially those in the government, are already afraid of us for our powers," said Minerva. "Add anonymity to that and they'll have a reason to start persecuting paras as threats like they did back in the Fifties."

Ment shrugged. "Whatever."

Sally felt her ire rising with the young psi, sitting smugly in all black with his sunglasses on indoors. She opened her mouth to take him to task when all their phones buzzed.

Emergency mandatory staff meeting. Fifteen minutes. Active watch duty or your own death only good excuses to miss. Juice.

"Emergency staff meeting?" Jason shook his head. "I don't like the sound of that."

"What do you suppose is going on?" asked Octane.

"It wouldn't be an active callout," said Sally, "or else he would have said."

The group of young heroes convened in the conference room, for once all showing up early. *Almost* all, amended Sally, as Carver raced in just as Juice was about to page him.

"Thank you all for coming," said Juice. He looked angry to Sally, and his face was drawn tight as if he were holding back great emotions. "I have been informed today that effective at three o'clock P.M. this coming Friday I am no longer the commander of Just Cause."

The room blew up in furious, astonished questioning. Juice held up his hand for silence.

"That's bullshit, man," said Jason into the silence.

Juice smiled. "It's not quite as bad as it sounds. Through Executive Order, the President has authorized the creation of a Parahuman Resources Agency. It will become the new governing body over Just Cause and other American parahuman organizations and individuals, as well as be a clearing house of information." He sat back in his chair. "I've been asked to head up the Agency."

"So it's a promotion?" asked Sally. "They're kicking you upstairs?"

Juice gave her a wry smile. "Not exactly. People in Homeland Security aren't too happy with me after the way I bucked their authority in the Archmage fiasco."

Sondra slapped the table. "For God's sake, they were considering using nukes, James! You want to talk about a fiasco?"

"I know." Juice shook his head. "And we were fortunate that our plan worked in the end, or the last year might have gone very differently. As it played out, we were right and that didn't sit well with some of the DHS people."

"Plus you knocked that one chick on her ass," said Sally to Doublecharge.

Doublecharge graced them with one of her rare smiles. "She had it coming, and it felt very good."

"The other thing they're concerned with is my popularity. When I put together a parapowered army on a moment's notice to rescue Jack and Stacey in Guatemala, the higher-ups noticed. They're worried about someone with that kind of pull not having direct supervision." Juice poured himself a tumbler of water from the pitcher at his end of the table.

"So they put you in charge of all American parahumans?" Jason actually scratched his head; Sally thought it was the most adorable thing she'd ever seen. "How does that work?"

"Keep your friends close and your enemies closer," said Jack. "Ancient Chinese secret."

"He's right, but it's more than that." Juice drained his glass. "Being the head of this agency means I don't have the autonomous authority I once did. I'll have to get DHS approval for everything, from budgets to personnel, licensing, you name it."

"You're the goat," said Sondra.

"I am, as you say, the goat. Powerless."

"This sucks," said Jason.

"Not necessarily," said Minerva.

"How so?" asked Carver. "Because it's pretty jacked up if you ask me."

"He won't immediately be in a powerful position, but he'll have access to the most complete database of parahumans, maybe in the world. And a time is coming when that will be important." Minerva folded her arms and seemed to shrink in on herself.

"What do you mean, babe?" asked Ment.

"They hate us, fear us. Sooner or later they're going to go to war against us. Better we have some insiders."

Juice set down his tumbler with a loud clink. "You're talking a war with parahumans against . . . everyone else? Forgive me, but that's preposterous."

"It almost happened before. In the Fifties." Minerva nodded toward Sally. "She knows. There are people, leaders, who would rather we went away altogether."

Juice cleared his throat to let everyone know that conversation on that particular topic was done. "Anyway, since I'm still commander of the team for two more days, we have some business at hand. That would be the question of leadership." He leaned back. His chair creaked dangerously under his weight, but Sally had yet to see a Just Cause chair break under his or Jason's considerable bulk. "In my mind, there's only one person eminently qualified to lead this team, so I'm appointing Stacey Martin, Doublecharge, to assume duties as commander upon my departure." He turned to her. "I trust you and know you will do a fantastic job. You can turn down the position or request time to consider it if you need to."

"No," said Doublecharge. "I appreciate your faith in me, James. I'll try to live up to the standards you've set here."

"Then that's settled," said Juice, and everyone applauded. Sally had operated under Doublecharge's direct command before. She'd be a tough, no-nonsense kind of leader, but Sally felt that might be what Just Cause needed moving forward into a murky future.

"You're going to need a second-in-command," said Juice. "Your own Doublecharge."

"Jack." Doublecharge didn't hesitate with her selection. Sally was surprised at her choice. Doublecharge and Jack did not see eye to eye on a lot of things, and Jack was forever needling her about her lack of humor. Then Sally realized that a good second-in-command had strengths to play off the commander's weaknesses. Jack was more tactically-oriented, able to tackle small problems efficiently and effectively, whereas Doublecharge had good overall strategic vision, understanding the big picture.

"Sorry, I appreciate the consideration, but I'm going to pass," said Jack.

"Why?" asked Doublecharge.

Jack ticked off the points on his fingers. "I'm already well-established as the team's PR guy, and moving into a leadership position will cramp me there. I'm popular and well-liked, and if shit's going to hit the fan, we'll need that more than we need me running things. I'm happy to back you up and run a squad if needed, but I'm too much a people person to make the hard decisions."

Doublecharge nodded. "Okay, that's a good self-assessment. I appreciate your honesty, Jack."

"Can you see me leading this team? *It would be inconceivable!*" He winked at Sally as he fed her the quote.

"*You keep using that word. I do not think it means what you think it means.*" She and Jack were both movie buffs, and they'd found kindred spirits in each other with their love of quotes.

"All right, you two," said Juice, more gently than he might have in other circumstances.

"My second choice is actually you, Sally," said Doublecharge, turning to look at her.

"M-me? But I'm just, I mean, I've hardly been here at all." Sally felt her ears and cheeks grow hot.

"You've shown outstanding initiative, a willingness to put yourself at great risk for the sake of your teammates and the people you serve and protect, and have an excellent track record already. In my mind, you're strong leadership material." Doublecharge smiled again.

"It's just . . . I mean, thanks for thinking of me and all, but I just don't think I'm ready. I'm still a kid, you know?" Jason squeezed her hand in support. "Even though I'm engaged. Oh God, I'm turning into my mother in spite of everything. She got married at twenty-one too."

"You could do far worse than to turn out like your mother," said Juice. "She was an outstanding member of this team."

"Sally, I understand. It was a tossup between you and Sondra. Sondra?" Stacey turned to the winged woman.

Sondra smiled. "Sure, I'll be second-in-command. Anything to get to tell Jack what to do."

Everyone laughed.

"Jack, go get me a cup of coffee," said Sondra.

Grinning like a fool, Jack pushed back his chair.

"Oh, I like this already." Sondra laughed, making the tips of her wings quiver.

"Sit down, Jack," said Juice. "I'm glad we're all full of jocularity, but my last piece of business isn't very funny at all." He sighed. "Orb's memorial service is on Friday. Regulations don't allow me to let more than two members to attend."

Sally knew that was because a supervillain named Destroyer had sneak-attacked a hero's funeral in 1985. Her father had died in that attack, and she could have as well, since her mother had been there, pregnant with Sally.

"Sally, one of those spots is yours if you want it," said Juice.

"Yes, please," said Sally.

Doublecharge raised her hand to interrupt. "I think Jack should be the other attendee."

Sally growled internally. It seemed that the team was forever conspiring to keep her and Jason apart. Well, that would change once they were married. She glanced down at the diamond sparkling on her finger and smiled.

"Good point," said Juice. "Although a funeral shouldn't be thought of as a public relations opportunity, it is important for people to see the face of Just Cause there. They need to remember that even though we have powers, we're still human."

Doublecharge leaned forward. "Please convey our sincerest condolences to the Second Team. Jack, please take it seriously."

Jack smiled. "Hey, even I know when to be subdued."

"Unless anyone else has business to bring up, I believe we're done," said Juice. "Sally, Jack, I need to see you for a few minutes."

The others filed out of the conference room, leaving Sally and Jack to speak with Juice.

"What's up, boss?" Jack flopped into a chair and put his feet up on the table now that Doublecharge wasn't around to chastise him.

"Two things. First of all, Sally, I'm sorry I'm not sending Jason with you. I hate that I'm separating you two right after the engagement announcement. I know that he knew Orb too, but you'll see in a minute why I'm sending you with Jack."

"It's okay," said Sally with a sigh. "It'll only be a couple of days and then we'll be back home."

"Your other classmates, the Young Guns, are coming to the memorial service," said Juice. "I want you to reach out to them. I know they're fiercely independent and have a solid anti-authority streak, but they're a resource in the Northeast and I want them to know that both Just Cause and the PRA will support them."

Sally had fond memories of the rest of her graduating class from the Hero Academy: Johnny Go, who wasn't nearly as fast as Sally, but could move along vertical surfaces and even upside-down; the super-strong and tough Bombshell, who looked like a female bodybuilder; Toxic, the Goth girl who could draw man-made poisons out of the air, ground, and water; and last of all Surfboy, who couldn't fly any higher than six feet off the ground and never had stopped trying to get Sally in bed. None of them had passed the psychological testing to get into Just Cause, and Sally thought they were likable, if unbalanced. "Sure, Juice. I haven't talked to any of them since Guatemala."

"The reason I'm sending Jack is a little murkier. According to MetalBlade, when Orb died he was in his lab, working feverishly on some kind of project. He'd been at it for almost forty-eight hours straight. He suffered a Grade Six cerebral aneurysm. He was dead before he hit the floor. MetalBlade suspects some kind of foul play and frankly, so do I."

"Wait, you think he was murdered?" asked Sally.

"I don't know yet, but his death was suspicious enough that we're bringing in Grace from Paris to conduct the autopsy. Jack, you're by far the most technologically-minded of anyone on either team. You've also got a detective's instincts. I want you to investigate Orb's death and see if you can uncover anything untoward about it."

"I can already see there's untoward stuff around it. Nobody works forty-eight hours straight unless obsessed or terrified." Jack stood up. "I'll pack my gear."

Sally stood as well. She didn't have much to pack, but she would spend every minute she had left before they left with Jason.

"Good luck, you two," said Juice. "I'm afraid you might need it."

Chapter Three

"Dream as if you'll live forever, live as if you'll die today."

—*James Dean*

December, 2006
Richmond, Virginia

After their goodbye loving, Sally and Jason sprawled on the couch in their quarters naked, enjoying the feel of skin-to-skin contact. They'd left all the lights off except for the one in the bathroom, and that door was mostly shut. It made the small apartment they shared in headquarters seem much less like a hotel room and more intimate. Jason lay back, one hand behind his head and the other resting on Sally's back, while she nestled between him and the back of the couch, finding the warmest spot like an affectionate cat.

She gazed up into his eyes and smiled. "I want a summer wedding."

"This summer?"

She toyed with the blond curls on his chest. "No, next year. I want to enjoy being engaged for a little while. Flash the hardware around. Give the press more fodder."

"Yeah, because if there's one thing they don't have enough of, it's fodder. And what have I told you about using big words around me?" He grinned.

She slapped his chest. "If *fodder* is giving you fits, I think you're going to have a heck of a time with our vows. Some of those words have three, maybe even four syllables."

"Vows? You mean like *a, e, i, o, u,* and sometimes *y*?"

"No, you silly boy. Don't you know anything about weddings?"

"No, and neither do you."

"Well, that may be, but I'm a girl and weddings are in our genes."

"I like you in jeans almost as much as I like you out of them."

Sally slapped his chest again. "God, you're awful. You've been hanging around Jack too much."

"Not as much as you." Jason made his face into a hangdog expression.

Sally scooted up his chest to plant a kiss on the end of his nose. "I'm so mad that they're not letting us go together. I promise you, we'll get dispatched together next time if I have to pluck every feather out of Sondra's wings."

Jason laughed at that.

"I'm sure my mom will plan us a wonderful wedding," said Sally.

"Why's that?"

"Are you kidding? I'm her little girl. This is her last chance to play dress-up with anyone."

"Until we have kids."

"Kids? Us?"

"Why not? I love kids. I bet we'd make some darn good ones, too."

"Well, I don't know. I mean, I don't want to do that right away. I'd rather just be your wife for a good long while first."

A glint appeared in Jason's eyes. "That's okay. We can practice."

"Practice?"

Jason moved his hands lower.

"Oh, I see. Practice is good." She covered his mouth with hers.

An hour later, Jason walked Sally to the hangar. Jack was already waiting for them in the jet. Sally had hoped they might get to fly in the *Rita*, the team's regular transport jet, but instead one of the Learjets was warming up on the tarmac. It made sense, she realized. Sending the tactical response vehicle for a decidedly non-tactical situation would be foolish and wasteful.

She jumped up and wrapped her arms around Jason, kissing him deeply. "Goodbye, baby. I'll be back soon. I love you."

"I love you too. Have a safe trip."

Sally shouldered her bag and hurried up the steps into the jet. The flight steward closed the door behind her as she flopped down into a seat and shivered from being out in the cold even for a few minutes.

Jack looked up over the forensic science book he was reading. "Why, hello. Is it time to go already?"

"Wiseass. I'm sorry I'm late. I was just . . ."

"It's okay. I was *just* too." Jack winked.

Sally got out her iPod and a book as the jet taxied to the private Just Cause runway.

"If you get bored, I brought movies." Jack pulled a couple DVDs from his bag. "I can only read so much of this stuff before I need explosions and inane dialogue." He waved his book at her.

"Explosions sound good to me." Sally closed her book.

He started one of them up, but the sounds of air racing past the jet's hull combined with the thrum of the engines to make Sally drop off to sleep before the end of the exposition. She opened her eyes once during the second act of the film. It was just the way she remembered it when she'd seen it the first time, so she smiled and went back to sleep.

Jack shook her awake as they were on final approach to Just Cause Second Team's headquarters in Richmond, Virginia. Sally yawned and stretched and then pressed her nose against the glass to look down. JCST was on an island in the middle of the James River. The pilot came in low over the river; to Sally, it felt like a strafing run, except this one ended with a gentle bump as the wheels touched down.

MetalBlade and his wife Icebreaker waited in the hangar as the jet taxied to a halt. MetalBlade was a handsome young black man from the first graduating class of the Hero Academy back in 2000. He wasn't a large man by nature, although hours upon hours of gym time had built up his shoulders like cantaloupes. Whereas Juice had a rich milk chocolate skin, MetalBlade's was more of a cinnamon color. He and Icebreaker hadn't been in old Just Cause headquarters in the World Trade Center, unlike several other heroes who'd perished that day. His efforts to save lives and rescue people during the tragedy of 9/11 had made him the obvious choice to run the Second Team while the remainder of Just Cause relocated to the new Denver facility.

If MetalBlade was the heart of the Second Team, his wife Icebreaker was its soul. Her skin was almost blue like glacial ice, and her hair was the color of fresh snow. Her exotic, supermodel looks made her the most popular member of Just Cause in online searches.

Sally and Jack stepped off the plane and went to shake hands.

"Sally, Jack, it's good to see you again," said MetalBlade. "I only wish it could have been under happier circumstances."

"Keith, Ingrid, we're really sorry about Orb." Sally shook hands with them, wondering if she should have done more.

Ingrid smiled at her and gave Sally the hug she hadn't been sure whether or not to offer. "Thank you, Sally. We all miss him very much."

"Juice and the rest of the team send their condolences," said Jack. "He also detailed me to assist in the investigation."

"That's a relief." Keith led them inside the JCST headquarters building, which was round and sprawling like a pancake of glass and steel. "Dr. Devereaux is flying in from Paris. She'll be here later today to conduct the autopsy."

"Didn't the Feds start an investigation?" asked Sally. As Just Cause was part of Homeland Security, the FBI would be involved in any investigation involving Just Cause personnel.

"Started and finished," said Ingrid. "They sent an agent around. He asked a few questions, watched the video we have of Orb's collapse, read the medical report, and closed the case as *Natural Causes.*"

"But you don't think that," said Jack.

"No, because we knew Orb better than anyone." Keith brought them to his office, which had a sweeping panoramic view of the James River. "The way he was working went beyond his normal obsessive pattern. No eating, no sleeping. Nothing but lab work for the better part of two days. He was desperate to finish whatever it was. We can't figure it out, which isn't saying much. Most of what he built was so far beyond anybody's understanding anyway."

"I'll see what I can do to make sense of it," said Jack. "Never had much respect for the Feds except in their ability to fuck things up."

Keith and Ingrid both burst out laughing. "Oh my," said Ingrid. "That felt good. There hasn't been nearly enough laughter around here recently. I see someone's sporting some new jewelry. Congratulations on your engagement. You and Mastiff make a cute couple."

Sally smiled as she looked down at her ring once again. "Thanks."

Keith said, "I thought you'd like to know that the Young Guns are here."

Sally smiled. She missed her old classmates. "Where are they?"

"I think they're in the rec room. We're not having the memorial until tomorrow morning. I hope you'll join us for dinner tonight."

"Count on it," said Sally.

"Definitely. I haven't eaten since two time zones ago," said Jack. "Would someone show me to Orb's lab?"

"Follow me," said Ingrid.

"Um, where would I find—" began Sally.

"Out the door, go left to the end of the hall," said Keith. "They're putting on their bravest faces."

Ingrid looked back over her shoulder, a frown creasing her forehead. "I guess everyone deals with their grief differently."

Sally wondered what she meant by that. As she approached the rec room, she heard the commotion of her former classmates and then she understood why Ingrid had seemed a bit upset. The Young Guns didn't sound like they were grieving in the least. She wondered how she ought to approach them. Keeping Juice's request that she spend some time with them in mind, she decided that a full frontal assault would be the best way to go, so she strolled into the rec room like she owned it. Surfboy and Johnny Go were playing on the Xbox and shouting bloody murder at each other while Toxic and Bombshell were perched on the couch, defiantly trying to watch *Beaches*.

"I see Fred and Shaggy, Daphne and Velma," drawled Sally, "but where's Scooby Doo?"

"Sally!" shouted the Young Guns together. Then Johnny Go was hugging her; he was one of the rare superheroes who she didn't feel like a dwarf beside. He grinned at her and flipped his black hair back out of his face.

"Hey, move aside, make room for the dude," said Surfboy. He shoved Johnny out of the way.

Sally raised a warning finger. "Don't touch my ass."

"But—"

"Touch my ass, and I let my fiancé eat you."

"Fiancé?" Bombshell's squeal sounded funny coming from someone well over six feet tall with muscles like a linebacker.

"Cool. Congrats," said Toxic, whose smiles were as rare as Doublecharge's.

Surfboy was very careful to keep his hands on neutral territory. "It's good to see you. How's life in the big leagues?"

"Good to see you too, Stefan," said Sally. "It's been a quiet year. Except for, you know, this." She flashed her ring.

"That's awesome," said Johnny. "Seriously."

"So how is New York?" asked Sally.

"Oh, dude, it's unreal. They say it's the City that Never Sleeps, but you don't really get that until you're in the middle of it." Stefan laughed and floated off the ground to hover like a guru.

"It's cool," said Toxic, who was as petite as Sally but seemed even smaller and more waif-like because of her Goth appearance. "People love us there."

"And the food! Oh my God, I have to work out twice as much now," said Bombshell.

"What about Orb?" Sally asked. "You guys heard anything new?"

Bombshell shook her head. "Just that he died real suddenly. Like a stroke or something."

"I'm going to miss him," said Toxic.

"Yeah, me too," said Johnny. "He made cool stuff."

Surfboy held up his liter bottle of Mountain Dew. "To Orb."

The others raised their drinks if they had them. Sally zipped over to the sideboard and retrieved a bottle of water to join in the toast.

Surfboy poured out some of his soda on the floor. "For my homie."

"Dude, that's probably going to stain the carpet," said Bombshell.

"It looks like you couldn't hold your bladder." Johnny snickered.

Toxic raised a hand. "It's all right, I got this." She drew out all the man-made chemicals that suffused the stain, leaving behind only water. A goopy cloud of yellow swirled above the spill until Toxic directed it into the drain of the sideboard sink.

"I can't believe you drink that stuff," said Sally. "Are you trying to kill yourself?"

They spent the afternoon together, eschewing the video games, after much protest from the boys, for poker around one of the small tables.

"And she's good at poker, too," grumbled Bombshell as she slid Sally the rest of her chips a couple hours later.

"I can't help that," said Sally. "Lucky draws. Plus I spent some time watching a real master awhile back." She couldn't tell them it had been when she and half of Just Cause had accidentally been sent back in time. The Department of Homeland Security had sealed all reports pertaining to that series of events, because they didn't want anyone to know time travel was actually possible.

Dinner was a subdued affair compared to the boisterous party Sally and Jack had attended only two nights before. The Second Team's kitchen staff prepared a buffet of appetizers and finger sandwiches, rightly guessing nobody would be very hungry. The entire Second Team turned out for it, with Superconductor remaining on call if the Command Center required him.

Nobody had worn their costumes; Sally was glad. So many heroes' outfits were brightly colored, and it would have seemed at odds with the somber occasion. She sat with the Young Guns and nibbled at a sandwich without much interest. Even Johnny and Stefan had toned down their normal exuberance. The only one who seemed perfectly comfortable in misery was Toxic, but Sally knew that was just part of her whole Goth act; she could cut loose and get just as silly as the boys. Only Bombshell was really as serious as she acted, and that's why she led the Guns.

"It's a pity Shannon couldn't be here," said Bombshell. "Anybody heard from her?"

Sally bit back tears. Their classmate Shannon had been with the Just Cause team who time-traveled, and had died on the prairie a hundred and thirty years in the past. Again, Sally couldn't discuss it. "I'm sure she'd be here if she could, Yogurt." Bombshell's nickname had been *Yogurt* as long as Sally had known her, because her parents saddled her with the awkward moniker of Dannan.

Macey, the energy blaster known as Mosaic, sat off to one side and sobbed quietly. She and Orb had been involved with each other, and the young woman only a year older than Sally was despondent over his loss. The shapeshifting Alloy sat with her, comforting her friend and teammate while Superconductor watched, a plate of untouched food in front of him. Switchboard, who had temporarily been with the primary Just Cause team during the Archmage crisis, pushed his food around his plate with little enthusiasm.

Sally knew how they all felt. Three years before, when she was a rookie, Just Cause had lost Glimmer and Forcestar at the same time, and it still hurt to remember both the enigmatic psi with his cheerful smile and healing abilities, and the earnest and honorable descendant of samurai who wanted so badly to be a hero that he'd died a hero's death.

She stood and raised her glass. "A toast," she said into the silence of the conference room. "To Evan—Orb —who died doing what he loved . . . inventing. May he live on forever in our hearts and minds."

Everyone raised their drinks. "To Orb."

Sally remained standing; she felt like more needed to be said. "I remember the first time I met him. Well, not him . . . one of his spheres. It was sitting on a shelf in the locker room at the Academy. Who knows how long it was there, watching me and the other girls change. I'm sure he got quite an eyeful though." Jack chuckled and a couple of the Second Teamers smiled.

"We always got nervous when he'd bring a new one to a training session," said Superconductor. "One time he had one that shot sticky webbing to bind opponents."

Alloy spread her hands wide, extending her fingers and growing spiderweb threads between them to demonstrate. "It was a great idea, except that whatever chemical he used mixed with my own chemistry to release nitrous oxide. Imagine my confusion when everyone else on the team dropped to the floor giggling like lunatics. Good thing I don't breathe."

"He was always so quiet and shy around people," said Macey with a sniffle. "But he was very kind. He didn't want anybody to know he did it, but every Saturday he bought a couple hundred sandwiches and handed them out to homeless people." She wiped her eyes. "I'm going to keep doing that for him."

Stories about Evan carried the group late into the evening until everyone was too drained to continue. A few of the heroes paired off: Keith and Ingrid, of course, but also Dannan and Johnny, which surprised Sally. Dannan was a giant beside the slender dark-haired boy, but they seemed like a happy couple.

She said good night to Jack, went to the guest quarters, and fell into a fitful sleep.

Morning came, and with it the arrival of Dr. Grace Devereaux from Paris. Her family had been tied to Just Cause since the Forties, when her grandfather Georges had first approached the U.S. Army with the idea of parahuman commandos. Sally's grandmother had been one of those super-soldiers. Grace's father Lane had been instrumental in the management of the Devereaux Foundation, which provided financial backing for Just Cause before it became a government entity. Grace had no head for business dealings, but instead turned her keen intellect toward the physiology of those who had abilities far beyond normal humans. She had studied under Dr. Musashi himself, the geneticist who first identified markers common to all powered people. Now she was the world's premier authority on parahuman medicine.

That she'd come personally to perform the autopsy on Orb said volumes about the nature of his death.

For the memorial service, the heroes wore their costumes, as was traditional, making for a strange dichotomy of brightly-colored sadness. They each added a black armband, which they would wear for a full month to honor the recently-deceased. A Baptist minister conducted the service. Sally hadn't even known Orb was religious at all, but she'd always been so wrapped up in herself during school that she barely got to know anyone very closely.

Friends and family gathered in the Just Cause Memorial Garden at one end of the island. It had been established after the original Memorial had been destroyed along with the World Trade Center in 2001. The garden was full of bright flowers and granite statues of fallen heroes. So many of them, with names that had become legendary over the decades: Strongman and Tornado; Extinguisher and the Steel Soldier; Lady Athena and Lionheart. More than Sally could count on all her fingers and toes. It was the hero's privilege to die so that others could live, and many of them had already made that ultimate sacrifice. In time, when the sculptor completed it, one of Orb would adorn a spot there as well.

Sally knew someday the garden would hold a statue of her there as well. She hoped she could honor the world the way the other heroes had. Orb's death might have seemed meaningless, dying alone in his lab instead of in the field, saving innocent lives or battling terrible villains, but Sally knew better. Nobody worked so frantically as a scientist desperate to find an answer. Whatever had driven Orb to his death, he'd been doing so to serve and protect the world somehow.

They just had to figure out what that reason was.

Sally couldn't focus on the minister's words during the service. Her eyes kept wandering to one statue in particular: a man in Just Cause coveralls with sideburns, curly hair, and a roguish smile. She knew the base of that statue by heart. *Robert Thompson, a.k.a. Audio, 1953-1985.* That was her father, who had been killed before she was even born, along with several others when Destroyer sneak-attacked Tornado's funeral.

The minister's eulogy drew to a close. Icebreaker and Alloy formally folded an American flag and presented it to Orb's parents while a Marine trumpeter played Taps. The simple tune never failed to bring Sally to tears, and she tried to keep her sniffles quiet out of respect.

"Present arms," called MetalBlade.

Superconductor and Mosaic stepped forward. Tears streamed down Macey's face but she dutifully raised her fist to the sky along with Superconductor.

"Fire," said MetalBlade.

Twin bursts of brilliant energy arced skyward: Superconductor's electric blue beam and Macey's sparkling multicolored bolt.

MetalBlade called for them to fire twice more. People throughout the garden sniffled as the funeral started to break up. There would be a reception for the civilians and any heroes who wished to attend. If Jason had been there, Sally knew he'd want to give the buffet table a good going-over. She would have stayed by his side, even though she couldn't think of eating. All she felt in the pit of her stomach was numbness, and standing around pretending to be social wouldn't help that feeling of needing to *do* something. She was a hero; she had to find some way to help.

She saw Jack duck out from the reception and knew something was up. She slipped through the crowd into the hall beyond and found Jack speaking to Grace Devereaux. "What's going on?" Sally asked.

"Forensic autopsy," said Grace. "Juice asked me to look into this personally."

"Can I watch?" asked Sally.

"You sure you want to stick around for this, kiddo?" asked Jack. "There's nothing pretty or glamorous about an autopsy."

"He was my friend," said Sally. "I feel like I should help if I can, especially if he was a victim of foul play."

Grace squeezed her shoulder. "You are a good friend," she said in her mild French accent. She'd been born to American parents living in France. Sally was jealous of her exotic-sounding phrasing. "You may watch, and I will tell you if it is about to get disgusting."

"Thanks, I think," said Sally. "Jack, did you figure out what Orb was working on when he died?"

"No chance. I'm like a chimpanzee banging rocks together compared to Orb. The kid was so far beyond anything I've ever seen with his developments. Maybe Harlan Washington could figure out, but he's not exactly in my contacts list."

Sally shivered. Harlan Washington was the man inside the Destroyer battlesuit who'd killed her father and nearly killed her on three separate occasions. "Yeah, let's leave him out of this."

Chapter Four

"An independent report being released this morning concludes that current U.S. laws and regulations cannot adequately protect the public against the risks of nanotechnology..."

—*Rick Weiss, Washington Post*

December, 2006
Richmond, Virginia

Grace began her preliminary examination of Orb. She noted the blood in one eye and mismatched pupils and agreed with the initial assessment of the staff doctor that Orb died from a subarachnoid hemorrhage. The name alone was enough to creep out Sally. She kept picturing a spider inside Orb's head, tearing open the blood vessels in his brain.

"Family has no history of similar problems," said Jack.

"Okay, let's open him up." Grace took out some power tools. Sally felt her stomach getting queasy. Grace looked up at her. "From here on out it gets gross."

"Sally, why don't you go review the security footage of his final moments?" Jack put some safety glasses over his eyes, not so much to protect them since he couldn't be hurt, but to keep his vision clear.

Sally gulped as Grace raised a blade to Orb's chest. "Let me know what you find." She hurried from the room in a flash, keeping her eyes well-averted so she wouldn't have nightmares later.

She found Ingrid in the administrator's office. The beautiful, icy blue woman sat twirling a pencil through her fingers and staring vacantly at the wall. She jumped when Sally knocked on the open door. "Sally. Please, come in. I'm sorry, I was off in my own little world."

"It's okay." Sally sat in the chair Ingrid indicated. "We're all a little out of it. Grace and Jack are doing the autopsy now. I . . . I couldn't watch."

Ingrid smiled. "I understand. I just can't believe he's gone. He was such a nice kid."

Sally paused. She felt uncertain about how to approach the delicate matter of the security video. Finally she decided it would be best to just jump right into it. "Listen, uh, can I see the video of when he died? Maybe it'll give us some clues."

Ingrid nodded. "We've watched it several times. It's why we suspect foul play." She wiggled the mouse on her desk and motioned to the large flatscreen monitor on the wall. "It's a little disturbing."

"Couldn't be any worse than watching the autopsy," said Sally.

The screen illuminated to show Orb working feverishly in his lab. He literally ran between tables, his fingers flying to attach components together. When he was waiting for computers to compile code, or for processes that couldn't be rushed, he paced frenetically back and forth. His eyes were deeply shadowed and so bloodshot they looked like they'd been dyed.

"God," said Sally. "How long was he like this?"

"This was on the second day. He'd been in there working for some forty hours straight."

"And none of you asked him what was so important?"

"Sally, do you really know just how obsessive he was about inventing? He'd pulled marathon development sessions before. Just never for this long."

"He looks frantic. Desperate, even." Sally watched as he ran over to a table to take a long sip from a cup with a straw in it. "What's that?"

"Protein smoothie," said Ingrid. "He didn't want to stop working to eat. Macey brought him those and fresh coffee. She tried to get him to tell her what he was working on but he screamed at her to get out."

"Like he was mad?"

"It's hard to say. His body chemistry had to be all screwed up after being awake so many hours. It's entirely possible the aneurysm was related to exhaustion."

Sally turned back to watch Orb work. Every once in a while he'd stop his frantic movements and dig his fingers into his hair, eyes wide and staring, jaw clenched. "He looks afraid. I mean really terrified," said Sally softly. "What's he so scared of?"

Ingrid's voice sounded choked up. "It's coming up here in a moment."

Orb bent double in mid-stride. His hands flew to his forehead and he winced in agony. He staggered to a nearby lab bench and braced himself against it. A trickle of bright arterial blood rolled out of his nose. He brushed it with his fingers and stared at it in horror. "No! No no no too soon! Too—" He collapsed.

Ingrid shut off the video. Sally found she was crying all over again, and for a few minutes the two women couldn't do anything except hug one another. Finally, Ingrid wiped her eyes. "The Command Center was monitoring him at Keith's order. They called paramedics in right away, but it was too late."

"He knew," said Sally. "He knew something was wrong. That's why he was rushing. He was trying to save himself. Maybe whatever he was working on was supposed to do that."

Ingrid sighed. "We're still trying to figure out what he was doing. We hoped Jack could shed some light on it."

"Not so far."

The administration desk phone beeped. Ingrid touched a button. "Icebreaker."

"Ingrid, it's Grace. You and Keith need to come down here to the lab right away."

Sally looked at Ingrid. "I'm coming too."

"Please do."

Ingrid called Keith and he met her and Sally at the lab entrance. They entered the lab and found both Jack and Grace hunched over a computer terminal, leaving Orb's body ignored.

"What have you got?" asked Keith.

"Evidence of foul play," said Jack grimly. "See for yourself." He and Grace stepped aside to let the others see the screen.

It showed a strange, featureless cube with four appendages. Two ended in pads covered with little hooks. One ended in a sharp spike. The last was long and flexible, like a wire whip. "What is this we're looking at?" asked Keith.

"A nanomachine," said Jack. "When we got into Orb's head where the artery blew out, we found dark streaks in his blood that shouldn't be there. We took a sample and this is what we found."

"There might be thousands, or more," said Grace.

"What are all those limbs?" asked Keith, pointing at the image.

"Near as we can figure, these two pads are to create a molecular bond. They're like opposite faces of a puzzle piece. If all the machines follow this design, when two of them encountered each other, they could connect. Over time, they would form a long chain." Grace pointed to the shorter appendages. "This long whip looks like an antenna of some kind. This spiky one is what did the damage."

"What probably happened is these things collected at the target spot in Orb's brain, using their antennae as a kind of internal Global Positioning. When they reached a critical mass, they triggered their spikes and shredded the artery." Jack's voice was soft. "He didn't have a chance."

A muscle jumped in Keith's cheek. "So he was definitely murdered."

"And he knew he was in trouble," added Sally. "He must have been trying to build something to stop the machines." She shivered. "He had such an affinity for tech. I'll bet he knew they were inside him the whole time he was working."

"If that's true, that helps us narrow down when he first became . . . I don't know what to call it. Infected?" Ingrid stared at the image of the nanomachine.

"Infected is as good a word as any," said Grace.

"Don't infections spread?" asked Sally.

For a moment, nobody said anything. Then Grace touched a key on the computer and the lab doors slid shut. "Command Center, this is Dr. Devereaux. I'm declaring an immediate medical emergency. Quarantine the medical lab. Furthermore, nobody is to come to or leave the island until I give the all-clear. We may have a nanotech infestation."

"Understood, Doctor. Let us know what you need."

"Will do." Grace turned to Jack. "Okay, your turn in the scanner."

"Me? But I'm invulnerable."

"People with immunities can still carry viruses. You and I had the most direct exposure to Orb after his death. If you and I both scan free of nanotech, and these three—" she indicated Sally, Ingrid, and Keith "—are also clean, then I'll be comfortable saying this was an isolated occurrence and not a contagion."

Sally chewed on her knuckles as Grace ran a full-body scan on Jack, paying close attention to his brain. "That's great, Doc, but will I be able to play the piano when you're done?"

"Part of holding still means keeping your trap shut," said Grace.

The scan lasted most of an hour, during which time Sally paced herself dizzy. Finally, Grace slid Jack out of the machine and pronounced him uninfected.

"Great," said Jack, pulling his shirt back on. "Pizza and beer on me tonight."

"Not so fast," warned Grace. "We have four more scans to perform before I'll sound an all-clear."

Grace scanned herself next, and then Sally. Sally found the sensation of being inside a narrow tube a bit claustrophobic, but she was so tired that she wound up falling asleep during the scan.

Eventually, after finishing with Ingrid and Keith, Grace determined that the nanomachines hadn't spread and that they were all, for the moment, safe. She cleared traffic to and from the island to commence once more. Just to be sure, she had some techs in Haz-Mat suits load Orb's body into a hermetically-sealed chamber. Grace would have to conduct the remainder of the autopsy remotely using surgical waldoes.

Jack took Keith, Ingrid, and Sally aside to discuss direction for the investigation. "Given the circumstances surrounding his death, I have no question that it was no accident."

"Well, wait," said Sally. "What if he made those nanomachines himself? If something went wrong, he'd be desperate to get them out of his body or otherwise shut them down. We have to consider that possibility, don't we?"

"No, if he'd designed them, he'd already have had a system in place to deal with an accident. This is Orb we're talking about here. The kid was a walking contingency plan," said Keith.

"Also, he was always very straightforward with us about his projects," said Ingrid. "He never once mentioned nanotech to us."

"He didn't mention to you that he was in trouble, either," said Jack. "That's out of character."

"He was scared. Terrified." Sally recalled the way Orb had seemed like a man haunted by invisible demons as he'd worked in his final hours. "He was probably afraid of contagion. He had to treat the nanomachines as an infectious disease. What would have been the first thing you'd have done if he'd reported it to you?" she asked Keith.

"We'd have tried to help him, of course."

"He wasn't willing to risk you. Any of you." Sally looked at Keith and Ingrid. "He couldn't take the chance that the machines would transfer into anyone else."

"And those machines appear to be a single-purpose, single-use device," said Jack. "An assassination tool—one that's disturbingly effective. They could be used to kill almost anyone undetectably."

"But why Orb? Who would want to do anything to him?" asked Sally.

"That's what we're going to find out," said Keith. "We'll try to put together his movements prior to his self-imposed lab sequestering."

"We've got some pretty sharp nanotech engineers working in the Bunker back in Denver," said Jack. "I'll take some samples with me and head back to Colorado. Maybe our CTF techs can shed some kind of light upon our mysterious little murderers."

"What about me?" asked Sally.

"Weren't you going to connect with the Young Guns per Juice's orders?" asked Jack.

"Yes, but I mean in the investigation."

"Sally, why don't you and Macey go through Orb's room. Maybe the two of you can find a clue about where he might have picked up the nano thingies or who might have done it to him," said Keith.

"Okay, I'm on it." Sally checked in with the Second Team's Command Center and they reported Macey's location to her. She was sitting on a bench by the dock, wrapped in a parka and stocking cap against the cold, watching boats move slowly up and down the James River.

"Hey, Macey," said Sally. "How are you doing?"

Macey wiped her eyes and sniffled. "As good as can be expected, I guess. It's finally hit me that he's gone. God, I'm going to miss him. I loved him, Sally."

Sally put her arm around the older girl. "I know, and I'm really sorry." The Second Team hadn't suffered the kind of losses that Just Cause had, and Sally had attended far too many funerals of her friends. She didn't want to think she was getting used to them, but at least she knew what Macey was going through.

Macey's shoulders hitched for a moment and then she slumped against Sally. "He was killed, wasn't he? Somebody did it to him."

"How do you know?"

"It's the only way I can cope. I have to blame somebody, otherwise I'm going to scream."

"Macey . . . There were nanomachines in his blood. We think they caused the aneurysm that killed him. Did he ever say anything to you about working with nanotech or someone who was?"

Macey's eyes widened. "No, never. You're serious? He really was murdered?"

"I'm afraid so."

"I'm going to find out who did it, Sally." Macey stared resolutely out at the river. "I'm going to find them and kill them."

Sally shivered, and not from the cold wind. The edge in Macey's voice didn't fit her otherwise bubbly, colorful personality. "Come on," she said at last. "Let's not sit out here and freeze. Will you help me look in Orb's—Evan's—room for any clues?"

Macey wiped her eyes and stood up, looking lost inside the oversized parka. "Yes, of course."

Arm in arm, the two young women headed back inside the headquarters building.

Orb's room was separated by some distance from the quarters of the other heroes, ostensibly because his love for tinkering at all hours of the day and night interrupted their sleep patterns. Sally felt weird walking into his room, like she was trespassing. Jason was a neat freak, and compulsively cleaned up even the smallest mess. He'd have been appalled at Orb's room.

Every horizontal surface was covered with tools, piles of components, and miscellaneous stuff which Sally would have called junk if she didn't know better. Macey picked a path across the floor to perch on the end of the bed. She picked up Orb's pillow and inhaled deeply with her eyes shut.

The moment Sally entered the room, one of the floating spheres which had been Orb's trademark lifted from the cradle of its charging station to zip across the room toward her. "What's it doing?" She didn't recognize the drone. Orb had only maintained a couple when they were at the Academy together and they were much less-advanced than the one which hovered before her now.

"Scanning you, checking you against the Just Cause personnel files," said Macey. "If you were unauthorized, it would issue a warning, and if that didn't work, it would stop you."

"How?"

Macey shrugged. "Lasers. Sonic thingie. Gas. The spheres are pretty efficient."

The sphere must have decided Sally had permission to be in the room and returned to its cradle. She got the distinct impression it was still watching her like a dog from its kennel. She wondered if it would come barking and growling at her if she touched the wrong thing.

That gave her an idea. "Wouldn't he have had at least one of his spheres with him when he got, you know, infected? There's got to be a record somewhere."

"Of course, but none of us can access it. Orb had that weird machine telepathy power and that's how he talked to his spheres."

Sally regarded the group of four spheres in their charging cradle. There wasn't an empty space. "These are all of them?"

"Yes, he never had more than the four."

Sally approached the spheres. As she drew closer, the activation lights on each one brightened and the spheres turned a little in their cradles, giving her the sense they were watching her. "Listen, you guys. I'm sure you know that Orb, Evan, is dead. He's not coming back. He can't talk to you or tell you what to do anymore. One of you has to know what happened. Isn't there some way you can tell us?"

The only response was the four spheres' unblinking lights as they stared back at her.

Chapter Five

The legacy of heroes is the memory of a great name and the inheritance of a great example.

—*Benjamin Disraeli*

December, 2006
Richmond, Virginia

"Come back to New York with us," said Johnny Go. He and Sally ran laps around the Second Team's indoor track, he along the wall and Sally on the floor. They averaged three revolutions per minute. Sally could have gone around it ten times faster easily, but didn't want to make it impossible to converse with her friend, so she limited her speed on his behalf

"And do what?"

"Just hang out. See what we're up to. It's not every day we get a celebrity visitor, even in New York."

"I'm no celebrity," said Sally, but deep down, she knew that among parahumans she really was.

"It'd be cool. You can see our setup there. I mean, we're the only team in New York, you know? Four of us against the City That Never Sleeps."

Sally laughed. "You don't really think of it like that, do you?"

"No, of course not. But you have to talk big if you're from the Big Apple."

"You're from Sacramento, Johnny."

He rolled a cartwheel along the wall, showing off. "Only born there. Once you're a New Yorker, you're forever a New Yorker."

Sally lapped around the track in a heartbeat, using her momentum to ride up the wall so she could get behind him and flick him in the ear.

"Ow! No fair!"

They tussled for a few moments at high speed before separating in a fit of laughter.

"Seriously, Johnny, I'd love to come visit you guys. Juice asked me to do that anyway. He's being put in charge of a new government organization for paras." Sally leaned back against the sloping wall of the track.

Johnny hung upside down beside her. The young man's abilities let him cling to any surface like he was a static-charged dryer sheet. He delighted in his powers and never bypassed an opportunity to show them off. "He's going to be a government stooge now?"

"Not exactly. He says they're doing it to take him out of power, but I don't get it. Why would they put him in a position of power if that was their goal?"

Johnny shook out his wild black hair. "There's power, and then there's power. The government's a bureaucracy. If he wants to get anything accomplished, he'll have a lot of checks and balances to work around. In Just Cause, he could make things happen with a phone call. It's easier to ask forgiveness than to get permission."

"You always were the smart one. I don't get why you're not in charge of the Young Guns." Sally bent down to touch her palms to the ground, keeping herself limber.

"None of us are really in charge," said Johnny. "We pretty much make decisions as a group."

"And inviting me to New York?"

"We'd all love to have you visit. What does Juice want with us?"

Sally headed for the track entrance. If she was going to New York, she needed to pack her bag. True to her normal sloppy form, she'd strewn her clothes and beauty supplies all over her temporary quarters in Second Team headquarters. Johnny padded after her. "He wanted me to let you all know that Just Cause and the Parahuman Resources Agency are behind you guys. You aren't operating in a vacuum up there."

Johnny shrugged. "Sometimes it feels like it. We lost our sponsorship and money's really tight."

"Maybe Juice can get you some kind of funding assistance or something. I'll ask him."

"That would be very awesome of you."

"Johnny . . ." Sally smiled at him. "You don't need to follow me into my quarters."

"Oh, right." He grinned back at her. "I'll just let everyone else know you'll be coming by for a visit. Dannan will be especially happy to see you."

"Yeah, how did you guys wind up together?"

He shrugged. "I don't know. We've all shuffled around. I was with Toxy for a while. Now she's kind of playing the field."

"And Stefan?"

Johnny snorted. "He's a cock with legs. Toxy and Dannan both threatened to cut his nuts off if he didn't leave them alone, so he's hooking up with civilian chicks these days."

Sally laughed. Some things never changed. "Listen, I'll see if I can give you all a ride back to New York. Jack took our jet back to Denver, but the Second Team can spare one to give us a lift up the coast. Government job perks and all that."

"Like I said, you are very awesome."

Sally pointed down the hall, away from her door. "Now get out of here before I give you a really swift kick in the ass."

Johnny laughed and trotted down the hall, spiraling around the walls and ceiling.

After collecting her scattered clothing and jamming it into her bag, Sally called in to Doublecharge to report what she and Jack had learned so far about Orb's death. Juice was already gone from the team, and Doublecharge admitted it felt strange not to have the big man around anymore. Sally mentioned the situation with the Young Guns and Doublecharge gave her approval for Sally to visit the Young Guns' headquarters in New York.

The flight back to New York was short, and Sally spent it chatting with her old classmates about music, movies, and other things of less-than-global importance.

The Young Guns grew quiet as the jet came in on its final approach and Sally saw firsthand the large hole where the Twin Towers had once stood. She'd only been fifteen when they'd been destroyed. The Hero Academy classes had been canceled and she and the other students huddled around the television in the dorm, holding each other and sobbing. They'd wanted to go help, but the Academy administrators flatly refused to let any of the students leave, and warned that any who did would be expelled. There was too much liability letting teenagers, even with parahuman powers, go into such a dangerous place.

So the students could only watch. Many Just Cause heroes had died that day. Juice and Doublecharge both survived the initial impact of the plane, and she'd nearly killed herself slowing his fall from the upper floors of the second tower.

Jack and Sondra hadn't been in the building at the time. As they hurried to help, a jumper had fallen right onto Jack. He never spoke about that.

Just Cause had suffered greatly that day, losing many experienced heroes, and only through Juice's efforts did the team ever recover to become a separate entity once more.

Sally stared down at the site, littered with heavy equipment and construction supplies. The first new building was already standing proud amid the big scar in the city. Dannan told her it was supposed to open within half a year.

"Do people still talk about it?" asked Sally as the jet made its final approach into JFK.

"Sometimes," said Dannan. "People have long memories about some things, even though in New York if it's five minutes ago, it's old news."

The jet touched down and taxied to a hangar where an unmarked van with tinted windows awaited the young heroes. A fat Hispanic man chewing on an unlit cigar lounged in the driver's seat, listening to salsa music on the radio.

"There it is," said SurfBoy. "The Young-Guns-mobile. And Pedro."

"Classy on both accounts." Sally looked at the dents in the van's fenders and the cigar-chomping driver.

"Hey, don't knock him," said Toxy. "You know how hard it is to find a regular driver in New York City who knows his way around?"

"*Buenas dias*," called Pedro as the heroes disembarked from the plane. "Who's your friend?"

"Pedro, this is Mustang Sally from Just Cause. She's going to hang out with us for a couple days. Make sure she gets anything she needs," said Dannan.

"Sure thing." Pedro helped the boys load luggage into the back of the van while Sally, Dannan, and Toxy made themselves comfortable inside.

"Pedro's a real find," said Dannan. "He's got the largest extended family I've ever even heard of. Second and third cousins everywhere. It's a good thing he's on the side of law and order, because he could give the Mafia a run for their money."

Sally laughed. "So where are you guys holed up, anyway? I heard you were in the old Just Cause warehouse on the river."

Toxy nodded. "We're still there. Technically it became city property after Just Cause left. The Mayor is letting us lease it on the cheap just to have a parahuman team at his beck and call."

"That's cool. I can't wait to see it."

"It's not much." Stefan floated into the van. "Without sponsors, we're struggling just to keep the lights on."

"How did you guys lose your sponsors?" asked Sally. "I know that it's a tough go when you're in the private sector, but I mean, you're superheroes. That's got to count for something."

"There's some politician who's got it in for us. She thinks we're a danger. She's got the talk radio people all up in arms about us. People with deep pockets don't like to open them for controversy. There's no angle in it," said Dannan.

"Plus there was that thing with the girl from Ocean Pacific." Johnny glared at Stefan.

"I told you, I never laid a finger on her," said Stefan. "We went out for drinks. She had too many shots. I flew her back to her hotel and she woke up with me standing there. And that's all."

"God, Stefan, did she file charges or something?" Sally couldn't believe her ears. How did she not know about the Young Guns' legal trouble with Juice specializing in parahuman case law?

"No, because there was nothing to file charges over. Because I didn't do anything except take her home. She was pissed, though, and they pulled their sponsorship the next day." He gritted his teeth. "My fault."

"Word got around. A week later we didn't have anyone willing to sponsor us," said Toxy. "That was six months ago."

An icy silence filled the interior of the van.

"Hope you brought a sweater," said Johnny. "It gets cold in that old building."

Sally watched the city pass by as Pedro negotiated the van through Manhattan traffic. Bedecked in holiday colors, the city was gearing up for New Year's Eve, only a day away. She shivered a little as she imagined the thousands of revelers in Times Square. Crowds made her feel nervous and claustrophobic. She wondered if the Young Guns would be working security for the event, and asked Dannan.

"Actually, no, unless we're called," said the muscular girl. "We've kind of got our own thing going on that night."

"Oh? What kind of thing?"

Dannan blushed. "We're hosting a . . . a rave."

Stefan turned around in his seat to look back at them. "We're having one tonight, too. Ten bucks at the door and a cash bar."

"You're having a party? You're *charging* people?" Sally couldn't believe her ears. "That's crazy!"

"We've got bills. Payroll. Transportation. Seriously, if it wasn't for Pedro's wide range of skills, we'd be in a world of hurt," said Johnny.

"I'm underpaid," said Pedro from the driver's seat.

"We're all underpaid," retorted Toxy.

The original Just Cause headquarters had been well-maintained by the organization for many years. Consequently, the large warehouse looked much better than many of the surrounding buildings, which were dilapidated with peeling paint and broken windows. The economic downturn had hit the neighborhood pretty hard, and only a handful of businesses remained amid the numerous abandoned buildings. Then after 9/11, Just Cause returned possession of the warehouse to the city, and it had gone downhill as well. Sally looked doubtfully at the fading paint and the bubbled tinting on the windows. The Just Cause logo over the main entrance had been replaced by a sharp, modern-looking logo for the Young Guns in yellow and black.

Several cars were parked outside the warehouse already. Two young men were setting up a rope barrier to guide party-goers. "My cousins," said Pedro as he guided the van around the side of the building toward an opening garage entrance. "They'll work the door, collect the cash. My brother-in-law Jaime is a weightlifter. He'll bounce anyone who tries to crash the gate."

"Oh," said Sally. The warehouse enveloped the van and she looked around with interest.

The layout had changed from when Sally's mother was on Just Cause. It used to be half the warehouse was set up for team training and half for offices and the dormitory. The division was still there, but most of the interior office buildings were sealed up tight, and Sally could see they were full of stacked boxes and piled-up furniture. The dormitory was in slightly better shape because the Young Guns lived there. Several of the other rooms had been demolished and replaced with round tables and mismatched couches and overstuffed chairs around them. A bar sat along one wall behind a floor-to-ceiling wire mesh security curtain. Sally could see a wide assortment of bottles on the shelves behind the bar. Overhead, she saw a gantry from which hung all manner of lights and speakers, as well as three things she thought looked suspiciously like dancing cages.

The heavy training room floor and walls had been coated with acoustic tiles and painted murals. Wherever she looked, Sally saw nothing that said *superhero headquarters* and everything that said *club*.

She felt a little disappointed.

A blast of noise walloped through the sound system. Stefan brightened up. "Oh, you want to meet the deejay? She's Pedro's . . . What is she, dude?"

"Second cousin, amigo." Pedro labored under the team's baggage.

"So, is this what you guys do?" Sally knew she should be tactful and diplomatic, but she knew Juice would expect an honest report from her, and she felt disgusted at what her old classmates had apparently become. "Party? Drink? Not very heroic. Not what we learned in the Academy."

Dannan stiffened. "It's not like that. We're still fighting the good fight."

"Are you?" Sally gestured at the training center-turned-dance floor. "Can you even work out in here?"

"We're not high-powered paras here," said Stefan. "I can sort of fly. Johnny is sort of fast and sort of sticky. Toxy controls pollution, for fuck's sake. Sort of. That's all we are, Sally. Sort ofs."

Sally shook her head. "Dammit, you guys are parahumans. Graduates of the Hero Academy. That counts for something."

"It doesn't count for shit when you can't keep the lights on," said Toxy. "Look, we'd love to be A-list heroes with government support and all, but we're not. We have to support ourselves." She gestured to the club. "And this is what works. You're old school, Sally, and that's great. This is what we do, and this is who we are."

Sally sighed. She knew it wasn't right, what her friends were doing. It wasn't how proper heroes were supposed to act. Was she really the stodgy one, part of the machine? She'd never had much of a rebellious streak, even as a teenager. Sally's mom had trained and raised her to be a hero from an early age. She'd never considered that there was any other way besides the Just Cause way.

Perhaps it was time to learn.

"Give us one night," said Johnny. "Let us show you how we do things here. I'm telling you, the people here love us. That's a big deal, because I can see the way society as a whole views parahumans, and it's not very favorable."

Sally had to admit to herself that he was correct in that assessment. "Okay, one night," she said. "Like my mom says, if it ain't broke, don't fix it. Show me that your way isn't broken and I'll go back to Juice with a favorable report. He'll try to get you some funding and support. But if all you're doing is . . . is partying, well, I just can't condone that, and I bet he won't either."

"I promise, we're really doing some good here," said Dannan. "You won't be disappointed."

Sally nodded. "I sincerely hope not. Without you guys, there's nobody here to fight the good fight."

"Well, there's Champion," said Stefan.

"Oh yeah, I forgot him. Have you met him yet?"

"No," said Johnny. "But we really hope to."

Sally nodded. From what little she'd seen on the reports of Champion, he seemed to be a good guy. Maybe he could be the example the Young Guns so desperately seemed to need. She smiled back at her friends. "I hope so too."

Chapter Six

"Why do we have parties? We already caught all the bad guys. What else is there to do but celebrate?"

—*Sundancer*

December, 2006
New York City, NY

The pounding bass from the big speakers drove relentlessly into Sally's skull like a railroad spike. She wished she was rebellious enough to really cut loose, let her hair down, and drink like the twenty-one-year-old she'd just become, because maybe an infusion of strong alcohol would make the beat tolerable. Instead, she huddled in a corner of the Young Guns' headquarters, as far away as she could get from the direct line of sound waves, a forgotten glass of Coke slowly sweating over her glove. She had nearly balked at the idea of wearing her costume, but the Guns had convinced her. Now she'd have felt more out of place if she hadn't worn it, for the entire place was packed full of hundreds of dancers dressed in homemade, store-bought, and expensive custom superhero costumes. Apparently, it was the happening trend for Young Guns' raves. She'd seen several Mustang Sally costumes sprinkled throughout the crowd, including a woman who had no business wearing form-fitting clothing, another who looked better in the costume than Sally herself did, and a man, which might have been the strangest thing of all.

Seeing a Mastiff gave her a nasty turn, because she missed Jason terribly, and it had taken all her nerve not to approach the young man and chew him out for daring to dress up as her fiancé.

The Young Guns themselves worked the crowd like seasoned professionals. Stefan floated at head level, chatting up girls, making sure everyone had whatever they needed. Toxy was somewhere in the crowd, dancing up a storm. Johnny scampered up and down the speaker stacks like a squirrel. Even Dannan, who Sally had always considered to be the serious one, twisted and gyrated on the dance floor with all the unbridled sexuality of a stripper in a college bar.

"Excuse me, may I sit here?" Sally looked up from her thoughts to see a guy in a Champion costume regarding her from behind his canary-colored full-face mask.

"Go ahead."

The man sat down. Underneath his costume, he was powerfully-built with the kind of musculature that came from spending many hours in the weight room and eating the right diet. His outfit was almost painfully traditional: bright yellow bodysuit with orange gloves, boots, and—of all things, marveled Sally —trunks. The yellow suit extended up to cover his entire head, leaving only white slits for eyes. Around his neck was clasped a flowing mid-calf-length red cape that seemed so lightweight that it almost moved on its own. A stylized image of the world spread across his broad chest. "Your ice is melting."

"What?" Sally could barely hear him over the booming music.

He motioned to her glass. "Your drink. You're not drinking it and your ice is melting. May I get you another drink if you don't like that one?"

Sally sighed. She'd spent much of the evening fending off guys who wanted to buy her drinks, guys who wanted to dance, and even a couple of girls, which was both flattering and weird at the same time. "No thanks," she said. "I'm engaged."

He shrugged it off. "That's an outstanding costume. It looks authentic."

"Thanks."

"You're not enjoying yourself, are you?"

"Is it that obvious?" Sally knew she'd have to give the guy a firmer brush-off; he wasn't getting the message.

"Why are you here?" The man in the Champion suit leaned forward over the table so he wouldn't have to shout over the music.

Sally felt uncomfortable at the implied intimacy. She glanced around, looking for an exit. "Is this some kind of an interview?"

"Perhaps. You're quite a celebrity in the parahuman world. Isn't it natural that I'd have questions for you?"

Sally's eyes widened as she realized this guy had made her; he recognized her as the real Mustang Sally instead of just another girl in a costume. "Who are you, really?" she asked.

He extended his hand. "Champion. Like you, the real one. Pleased to meet you, Sally."

Sally shook the proffered hand. "Is it really you?"

Without a word, Champion floated out of his seat and spun in a graceful circle. A glow visible even amid the bright, colorful lights of the club emanated from him momentarily before he sat back down again.

"Very cool," said Sally. "I saw you on TV a few days ago. What are you doing here?"

"I came to speak to the Young Guns. It seemed like this rave would be a good opportunity to find them all in the same place. Besides, I like a good dance beat."

"I'm more of a rock and roll girl," said Sally. "What do you want with the Guns?"

"Actually, I'm hoping to recruit them."

"To do what?"

"Is this an interview?"

Sally couldn't see his face under the full mask, but sensed that he was smiling beneath it. "Maybe. I am a duly authorized representative of the Department of Homeland Security. Investigating parahumans is part of my mandate."

"You mean the Parahuman Resources Agency."

"News travels fast." Sally felt a little peeved. Champion seemed to know far more about everything than she did. "Faster even than me."

Champion laughed. "Indeed. The speed of gossip cannot be measured by traditional science."

"Seriously, though, why do you want to recruit the Guns, and why the mask? You know you're breaking the law by hiding your identity."

Champion held out his hands, wrists together. "Arrest me, if you wish. I am protecting my loved ones by keeping my identity a secret. I'd take my case all the way to the Supreme Court, and I might just win. Wouldn't it be nice to take off your mask and be able to live like a normal person when you chose?"

Sally shrugged. "It's not any different than being a movie star."

"True, and you're also stalked by the paparazzi. I've seen the photos. Wouldn't you like to leave that behind?"

"I guess. I don't know. I haven't really thought about it." Sally smiled. "On the other hand, you haven't answered my question."

"Of course. I've been following the exploits of the Young Guns for quite some time. They're impressive in their own way. Quite a unique blend of abilities. They're undisciplined, though, and don't give a very good representation of the parahuman presence here in the World's City. I thought perhaps they might benefit from some leadership."

Sally took a sip from her watery Coke to cover her surprise. Here was a man who had observed exactly the same thing as her. Perhaps he could be a solution to the problem of the rowdy Young Guns.

Almost as if illustrating her point, Johnny Go stage-dived from a ledge onto the waiting crowd below. They cheered and bounced him around like a human trampoline. Somewhere amid the crowd noise and thumping bass beat, Sally heard glass breaking and hoped nobody was hurt.

"I think that's a great idea," she said. "I'm going to talk to the PRA and see if they can get some kind of funding for the Guns. They're doing this so they can pay bills." She motioned at the rave filling the building.

"Another reason I'm hiding behind a mask is that I'm quite wealthy, and it would look awkward in my social circle if I was flitting around in tights, fighting supervillains," said Champion. "The wealthy can be quite . . . judgmental."

"I guess. Well, I'll see what I can do. I don't know how the PRA will react to you keeping your identity hidden. You might have to at least share it with them. I'm sure you already know it's a new agency, and they've got a lot to figure out."

"I'm sure Director Forsythe is up to the task."

It always sounded weird to Sally when people referred to Juice by his civilian name since he'd always been Juice to her since she was a baby.

Urgent red lights began flashing around the room. At first, Sally thought it was just part of the whole club scene, but then she saw Stefan flit over to the bar where he was joined by Johnny and Dannan. Toxy pushed through the crowd, using a wedge of secondhand smoke to shove recalcitrant dancers aside.

"Something's up," said Sally to Champion. "Come on."

She zig-zagged through the crowd in the blink of an eye. Champion followed her, using the expediency of flight to avoid the throng.

"Oh, hey! Is that the real Champion?" Johnny grinned up at the muscular man with the cape.

"It is," said Sally. "What's going on?"

"Emergency call from the Mayor's office," said Toxy. "Stefan's checking it out." Her costume looked like a Catholic school girl gone horribly wrong: little plaid miniskirt, buckle boots, white oxford shirt unbuttoned and tied at her midriff over a ripped black belly shirt with a skull-and-crossbones emblem. A black blazer jacket with a matching logo over one lapel completed the ensemble. Her eyes swam amid thick, black shadow and eyeliner, and Sally thought she looked like a raccoon.

Stefan had a telephone handset to one ear and his fist jammed into the other so he could hear. As Surfboy, he wore an outfit that closely resembled a wetsuit except for the boots and discolored spots where he'd been required to remove ex-sponsors' patches.

"Awesome cape, dude," said Dannan. Her costume was minimalist—cutoff denim shorts, sneakers, and a denim vest over a sports bra. With her strength and muscular density, she had to get up close and personal in combat, and she explained it was simpler to buy clothing off the rack that she didn't mind destroying regularly.

"Thanks," said Champion. "What's the story?"

Stefan hung up the phone. He looked both excited and terrified. "There's an, um, oil tanker. They had an accident on board. A fire or something. The pilot and captain are injured or dead or something. They've got no navigation and can't shut the engines down because of the accident." His face went pale underneath his carefully-maintained tan. "It's steaming in toward the New Jersey coastline at full throttle. It's fully-loaded, too. If it hits, we're talking the worst catastrophe ever."

"Holy shit," said Dannan.

The Young Guns stood around, looking at each other, dumbfounded.

"Oh my God," said Sally in exasperation. "What are you doing? Let's go already!"

"What can we do?" Toxy shrugged. "How are we going to stop a tanker with our stupid little powers?"

In the blink of an eye, Sally was right in her face. "We'll figure it out when we get there."

"Agreed," said Champion. He glowed like a searchlight and nearby dancers recoiled with shrieks.

Sally zipped over to the deejay's booth, located the master volume control, and shut it down before the woman in the booth had a chance to move. "Microphone. Now."

The woman handed her a wireless mic. Sally cleared her throat and considered what would be the best way to make the announcement. "Ladies and gentlemen, the Young Guns have to go be real superheroes for awhile. Wish them luck. They'll be back soon."

People started to clap and cheer, and somebody took up the chant "Young Guns! Young Guns!" Soon the entire crowd echoed the refrain as Sally rejoined the others.

"Nicely done," said Champion. "You've got a good sense of how to motivate others. I approve."

Sally blushed. "I don't really know what I'm doing."

Champion turned to the Guns and Sally didn't miss how smoothly he'd taken over the leadership role. "Let's go, team."

He turned and flew out the doors with Sally pacing him. Johnny Go was only a step behind them while Toxy floated after on a solidified cloud of smog. Dannan leaped onto Stefan's back and rode him like the surfboard of his namesake.

The six heroes hurried down the crowded waterfront. Lots of ships had come in to port so their crews could celebrate New Year's with their friends and family. Large tugboats were threading their way through the crowded harbor, presumably to try to intercept the out-of-control freighter and stop it before it impacted somewhere along the coastline, but Sally knew most of them were not really set up for anything but harbor work. Their crews were risking their lives to take the tugs out into the sea.

"There!" Champion pointed toward the horizon, where they could see the shadow of a large ship against the dark water and low clouds. It had a ruddy glow around it that suggested fire.

Sally glanced over at Johnny. "You still fast enough to cross open water?"

"Watch me," he retorted with a grin. "You still can't figure it out?"

Johnny accelerated and ran down a boat ramp right across the water.

"Shit. Shit!" Sally skidded to a stop right at the edge of the ramp. She'd spent years trying to run across water and had never succeeded where other, slower speedsters could leave her far behind. The physics should have allowed her to skip across the surface like a thrown flat stone, moving her feet like a speed skater, but every time she'd ever attempted it, she wound up having to swim back to shore in soaking wet humiliation. Maybe Jason was right and it was some kind of psychological failure on her part.

But analyzing her inability wasn't going to get her any closer to the incoming tanker.

Champion swung around, recognizing her frustration, and lowered a hand to her. She reached up and grabbed hold of his wrist as he clamped his fingers around hers. He pulled and lifted her into the sky as if she weren't any heavier than purse. "Thanks," she said as the ocean and horizon swung crazily back and forth in her vision. She forced herself not to panic at being dangled over a long drop with a hard stop at the bottom. She'd fallen much further when she'd fought Destroyer in Guatemala, slipping off his battlesuit as he flew to freedom. It had been thousands of feet, and she'd had plenty of time to panic before a last-minute rescue saved her life. She swore not to freak out again, but she was already gasping for air as the tightness in her chest threatened to overwhelm her.

Champion twisted himself in mid-flight, pulling Sally up to him where he could put both arms around her waist, supporting her from above like they were tandem skydiving. "Better?" he called over the rush of air.

Sally licked lips that had gone dry and chapped. "Yeah. Sure."

Beneath them, Johnny Go skated across the waves, flanked on one side by Toxy as she rode on a solidified cloud of pollution and on the other by Surfboy, skimming the surface with Dannan perched on his back like he was, well, a surfboard. As they approached the distressed vessel, Sally could see a column of black smoke issuing from the stern and flames roaring around the bridge. An out-of-control, burning oil tanker; Sally couldn't think of much else scarier.

Champion lit himself up like a beacon behind Sally, his heat seeping in through her costume, and swooped down toward the deck to set her gently upon it. Crewmen saw their approach and ran over, frantically shouting over each other.

"Lower a Jacob's ladder," shouted Sally over the roar of water past the ship's hull and the flames. Crewmen hurried to comply with her order.

Johnny scampered up over the side of the tanker, having run right up the hull. "Johnny, run around the lower hull and look for any damage," said Sally. He nodded and went back over the rail.

Sally leaned over the rail and waved at Toxy. "Any oil in the water?"

"Just the usual amount." Toxy stepped off her cloud of pollution onto the deck. The cloud behind her broke apart into dust and blew away on the breeze.

Johnny returned to Sally's side. "Hull looks okay."

Champion, impatient with the crew's apparent slowness, pulled Dannan and Stefan up onto the deck himself. They regrouped to plan their next move while being assailed by panicking crewmen, some shouting and talking over one another at the heroes while others fought the fire in vain with handheld extinguishers.

"Hold it," shouted Champion. "Who's the captain?"

"I guess I am," said a burly man with an iron cross tattoo on his neck. "Matt Lepper, Second Officer. Ranking survivor."

"What happened?"

"Some kind of explosion in the engine room. It severed control circuits. The halide system malfunctioned and now we've got this fucking fire. I've got eight guys dead or missing, including the Captain. We can't shut down the engines or steer, and we can't get into the engine room because of the goddamn fire and toxic gases."

"Keep your men well back," said Champion. "We'll douse this fire and then see about getting control restored to you. A fleet of tugs is on their way, but we'll try to get your engines stopped first."

Champion was a strong, powerful leader, observed Sally. He had an excellent sense of command and issued orders like someone used to having them followed. She wondered if he might be a military officer underneath his mask. That would explain him hiding his identity.

"Mr. Lepper, why aren't you using the main pumps?" asked Champion.

"Our entire electrical system is down. Computers too. We're trying to get the pumps going manually, but I'm short-handed as it is."

Champion turned to Sally and the Young Guns. "Toxic, see if you can assist with the front-line fire-control teams. You other four, go help get the main pumps going. We've got to get the fire out so we can stop the engines or turn the ship."

"Who died and put you in charge?" asked Johnny Go.

Champion rounded on him. "As many as eight crewmen have already died. I won't have any more casualties on my watch. You're a goddamned superhero. Start acting like one!"

Johnny shut his mouth with a snap. Sally couldn't help but be secretly pleased at how easily Champion kept the situation under control. Juice couldn't have done it any better.

"Come on, Bombshell," Sally said to Dannan. "We'll tackle the starboard pump. Let the boys fix the one portside."

As they descended into the bowels of the ship, Toxy and Champion began their own actions to save the ship. Toxy drew a thick, foamy substance from the waves. Wherever it touched, flames retreated. Champion flew to a point just off the port bow and discharged blast after blast of energy into the sea, vaporizing great swaths into steam. He timed every blast with precision until waves slapped rhythmically against the ship's hull, slowly but inexorably nudging it a few inches off course with each swell.

A heavy steel plate had fallen against the pump, blocking access to the manual engage switch. Two crewmen were trying to lever the piece aside without the least bit of success.

"I got it," said Dannan. She dug her fingers into the plate's edge, flexed her shoulders, and pulled it away. "Clear?" she grunted.

Sally grabbed the two astonished crewmen and tugged them over to the bulkhead. "Go for it."

Dannan dropped the plate flat on the floor. It kicked out a burst of air that ruffled Sally's braids when it hit. She barely got her fingers into her ears in time to block out the loud clang.

One of the crewmen slapped the activation switch and the pump roared to life. He reported back to the Second Officer and then both crewmen hurried back up to the deck to help battle the fire.

"Let's go see if the boys need help," said Sally.

"I'm sure they do. They're boys," said Dannan, as if that explained everything.

They hurried to the opposite side of the tanker only to be met by Johnny and Stefan halfway. "The other pump's fucked," said Stefan. "It's working, but has no suction. There's got to be a broken pipe somewhere."

"We got ours working," said Sally. "That's better than nothing. Let's see what we can do about getting this beast stopped."

The four young heroes rejoined Toxic as she battled the blaze with more of the foamy goo drawn from the ocean. Sally had long ago learned not to ask her exactly what pollutants she drew from the surrounding environment. Toxy's obsession with the worst grime created by humanity bordered on psychopathy, and asking her about details was to invite a ranting lecture about the evils that men do to the world.

Between Toxy's power and the recently-repaired water pump, the crew was making good headway against the fire. Sally found the Second Officer and asked what the heroes could do to help.

"We could really use you super-fast types to scout down belowdecks toward the engine room. If we can get in there, we can shut down the engines manually and turn the rudder," said the soot-stained man.

"Consider it done," said Sally. "Have you got an extra oxygen mask for Johnny? I've got my own." In her last redesign of her red-and-yellow costume, Sally had asked for and received a small self-contained oxygen supply built into her breathing mask, which she had to wear when running at extreme speeds to keep from damaging her lungs. With the extra air, she had two minutes of safe oxygen, which didn't seem like much, but she could accomplish more in two minutes than a brigade could in two hours.

Lepper handed a mask to Johnny. "Okay," he said. "There's a stairwell that leads right down to the engine room. I'll show you where it is. If it's structurally-unsound or blocked, don't risk it. If you can get all the way down, report back up here and we'll get someone down there to try to shut everything down."

Sally looked at Johnny. "Ready?"

"As I'll ever be," he said.

The two heroes descended into the depths of the burning ship.

Chapter Seven

"We must embrace pain and burn it as fuel for our journey."

—*Kenji Miyazawa*

New York City, NY
December, 2006

Emergency lights glared dully red amid the smoke and flames. The heat in the stairwell had been so great that the steel bulkheads were warped and rippled. Water from the functional emergency pump and Toxy's white goo preceded Sally and Johnny down the stairwell.

"Careful, it's still really hot down here," she said. Sweat soaked through her costume after only a few seconds, and every breath of hot air felt like she was inhaling a furnace. The fire was a constant crackling in the background, punctuated by the groans of scalding metal being slowly forged into new shapes by the heat.

Johnny nodded, choosing his path carefully down the walls and eschewing the steps.

Despite their caution, they only took seconds to descend to the bottom of the stairwell at their super-speed. The temperature grew uncomfortably warm far too fast for even Sally's liking, and she was from Arizona. She estimated it was a couple dozen degrees warmer than the hottest days of summer. Maybe as much as a hundred and fifty degrees. Working in that heat could be potentially fatal if it took more than a couple of minutes.

Their progress halted at a rippled and bowed-out emergency door. Automatic systems must have shut it before the wires were destroyed in the fire following the explosion.

With a thud, Johnny slipped off the ceiling to tumble down next to Sally. She wasted some of her air to ask if he was all right.

He didn't reply.

Sally didn't hesitate. She wasn't heavily muscled like Dannan, but she had enough wiry strength in her slender frame to get Johnny up and over her shoulders in a fireman's carry, just the way Jason had showed her. She struggled up the stairs, unable to move at any kind of super-speed. Halfway up, she ran out of canned air. Her head immediately started to spin and she gasped, terrified that she'd lose her balance, sending both of them tumbling down to the bottom, breaking who-knows-what on the way down. Nevertheless, she kept her feet pounding on the steps, bent forward to let her arms help support hers and Johnny's weight. The smoke and fumes grew thicker as she climbed, until her eyes were streaming behind her goggles and she was seeing triple of everything.

Strong hands wrapped around her and pulled her up the last several steps to the clear air of the deck. Somebody took Johnny from her and Sally sank gratefully to her knees, drinking in breath after breath of sea air.

"Are you okay?" A sailor squatted down beside her.

Sally nodded and coughed. "I'm fine, I swear. Check on Johnny."

"Looks like his mask didn't seal properly," said someone else.

"The fumes are bad down there," said Sally, feeling strength return to her with each breath. "And the door won't open. We'll need Dannan to wrench it open and Toxy to clear the way."

Dannan looked up from where she knelt, cradling Johnny's head in her lap. He coughed and moaned. "Is he going to be okay?"

"I'm sure he just got a lungful of bad air," said the seaman. "Lucky Mustang Sally got him out quick enough. He'll be fine."

Dannan bent down to kiss Johnny. "He better be." She stood. "Okay, let's go."

"Listen," said Second Officer Lepper. "When you all get that door into the engine room open, shut off the engines. You can do that before any of us can." He gave Sally a quick rundown on the emergency shutdown procedure. "After you do that, swing the rudder all the way around to starboard. We can circle for days if we have to."

Sally listened carefully to his directions on how to do that; she knew there wouldn't be time to check back with him. They might only have seconds in the engine room if it was flooded with toxic fumes.

"Once you've got that done, get the hydrants in there open. I don't care if you break them and flood the place. Just make sure it's good and wet in there. And then get out."

"Don't worry, Mr. Lepper," said Sally with a confidence she didn't really feel. "We'll save your ship."

"I don't care about the damn ship now. I just don't want to crack up against the coastline. We're carrying millions of gallons of crude."

"It's New Jersey," said Stefan. "Might be considered civic improvement."

Off to the starboard side near the bow, Champion fired blast after blast of energy into the water. Even as large as the tanker was, Sally could feel it swaying rhythmically as waves pounded against the corner of the bow, slowly but inexorably turning the vessel.

It was a heroic effort, thought Sally, but probably wouldn't be effective unless there were ten of him and the tanker a tenth of its size.

The only option was to enter the engine room.

"I'm out of canned air," said Sally as she stood up. "Got another mask handy in case I have to get in where Toxy can't help?"

"Here, take this one," said the crewman attending to Johnny. "It's mostly full."

"Thanks." Sally fitted it over her head. "Toxy, can you clear a breathable tunnel?"

"Yes, I think so." Soot swirled like a living thing around the girl's ankles.

"Not really any room for me to fly down there," said Stefan. "I'm no help at all."

Sally squeezed his shoulder. "It's all right. Not everyone's powers are useful in every circumstance. Stay with Johnny in case he needs help."

Stefan nodded. He looked miserable, the way his shoulders slumped.

Sally turned to Dannan and Toxy. "Come on, ladies, let's go save this tub."

They descended the stairs toward the bent and warped bulkhead door. Toxy took point, guiding fumes around the three heroes until Sally felt like she was moving through a tunnel made of smoke. Sally followed Toxy and watched for signs of structural failure or other impending disaster. Dannan brought up the rear, ready to offer her strength to protect the others at a moment's notice.

The descent was less harrowing than it had been before, thought Sally. Johnny was a nice guy and all, but his powers were kind of a liability in this situation. Having Toxy keep the poisonous fumes away helped tremendously, and in no time at all, the three heroines faced the warped door sealing off the engine room.

"Stand back," said Dannan, "and watch for flying splinters." She dug her fingers into the door's edge, braced her feet against the adjacent bulkhead. For what seemed an eternity to Sally, Dannan strained against the recalcitrant door. Her muscles stood out under her skin like bunched cables. Sweat rolled down her cheeks and her face grew red with the effort. The door creaked and groaned as Dannan applied her strength to it. Just when Sally was ready to call it off and have Champion come down to try to blast through the door, it slid open several inches with a ragged sound of tearing metal.

"That's it." Dannan gasped for breath. "I can't move it any more than that."

Water spilled out of the engine room, flooding the small landing on which they stood, to a depth of almost a foot. Fresh smoke poured out through the gap from fuel oil patches that burned while floating on the surface. Sally peered through the opening. Inside, the engine room looked like some artist's twisted representation of hell, with random patches of flames and broken, tangled equipment scattered throughout from the explosion.

"No way," she grumbled. "It's such a mess in there I wouldn't even know where to start."

"Nobody else is going to fit through that crack," said Dannan.

"Okay," said Sally. "New plan. We need a crewman down here who can talk me through this. Toxy, can you do anything about the fires?"

Toxy nodded. "I think I can trigger the halon system from here. It should have gone off, but something stopped it. Corrosion ought to do the trick."

"Isn't corrosion slow?" asked Sally.

Toxy grinned, her teeth bright white in the soot staining her face. "Not when I do it. Give me some room to work here, Yogurt."

Dannan obliged by stepping aside. "Be careful. That crack is like the barrel of a gun if something explodes in there."

"That's why I'm a superhero, right? Only superheroes like us are dumb enough to run to a bomb that's on fire." Nevertheless, Toxy crouched right by the edge of the door and raised her hands to the narrow gap that Dannan had opened.

Seconds ticked by. Sweat poured off all three young women. Sally felt her heart beating a rapid staccato in her chest. All she could think about was Jason and how upset he would be if she got herself killed right after agreeing to marry him. Something crashed in the engine room and a wave of fresh heat boiled off the scalding hot metal. Toxy shrieked and yanked her hands back. They were angry red and blackened at the fingertips.

"Dannan, get her out of here," said Sally.

"N-no," said Toxy. "I almost got it." She raised her hands once again. "I can m-make my own burn cream. I can feel the halon. It's ready t-to come out."

"Okay, if you're sure," said Sally. She wasn't going to second-guess Toxy; without her, she knew that someone would have to get into the engine room while it was on fire, and the only one who could do that now was her. She adjusted her breath mask. "Ready when you are. Soon as you trigger the halon, you get upstairs and get something on those burns."

Toxy nodded. Tears mixed with the sweat and soot, making her face zebra-striped. "Go."

A muffled whoosh came from inside the engine room as Toxy forced the halon system to discharge. The gas burst outward, smothering the flames with a thick white fog. The blast of cool air from the crack in the door felt cold as an arctic chill compared to the inferno that had raged only seconds before. A strange, thundering roar emerged from the engine room that seemed to pound at Sally's ears from all directions. She couldn't see, could barely think, but knew she had to act.

She squeezed through the crack in the door. For a moment, she was afraid she might have gotten stuck, but she wriggled at high speed and her low friction-coefficient suit did the rest. She staggered into an apocalyptic hell that would haunt her forever. The fog made it impossible for her to advance except at—for her —a snail's pace. Ruined and burned equipment was everywhere, with giant pipes and railings buckling from the fire's tremendous heat. She knew from Lepper's instructions that there was a narrow stairwell ladder leading down to the main floor of the engine room, and that was where she'd find the manual shutoffs for the engines.

She found the stairwell right away, but it was twisted from the heat and dangling precariously over a drop into more fog. She didn't have time to be cautious. She'd run out of air while she sat at the top of the stairwell, afraid of a little fall. She was small and light. Heck, in training one time, Jason had lobbed her up onto the roof of a six-story building as if she were no more than a basketball. He couldn't do that with anyone else. She'd just have to get down the stairs faster than they could collapse.

She'd worry about how to get back up them later.

Speeding down the stairs in a blur, her feet barely touching the twisted metal, she reached the bottom in a second and leaped out of the way as the stairwell came crashing down in pieces. The strange roaring continued and she realized it was the engines, running well beyond their maximum safe RPMs. She had to hurry.

She went from station to station, repeating the instructions Lepper had given her. Fallen equipment tried to trip her as she stepped around it. Hanging cables and wires reached for her in their greed, longing for a careless hand or foot to wrap around. She dodged past it all and shut down the next station. Then the next. Then one more.

Her breather unit whistled as she took a breath, warning her that she had nearly exhausted her supply. Halon wasn't poisonous; she knew that much. At least, it wasn't super poisonous. Getting a lungful or two of it wasn't going to kill her. So long as she got the engines shut down, she'd deal with the aftereffects of halon exposure. She had a quick metabolism; she wouldn't be sick for long.

The dizziness hit her right away. She felt like she'd had too much champagne or been too close to someone enjoying a bit of recreational weed at one of Jason's concerts. Her vision blurred and she couldn't read any labels without squinting and concentrating, which grew more difficult the longer she spent breathing in the concentration of halon gases. She stumbled through the fog, holding onto a twisted railing for support. The stink of hot metal and burned fuel permeated the air, and her head throbbed. She couldn't tell if the roaring she heard was the sound of the halon killing the fire, the engines racing, or the blood pounding through her ears. How many stations had she visited? She couldn't remember. She thought she must have gotten to all of them. Surely there couldn't be more. And why was the world tilting?

Her head banged off the railing, hard enough to make her see stars in her eyes. She felt sick to her stomach and wondered if she'd just given herself another concussion. She'd had two within the past two years, and the Just Cause doctors had warned her that repeated concussions would lead her to an early retirement and possible long-term damage. *You only have one brain*, they said. *Try to take better care of it.*

Jason would still love her, though, even if she wound up a drooling vegetable. She checked her mouth, just to be sure that it wasn't leaking.

A figure loomed out of the fog over her. At first, Sally thought it was an alien or a supervillain or something from the monstrous head, but then she realized it was Dannan, wearing a firefighter's breath mask on her face. "Hey, Yogurt," said Sally. "What's goin' on?"

Dannan crouched down and strapped a fresh breath mask over Sally's face. The muscular young woman's denim was ripped and tattered, but her skin was unmarked as ever. "Sally, you did it. You got the engines shut off."

"Oh good," said Sally. She breathed deeply of the clean air in her mask. Her head was already clearing from it. "I hit my head. Rung my bell pretty good. Can you find the rudder controls?"

"Yeah, the guy was worried that you might need help. I damn near broke the whole ship trying to get that door open, but I did it." Dannan winced. "I'm going to be sore, though. You know how long it's been since I was actually sore? This superheroing stuff is hard work." Her demeanor grew more serious. "Are you going to be all right?"

Sally nodded. "Yeah. Let me just catch my breath." She inhaled more sweet oxygen and let it work its magic in her blood.

"You sit tight. I've got to get the hydrants open and then they're going to come down and get the rudders to work." Dannan vanished into the fog again.

Sally leaned back against the console beside her. She felt tired enough to sleep for a week. As her eyes fluttered, she heard the *bang-whoosh* sounds as Dannan smashed open the engine room hydrants. The splashing of flowing water was almost like a lullaby to Sally and the next thing she knew, someone was shaking her awake.

"You all right, Mustang Sally?" It was Lepper, the Second Officer. He crouched down beside her. She heard men shouting and the banging of tools, and off to one side the walls flickered with the reflection of bright blue light from someone welding. That couldn't be safe, for there was a lot of water on the floor. She realized how much the surviving crewmen were risking to get control of the ship back, and what was she doing? Sitting around taking a nap.

She struggled to her feet. The engine room swayed around her and she had to clutch at Lepper for support.

"Easy, girl, you've had a hell of a day."

"So have you. What can I do to help?"

"Down here? Not much. We've got the ship turned and the fire out. Best thing for you now is to get back topside. There are choppers on the way for the wounded. You heroes did real good. If it hadn't been for the five of you, we'd have plowed right into the shoreline and that would have been the worst catastrophe since . . . Well, it would have been pretty bad."

"Just doing our jobs." Sally coughed behind her oxygen mask. The halon gas had left an odd, greasy taste in her mouth.

The stairwell was a twisted, ruined mess. Someone—probably Dannan—had yanked the wreckage free and tossed it aside. The crewmen had strung a cable sling around a support girder to raise and lower people into the engine room. Lepper showed Sally how to step through the safety harness attached to the sling. "It's as safe as it can get," he said, "but I'm going to give you an extra clamp because you look like you're about to faint."

Sally nodded, too tired to argue. "Hit my head. It's okay, though, because my boyfriend—I mean my fiancé—says I don't keep anything in it." She let Lepper check her straps and add a second carabiner to the cable to help keep her upright. He pulled his hand out of his work glove, put his fingers to his mouth, and cut loose with a piercing call-a-New-York-cab whistle. A moment later, Sally felt herself lifted from the deck through a miasma of steam, smoke, halon, and whatever other chemical vapors were filling the engine compartment.

Stefan was at the top of the cable along with Toxy and two crewmen. They reached out and pulled Sally to safety. She let herself be passed from hand to hand and escorted out into the daylight. The sea breeze perked her up almost immediately, and she shook her head to clear it. Instead of barreling straight toward the New Jersey coastline, the tanker's prow was pointed to the north instead. A fleet of tugboats was moving into position around the enormous vessel, with their crews readying towlines. Three helicopters were approaching like anxious bees, including one heavy Coast Guard chopper that could probably carry most of the tanker crew contingent all by itself.

Champion stood on the deck, his cape blowing majestically in the wind. Johnny Go sat at his feet, looking pale but cheerful.

"How's Johnny?" Sally asked.

"He's fine," said Stefan. "And so am I, thanks for asking. I've been fighting fires." He grinned. "You know, doing real superhero stuff."

"He's been floating because he's afraid of burning his tootsies on the hot deck." Toxy giggled.

"Is this what it's like in Just Cause?" Stefan asked. "The Big Show?"

Sally wrinkled her nose. "Well, I look like I fell down a chimney, feel like I came out second best in a car accident, and I smell like a racehorse, so yeah, this is what it's like. Superheroing is a dirty job."

"But someone's got to do it," said Dannan as she walked up. Her denim had finally given up and she'd pulled on a spare set of crew coveralls to keep the lonely seamen from ogling her muscular nude form.

"You all did an outstanding job," said Champion. "I don't know what I would have done without the five of you to help. Yes, even you, Surfboy," he said in answer to the unasked question. "I see far more potential within you than you likely see within yourselves. If you're amenable, I'd like you to form a team with me."

"I already have a team," said Sally.

Champion's masked head bobbed up and down. "Of course. Perhaps the Young Guns might see it as an opportunity to grow and develop and earn the respect they should already be receiving."

"We'll have to talk that over," said Dannan. In Sally's eyes, she seemed to bristle at the suggestion that the Young Guns weren't quite all that, but she didn't expound further.

Conversation would have been impossible for them anyway, for the large Coast Guard chopper set down upon the tanker's helipad, deploying a small army of relief crew and medics. Over the next half an hour, the heroes were too busy helping to move the wounded or assisting with connecting lines to tugboats to have any kind of dialogue.

Sally offered to help however she could, but when a medic found the lump on her head from where she'd hit the rail with it, she was given strict orders to stay with Johnny Go and not to exert herself unnecessarily. It galled her that she was stuck sitting around while everyone else was doing something to help with the tanker, although deep down she knew that her powers were even less useful in mop-up operations than Stefan's might have been, had he not hit upon the perfect usage of his abilities.

Stefan found himself pressed into use as a high-speed shuttle, able to zip back and forth across the deck carrying tools, lines, radios, and even men who weren't too injured to require stretchers. The look of pride plastered across his stubbly face filled Sally with cheer.

As long as she'd known him, he'd been generally disgusted with his relatively useless power of low-altitude flight. At last, he had found a situation in which he became a valuable, almost indispensable asset. Sally suspected that over time, he would use this experience to help find new ways in which his power would be useful. If only he had a training program, like the one Just Cause used in the Combat Training Center beneath the headquarters.

Toxy went to work cleaning the air below decks so the crews could work in safety. A steady stream of noxious goo funneled up the stairwells to run down the sides of the tanker and float around the hull like brownish green scum. Sally wished she would have channeled it into some kind of container or empty hull tank instead of polluting the ocean with it. She'd benefit from better training in the use of her powers too.

Dannan helped with the heavy lifting and clearing of damage in the engine room. She was as strong as a crane, and under the direction of the engineers, she managed to strip damaged equipment and interior bulkheads away at an incredible rate.

Champion seemed quite resourceful and came across as wise. Sally considered that his plan for the Young Guns might be a benefit to all of them. She figured she'd make an official recommendation of it. Her membership in Just Cause had to carry some weight when it came to stuff like that, and besides, she had a close and personal friend in charge of the Parahuman Resources Agency. One phone call to Juice and she should be able to get Champion and the Young Guns some real resources.

He'd want to know who Champion really was, though, and that was something she would have to work on. He showed no signs of removing his mask, even when it became drenched with sweat from his labors flying heavy cables between the tanker and tugboats. It must have been incredibly uncomfortable with the chilly sea breeze. When he finally dropped down beside Sally after running the final cable, tiny ice crystals speckled his costume where either his sweat or seawater had frozen within the fabric.

"You must be chafed raw," said Sally. "You should really get out of that outfit and into something warm."

"I'll be fine," said the masked hero. "I don't feel pain. I'm more concerned about you and the blow you took to the head."

"I'm fine too. Listen, I think it might be a good idea for you to work with the Young Guns. I'll talk to them about it, okay?"

"Thank you. I will do my best to help them to become better heroes."

"Any chance I can get you to identify yourself? It'll make things go a lot smoother when I talk to my boss after filing my report."

Champion shook his head. "Farewell, Mustang Sally, and my other new friends." He nodded toward Dannan, Stefan, and Toxy, who'd rejoined Sally and Johnny. "We'll speak again." Champion lifted away from the deck and accelerated toward the coast like a yellow and red missile, easily outstripping a pair of news helicopters that turned to follow him.

Sally watched his flight until she couldn't see him anymore in the coastal haze. She turned to the Guns, feeling happy. They'd averted a huge disaster and a celebration was in order. "First round's on me, you guys." Her head twinged and she winced. "I think I might need a double of something."

Stefan grinned. "Now you're talking our language."

Chapter Eight

"Nothing has such power to broaden the mind as the ability to investigate systematically and truly all that comes under thy observation in life."

—*Marcus Aurelius, Meditations*

Richmond, Virginia
December, 2006

"Another head injury?" Grace Devereaux clicked her tongue in disgust at the note in the report from the first responders.

"It was nothing." At first, Sally had been pleased that it was Grace who conducted the mandatory post-deployment medical check instead of the Second Team's resident doctor, but that pleasure had quickly dissipated when she realized that the woman wasn't just going to sign off on things and let her get on with her day. She hadn't even had a chance to call Jason since first arriving on the East Coast and the bespectacled woman in the lab coat was adding yet another delay. Patience wasn't one of Sally's strong suits, and she had to keep herself from tapping out a rapid tattoo of a drum roll with her fingers on the examination bed. "It's not even swollen anymore. I recover from injuries really fast. You know that better than anyone."

"There are injuries, and then there are *injuries*, young lady. Any lingering headache or nausea?"

"No. I'm fine, I told you. It's not like I got clocked by a supervillain or something. I just banged my head on a rail."

"Which could cause a concussion just as easily as getting clocked, as you call it, by a supervillain." Grace took a penlight and shone it in Sally's eyes. Sally tried not to squint as she suffered the examination. "Ever think about wearing a helmet?"

"I can't run with one on. It interferes with my sense of balance." Sally sighed, trying to convey her impatience with the doctor, even though she knew the woman meant well.

"Ah. Are you feeling off balance now? A little dizzy?"

"I'm hungry. Does that count?"

"No. Any changes in your vision? Blurriness? Feeling foggy-headed?"

"No, no, and no. I swear, I'm fine, Grace."

"That's *Doctor* to you until I clear you. Tell me how you hit your head and what happened after."

Sally dutifully recounted the events leading up to her breathing too much halon and falling against the railing. She made sure not to leave anything out; she'd been checked for concussions before and had failed those tests. "I think that's everything except maybe the part where I looked at Champion's ass when his cape blew aside. It was like a juicy melon."

Grace snickered. "Oh dear me."

"So am I cleared?"

"No, I'm afraid not."

Sally's mouth fell open in dismay. "What?"

"According to your records, this is your third traumatic head injury in as many years. I'm going to err on the side of caution here. Forty-eight hours light duty. No deployment and you're not to return to Denver until I've had a second look at you."

"But Grace, come on! I just got engaged!"

Grace shook her head. "Yes, and congratulations to you. Jason's a fine young man and I think the two of you make a lovely couple. But I'm sure he'd agree that it's better to be safe than sorry. Sometimes the pressure changes of air travel can exacerbate concussion symptoms."

"Then I'll run."

"You will absolutely do no such thing. Forty-eight hours. I've already notified Doublecharge and MetalBlade. You'll remain a guest of the Second Team for the next two days." Grace's harsh demeanor softened a bit and she squeezed Sally's shoulder. "I'm sure you'll test just fine and I'll release you then, but if I release you prematurely and something happens, I'd feel terrible. I'm just looking out for myself, Sally."

"Yeah, you're super selfish. It's all about you." Sally rested her chin on her hands. Two whole days. Sure, she loved the Second Teamers, and hanging around with them was fun, but now it felt like an enforced punishment.

Sally dressed in some track pants and one of Jason's sweatshirts—it fit her like a cottony tent and smelled of him and that was exactly what she needed; she'd already sent her costume to the Second Team's on-call tailors to have it cleaned and repaired for her next deployment, which wouldn't be coming for another forty-eight hours thanks to the good doctor. She returned to her guest quarters to call Jason.

"Hey, babe, you made the news," he said when she reached him.

"Yeah, I can't wait for the gossip rags to start speculating that I'm having an affair with Champion. Has it started already?'

"Not as far as I know, but you know I only look at those mags for the bikini pictures. Reading's not my strong suit."

"Oooh, I wish you were here so I could throw something at you."

"I wish I was there too. Two more days is two too long." He paused. "That's awesome. I'm going to write a song about that."

Sally smiled. The oddest things inspired Jason to write music, but once he finalized an idea and his band played it, it would inevitably become her new favorite song. "I want a writing credit if you do."

"You got it, babe. So, what's Champion *really* like?"

"He's really smart and observant. He actually reminds me a lot of my grandpa Adrian before he died. He's the kind of guy who's pretty hard not to like, even though his costume is the most dated thing I've seen since, well, ever."

"I don't know. I was thinking about adding a cape. Capes are cool."

"No, babe, they're not. I promise. Talk to anyone. But Champion makes it look good. He wants to work with the Young Guns. I think he'd be a really good influence on them. They're, um, they're not quite getting the whole *being a superhero* thing."

"You find out who he really is yet?"

"No, he's still masked up."

"PRA isn't going to like that."

"I'll talk to Juice. Maybe they can issue some kind of special dispensation or something. It must be nice to be able to take off the mask and just be normal instead of a celebrity superhero. I can't even sunbathe without some asshole in a hot air balloon with a telephoto lens trying to catch me topless."

"That only happened that one time, and Sondra just about made that guy wet himself."

Sally grinned as she recalled how furious her winged friend had been and the way she'd yanked him right out of his basket and spun him around in midair before divesting him of his camera. Juice had called her up on the carpet for that one and she'd had to write an apologetic letter, but peppered it with none-too-subtle threats that Juice had overlooked.

Jason sighed. "You weren't even topless, which is a crime as far as I'm concerned."

"What, you want everyone to get a load of my teensy boobs?"

"They're darling boobs. I miss them."

"I'll send you a picture of them." She sighed. "I miss you, Jase."

"I miss you too, babe. Get yourself cleared and I'll see you in two days and a couple hours."

"You better not be on duty when I get home."

"I'll swap with Carver. He owes me a favor anyway."

"I love you," Sally whispered, wishing she could reach out and touch him, even for just a moment.

"I love you too, babe." The words came to him easily. It had been so hard for him the first time to say it.

It was why she loved him.

Well, she had two days to kill. Might as well make the most of them, she figured. She logged into the Just Cause private website and spent an hour pecking away at the keyboard for her report on the deployment with the Young Guns and Champion. The system automatically linked to and updated the files for all the heroes Sally mentioned in her report. Curious, she clicked on the link for Champion to see what records Just Cause had on the elusive hero. As she suspected, his file contained numerous reports of his appearances, with links to relevant online news articles or archived scans of print documents. Most of the information in his file brought more questions than answers. His observed powers were flight and an undefined generic energy blast, and that was the sum total of it. "That's useless," she grumbled.

There was a new PRA link right on the Just Cause website. She clicked through and spent some time surfing around the website. Juice had his own page on it with his biography and a nice picture of him in a suit in his office instead of in his costume. She wondered how he was doing at his new job. She started to compose an email to him, but then decided she'd just call. She didn't have his direct line yet, but the JCST Command Center should have it.

"Hey, Sally."

Sally turned to see Mosaic—Macey standing in the doorway. Like Sally, she was dressed down in comfortable civvies. Her eyes were red rimmed and her face looked blotchy, as if she'd just finished a good long cry. Sally got up from her terminal and embraced Macey. "Hey, Mace. How are you doing?"

Macey sniffled. "I'm getting by, I guess. I can't keep sitting in my room with the shades drawn. All it does it hurt more. What are you doing?"

"I just finished writing up my report on the oil tanker thing."

"Oh, cool. The way you guys handled that was top-notch." Macey wiped her eyes.

"We did all right."

"You stopped the ship and nobody died after you got there. I'm not sure you could have done any better."

"I guess you're right. I always feel like there's more I could have done. More I should have done."

Macey smiled. "That's why we're good heroes. We all feel that way." She pulled a chair over from the wall and flopped into it beside the seat where Sally had been working. "And you met Champion."

"Yeah. Nice guy. I was looking at our file on him, to see if there's anything I can add."

"Is there?"

"I don't think complimenting the tone of his butt would be appropriate for the database."

Macey burst out into giggles. The laughter was infectious, and both girls' laughter filled the utility office for a couple of minutes. "Oh, that felt good. I haven't had a lot to laugh about recently."

Sally sat down beside her and took Macey's hand. "I know. I'm really sorry."

Macey looked down at her other hand, making light sparkles dance around her fingertips. "It's so hard to accept that he's gone. I keep waking up thinking he's there but it's only his spheres floating around the room. I think they're sad, like they don't know what to do."

"There's got to be a way we can get into them," said Sally. "Evan must have had some kind of contingency in place. One of them has to have been with him."

"I've been wracking my brain, but I can't think of anything. Evan never said. It's like they're waiting for instructions, but they're never going to come." A tear trickled down one cheek.

"Stop that. There's got to be a way. You know what we need? Hot chocolate and a parahuman who understands machines like Evan did. Who can talk to them." Sally stood and tugged Macey out of her seat. "Come on. Hot chocolate now."

The two girls went to the JCST commissary and Sally mixed up two large mugs of her favorite doctored combination of rich hot chocolate with marshmallows and caramel drizzled on top. Macey looked at hers. "I'm getting fat just looking at this. I'm not going to be able to fit into my costume."

"It'll stretch. You're allowed. I'll give anyone who says otherwise a really fast kick in the ass." Sally blew on her steaming hot drink. "This is the only way I can get through the winter. I'm a warm weather girl."

Macey tasted hers. "This is good. Thank you. How are we going to find someone who can do what Evan did? That can't be a common ability."

Unpleasant thoughts of Destroyer surfaced in Sally's mind. The man inside the suit, Harlan Washington, probably had that same kind of machine empathy that Orb had. It was the only logical way to explain how Destroyer could build such powerful and frightening battlesuits. Sally pushed away thoughts of him. The man wasn't worth her attention, and she'd have to be far more desperate to ever consider seeking him out for help.

And then it came to her. "You know, I'm good friends with the director of the PRA. I bet he has information in his database that we don't have. Let's give Juice a call." She pulled out her phone and speed-dialed the Command Center.

"Command. Go ahead, Sally," said the operator.

"Hi. Can you connect me with Juice, er, James Forsythe of the Parahuman Resources Agency? I don't have his direct line."

"One moment. We'll forward you from here."

Sally activated the speaker on her phone and set it on the table between her and Macey.

"James Forsythe. Go ahead, Second Team." Juice's voice carried the weight of his authority even through the tinny speaker of Sally's phone.

"Hi Juice, it's Sally."

"Sally. It's good to hear from you. Nice work on the tanker incident. I'm reading your report now, as a matter of fact. You could stand to use spellcheck a little more judiciously."

Sally glanced at Macey. "Yeah, I know. Sorry. I was in a hurry. You know me."

"Yes, of course. What can I do for you?"

"Okay, so I'm on light duty for a couple of days and thought I'd do a little investigating on Orb's death with

Mosaic. We're trying to find someone who might have the same kind of machine empathy or something similar to it who could help get information out of Evan's spheres to maybe shed some light on how he got infected with nanobots. You've got access to more information there than Just Cause, don't you?"

"Some, yes," said Juice. "I'm not at liberty to discuss exactly what, though."

He sounded a bit troubled. She wondered how much information the PRA actually had on parahumans in America and around the world. If there was a lot, it could be a really dangerous database. Juice would make sure that it wouldn't get used for the wrong purposes, though. There wasn't anybody better than him to head up the Agency. "I'm not asking you to divulge any national security secrets. Just help me find out who killed Evan so we can bring them to justice. That's okay, isn't it?"

"Of course. I'm looking now. Hmmm. This is interesting. Kali."

"You mean like the goddess?"

"Yes, but this is also someone's name. She's listed in our database as a parapowered hacker, but her account is locked and flagged."

"Aren't you the director? Unlock it."

He paused. "I can't. I'm not sure why. My override authority doesn't appear to be sufficient enough to break the seal."

"Who has authority over you?"

"The director of Homeland Security, the director of the NSA, the President, my wife. Pretty much everybody important."

"Can you get authority to unlock that file? A parahuman hacker might be just what we need."

"It's not quite as easy as that, Sally. In this position I have to follow certain procedures because I'm a lot more answerable than I was in command of Just Cause. However . . ."

"Yeah?"

"Sally, I'm going to have to get back to you. I'll see if I can get this information to you another way. It's best if you don't ask any more questions along this path."

"Oh. Okay. Talk to you later, boss." Sally put her phone away.

"What do you think that's all about?" asked Macey.

"Super secret government conspiracy stuff," said Sally. "He's got to go meet some guy in a raincoat and sunglasses in a diner who'll give him the information he needs."

"Is that how it works in government?"

"Don't you watch movies? Of course it is." Sally finished her hot chocolate, which had cooled enough that she could drink it fast, letting the thick, sugary concoction coat her mouth and throat. "It might be a little while. He's probably got to have a shootout and car chase first. Maybe both at the same time."

Macey snickered. "Nerd."

"Now I want to go watch a spy movie. Like I told Juice, I'm on light duty already. Want to catch a flick?"

Macey nodded. "Sure. Might be a good way to keep my mind off other things."

They retreated to the JCST lounge and Sally picked out a movie neither of them had seen before. They curled up on couches and settled in to watch. Icebreaker wandered into the lounge, preceded by a chilly breeze. "Oh, I love this one. May I join you?"

"Sure," said Macey. The woman some tabloids called the Ice Maiden sat well away from Sally and Macey so the cold temperatures that she naturally exuded wouldn't bother them. By halfway through the first act, Superconductor had joined them, bringing with him a huge bucket of popcorn to share around.

Sally was so engrossed in the movie that she didn't notice when she got the text. Macey leaned over and whispered, "Your pocket is buzzing."

Sally pulled out her phone, wondering if the message was from Jason, but instead it was from Juice. It gave a name, *Vanitha Bhat*, and an address in Boston.

Sally smiled. She knew she wasn't supposed to go off running around per Grace's orders. However, Grace's exact words were that she would be a guest of the Second Team for a couple of days, and if Macey went to Boston with her, well, she was technically following the letter of the law if not the spirit. "After the movie's done, how do you feel about a short trip?"

"Where to?" asked Macey.

"Boston."

Macey smiled. "Boston sounds good."

Chapter Nine

"The Internet is the first thing that humanity has built that humanity doesn't understand, the largest experiment in anarchy that we have ever had."

—*Eric Schmidt*

Boston, Massachusetts
December, 2006

It had taken a mixture of smooth talking from Sally and honest entreaty from Macey but Keith finally relented and allowed Sally to leave the base on the investigation. "I know I'm not supposed to do anything but light duty," said Sally, "but asking questions has to qualify, right? It's not like I'm stopping an oil tanker in its tracks."

"Let's hope that doesn't come up again. Ever," said Keith. After Sally assured him that it wouldn't bother her poor, tender head in the slightest, he authorized them the use of one of the Second Team's auxiliary jets and an hour later, the two young women sprawled across the seats while the jet ate up the miles between Richmond and Boston.

Macey had all four of Orb's spheres with her. They had a carrying case which Orb had never used. It sat open beside her and the four spheres hummed quietly as they made slow circuits around the airplane cabin. Every once in a while one would approach Sally, lights blinking and tiny appendages unfolding from within its depths. She would reach out to touch it and it would zip away like a skittish cat, making what she imagined were scolding noises.

"I think it likes you," said Macey.

"Can it even do that? I mean, are they smart enough to *like* anything?"

"Evan always said they each had their own personalities. I don't know that they're intelligent—at least, not like we'd understand intelligence—but I think they're smart. Does that make sense?"

"Sure. What are their names?"

Macey blinked. "I don't know if they have names. Evan never told me. He didn't communicate with them on a verbal level. A name might not be a concept they even recognize."

Sally held up her hand, letting the curious sphere approach closer. She held her breath, not daring to move, as the device brushed against her fingertip with the most delicate touch before shooting up to float near the ceiling. "Well, they belong to you now, right? I mean, you've inherited them. Four new mouths to feed. You may as well name them." She pointed to the one who'd touched her. "Curious."

Macey nodded. "Yeah, that works. And that one's Angry." The sphere in question made an electronic raspberry sound at her. "Sneaky," she said, noting the device that was hovering low between the seats as if trying not to be seen. "And Thinker. That one's the oldest. I always felt like it was sort of the ringleader of the group."

"Curious, Angry, Sneaky, and Thinker. People are going to think you've adopted four of the Seven Dwarves' less-interesting cousins."

The JCST jet landed at a small airport on the south side of Boston. The two girls coaxed the four spheres back into their carrying case and headed out to rent a car. "You'll have to drive," said Sally. "I don't have a license. Driving scares the hell out of me."

"Says the girl who can run at supersonic speed."

"No, I'm not that fast. Not yet, anyway. Maybe I'll try that someday. Jason's been trying to teach me to drive his Blazer, but I can't do more than circles in a parking lot. I go to pieces if there's any kind of traffic."

"No problem. I'm a good driver," said Macey.

"*Definitely. Definitely a good driver.*"

Macey looked askance at her. "What is that? Some kind of quote?"

"It's from a movie," said Sally. "If you haven't seen it, there's no point to try to explain."

The rental clerk didn't recognize either of them, which was fine with Sally since she didn't really want to spend her day fending off well-meaning autograph seekers and paparazzi. He didn't even blink when Macey passed him her Just Cause Visa card. They got a boring, sensible sedan with a GPS. Sally plugged the address associated with Vanitha Bhat into it and then settled in for an impatient, nerve-wracking hour drive through heavy Boston traffic with slush blatting down onto the windshield.

"I wish I could control the weather," said Macey. "I hate winter."

"Me too. People shouldn't live in climates like this. Unless they're Vikings or something."

"Blonde hair like yours and you're not claiming Viking ancestors?" Macey laughed.

"Maybe. Hey, keep your eyes on the road, huh?"

"You really don't like cars, do you?"

"No."

Macey wove through traffic, her jawline standing out in sharp relief as she chewed gum like it was keeping her alive. Sally did everything she could to avoid actually looking out at the cars, convinced that they would be killed in a horrible accident at any moment, leaving Jason to pine away for the rest of his miserable life.

At last they pulled up to a series of row houses in an older part of town. Even though daylight was waning, Sally could still make out house numbers and checked them against her information. "That's it," she said. "The third one in." A steady bluish white glow came from a first floor window, suggesting a television or computer monitor. "I think somebody's home." She checked the time on her phone. "You don't think it's too late to visit, do you?"

"Visit? Maybe if this was a social call, but this is a murder investigation." Macey spat her gum out into a wrapper and dropped it in the trash bag the rental company had provided. "If it's too late, we'll apologize."

"You're right," said Sally. "I'm sorry. This has almost been a fun trip. Guess it's time to go to work now." She pulled down the visor and turned on the lights on either side of the mirror to check her face. She'd gone with a professional look, subdued makeup without any wild colors, hair pulled back into a single conservative braid, and a muted charcoal business suit over a white blouse. Because she wouldn't be Sally without something red, she had her cranberry overcoat in the back seat and a white scarf to complement it.

Macey shut off the engine and got out. Faint traceries of colorful energies swirled around her in the growing darkness.

"Hey, you're glowing," said Sally as she shrugged into her coat.

"I do that when I'm upset," said Macey. "It's just a thing. Harmless."

"Yeah, but it's also obvious. Let's not attract undue attention. This girl is a civilian but she's also on a PRA watchlist, which means she's some kind of potential problem. Let's not turn a potential problem into an actual one."

"Now you're the one who's right." Macey pulled on her own overcoat and her glow vanished. "I'll do my best to keep it under wraps. Would you take point on the questioning?"

"Me?" Sally blinked. "I've never done this before."

"Me neither, but you seem a lot more sure of yourself." Macey touched Sally's arm.

"I'm faking it."

"Me too. Please, Sally?"

Sally nodded. The two women went to the door and Macey rang the bell. They listened and Sally heard the rustling sound of someone approaching. She steeled herself and tried to pretend she was a character from a cop movie. How hard could it really be?

The door opened and the two heroes saw a young Indian or Pakistani woman who looked like she was roughly their age. She was curvy but not necessarily fat, although she hid much of her body underneath baggy sweatpants and a Boston University hoodie. Her thick, black hair was pulled up into a "pineapple" hairdo. "Can I help you?"

Sally was ready. For the first time ever since she'd first become a member of Just Cause, she pulled out her badge and held it up for display. "I'm Salena Thompson and this is Macey Fontaine. We're with Just Cause. Are you Vanitha Bhat?"

The young woman's eyes widened. "What do you want? I didn't do anything!"

"We're not accusing you of anything," said Sally. "Are you Vanitha? Because if so, we need your help."

"My help?" The young woman glanced back over her shoulder.

She couldn't have telegraphed guilt better than if she had a sign around her neck, Sally thought. But whatever it was is she was doing, Sally figured they could overlook it so long as she was willing to help them unlock the mysteries inside Orb's spheres. "Ms. Bhat . . . Vanitha, I promise you we're not here to arrest you or question you or anything. Honestly, we wouldn't even be here if we had someone within our own organization who could help us."

"I d-don't understand. Help you with what?"

Macey held up the case containing the spheres. "These." She opened the lid and the four spheres flew out. Angry scolded the two heroes for locking them up, Thinker hovered right by the case as if considering returning to rest, Sneaky dropped down to hide within the folds of Macey's coat, and Curious buzzed right past Vanitha into the house, causing the girl to utter a startled squeak.

"It won't come back out before it's had a good look around," said Sally. "Maybe we could come inside and talk to you? It's too cold to think out here."

Vanitha glanced back once more, raising Sally's hackles. What was the young woman hiding? If Sally had telepathy, she'd have been rampaging all over the young woman's mind to convince her to say all right. As it was, Sally had to force herself not to take an aggressive step forward and to unclench her fists. "Yeah, I guess that's okay. Come on in. Do you, uh, do you want a beer or anything?"

"No thank you," said Sally. "We're on duty."

"Kind of late, isn't it?"

"We're Just Cause." said Macey with the ghost of a smile. "We're always on duty."

"Yeah, that's . . . Wow, I never thought I'd run across any of you guys," said Vanitha. "Listen, let me just shut down my system, okay? Then you can have my undivided attention."

"That's fine," said Sally, itching to see what it was Vanitha was doing. Juice had said she was supposed to be some kind of *über*-hacker. Maybe she was hacking into some government agency or corporate data files even as she was speaking to them. Sally thought about it for a moment and then realized that she didn't really care what the young woman was up to, so long as she could help solve Evan's murder.

The first thing Sally noticed about Vanitha's narrow row house was how little it had in the way of furnishings. A ratty love seat slouched against one wall with what looked like a secondhand end table holding a lamp with a dusty shade and a half-full water bottle. A large and expensive flatscreen television hung on the wall opposite the couch, with a modular rack beneath it holding several different gaming consoles. No artwork decorated the walls, the carpet was a bland, neutral color, giving the entire room an appearance that made it seem barely lived-in.

Vanitha's computer setup, on the other hand, looked like something from a big-budget science fiction movie. Sally, being a sci-fi junkie, heartily approved of the spherical chair with large speakers installed in it, the forest of a dozen different monitors on an articulated framework, and the rack of servers that might have given Vanitha more computing power than Just Cause itself. Vanitha reached out to one of her terminals and Sally almost missed that she didn't touch any buttons but instead dragged her hand across a USB port, instantly making all her monitors switch from the massive amounts of data they'd been displaying to a serene spacescape image that spread across the entire field.

Über-hacker, thought Sally. "What do you do, Vanitha? For work, I mean."

"I'm a freelance computer application and security consultant for about half of the Fortune 500 companies."

Sally blinked. That kind of client base suggested that Vanitha was worth millions. She certainly didn't look the part in her frumpy sweats and tiny row house in a less-fashionable part of Boston. But when one was rich, Sally supposed, one could dress and live however one chose.

Vanitha motioned for the two women to sit on her love seat, while she herself flopped into her spherical chair and spun it around to face them. Sally noticed the chair was not only mounted upon a gimbal but had its own shock absorbing system as well. Vanitha drew her legs up underneath her, letting the chair envelop her like a cocoon, and said, "Now, how can I help you?" The sphere Curious peeked around the edge of Vanitha's seat and she shrank back. "Hey, you, back off."

The sphere scooted back several inches as if taken aback, and then dropped down almost to the floor where it flew slowly back to Macey and parked itself inside the case beside Thinker. It reminded Sally of a dog that had been chastised. "You seem pretty well plugged into the world. You know about the death of the Just Cause hero Orb, right?" asked Sally.

"Yeah. He was in a couple of forums I belong to. We —that is, the other forum people—were talking about it. It's sad, you know?"

Macey coughed into her hand and Sally could see that she was holding back tears. "Yeah, we know. He was a friend of mine. We went through the Hero Academy together." She raised an eyebrow. "You're a parahuman, aren't you?"

"Yeah, but I don't really talk about it."

"What's the story with your abilities?"

"They're, um, computer-related."

"You *really* don't talk about it, do you?"

"No."

"Your PRA file was locked. We hardly know a thing about you."

A flash of pride flickered across Vanitha's face. "Yeah, I put it there. The lock. If it got out what I could do, I think I'd be declared threat to national security and be made to disappear. Or wind up as a government stooge. No offense."

"None taken," said Sally. "Ms. Bhat—"

"Vanitha, please. Ms. Bhat is my mom, and we don't see eye to eye."

"Vanitha, then. I promise you that we're only here to ask for your help. We're not going to arrest you or kidnap you into the PRA or anything like that. I don't care what you've done in the past, or what you're going to do in the future. Right now, we need you to help us solve Orb's murder. You have the right to refuse to do so, but by the authority of the Parahuman Resources Agency, we can get a court order compelling you to assist us." Sally felt her cheeks grow hot. "But I really don't want to do that. It'll make me feel like an asshole. Will you help us?"

Vanitha leaned forward in surprise. "He was murdered? Not cool. I didn't know him personally but like I said, we were on a couple of the same forums. He seemed like a really nice guy. Way too smart for most people, though. I'll help. I mean, I will without a court order. You came in here and were really nice about it. And if you're being dishonest, you're at least being polite. Not everyone is so cool with me when they know what I can do. That's one reason I never went into the superhero business."

Sally motioned to the case in Macey's lap, containing only Thinker. Angry was slowly orbiting above Macey's head like it was on guard duty, Curious was poking around the server farm, and Sneaky was nowhere to be seen. "Orb never went anywhere without at least one of these guys with him. We're pretty sure that there must be some kind of hint about his murderer locked up inside one of them."

"Or how the nanites might have gotten into him," said Macey. Her eyes grew wide as she realized she'd given away a secret germane to the investigation.

Vanitha's eyes widened as well. "Nanites? You mean like those critters in your training centers?"

Sally gritted her teeth. They'd been told to keep a lid on the nanotech angle, because if it got out into the press it could cause a tremendous panic. "No, these are something different. More sinister. They were the murder weapon." An idea occurred to her. "Is that something you can hack? Maybe you could get us some more information from them."

"I have no idea." Vanitha wandered across into her small kitchen and took a bottle of soda from the fridge. "You sure I can't get you something?"

"We're fine," said Macey. "Nobody can communicate with the spheres the way Orb could. Can you?"

"Let me see one and I'll tell you." Vanitha held out her hand.

"What exactly can you do?" asked Macey. "Your powers, they're not destructive, are they? You're not going to hurt the spheres?"

"No, of course not. That would be rude." Vanitha smiled. "I'm a hacker's dream. I can get inside any system with a hard line and control it from the inside. If it's got a chip in it, power, and a port, it can't keep me out. There's no password I can't get past, no encryption I can't break through, because in the end it's all ones and zeros, and that's my language."

"Can we see a demonstration?" Sally understood why Vanitha wanted her privacy; if she was really as powerful as she claimed, she would be the ultimate cyber-spy and cyber-weapon. Any government would want to use her for espionage or black ops activities. Any corporation would want her to destroy its competitors.

Vanitha spun her chair around to face her computers. Sally and Macey approached to get a better view. The young Indian woman reached over to touch one of her towers, and she vanished, leaving behind only her clothes. Sally gasped. It had happened even faster than she could see with her accelerated perceptions. One moment Vanitha was sitting there in her chair, a slight smile on her face, and the next she was gone. She must have traveled at the speed of light, Sally thought.

All the screens powered up on Vanitha's system. A shining figure appeared, divided between several screens at once. The figure resolved into a woman with ten arms, dark blue skin, and flowing dark hair. She wore nothing but a necklace of severed human heads and a skirt of human arms. Her face was twisted into a snarl, with pointed razor-sharp teeth framing a lolling tongue. "I am Kali, the Goddess of Death, the Queen of the Timeless Black." The voice thundered from the stereophonic speakers built into the sphere chair as well as booming out from multiple subwoofers beneath the monitor framework. "Look upon my works, ye mighty, and despair."

Sally sniffed. "That was some poet. Shelley, right? I didn't just study superheroing in school." Nevertheless, despite her blasé statement, she was impressed. Vanitha seemed to be completely inside the computer, like Flynn being zapped onto the Game Grid by the MCP in *Tron*.

Kali sucked her tongue back up into her mouth, smiled, and shrugged—which was far more impressive a gesture when magnified by ten arms. "Kali is my online avatar. She's how the forum people know me."

"She seems kind of, the opposite of subtle. I always thought hackers were supposed to be sneaky in the way they did things," said Macey.

Kali seemed to shrink in upon herself and transformed into a hummingbird icon, flipping around from screen to screen on wings that looked as if they were made from diamond. "I can do subtle and sneaky. Plenty of times when that's what I need. But there are plenty of other times where loud and badass is better, and that's when I'm Kali." The hummingbird paused long enough to hover on a single monitor screen. "Um, would you mind turning your backs? I don't come out dressed."

Sally glanced over at Macey, who shrugged. "Sure thing." Sally hoped it wasn't a trick of some kind. She kicked her altered time perception up to maximum, focusing her attention on anything that might be some kind of threat.

She heard the creak as Vanitha's weight returned to the sphere chair, followed by the rustling of cloth as the young woman pulled on her sweats again. "Okay, I'm ready," said Vanitha. "Thanks for being cool about it."

"You're welcome," said Sally. "So can you begin now? Or do we need to do something else first?"

Vanitha grinned. "Hungry? There's a really great Thai place not too far away, and they deliver."

Sally smiled back. "Dinner's on me."

Chapter Ten

"Investigation may be likened to the long months of pregnancy, and solving a problem to the day of birth. To investigate a problem is, indeed, to solve it."

—*Mao Zedong*

Boston, Massachusetts
December, 2006

While the three young women dined upon spicy fried noodles, green papaya salad, and seafood curry, Vanitha examined Orb's spheres one at a time. Although every one of them took some convincing, eventually they all floated over to her and allowed themselves to be poked, prodded, turned around, and to let her dissolve a finger into their data ports. Each time she performed the task, she'd stop eating and talking, sometimes even with her hand partway to her mouth. More than once, Sally reached over to catch a potential spill.

"Thanks," said Vanitha after the third time. "I really shouldn't be eating while I'm doing this, anyway."

"It's all right," said Sally. "As long as you think you're going to be able to help."

"I believe so. These are fascinating devices. The way they're built . . . It's like no system architecture I've ever seen. And their schematics are unreal. For someone else to build one of these creatures, I'd think it would take a medium-sized factory. And all that is crammed into something only as big as my morning grapefruit."

"Are they intelligent?" asked Macey. "I always got the sense that they were, you know, smart."

"I don't think they qualify as AI, if that's what you mean," said Vanitha.

"Artificial Intelligence," said Sally. "Why not? There've been other AIs. The Steel Soldier. Carousel from the Lucky Seven." She'd never met the Steel Soldier as the robotic warrior had been blown apart by Destroyer in the attack that killed her father, right before she was born. Carousel, on the other hand, was a good friend of hers, and they'd served together when Sally trained with the Lucky Seven. Carousel was a creation of liquid metal, much like the T-1000 from the *Terminator 2* movie, but unlike that monster, she had been built with the idea of becoming a force for good. Although her creator had perished in a lab accident that also destroyed his notes and files, his legacy lived on with her as a member of the widely-regarded Lucky Seven.

"These things aren't intelligent. At least, not like you and I. They're more like . . . like dogs. Loyal, devoted, smart enough to be trained and follow directions."

Macey said, "Evan always treated his spheres more like they were pets than tools. Once I even caught him petting them."

Sally chuckled, but then covered her mouth and made herself regain her composure. "I'm sorry," she said.

"No, it's okay. I thought it was funny too." Macey's brave smile crumbled and her eyes filled with tears. "Vanitha, m-may I use your bathroom, please?"

"Yeah, go ahead. Just off the kitchen."

Macey practically ran away from the other two and slammed the door behind her.

"What's the matter with her?" Vanitha asked Sally. "She close to Orb?"

"Yes. She was his . . ." Lover? Girlfriend? Sally had no idea what the proper term was under the circumstances.

"I get it. That sucks. Really, really sucks." Vanitha glanced back in the direction of the bathroom. "I hope she's not puking in there. There's no fan."

Sally shook her head. Vanitha clearly spent far more time dealing with people online than she did in real life. It showed in her direct, almost transparent way of speaking. "Listen, if you're done eating, maybe you could get started? Seeing some of what might be stored on those spheres could be pretty painful." She nodded toward the bathroom as well.

"Oh, right, right." Vanitha set aside her food. She cracked open a highly-caffeinated energy drink from her fridge and drained it like a sorority girl at a mixer. An unladylike belch escaped from her lips. "Phew. Sorry. Helps me focus." She sat down in her chair and folded her legs into a half lotus. "Come here, you precious little boys."

The four spheres zipped over from wherever they'd been around the house to hover in front of Vanitha.

"I think they like you," said Sally.

"They're just happy to have someone talking to them," said Vanitha. "You fellows have hardline connections. Go ahead and sync up, if you would. That'll make this go a lot faster." She winked at them from behind an errant curl that had fallen from her pineapple hairdo. "This isn't going to hurt at all, I promise."

The spheres reoriented themselves into a square. A wire-thin antenna emerged from each orb to join with a similarly tiny port on another. Vanitha pulled a unit down from the top of her chair. A cable trailed from it and eventually connected to one of the boxes on the server farm. She twisted a dial on it until it reached a setting she liked. She connected a dangling antenna from one of the spheres into the unit.

"Welcome to my big world, boys," said Vanitha. "Let me slip into something a little more comfortable for spelunking data and we'll be off."

Macey returned from the bathroom. Her face looked puffy and her eyes were reddened but she managed a smile. "Sorry about that."

"It's all right," said Sally.

"Yeah, no big deal," said Vanitha. "Okay, so I don't know what I'm going to find, but what I can locate and translate, I'll put up on the screens for you. I hope you see something you can use."

"We'll be able to talk to you, right?" asked Sally.

"The mic's already hot and the speakers are buzzing."

"Then let's get going." Sally squeezed Macey's hand.

Vanitha vanished into her terminals. The hummingbird reappeared on the monitors and buzzed around briefly, trailing glowing sparks like Tinkerbell in a Disney cartoon. The sparks coalesced into the Kali figure once more. Kali's wagging tongue slipped back into her mouth and she spoke. "I'll share things with you as I decode them. I can't be sure anything I uncover won't be damaged in the process, so I don't want you to miss anything."

Sally glanced at Macey. "We understand."

Images and brief clips of video flashed on the screens, overlaid with a mishmash of sound, the entire thing being the visual and audio equivalent of turning the tuning knob on an old-fashioned radio. Many of the images and videos featured Evan and Macey together, as if the spheres put in extra effort to monitor the two of them. Macey sniffled and Sally expected her to run back to the bathroom once again, but instead the young woman wiped her eyes and stood before the monitors. "Why's it all jumbled like this?"

"They've suffered some kind of damage to their memory. Corruption, fragmentation, missing data," said Kali. She flashed a knife for emphasis.

"Like a virus?" asked Sally.

"I don't know what caused it. But there's a lot of memory damage. I've got some timestamps that I can read, though. How far back do you want me to go?"

"Two weeks," said Macey. "I know he was okay that far back. I'm guessing that . . . that whatever happened, he figured it out right away and went to work in his lab right away too."

"Okay, two weeks," said Kali. She pulled an image fragment out of the blurry mixture and centered it in front of her necklace of heads. Although black blotches marred the picture, it was a recognizable shot of Evan and Macey in a suite together. He was sitting in bed, hair tousled and shirtless, looking smug and satisfied, while she was emerging from the attached bathroom, naked but for a skimpy pair of panties.

"Oh," said Sally. "Um, maybe not that one."

"Sorry," said Kali. "First thing that came up with the timestamp. Are you okay?" The solicitous tone didn't match her monstrous appearance, but Sally was growing used to the cognitive dissonance.

Macey wiped her eyes. "Yeah, I'm getting there." She took a shuddering sigh.

"Okay, I'm fast-forwarding. The damage is really bad here. I'm not sure I'll be able to get more than a few still images out of all this mess. These poor critters really got their heads nuked."

"Nuked." Sally rolled the word around her mind. "Whatever you can get us. Anything might be the clue we need to move forward."

"I'll need some time."

"Take all you need," said Macey.

Kali's tongue popped back out and virtual blood dripped from her outfit of severed body parts as she concentrated upon filtering through all the garbled data trapped within the memories of Orb's spheres.

"What do you think?" Sally asked Macey. "It can't be a coincidence that all of the spheres' memory files are corrupted."

"Someone was covering their tracks. The killer." Macey grimaced and turned a little green.

"You all right?"

"I will be. Heartburn from dinner."

"I got something," said Kali. "The timestamp is about three days before his death. It's a blurry capture from about a half a second of video. Not sure if it'll be any help."

"That's the time frame we're looking for," said Sally. "Let's see it."

Kali opened her hands as if she were opening a book and the image appeared, framed by her hands. It was definitely Evan, or at least, his profile. He was half-in, half-out of the camera view and dressed in civilian garb. Behind him was a reddish-brown wall with some white lettering on it.

Sally squinted, trying to make sense of the clouds that were words. "I can't make it out," she said.

"Me neither," said Macey. "Can you maybe *C.S.I.* it up for us?"

"*C.S.I.* it." Kali sounded disappointed. "You think it's as easy as all that?"

"Well, it *is* on television," said Sally. "You telling us that a hacker of your skill and talent can't do better than a bunch of hack television writers?"

"I know what you're trying to do, and it won't work. Image reconstruction is a long and involved process."

"Then I guess you'd better give the picture to us in a copyable format so we can put our own people to work on it."

Kali hooted laughter. "Your people? Please, I've seen what passes for experts in the Just Cause personnel files. I could work circles around them."

Sally winked at Macey. "Nah, I don't think so."

"Excuse me a moment," said Kali.

"What's up?" Sally stared at the blurry image, wishing her accelerated perceptions allowed her to see beyond the blurs.

"I'm borrowing some software from the FBI."

"Borrowing?"

"You want to argue semantics or solve a murder?"

"Do whatever you need to," said Macey.

"Okay, running some filters now." The image grew darker, then lighter, then darker again, almost opaque. A grid appeared over it and contracted until each square must have only contained a few pixels. Kali grinned, showing her filed teeth. "Watch this." She took her lowermost left hand and wiped it across the image. In its wake, it left behind pixelated but legible letters.

"*-lems, sma-*," read Sally. "That's not very helpful."

"It's more helpful than you might think." Kali smiled again. Sally suspected the grim blue visage would haunt her nightmares for quite awhile. "Evan probably didn't travel any significant distance, right? He would have had to file something if he was going to take a Just Cause jet or fly privately, right?"

"Yes," said Macey.

"That means wherever he went was within daily driving distance of Richmond. The font of those letters is common to businesses, and that comma suggests to mean that it's not a corporate logo so much as a slogan."

"I'm with you," said Sally. "*-lems* isn't a very common suffix. Um, *emblems*. What else?"

"*Problems*," said Macey.

"There are a couple of others, but they're really uncommon words like *golems* and I already eliminated them with a search. I think it's *problems*."

"Okay, *something* problems, *sma-* something."

"Smart? Smack?" said Macey.

"Small," said Kali.

"You sure? You sound sure," said Sally.

"The full phrase is *Big problems, small solutions.* It's for a company called ScaleAbility, and you'll never guess what they do."

"Nanotech," said Sally.

"Look at the big brain on Mustang Sally," said Kali. She brushed the window aside and opened a new one featuring the company's website. "They're in Chesapeake, plenty close to Richmond, they work with nanotechnology, and we've got an image placing Evan at their facility shortly before he died. Looks pretty suspicious to me."

Macey stood. "Let's go."

Sally looked at her. "Go? We can't go yet. That's not only a potential crime scene, but there could be a killer there who can infect you with nanites. We can't go rushing off. And believe me, if anybody knows rushing off, it's me."

Macey wilted before her. "Oh God, what if they get away because we're sitting around?"

Sally took her hands. "First of all, if they get away, we'll catch them again. Second of all, nobody's sitting around. Vanitha . . ."

"Yeah?"

"Would you rejoin us out here in the real world? It's weird to keep talking to you like this."

"Yeah, okay. Hang on. Incoming naked Indian chick."

Sally and Macey obliged by turning away from the computers and a minute later Vanitha was fixing her hair back up into a pineapple ponytail once more. "Vanitha, thank you for your help. You've given us a good lead," said Sally.

"No big deal. It was fun. You never know what you're going to run across when you do what I do."

"If you would like, I will commend you in my report. On the other hand, if you'd rather keep things on the down-low . . ."

Vanitha nodded. "Yeah, I didn't mind helping you guys out. You were cool and polite, and you bought dinner, anyway. But I don't want to be on call for Just Cause or anyone else. You need anything else, come on back, but keep it just between us, all right?"

Sally shook her hand. "It's a deal." She buttoned her coat against the chilly evening.

Macey likewise bundled up and held up the case for Evan's spheres. "Come on, you. Let's go."

"Um . . ." Vanitha looked over at the four hovering orbs. "You don't suppose I could hang on to them for a couple of days? I've got an idea about how to fix the corruption in their software. Make them whole again, you know?"

"You can do that?" asked Sally.

"I don't know, but I'm game to try. I might even get some more good data off them. Either way, it'll take some time."

Macey's eyes narrowed. "What are you planning? You're up to something."

"No, I'm not."

"You're a hacker. You want to do something with them. To them."

Vanitha's eyes narrowed as well. "Maybe I just want the challenge."

Sally stepped between them. "A couple of days is fine. But you have to promise you're not going to do anything . . . illegal or immoral or whatever with them. You said they're like pets. We'll let you watch the dogs for a couple of days and then come back to collect them."

Vanitha nodded. "I'll make sure they get plenty of kibbles and take them for regular walks."

"I don't know . . ." said Macey.

"It'll be all right," said Sally. "Thanks, Vanitha."

"No problem. Go get that guy. Let me know how it turns out."

"If we can, we will." Sally handed Vanitha one of her business cards. "If you change your mind about wanting to be on call, or have anything you need to pass along to Just Cause, call me."

Vanitha sniffed ever so slightly. "Call you. Sure. I think I have a phone around here somewhere."

Sally smiled. "You can email me too. For that matter, you can probably Kali yourself right onto my computer. Just warn me if you're going to teleport to me. Or whatever it's called. Then I can at least have a bathrobe handy for you."

"Thanks for your help," said Macey. "Take care of those spheres. They're all I have left of Evan."

"I'll try and get more memories cleaned up for you and convince them to share with you."

Sally and Macey stepped out into the chilly night. A few lonesome snowflakes tumbled down from high clouds. Sally shivered. "Winter," she grumbled.

"What's our next move?" asked Macey.

"Back to Second Team HQ," said Sally. "You drive back to the airport. Coffee's on me." She pulled out her phone. "We've got a raid to plan."

Chapter Eleven

"Mistakes were made. Just Cause is taking steps to ensure that the unfortunate events in Waco will not be repeated in the future."

—*Juice, TIME Magazine, June 6th, 1993*

Richmond, Virginia
December, 2006

"So that's my proposal," said Sally. She was in the Just Cause Second Team's conference room along with Macey and the rest of the team. They'd arranged a video conference with Just Cause back in Denver as well as Juice from his office in Washington. Although she'd tried to be careful to keep herself in the view of the webcam mounted on top of the workstation, she'd still found herself pacing back and forth several times and had to force herself to sit back down again. Nerves were nerves, and she'd never been a fan of public speaking.

"That's good work, Sally," said Juice. "Very thorough. I'm impressed."

Sally felt her cheeks grow hot. "I'm on light duty. Figured I might as well exercise something besides my legs for once."

Jason grinned in the small inset window on Sally's monitor. It was one of the grins that usually encouraged her to climb up his gargantuan frame for a heavy makeout session. She smiled, wishing she could fulfill that fantasy.

"I've seen enough here to be satisfied of the urgency of your request," said Juice. "I'll have a Federal warrant to you within an hour. What else do you need?"

"Just some personnel," said Sally. "Doublecharge, can you spare Minerva, Ment, and Jason? We'll need Ment's psionics for questioning and Minerva's wild-card powers could make all the difference if there's any kind of nanotech outbreak."

Doublecharge didn't look impressed. "And what about Jason?" Sally knew that at some level she still disapproved of the relationship between her and Jason, feeling that it was unprofessional.

"Intimidation, boss." Jason turned away from his own camera to look at Doublecharge. "Crunchies tend to behave themselves around me."

Doublecharge started to say something but Juice interrupted her. "I agree, Stacey. And Jason, I'll thank you not to use that term ever again."

"Sorry, boss."

Juice leaned forward until his face almost filled the view of his webcam. "Stacey, Keith, I'm not about to tell you how to run your teams, but you both know that I think very highly of Sally, and I believe she's got a solid lead here, and the official PRA recommendation is that you act quickly. I'm doing what I can to keep the lid on the nanotechnology angle. There are some senators that would damn near start a civil war over something like this. They already don't like that Just Cause has nanotech and the U.S. Military doesn't."

"I understand, James," said Doublecharge. "Sally, you've got the full support of Just Cause behind you on this. I'll dispatch Ment, Minerva, and Mastiff as soon as we're finished with this call. What about Jack?"

"Jack?" Sally thought about it. He was very good at the insurgency type of thing, but without innate parahuman powers beyond his invulnerability, he tended to carry an arsenal with him into combat, and that could be overly frightening to civilians.

"Yes, Jack," said Doublecharge. "Take Jack. Please."

And then Sally realized that Jack had gotten thoroughly under the Just Cause leader's skin. Sally knew she shouldn't laugh, but she struggled to hide a smile. "I think Jack is more valuable where he is right now. Let him know that when we do need him, we'll call on him."

Juice made an amused snort and covered it quickly with a cough.

"Very well. We're at your beck and call, Sally," said Doublecharge through gritted teeth.

"Likewise, the Second Team is at your disposal," said MetalBlade.

Sally glanced over at Macey, who nodded in encouragement. "Um, okay. That sounds good. I guess that's all I have for now. We'll wait for the Just Cause members and the warrant to arrive and then we'll work out our plan."

"Just Cause out," said Stacey.

Jason winked into his camera just before the Just Cause feeds went dead.

"Sally, I'd like to speak to you in private once we're done here," said Juice.

"You can use the conference room," said MetalBlade. "Come on, everyone, clear out and give the young lady some space." He and Icebreaker led Alloy, Superconductor, and Macey out of the conference room.

Now in a less formal setting, Juice leaned back in his chair, which creaked under his considerable weight, and thumped his feet up onto his desk with obvious relish. "I love this desk. Most solid piece of furniture I've ever had. It weighs in at eight hundred pounds. Can you believe it?"

"It's a really nice one," said Sally. "You sure you don't want me to run on up there? I could be there in like ten minutes."

"That's tempting, but I don't believe Grace has cleared you for full duty yet, and I'm not brave enough to override her. No, this will be fine."

"Okay. What's up?"

"Your masked friend moves pretty fast. A corporation that appears to be a front for Champion successfully purchased the old Just Cause headquarters from the City of New York this morning. I've received word that construction equipment and supplies are already moving into the area."

"He bought the warehouse? Why?"

"We don't know. The purchase money came from an account in the Caymans. We have people trying to trace information back but this guy has been very careful to hide his identity. We can't find anything on him, and that makes me very uncomfortable."

"Yeah, I get that too. It feels like there's a lot more going on behind his mask than just keeping his loved ones safe."

"Sally, you've had more contact with him than anyone else has. At the moment, you're my only expert on Champion."

Sally swallowed, her mouth suddenly having gone dry. She poured herself a glass from the pitcher at the center of the conference table. "I suggested that he might connect with the Young Guns. He seemed really, you know, competent and professional. They really need someone like that to influence them."

"But not necessarily him?"

"I don't know. The more I think about it, the more I'm not sure. What does that mean?"

"It means you have a healthy dose of suspicion. That's an important quality for a good leader."

Sally drained her water. "What do you mean?"

"Let's just say I've got my eye on you, Sally. You've done nothing but impress me during your tenure with the team, and I don't doubt that you'll be leading one of the teams before too long. Maybe one of the new ones."

"New teams?" Sally blinked.

"There are a lot of kids in the Hero Academy pipeline now. We're tracking them as early as elementary school. There's a big bubble coming, both in the number and potential power level of heroes. Those kids are going to need to be placed on teams, and those teams need to be under the aegis of Just Cause and the PRA. And those teams are going to need veteran leaders."

Sally laughed. "Veterans? I'm twenty-one."

"And you've already seen far more action than many superheroes twice your age," said Juice. "So that's something for you to keep in the back of your mind. You're a superstar, Sally, and I know you've still got many great things you'll accomplish."

Sally felt her cheeks grow hot. "If you say so."

"I do, and I'd like to think I'm a pretty good judge of character. But that's all stuff to worry about later. What I'd really like you to do is see if you can find out what Champion is up to. If you can uncover his identity, so much the better. It worries me to no end that there's a fellow as apparently powerful as him that we know nothing about, and on top of it all he's rich enough to drop a boatload of money on a former superhero team headquarters."

"You think he's a . . . a *supervillain*? Like Destroyer or Misrule?"

"I don't know what to think, except that I'm having a hard time trusting him with as little information as there is about him."

"I'll call the Young Guns. See what they might know."

"Do that, but keep it on the down low. Right now this is just between you and me, and it's an unofficial investigation. You follow me?"

"Yes, sir."

"Knock off that *sir* stuff. We're well beyond that."

"Okay, uh, Juice."

"And be careful. There's no telling what he may be up to."

"It might not be anything."

"And if it isn't, I'll trust you to report that back to me as well."

"I will."

"Good luck with your raid. Report in as soon as you've got something." Juice smiled and broke the connection, leaving Sally sitting alone in the conference room. She started to mess around with the idea of putting together a PowerPoint presentation for her plan, but quickly discovered she was incompetent with the software. She called in a specialist from the Command Center and outlined her needs to him and he promised to put something professional together and email it to her for review.

She had several hours to kill. Jason and the others would arrive in the early evening. The raid would happen in the morning, and then there were only three more days until . . .

"Oh my God, I haven't done any shopping!" said Sally aloud. How had she forgotten something as important as Christmas shopping?

Well, for one thing, she'd turned twenty-one, gotten engaged, attended a funeral, and saved the entire East Coast from an out-of-control tanker in the past two weeks. She had to have been owed some kind of slack for that. Nevertheless, she was going to have to bite the bullet and hit up the stores in Richmond for everybody on her list. She pulled out her phone and called Macey.

"Mace, I'm a mess," she said when the young woman answered. "I spaced out my Christmas shopping and I don't know where to go. I've got to get it all done today, because I don't know when I'll have time afterward. Save me, Obi-Wan Ke-Macey. You're my only hope."

Macey laughed into the phone. "That's from a movie, isn't it?"

"*Star Wars*. Only a classic, Macey."

"I've never seen it."

"Never . . ." Sally shook her head in disbelief. It amazed her that there were still people in the world that hadn't seen it. "Okay, I know what we're doing after we shop."

"There's a mall not too far away. How many people do you have to shop for?"

"Um . . ." Sally counted off on her fingers. "Fifteen, plus Jason. Oh, no. I don't know what to get him. He got me an engagement ring. What do I do after that?" She paused in her panicky tirade as her brain caught up with the rest of her. For having accelerated perceptions, at times she still managed to shove her foot into her mouth with impressive speed. "I'm so sorry, Macey. That was really insensitive of me."

Macey sounded like she was smiling. "No, it's okay. I'm dealing with it. I may cry some more. A lot more, actually. But for now, I'm okay."

"Still, sorry for being an asshole," said Sally.

"There's a store in the mall that sells actual records. I mean, like, vinyl. Jason's a musician. He's got to be into stuff like that, right?"

"I wonder if they have any Jimi Hendrix . . ."

The two girls went to the mall and lost themselves in the mix of holiday shoppers. For Sally, it was like surfing waves made of people. With Macey's help, she found gifts for everyone on her team, her mother and grandmother—whom she wouldn't have time to visit until after the new year—and Jason. She had a long discussion with the skinny unshaven man behind the counter who had a pierced septum and hair that might have never seen a comb. It turned out that he actually owned a Velma's Glasses CD in his personal collection and was thrilled to meet Sally. She left the shop with a turntable player and three vinyl records for Jason: two Jimi Hendrixes and an early Stevie Ray Vaughan. Satisfied with the outcome of her shopping, Sally bought a giant cinnamon roll for her and Macey to share, and they got so sticky that they both had to scrub off their hands and faces in the mall bathroom before heading back to the car.

They returned to Second Team HQ and followed up their shopping bonanza with a gift-wrapping party that turned the dormitory lounge into a mass of paper and ribbon scraps. "Jason is such a neat freak. He'd ignore everything else in here just to pick up." Sally tossed an empty wrapping paper tube across the room as if to illustrate her point. "I could be naked and he'd still go collect that first."

Macey giggled, but then she grew sober. "Do you have a plan to move on that nanotech company?"

Sally nodded. "The trick is that we have to hit them fast so nobody has a chance to do anything like deleting files or destroying research. Or release nanotech into the wild. God, that's terrifying just to think about. With Minerva there to supercharge him, Ment can knock out everyone in the building in just a few seconds. I can sweep the building to shut down any running equipment. Superconductor can generate an electromagnetic field around the building that should shut down any nanotech threat."

"Are you sure a subtle approach wouldn't be better? Maybe Kali could just read through all their data files or something. Give us some better intel."

"I thought about that," said Sally. "But if we make any kind of slip in an on-the-sly investigation, we could tip off the suspect and then we might lose any chance at bringing Orb's killer to justice."

"That makes sense. What about the rest of us?"

"You know how they say no battle plan ever survives contact with the enemy? That's where you guys come in. What if there's a parahuman there in the facility? Or they have unusual or advanced technology? Maybe there's something that only you can stop, or only Icebreaker or Alloy."

"What about MetalBlade?"

Sally snickered. "If there's any sword-fighting to be done, he's our guy."

The afternoon passed quickly. Sally made Macey sit down and watch *Star Wars* while she reviewed her PowerPoint presentation on her laptop. Macey's bemused expression told Sally that she just didn't get it. Sally didn't mind, though. She mouthed along with every line and enjoyed sinking into someone else's fantasy universe for a little while.

And then Jason arrived.

He tried to be subtle and nonchalant as he sauntered into the lounge with Ment and Minerva behind him, but Sally caught a whiff of his shampoo on the breeze from the ventilation. She turned and let her perceptions accelerate to maximum so she could drink in every detail about him. His face was frozen in the act of forming his trademark goofy grin. Blonde stubble dotted his chin and cheeks and his hair was flopping down in his eyes as usual. Sally launched herself at him in a blur and wrapped her arms and legs around him, planting kisses all over his face. He shouted with laughter at the affectionate attack and returned the favor.

"Get a room, you two," said Ment. He was squeezing his head between his hands. "I hate flying."

Minerva brushed her fingertips across the back of his neck. "How's that?"

His eyes widened. "Better. What did you do?"

Minerva fixed him with an unsmiling gaze. "Do you really want to know?"

After a pause, Ment said, "Uh, no, I guess not."

Minerva was the granddaughter of Lady Athena, one of the heroes who founded Just Cause in the Fifties. Her powers were wide-ranging and mysterious and poorly-defined. Dr. Devereaux had said on more than one occasion that she didn't think Minerva was so much a parahuman as a posthuman, but even she couldn't say exactly what that meant. Sally had seen her supercharge other heroes' powers, and even brought back Jack from a fatal, magically-inflicted wound that had bypassed his normal invulnerabilities. She hoped the slight, dark-haired girl's powers would be the unexpected ace in the hole when they hit ScaleAbility in the morning.

"How was the flight?" asked Sally.

"Noisy," said Ment. "And bumpy."

"It wasn't bad," said Jason. "Starving, though."

"Tell you what. Let's all take an hour and a half to eat or nap or whatever, then we'll meet in the conference room to plan tomorrow's strike," said Sally. She pulled out her phone, speed-dialed the Second Team Control Room, and asked them to relay the ninety minute time frame to all other JCST members.

"Ment, Minerva, you can freshen up in one of the guest suites, or there's food down in the commissary," said Macey.

"Food, please," said Minerva. Ment nodded in agreement. Macey led the two of them down the corridor.

"Food, please," echoed Jason.

"You can eat later, mister." Sally felt tingly all over. She loved how Jason brought that alive in her. "We're having *whatever* instead."

"Whatever's good too." Jason took Sally's tiny hand in his huge one and they went the other direction, toward Sally's guest suite.

Between whatevering and then needing a shower afterward, Sally was nearly late to her own meeting.

Sally skidded into her seat, her hair still damp at the ends. Jason yawned, ambled over to the beverage bar, and confiscated an entire coffee pot, as was his wont.

"Glad you could join us, Sally," said MetalBlade in a tone that suggested he knew exactly why she and Jason were late.

Icebreaker reached out and squeezed her husband's hand. "Let's go ahead and get started."

Sally turned on the PowerPoint projector. She clicked the control and instead of the feared and fabled Blue Screen of Death, she got her intended starting slide showing the front of ScaleAbility. "This is ScaleAbility, a small company focusing upon nanotechnology-based solutions to various large-scale problems. They have patents, for example, in ocean desalinization and smog control, as well as in some medical applications." She clicked another slide. "It's the medical applications that particularly concern us, as we've discovered evidence placing Orb at this facility only two days prior to his death. Given the nanotech involved in his death, we've obtained a warrant to search this company's personnel files and database of projects current and past to see if we can find a connection and possible suspect."

"Is the nanotech related to what we use in the Bunkers?" asked MetalBlade.

Sally smiled; she'd anticipated that question, and dialed up a new slide. "I had one of the CTF engineers take a look at the bugs that killed Orb, and she said they were of a completely unfamiliar design to her. The CTF nanites are really, um, specialized in their construction, and even if someone could copy the tech, they wouldn't function any differently under different circumstances."

"Basically, they're no good unless someone wants to build another Bunker," said Jason. Sally glanced over at him. "What? I do read, you know."

Sally returned to her presentation. "According to the company website, they're shutting down all nonessential operations the day after tomorrow until January third, so if we're going to get in there and have a lot of people to interview, we need to do so tomorrow." She clicked onto a new slide. "Given the extreme risk of nanotechnology as a murder weapon, the PRA has authorized us to conduct a raid instead of a simple service."

Sally's next slide showed the tactical deployment of the team. She'd double checked her strategy with Doublecharge back home and MetalBlade. Then she'd called Juice and had him triple check her. None of them had found any fault in her plan, and Juice had been very complimentary of it, telling her that he'd had no idea she had such a good head for tactics. "Here's what we're going to do . . ."

Chapter Twelve

"Parahuman abilities are just tools. The real successes come from planning, lateral thinking, and the ability to make shit up on the fly."

—Seahawk, Playboy Magazine, October 2000

Chesapeake, Virginia
December, 2006

For the fiftieth time since the unmarked van came to a halt on the street across from ScaleAbility, Sally checked the time on her phone.

Three minutes had passed. And forty-seven seconds.

"Not good at waiting, huh?" asked Macey. She wore her costume, all bright primary colors with subtle speckled patterning that looked like scales in shifting light.

"Comes with the territory," said Sally. She tightened the laces on her chunky yellow boots with their vulcanized rubber and ceramic soles. They'd been custom made for her, and even though they didn't make her run appreciably faster, she always felt faster with them on.

Ment and Minerva sat with them in the back of the van, also wrapped up in their costumes. Regulations required Just Cause members to wear their costumes during all but covert deployments. For legal purposes, they were considered a badge. Ment's costume didn't make him look so much like a walking representation of legal authority as it did an extra from the *Matrix* movies. His long black coat was belted tight around him and his sunglasses were on even in the darkness of the van. Minerva wore her bronze breastplate and crimson tunic with a burgundy hooded cloak over the whole thing. Her helmet sat on the seat beside her and she warmed Ment's hands between hers.

Sally started to check her phone again but stopped herself. "This is stupid." She thumbed the radio switch on instead—after glancing at the time, of course. "All positions report."

"Team Two in position," said Metalblade. He and Icebreaker were covering the facility's loading dock. "All clear."

"Team Three all clear," said Jason. He was watching one of the side exits on his own.

"Team Four ready," said Alloy from her position on the opposite side of ScaleAbility.

"Team Five, ready and waiting," said Superconductor. He was flying high above the building.

"We're good to go," said Minerva.

Sally took a deep breath. She hoped Vanitha's assessment had been correct. She hoped her own plan was a good one. She hoped nobody would get hurt. Especially not Jason. She swallowed hard, nervous tension making her throat ache. If this was what it felt like to be in command, she'd gladly leave it to others in the future.

Nevertheless, everyone was counting on her at the moment, so she couldn't delay any longer. "Team Five, drop the curtains."

"Roger that." Sally watched through the van's side window as Superconductor dropped down until he was only a couple of dozen feet over the highest point on the ScaleAbility building. He spread his arms wide. Blue and purple lightning arced first between his fingertips, then spread inward towards his center and outward in a radial pattern to encompass the entire building. He poured on the power, channeling it like a human Tesla coil. Where Doublecharge's abilities tended to focus primarily on lightning-based applications, Superconductor made use of much more of the electromagnetic spectrum. His rays and fields could be the bane of unshielded electronics, and that was what Sally was counting upon to keep any nanotech from breaking containment.

"Team Four, lights out."

Ment was one of the most powerful telepaths that had ever come through the Hero Academy. Indeed, he was likely one of the top three or four most powerful in the entire world. Unfortunately, he lacked the ability to control his powers, and only through supreme acts of will and concentration could he temper his raw ability enough for it to become usable. That's where Minerva came in; she could tie herself into his power stream and give it the focus he lacked, like putting a lens over a floodlight to concentrate it into a tight beam. When they synced together the way they were for the mission, they seemed to share a single consciousness. It wasn't any wonder to Sally that they were in love with each other. She wondered what it was like to be so intimately close to someone as they were to each other. She imagined that to Ment and Minerva, she and Jason must seem as distant as if there were an ocean between them.

The power spread out from Ment, channeled through Minerva's senses, into the inhabitants of ScaleAbility.

"Twelve minds," murmured Minerva. "Triggering delta waves. Done. They're all soundly asleep."

Sally had experience with a couple of different psionicists during her time in Just Cause. Glimmer had already been a member of the team when she joined, but she'd only had a couple of months to know him before he was killed in Guatemala by the super-criminal Destroyer. Later, she'd met and worked with Switchboard of the Second Team. Ment was by far the most scary powerful of the bunch. The ease with which he knocked a dozen people unconscious with a thought was sobering. Fortunately he needed Minerva to focus him, and she would help him keep his temper if he should ever grow angry toward Just Cause.

"This is Team One," said Sally into her phone. "Moving in." She stepped out of the van, shrugging out of her overcoat as she did so. The cold seeped through her body suit in seconds, and she felt goosebumps rise all over. She jumped up and down a couple of times, slapping her arms to try to warm up. "Winter. Why am I always doing this in the winter?" she grumbled. "Macey, watch my back."

"I've got you covered to the front door," said Macey, or Mosaic as she called herself in the field. "After that, you're on your own until we get your all-clear."

"Right." Sally was done with formalities. It was time for action.

She ran.

To the van inhabitants, it would have looked almost like she vanished and reappeared beside the building's main entrance, but she actually covered the distance between them with her ability to accelerate and decelerate instantly. She accelerated her perceptions to maximum so she would have plenty of subjective time to observe, report, and rescue if necessary.

The door seemed to open with glacial slowness, but Sally could already see the receptionist slumped across her desk. She didn't appear to be in any danger, so as soon as the door was open enough for Sally to slip through, she burst into the building to conduct her search.

Three more people were in the front offices just off the main lobby. Two had their heads down on their desks but the third, a jowly man with a too-small mustache and glasses, had crumpled into a heap against a wall. Sally took a few precious seconds to rearrange him into what she imagined was a more comfortable position, stretched out on the floor. That was four people accounted for, eight remaining.

She found a fifth man in the security office. He wore a uniform with an unfamiliar logo on the arm. Sally figured he was probably a contractor, handling the security for ScaleAbility. Once she and the other heroes had the facility secured, she could verify that. She was pleased to note that there were six video screens in the office, each one cycling through either two or three cameras regularly. With the building under so much scrutiny, she knew that there would be a record of Evan, either as a visitor or trespasser.

Satisfied that she'd accounted for everyone in the front offices, Sally headed back toward the research labs, only to be temporarily stymied by a secured door that required a keycard. She went back to the front offices and checked each sleeper until she found a likely candidate. Grasping the purloined card firmly in her gloved hand, she slid it through the reader. The first time she did it far too fast for the sensor to get a clear reading, so she made herself slow down to a speed approximating human-normal and tried again. The light on the keycard box switched from red to green and the door unlocked. She slowed herself even further so she could be understood and spoke into her phone. "Team One. Five targets secured in the front. Moving into the back."

The labs would be more dangerous, so Sally made sure to explore them at a more leisurely pace. All she needed was to blow through an area too quickly and catch up something that could hurt or even kill someone in her wake.

The first lab she came to was empty, but the second had two researchers in it. Both were asleep on the floor. She made a quick circuit of the room to see if she could identify whether anything dangerous was running unattended, but after a few seconds of staring at completely unfamiliar equipment, Sally was forced to conclude that she wouldn't have known a dangerous experiment unless it sat up and tried to bite her. Fair enough, she decided. The researchers themselves would have to make sure things were shut down in a safe and appropriate manner once they were awakened.

She found two more researchers in a third lab and a third in the final lab, leaving two people unaccounted for. Steeling herself for icky possibilities, she checked the bathrooms. They were empty as well. Nobody was in the halls either. Where could they be? Sally slowed herself down again and keyed her radio. "Team One reporting, all but two personnel accounted for. I've looked in all offices, labs, bathrooms, and halls. Does anyone have any ideas?"

"Try the supply closets," said Jason.

"Why would two people be in—oh." Sally felt her cheeks grow hot as she realized exactly why two people might be in a supply closet. After all, she and Jason had nearly gotten caught once back in headquarters. "Checking on that now. All teams, move in and relocate the sleepers into the conference room. Team Five, maintain your shield until we give you the all clear."

"Roger that," said Superconductor. "Freezing my ass off up here, by the way."

Sally did indeed find the remaining two sleepers in a supply closet. From their half-undressed state and the way the man was draped over the woman in their sleep, it was obvious that developing nanotech hadn't been first and foremost thing on their minds. "Ahem. Team Three, I'm going to need some help here. Supply closet off the main hallway between Labs Three and Four."

After waiting for what seemed like an eternity, Sally heard Jason's heavy footsteps in the hallway outside. She disengaged her throat mic and stuck her head out the door. "In here, babycakes."

He grinned. "Just like old times, huh? Thanks for not calling me that on the radio, by the way."

"What, are you embarrassed by it?"

"Not when you say it, just when other people hear it. Oh . . ." Jason realized what he'd walked into when he saw the two sleepers on the floor. "I didn't realize you were serious. I thought you wanted to make out."

"We're working, silly boy. Which reminds me . . ." She turned her microphone back on.

Jason looked down. "These two were working too. Just not on nanotech."

"Well, what are you waiting for? Pick him up and get his pants back on him. At least we can preserve their dignity when they wake up."

"But he's bare-ass naked," said Jason. "His deal's all dangling around down there."

"Yes, I guess it is," said Sally. "And do you really want me to handle that or would you rather do it?"

Jason thought about it for a few seconds. "I see your point. You didn't look at it, did you?"

"No," lied Sally. She had, of course. She was only human. And curious. Her only actual experience had been with Jason, and he was quite pleasant in that regard. She wondered how close the two researchers were. Were they in love? Or were they just what Sondra called *chew toys* to each other?

Jason's face registered pure disgust as he carefully lifted the man off the woman. "Oh, man, it's all just right there, isn't it?"

"Don't you guys all walk around naked in the locker room and shower together? Flick towels at each others' asses? That's like a jock thing to do, isn't it?"

"I wasn't ever a jock. They don't let kids with parapowers play sports."

"You know what I mean."

Sally found the woman's underwear, coolly appraised them for tastefulness, and then slid them up the woman's hips. She noticed the woman had a small heart tattooed just above her bikini line. "Hey, would you ever want me to get a tattoo?"

"Sure, if you want. I think tats are sexy."

"We could get matching ones."

"I can't get a tattoo. Needles won't go through my skin." Jason shrugged. "Closest I could manage would be a drawing with a permanent marker. Or what's that stuff called? Hannah?"

"Henna," said Sally. "I never thought of that. Your skin being tough like that, I mean. I know you're tough, but it's on all the time. I mean, I can turn my perception and my speed on and off."

"It's cool that you can do that." Jason grimaced as he wrestled the man's pants back on. "It would suck if you were stuck on fast forward all the time. Everyone would be like statues around you all the time."

Sally shivered. She'd had nightmares about getting her perceptions stuck in overdrive, and Jason had managed to touch exactly on that fear. She turned away and got the woman's pants back on. "You can still feel things, right? I mean, when I touch you, you feel it?"

"Of course I do, babe." Jason stepped over and kissed the nape of her neck, making her shiver. "I feel everything. But the stuff that hurts only hurts. It doesn't do any harm."

Sally turned around and hugged him tight. "I'm glad. I worry about stupid little things like that."

"You don't need to. Not with me."

Sally was tempted to take advantage of the privacy of the supply closet as the two researchers had, but that would have been foolhardy given that they were still involved in a live raid. "Let's get these two lovebirds to the conference room."

ScaleAbility's conference room was much smaller and less modern-looking than Just Cause's, with blond wood accents on the walls and a large flatscreen on one wall. The heroes arranged the twelve sleepers in chairs around the table and then took up strategic positions around the room.

It was entirely possible that one of those dozen was a murderer.

Jason brought in two dozen donuts and a flat of water bottles. He set them at the center of the table. It had been his idea and Sally had seen the wisdom in it. "How would you feel if somebody just nuked your brain?" he'd asked her. "We don't know that any of those people are guilty of committing murder. We don't even know that it *was* a murder. Evan's death could have been accidental, right? And we're going to come in all heavy-handed with our costumes and powers. These people are going to be scared, and angry, and they're going to hate us. If we want them to cooperate, we've got to make them see that we're not the bad guys in this scenario."

"And donuts will do that?" Sally had asked, skeptical.

"It would for me." He'd grinned. "Bad guys never bring you donuts."

Ment was pacing back and forth along one wall, with Minerva tagging along beside him, trying to maintain some kind of calming physical contact with him. When he used his abilities, it made him jumpy and nervous, and prone to making bad decisions. If Sally had access to another telepath within the Just Cause system, she'd have tried to use that person instead. Unfortunately, psionic abilities were the rarest among parahuman powers, and so she had to make do with what she had.

"I don't see why I can't just read their minds, find out who did it," Ment grumbled.

"Because it's a violation of their rights," said Sally. "We've been over this. Supreme Court ruled that an individual's thoughts are protected under the Fourth Amendment. You took Ethics at the Academy."

"Yeah. And I passed it." He glared at her from behind his sunglasses.

"Take those off when we're indoors. The sun doesn't shine on you twenty-four hours a day." Sally glared back at him. She indicated her own goggles, riding high on her forehead so her face was clearly visible.

He took them off and hung them from his collar.

"Besides, evidence obtained telepathically isn't admissible in a court of law."

"That's stupid."

"Maybe so, but it's the law. You keep out of these peoples' heads or I'll put you on report. You wake them up and then you back off, Ment."

Ment glanced over at MetalBlade. The man was wrapped up in the dark iron armor that he drew out of the ground, but he'd kept from forming the helmet that normally obscured his face in battle. "This is Sally's operation," he said. "We're behind her one hundred percent."

"Thanks, Keith," said Sally. "Now can we stop arguing the law and get to work on finding our killer?" She glared at Ment.

"Yes, all right," he said through gritted teeth. He crouched against a wall for a moment and then shied away when Minerva reached out to him. "I'm fine. Leave me alone."

"I don't have to be a telepath to know what you're thinking," said Sally. "And it changes nothing."

Jason cleared his throat and casually cracked his knuckles. It sounded like rocks falling in a pile. The subtle unspoken threat wasn't lost upon anyone in the room, least of all Ment. The telepath's father had been a minor-league supervillain in the '70s, and Sally knew the young man had worked hard to overcome that reputation. She was trying not to blame him for his attitude, knowing it was a side effect of his powers.

"Sorry," said Ment at last. "Minnie, please." He held out his hands to Minerva. She took them in hers and the tension washed out of his face like it had drained from a sink. "Okay, I'm better now. Sorry I'm such a dick about it. I suck at being a hero."

"No, you don't. We all have side effects of our powers that we have to live with," said Ingrid— Icebreaker, MetalBlade's wife. Her normal body temperature was only a couple of degrees above freezing, and her blood was like organic antifreeze. Sally had often wondered about the mechanics of intimacy between her and Keith. Whatever was required, the two of them seemed to have worked out those details, for they seemed quite happily in love and had been married for years.

"Is everyone ready?" asked Sally.

Everyone indicated they were.

"All right, then. Wake them up."

Chapter Thirteen

"The true mystery of the world is the visible, not the invisible."

—*Oscar Wilde*

Chesapeake, Virginia
December, 2006

For a moment, there was chaos in the conference room as the ScaleAbility employees, suddenly awakened, started to finish their sentences and actions until they realized that *something had happened*. The two lovers discreetly checked their clothing and then stared around the room at the colorful visitors.

"Ladies and gentlemen, may I have your attention please?" said Sally. "We're very sorry to have approached you like this. I am Mustang Sally and these are members of Just Cause. We are investigating a nanotech-related death and we need your help."

One of the men whom she'd found in a front office stood up. "What's going on here? How did we get in here? I was in my office."

"Sir, I can assure you that you're in no danger and that at no time were your rights compromised," said Sally. "Due to the nature of your research and the investigation, we couldn't come here under the, um, the auspices of a traditional warrant." She held up the document signed by a federal judge. "Although we do have one here."

"Are we under arrest?" asked one of the researchers.

"No, ma'am. We need to ask some questions and then we should be on our way and let you get back to your work." Sally squeezed her shaking hands together behind her back. She hated public speaking but knew that as point on the investigation, she needed to be the one speaking to the civilians. She was also one of the best-known parahumans on Just Cause and indeed in the entire world. That reputation would carry a certain amount of *gravitas* that would help keep things from getting out of hand. "Mosaic, if you would please?"

Acting like a human PowerPoint projector, Macey projected a holographic image of Evan in the center of the table, rotating it around so everyone could see it clearly. Sally bit her tongue. The image was so realistic that she felt like she could have reached out and touched it. Macey was putting forth her best effort. "This is Evan Roberts. He died earlier this month due to a stroke caused by nanotech devices," said Sally. "We've been able to trace his movements to this facility." Macey recreated the static image that Vanitha had been able to retrieve from the orbs. "As you can see, we've been able to place him at this location. We're going to be pulling each of you aside to question you further. We're also going to review your security footage and personnel files, and the warrant gives us legal authority to do these things. Once we've done that, as long as we don't need any further information, we should be leaving you. Does anyone have any questions or statements to make before we begin?" Although she was addressing everyone in the room, Sally focused her attention specifically upon the receptionist and security guard, who were most likely to recall having seen Evan during a visit. She thought she saw a spark of recognition on both of their faces.

The man from the front office spoke again. "Personnel files? Are we suspects?"

"Not at this time," said Sally. "As I said, we're just beginning our investigation at the moment."

He nodded. "All right, then. I'm George Appleby. I'm the CEO here. We'll do everything we can to comply and to assist you in your investigation. I hate the idea of a death caused by nanotech. We've always done our best to prevent such things. Karlie, if you'd pull the files for them, and Troy, the security footage."

"We'll begin questioning with the two of you," said Sally. "I'm afraid the rest of you will have to stay in here until we're finished, but we've brought you some refreshments. Did anyone have any work going on that requires your immediate attention?"

The researchers all shook their heads. The woman who'd been found in the supply closet blushed to the roots of her hair. Sally felt sorry for her. She made a mental note not to bring up the compromising position at all.

"Mosaic, if you'll start reviewing security footage, I'll begin with questioning . . . Karlie, is it?"

The receptionist nodded.

"Let's go back to your desk," Sally said. "You have personnel files there?"

"Yes, ma'am," said Karlie.

"Ma'am," repeated Sally with a tinge of disgust in her voice. "Yeah, you can just call me Sally, okay? *Ma'am* makes me think I'm the one in trouble."

"Am I in trouble?" Karlie's voice quavered a bit.

"I seriously doubt it." Sally looked around the reception desk. "You're very neat. My fiancé would approve."

"Oh. I can't stand clutter," said Karlie. "That guy who died, that was your teammate, right? I saw on the news that he died. I never put it together that his death was the one you're investigating."

"Yes." Sally saw no point in elaborating further. "Do you remember him coming here? It would have been about two weeks ago."

"You know, I think I do. What day? Do you know?"

Sally gave her the date and Karlie pulled up her appointment book on her computer. "Mark Moriwaki," she murmured.

"I'm sorry?"

"Your friend had an appointment with Dr. Moriwaki. He's a reproduction specialist."

"You mean like making copies of nanotech devices?"

Karlie laughed. "No, like making babies. He's been working on a project using nanites to assist with overcoming infertility."

Sally blinked. "They can do that?"

"Yes. Well, with rabbits, at any rate." Karlie smiled.

"Funny, I didn't think rabbits needed any help breeding," said Sally. "So what was Evan doing with Dr. Moriwaki, then?"

"Some kind of consulting work, I'm sure. I only sort of know what's going on here at any given time. It's mostly so I know who needs to take any particular phone call."

"Which one is Dr. Moriwaki?" asked Sally.

"He's not here. I'm sorry. He started his Christmas vacation last week. I think he was going to Belize with his wife."

Sally grimaced at the notion of Central America. After seeing her friends killed in Guatemala and nearly dying herself, she had no desire ever to return to that part of the world. "Was he working with anyone else here? A partner on his project?"

"No, at least, I don't think so." Karlie opened a project monitoring program on her computer. "The researchers here are given pretty much free rein over their projects. They pitch them to Mr. Appleby, and if he approves them, they get their development funding and their name on their design and ScaleAbility markets their work and earns the bulk of the profits."

"They pay well here? I'm not looking for a job, I mean. I'm trying to think of a motivation for someone to use ScaleAbility tech to commit murder."

Karlie shuddered. "I wish that hadn't happened. I like working here, but now I'll always think of that."

"I'd like to see Dr. Moriwaki's file, please," said Sally.

"Of course. Give me a moment," said Karlie.

Sally pulled out her phone. "Mosaic?"

"Go ahead, Sally."

"Pull the security feeds for Mark Moriwaki's lab for the following time . . ." Sally passed along the time frame that Evan's appointment had been scheduled, padding it for half an hour on either side.

"Got it, we're looking now."

Sally turned back to Karlie. "Could Mr. Appleby identify who built a particular nanotech device if he could see it?"

Karlie shook her head. "I don't know for sure, but I don't think so. He's the money guy. You want to talk to Dr. Marzano. She's the senior researcher on staff."

"She's here today?"

"Yes, ma'am. I mean, Sally. Do you want me to call her in?"

"Please."

Dr. Christine Marzano was as close to a fireball in human form as someone could be without parahuman abilities. She was every bit as short as Sally, with a thick mass of black ringlets pulled back in a silver clip, but she had a presence about her that filled the room. Sally had been terrified that she would be the researcher who'd been in the compromising position in the storage closet, but she'd been in one of the front offices instead. "How can I help?" she asked in a brusque but not unfriendly way.

Sally held up a thumbdrive. "I've got some images we were able to take of the nano thingies we found in Evan's body. We were hoping you or somebody here could identify them."

"Of course, I'll take a look. Can we go to my office?"

"Yes," said Sally. "Karlie, do you have the personnel files in hard copies?"

"I do," said the receptionist. "This stack right here." She handed the folders to Sally.

Sally switched her perceptions to high speed and flipped through Moriwaki's file. He was an MIT graduate, and he'd specialized in nanotechnology right from the start. A PhD figured prominently in his file, as did a half dozen patents in the field. He'd come to ScaleAbility right out of school, and from what Sally could see, he'd been targeted by one of Appleby's headhunters. He was married to a biochemist who worked at a nearby firm. They had no children.

Nothing in his file suggested that Moriwaki was even capable of committing a murder. Sally began to wonder if perhaps Evan's death had been accidental somehow. But then she shook her head. If he'd been accidentally dosed with nanotechnology, he'd have sought help. Instead, he'd worked feverishly to try to save himself without involving anyone else. To Sally, that suggested that he knew exactly what had happened and was somehow trying to protect the others. What if the nanites had been contagious? Sally shivered at the thought of a nanotech plague. It was even scarier to consider than a viral plague. At least viruses could be isolated and treated, but how could anyone fight nanotech? More nanotech, probably, she thought. That was the logical science fiction way to do it. Bugs hunting bugs. Layers upon layers of nanites fighting other nanites. Nothing could go wrong with that, right? That was *also* the logical end result in science fiction tales: the world dissolving into shapeless gray goo.

Sally finished with Moriwaki's file and her instincts said that he probably wasn't her guy, but she knew not to discount anything until the investigation cleared him . . . or didn't. She slowed her perceptions back down so she could interact with Marzano more easily.

Marzano plugged Sally's thumbdrive into her desktop computer. "You don't have to wait over there," she said. "Come on around here so you can see what I'm looking at too." She smiled. "I don't bite."

Sally moved to look at the monitor. It showed the best resolution images of the nanites that had infested Evan that the Second Team's technicians had managed to take. Even though the Second Team had a nanotech-based Combat Training Facility like the one in Denver, there wasn't any way they could repair nanites themselves. When the microscopic machines became damaged, as they often did, they were broken down into their raw materials and used to make replacements by the machinery built by the heroes Particle and Architect. Consequently, the only way they had to examine nanotechnology was with the electron microscope in Evan's lab.

"Hmmm . . ." said Marzano as she scrolled through the available pictures. "It's a simple, basic design. We use a lot of these here as foundations for more complex nanites. You see these?" She pointed to four claw-like appendages extending from the nanite's sides like the points of a caltrop. "These are grippers. They will chemically interlock with other nanites and with other targeted molecules to form a kind of fabric. When they achieve a critical mass, the entire group will contract. They're useful as molecular fasteners or sutures."

"Or as a murder weapon," said Sally. "They closed off a blood vessel in Evan Roberts' brain, causing a cerebral aneurysm."

Marzano shook her head. "That's horrible. I hate that it was our technology that did it. Mr. Appleby has always been concerned about the weaponization of nanotech. Oh!"

"What is it?"

"That right there." Marzano pointed to the screen. "That's part of one of our ID numbers. It identifies the base manufacturer, the lab, researcher, generation, and project number." She opened a second window on the monitor and scrolled through a list of numbers. "Evie Lincicome. This is her work."

Sally texted Macey to also check on Evie Lincicome's lab, and then sent another text to Jason that she should be the next one they questioned. Macey texted back a moment later that the same interference that had corrupted Evan's spheres had apparently affected the building's security cameras as well. Sally thought maybe Vanitha could be helpful, and decided to call her later.

An incoming text message from Macey caught Sally's eye. *Ask abt tall blond guy. Took somthn from Evie's lab. Didn't see him here.*

"Ms. Marzano, besides Dr. Moriwaki, do you have any other employees who aren't here today? Perhaps out for the holidays?"

Marzano opened her calendar. "Just two. Deirdre Savoy—she's our accountant—and Henry King. He's a tuning specialist."

"Tuning?"

"Nanites are very simple machines. You can't pack a whole lot of processing power into an individual device. They're more effective in large groups, of course. Since the colonies don't have anything like a CPU, programming them is more like controlling an ant colony. Where the ants use pheromones, we use specific tonal frequencies to activate specific functions. That process is, um, proprietary."

"And King is your tuner? He programs the nanites?"

"That's as good a way as any to describe it."

"May I see his file?"

"Of course." Marzano opened a folder on her computer. "That's odd. It's empty." She navigated to another location. "Here as well. Even the backup is gone."

Sally felt a thrill of vindication. The missing personnel file felt like their first solid clue pointing toward a suspect. "Do you keep hard copies anywhere?"

"I don't, no, but Karlie might." Marzano touched her intercom. "Karlie, do you have a hard copy of Henry King's file? It's missing from the server."

"Yes, ma'am. Just a moment."

Macey sent a picture to Sally's phone that she must have snapped of the grainy surveillance video. Sally held the phone up to Marzano. "Is that King?"

Marzano nodded. "Yes."

Karlie entered Marzano's office with a manila folder in hand. "I know you guys are trying to go paperless here, but I'm an old-school kind of girl. Sometimes you just want papers to shuffle."

"Good thing, too," said Sally. She took the folder, opened it, and her heart sank. Although the file was clearly labeled *Henry King*, the photo paperclipped to the first page showed a man Sally knew by face, if not in person.

The man who called himself *Henry King* had another name: *Heinrich Kaiser*. He was the world's first lab-created parahuman, having been forged in a secret Nazi reactor towards the end of World War II. Just Cause had a disturbingly thin file on Kaiser, because he'd spent so much of the past sixty years working behind the scenes on a long-reaching mysterious project. They knew he'd stopped aging at the time of his creation, and that he could fly and . . .

"Radiation bursts," said Sally. "Jesus."

"Radiation?" asked Marzano.

Sally thumbed the open frequency on her phone. "All Just Cause personnel stand by. Superconductor and Minerva, I need you to check for residual radiation in this facility and its personnel."

Minerva and Superconductor acknowledged her.

"What's the matter, babe?" asked Jason over the open frequency. Sally wished he was beside her to put an arm around her shoulders. The last time she'd faced Heinrich Kaiser had been in Guatemala, when he'd allied with Destroyer to try to recreate the same reactor that had made him. Between the two of them, they'd slaughtered thousands of residents to build a telepathically-controlled army of ready-made parahumans. Doublecharge and Crackerjack had been tortured, and Glimmer, Forcestar, and some other non-Just Cause heroes had died as well.

Having Kaiser involved in Evan's death made everything seem far more sinister. It meant that Evan's death wasn't an accident in any way, shape, or form. Everything Kaiser did was according to his plan. And if that plan called for a single Just Cause hero to die, that hero's days would be numbered.

Evan had *known* something, something that Kaiser needed to keep a secret, and he'd made sure the young man would never pass along that secret.

"Evan's killer," said Sally. "I'm pretty sure it was Heinrich Kaiser." She shivered. "And he knows how to program nanites."

Chapter Fourteen

"Propaganda should be popular, not intellectually pleasing."

—*Joseph Goebbels*

Chesapeake, Virginia
December, 2006

Sally figured it was nothing short of a miracle that they'd been able to get a no-knock warrant in less than an hour for Henry King's bungalow two days from Christmas. She'd personally run to the home of the federal judge that had agreed to sign the document, thanked the iron-haired woman for her time, and raced back to meet the rest of her task force. Despite her breath mask and goggles, the icy air seeped through every possible crack and seam in her winter-issue uniform to leave her shivering and feeling like her entire body was chapped raw.

Jason handed her a steaming hot chocolate with a shot of espresso in it, and she smiled as she sipped it.

The first day she'd joined Just Cause as an intern, he'd taken her for a tour of the facility that culminated in them drinking hot chocolate in the cafeteria. Sometimes she couldn't believe it had only been three years. They'd passed by like she'd been running through them at top speed.

Sometimes, she had.

"How's it look?" she asked Minerva. The young woman stood in front of the bungalow, her arms outstretched, eyes closed, and mouth agape as if she were tasting the air. Her cloak blew in the wind, but she wasn't visible to anyone but her teammates. Macey had used her light-bending abilities to create a cylinder of invisibility around the Just Cause van and its inhabitants.

"I don't believe anyone is home," said Minerva. "I don't detect any trace of explosives or dangerous chemicals. Not even normal household chemicals."

"No mental signatures," added Ment.

"There's power to the building, but nothing's drawing it," said Superconductor, alighting beside Minerva. "I think this is a dead end."

"Let's be sure. Jason, you're up" said Sally.

Jason grinned. He pushed his hair back and pulled the half-mask up over his face. He didn't wear the mask that often. Jason had freely admitted to Sally that he only wore the mask at all because he liked the aesthetic it gave the rest of his costume. Half the time it stayed crumpled down around his neck anyway, though, because he said it itched. He cracked his knuckles and stepped out of the van into the chilly air.

Sally accelerated her perceptions to watch as he lumbered up to the door at what was for him a dead run. The play of his muscles beneath the outer velour layer of his brown and gray costume almost drove her to distraction. As he took the steps onto the porch, Sally grabbed the signed warrant in its envelope and sped across the walk to accompany her fiancé.

Jason shouldered into the door, which splintered into fragments. "Just Cause," he bellowed like he'd practiced it. "We have a warrant." He proceeded to stagger into the front room of the bungalow and skidded to a halt amid the wreckage of the door and surrounding framework that his broad shoulders had broken.

The room was empty of any furnishings. A great cloud of dust roiled around the confused Jason. Sally's heart sank. She made a rapid circuit of the house and verified her fears. "It's empty. Nobody's been in here in months."

"Why would Kaiser have an empty house?" Jason brushed debris from his uniform.

"Safe house, maybe. Maybe he needed a physical address so he could get that job at ScaleAbility," said Sally. "That's not beyond him by any means."

"We're still going to search it, right?" Jason looked disappointed. Sally knew he'd been looking forward to getting to play action movie cop for once.

"Yeah, babycakes, we are." Sally didn't tell him she'd already checked everything out. Besides, there was already the chance she'd missed something at her accelerated pace. She called Juice but got his voice mail saying that he would be out of the office until the beginning of January. Should she call him at home? No, she decided. She'd send him an email report later. She had enough authority on her own as a member of Just Cause to order a federal investigation.

They notified the Chesapeake Police Department that the house was considered an active crime scene until a forensics team went over it with a fine-toothed comb and then the Just Cause heroes cleared out to return to Richmond.

After a short and disappointing debriefing session, Sally sent in requests to the feds to investigate Henry King a.k.a. Heinrich Kaiser. She specifically asked for them to try to track his movements between when he'd departed from Guatemala in 2004 and turned up at ScaleAbility during the past year. She added *murder suspect* to his sparse file and then closed her aching eyes for a minute.

When she awoke, Jason was lowering her into bed like a mother laying a baby down. "Hey," she murmured. "What time is it?"

"Dinnertime, if you want." He kissed her cheek. "I picked up pizza from a place Keith told me is fantastic. I'm reserving judgment until I taste it, though."

Sally wrinkled her nose. "How much tasting did you already do? You smell like pepperoni."

"I'm reserving judgment until I taste the second pizza." Jason grinned. "The first one was delicious."

"You're going to get fat if you keep eating like that," said Sally. She unbraided her hair and worked on a tangle. "Maybe you should start running."

He nuzzled her neck. "I'll get right on that."

"Liar." She buried her hands in his thick, shaggy hair and turned his head so she could kiss his lips. Or rather, he let her turn his head. Sometimes, being strong enough to throw a car across a highway meant he had to relax and let Sally take the lead.

"Your pizza's going to get cold," he said in between Sally's kisses.

"I like cold pizza," she said. "It can be dessert, Mr. Main Course." Her hands moved lower, and he smiled against her lips.

Later, a warm glow filling her from their loving, a drowsy Sally nestled in Jason's arms. She kept thinking that she was hungry and she should go find the pizza he'd brought, but then she'd drift off to sleep. She was warm and comfortable, and his heart thumped its reassuring rhythm against her cheek.

A knock on her door brought her instantly to full alertness. Still naked, she flashed to the door and squinted through the peephole. The amenity might have seemed out of place in a secure superhero headquarters facility, but team psychologists had determined it beneficial for inhabitants to be allowed to peek through the door, even when more advanced monitoring systems were available.

"Sally, are you in there?" It was Alloy. The young woman's flowing and rippling metallic body seemed even more distorted than normal through the fisheye lens of the peephole.

"I'm here. I just woke up. What's the matter?"

"Um, are you dressed? Keith just asked everyone to head down to the conference room ASAP."

Sally sped up her perceptions, dashed across the room to find her discarded clothing. As usual, her suitcase looked like a bomb had gone off in it and her riffling through it at super-speed wasn't doing anything to improve the state of her clothing. She found clean underwear, yoga pants, a tank top, and one of Jason's voluminous hoodies that smelled like his shampoo. She pulled everything on, stepped into her moccasins, and opened the door. "I'm ready. Um, do I need to wake up Jason?"

"I'm up, babe," said Jason from the bedroom. "Someone stole my sweatshirt. You wouldn't know anything about that, would you?"

"Nope," said Sally. Alloy giggled, a tinny sound like soft wind chimes.

Jason wandered out of the bedroom in sweat pants and his *Property of Just Cause—XXXL* t-shirt. "Hope Keith doesn't mind slobs in his conference room. Juice was cool with it, but Doublecharge is a real Nazi about it."

"He'd have called for duty uniforms if it was for a deployment," said Alloy. She headed up the hall, not so much striding as flowing like a humanoid-shaped superfluid.

"Well, come on, sleepyhead," said Sally. "Let's go see what's so important that I had to miss my pizza."

"It's still there. I promise I didn't eat it in my sleep."

Sally and Jason joined the other heroes in the Second Team's conference room. Several of them were clustered around an auxiliary monitor that was showing Monday Night Football. Jason looked in to check the score. "Falcons losing to the Redskins. Naturally. I swear, that team hates me." He made a petulant, brushing-off gesture.

"You don't have any money on it, do you?" asked Sally, who thought football was second only to baseball in the category of most-boring sports.

"No, it's just, you know. They're a bunch of heartbreakers. They can't win for losing."

Keith stepped up to the head of the table. He was dressed in comfortable lounging clothes like everyone in the conference room except Superconductor, who was on monitor duty and therefore required to wear his costume. "Ladies and gentlemen, I'm sorry to interrupt your evening, but we've had a situation arise and quite frankly, I'm not sure what to make of it."

"Is it that commercial?" asked Ment. "We saw it while we were watching the game in the lounge."

"What commercial?" asked Sally.

"We have a recording of it," said Keith. "Ingrid?"

Ingrid raised the remote at the large wall-mounted monitor. It lit up to show the last play at the end of the half and then cut to a station identification blurb followed by a commercial break.

The screen filled with the image of Stefan of the Young Guns, although he'd drastically altered his appearance. Gone was his shaggy blond hair, replaced by a military-looking cut. Instead of his customary wetsuit, he wore a tight-fitting yellow bodysuit with red trim and an unfamiliar logo on the chest that resembled a stylized letter *C* encapsulated in a swooping diamond shape. "My name is Surfboy, and I wasn't good enough for Just Cause."

The camera made quick cuts to the other members of the Young Guns. All four were similarly attired to Surfboy, and each one announced his or her name and that they also weren't good enough for Just Cause."

"What is this?" Sally murmured.

"I don't know," said Jason.

The camera cut to Champion, standing amid the four Young Guns heroes. "They may not be good enough for Just Cause, but I promise you they are good enough to be heroes, to save lives, protect property, to show leadership and fortitude in the face of danger, and to be champions for law and order." The camera pulled in tight on his mask. "My name is Champion, and I can see the potential in these young heroes, like I can see it in so many others. How many times have you needed help? And how many of those times did Just Cause come to your aid? They are a government organization, and they only deal with the problems of our government."

"That's not true!" said Sally.

"Hush," said Keith.

"The problem with Just Cause is that it is inaccessible to everyday people like you, and that is why I've created the Champions. Real heroes who are ready, willing, and able to help you with all manner of problems and needs from small to large. With the Champions, you always know you are getting the best possible assistance we can provide, and we do so out of our moral obligation, not because we are being paid by your tax money."

The camera returned to Surfboy. "Do you have a parahuman ability that you thought was too slight to make a difference? Or you're afraid to use it because of unwelcome attention? We accept any and all parahumans into the Champions. We'll even accept non-parahumans who can meet our requirements. We are a non-discriminatory organization."

"Our identities are known," said Toxic, who looked strangely unfamiliar without her trademark punk getup. "But yours doesn't have to be. With us, you can remain safely anonymous. You never need to worry that your loved ones will be in danger."

"Check out our website for more information," said Johnny Go, and the words *ChampionProject.com* appeared on the screen. "We're always accepting new members, from anywhere and any background."

The camera cut to the four Young Guns heroes as they each pulled masks up over their faces. "Come be a Champion with us," they said together.

Some fine print appeared at the bottom of the screen. Sally threw her perceptions into overdrive so she had time to read it before the commercial ended. *Paid for by the First Church of the Parahuman, a 501(c) (3) organization. Not affiliated with Just Cause, the Parahuman Resources Agency, or the Department of Homeland Security.*

Ingrid stopped the recording and Keith turned his back on the monitor to face the Second Team and their guests. "This went out over the air fifteen minutes ago. From what our tech people can tell, the Champion Project website is registering thousands of hits every minute. It's already on YouTube and other video-sharing sites. People, this is huge."

"What's the big deal?" asked Switchboard. "So Champion wants to make a cut-rate superhero team. There are other private teams already, like the New Guard, the Lucky Seven, and those Bible-thumpers down in Atlanta."

"Divine Right," said Sally.

"It's not that he can't make his own team," said Keith. "The issue is with secret identities. He's already been flaunting his willingness to go against the Unmasking Act, and he's not only willing to take on others to do the same, he's encouraging it."

"I never saw it as that big of deal either way," said Jason. "He wants to keep his identity a secret. So what? Maybe he doesn't like having paparazzi follow him every time he wants to take his girlfriend to a nice dinner or see unflattering photos of him posted in the rags."

Sally knew exactly what picture he was referring to; he'd had chicken grease on his chin and a half-full bucket in one arm with a headline suggesting that he was *Too Big For His Costume?* "Jason's right. Are we really going to make a big deal about a fifty-year-old law?"

"Laws are the foundation of this country," said Ingrid. "And the Unmasking Act was put into place for a very good reason. Without it, we wouldn't ever have been granted the authority to enforce the laws, because of the Confrontation Clause in the Sixth Amendment."

Ment raised his hand. "I was sick that day. Which one is that? The right to remain silent?"

"No, the right for the accused to cross-examine the witnesses against him or her," said Minerva. "And you weren't sick, you were hung over."

"Traitor," mumbled Ment.

"An anonymous witness, like a masked parahuman, can't testify in a trial," said Minerva. "Their testimony isn't admissible, even if it is crucial to the case."

Ment looked like he wanted to sink right into the table. "Okay, all right, I get it."

"Also, you just incriminated yourself," added Jason. "You might want to look into that."

"People, please." Keith raised his voice. "Everything we can see so far on Champion's website suggests that he's not just looking to build a new team, but a wide-ranging organization. Think about this. For every one of you who graduates the Academy and joins Just Cause, how many of your classmates don't get selected? How many more parahumans out there don't have significant-enough abilities to warrant Hero Academy admission? Or have no interest in pursuing that kind of career?"

"I thought that parahumans were about one in five million people or so," said Ment. "I wasn't hung, er, sick *that* day."

"Those are Musashi's original estimates. More recent data suggests it may even be more than one in a million. Suddenly instead of forty or fifty parahumans in the U.S., we could be looking at ten times that amount," said Ingrid.

Keith folded his arms in solemnity. "And Champion wants to recruit all of them, and it doesn't sound like he's going to be doing the exhaustive background checking that we do."

"He could be recruiting criminals into his organization," said Alloy. "He could even be one himself. Don't we know where he is now? Why don't we go arrest him for violating the Unmasking Act?"

"That could be a problem," said Sally. "He's awfully popular. He's been doing a lot of good out there, and heroism goes a long way in the public eye. In their perception, he stopped that oil tanker."

"Babe, did you hit your head that hard? If I recall, *you* stopped that oil tanker," said Jason.

"Maybe yes, but I was deep down in the engine room. He was flying outside, blasting the ocean into steam. That's flamboyant, and flamboyance makes great press. All the pictures are of him. People are going to remember him, not the rest of us."

"He's capitalizing on his reputation," said Keith. "And if we bust him, especially now that he's opened this can of worms, we become the bad guys. Jealous at the attention he's getting."

"Hey, did you guys see the fine print at the end of the commercial?" asked Sally. "Has anyone ever heard of the First Church of the Parahuman?"

Everyone shrugged.

"It said it was 501(c)(3) status. I think that means it's tax exempt. That means that someone in the IRS decided it was a real church." Sally felt herself starting to talk much faster and struggled to keep her accelerating perceptions in check. "If it's a church, it's got to have rules and stuff. What if their rules require everyone to be masked? And permit anyone to remain anonymous?" She got up, too excited to sit still anymore, and started to pace back and forth. "That could be a First Amendment issue. We're going to have the ACLU all over us if we take any action against an established religious organization."

"But they're not real," said Jason. "Champion has to have made up the church just for this purpose."

"I don't doubt it," said Sally. "But imagine the uproar if we went after a more popular church."

"They're a cult," said Keith. "And they're acting more like a militia than anything else. That makes them dangerous."

"We can't treat them like a cult. I remember Juice telling me about the Branch Davidians." Sally drummed her fingers on the conference room table in a rapid tattoo. "That was a nightmare that lasted for a long time, and had lasting implications."

Ingrid stood. Her motion radiated cool air throughout the room. "I think we need to consider that we're already looking at this like Champion is our enemy. We don't know that he's just another garden-variety despot looking to take over the world. If they're true, his statements express his desire to help people. Shouldn't we wait until he proves otherwise? We should give him the chance to do what he says. Maybe this is heralding a new era in parahuman relations."

Alloy nodded. "It's not so much a factor for me, but I bet there are plenty of paras out there who haven't done anything positive with their abilities because they're ashamed, embarrassed, or afraid. If Just Cause hadn't taken me, Champion's offer would have sounded pretty appealing to me."

"It's going to sound appealing to a lot of people, I think," said Keith. "And that's the problem. There could be a whole lot of new parahumans turning up who we know nothing about. How many criminals out there could use his organization as a place to hide?"

"With all due respect," said Sally. "We've got a whole lot of questions and no answers. I think that maybe the best thing to do would be to go to the source."

"You want to knock on his door and ask what he's up to?" Keith gave a wry smile. "I'm sure he'll tell you."

"Not as such," said Sally. "But I've got an . . . independent agent in mind who might be able to get us a little more information."

Macey nodded, knowing that Sally meant Vanitha. "Yeah, I think that we might be able to shed some light on things with her help."

"Her?" asked Keith.

"Yes, and that's all I can disclose for now. I made a promise not to reveal my sources."

"Very well," said Keith. "Go talk to your independent agent, as you called her. See if she can indeed help us understand more about what kind of motives Champion might have beyond those he stated."

"I can't promise anything, but I will ask her." Sally sat in her chair but only for a second. She was back up pacing again in a flash.

"Babe, you're making me tired just watching you," said Jason.

"Sorry," said Sally. "I'm just . . . I don't know, nervous about this Champion thing, I guess."

"You've met him," said Keith. "Did you get any sense he was going to do something like this?"

"No. He was very polite and gave every indication that he wanted to help the Young Guns with some firm leadership."

"Well, he's certainly done that." Keith sighed. "I've got a bad feeling about this."

"*That's no moon, it's a space station,*" quoted Sally.

"What?" Keith's face was blank with confusion.

Sally rolled her eyes. "It's a hard world when a girl can't even quote *Star Wars* without losing civilians in the process." She took Jason's hand and led him toward the conference room door.

"Wait, civilians? What?"

Jason grinned back at Keith. "It's on Netflix, MetalBlade. You should put it in your queue."

Sally squeezed Jason's hand, reveling in her moment of geek superiority.

Chapter Fifteen

"The world is full of obvious things which nobody by any chance observes."

—Sherlock Holmes, *The Hound of the Baskervilles*

Richmond, Virginia
December, 2006

Sally munched on cold pizza while Jason sprawled on their bed, wrestling with lyrics for a song he was working on for his band, Velma's Glasses. The crust was delightfully thick and chewy, even having sat for a couple of hours in the box. Sally wished she had some honey to drizzle across the heel of each slice, making dessert out of dinner. She and Sondra had visited a restaurant back in Colorado where that was the standard practice and ever since then, Sally couldn't really enjoy pizza without a bottle of honey at hand.

Vanitha Bhat had asked that she not be on call for Just Cause, but maybe it would be all right for Sally to contact her. She needed to follow up to see if the hacker had been able to retrieve any more information from Evan's spheres. She wondered if Vanitha had seen Champion's ad yet. It seemed like the sort of thing that might appeal to her if she was looking to utilize her abilities without exposing herself to unwanted attention.

Sally unlocked the desktop computer and logged into her account. Besides her normal clutter of screen icons, a new one hovered in the lower right hand corner of the screen. Despite its size, it seemed like an incredibly complex geometric pattern of nested squares and circles. Sally was sure she'd seen something like it before. Then she snapped her fingers. It had been on a peripheral monitor in Vanitha's home studio. For a moment she was offended that Vanitha had so casually hacked into her account to place it there on Sally's screen, but then Sally realized she'd essentially given the young woman an invitation to do exactly that.

Sally clicked on the icon.

For several seconds, nothing happened, and Sally wondered if perhaps it was nothing more than a typical hacker prank, or Vanitha was sleeping, or busy doing work for one of her Fortune 500 clients. But then a chat window popped open, headed by a user named Kali.

Hi Sally.

Hi, Sally typed back. She paused, wondering how she should broach the subject of Champion with Vanitha. The hacker didn't seem enamored with niceties like tact, so Sally decided she might as well just go for broke. *Have you seen Champion's ad?*

Yes, Vanitha replied. *Interesting notion.*

Are you thinking of joining him?

Shit, no! I have better things to do than run around in a spandex suit pretending to follow some fake religion.

Sally nodded, even though nobody was there to see it except Jason, and he was busy trying to come up with a rhyme. "Hey, babe, you think *youth* and *truth* are rhymed too much in music?" he asked.

"I have no idea," said Sally. "You know more about it than me."

"*Forsooth?* No, that's just stupid. Nobody uses that. Hmmm. *Booth?*"

Sally typed, *You think it's some kind of scam?*

Yes. Vanitha's reply was immediate, encouraging Sally to type her next sentence.

Want to help me look into it further?

Yes. Is it safe for me to drop in?

Sally looked up at Jason. "Hey, I need a little privacy."

"For what?"

"You know how I mentioned my contact who might be able to help? She's going to stop by."

"Can't I meet her?"

"Not without her permission. And, um, she shows up naked."

Jason grinned. "That's kind of hot."

Sally didn't have anything to throw at him but a piece of pizza crust, but she hurled it anyway. The less-than-deadly missile bounced off his nose.

"Ow," said Jason, more out of surprise than any actual pain. "Don't waste the crust. It's good crust." He retrieved it from the sheets, inspected it for stray hairs, and then crammed it into his mouth. "Om nom," he said, chewing with his mouth open for Sally.

"Ew. Go away. I can't believe I said *yes.*"

Jason swallowed and gathered up his things. "Wait until you experience my beer farts. If you don't leave me after that, nothing will drive you away."

"I can hardly wait."

He paused by the door. "Listen, Sally, I trust you. You know that. But you might want to keep it quiet about letting someone teleport into the middle of a superhero team's headquarters, you know? These are paranoid times."

Sally zipped across the room and flung her arms around Jason's thick neck, planting a strong kiss on his lips. "Thanks, babe. If she's okay with it, I want you to meet her. She's nice. And it's kind of refreshing to talk to someone who isn't a superhero all the damn time like everyone else I know."

Jason laughed. "You want to invite her to the wedding, don't you?"

"Yes!" Sally grinned. "Now go away. You don't get to see other girls naked anymore."

"I'm going, I'm going. Call me when you're all done." He held up his phone. "And then we can talk about seeing you naked." He pulled the door shut behind him, leaving Sally alone in the room at last.

There was no way any of Sally's clothes would fit Vanitha's curvy frame, but Jason had a bathrobe hanging on the suite's bathroom door. Sally teased him about wearing it, but he always shrugged it off, saying that a true Southern gentleman didn't walk around in the altogether after a shower. It would have to do.

Coast is clear, Sally typed.

Stand back from the computer.

Sally accelerated her perceptions to maximum and watched as pixels seemed to flow outward from the screen like a special effects shot in a movie. The pixels swirled around and solidified into Vanitha's body. Sally held open the bathrobe and hung it over Vanitha's shoulders as she slowed her perceptions back to normal.

"Thanks, uh, I think," said Vanitha. She slipped her arms into the sleeves and tightened the robe as best she could across her large chest. She sniffed at the terrycloth. "Your boyfriend's?"

"Fiancé." Sally smiled. "Mastiff."

"At least he uses a pleasant soap."

"I picked it for him. He used to just wash himself from head to toe with shampoo."

Vanitha chuckled. "Boys will be boys."

"How's your work going on the spheres?"

"Not bad. I've got six of my servers running frame-by-frame algorithmic reconstructions . . . I can see I've already lost you."

Sally nodded. "Sorry."

"I'm not sure how much uncorrupted data I can pull off of their hard drives, but whatever's there, I'm going to get."

"Good."

"In the meantime, I'm preparing an experiment with one of the spheres. With its permission, of course."

"What do you mean, *with its permission*? And what kind of experiment?"

"I asked it if I could remove some of its components and replace them with pure storage capacity and it said that would be acceptable. So I'm going to see if it can contain Kali."

Sally blinked. "You're going to put yourself into one of those spheres?"

"It might be nice to be more mobile. To be able to go places where there aren't hardline data connections." Vanitha's face turned wistful. "I always wanted to fly. That's the closest I'll ever get."

"I fell a really long way once. That pretty much cured me of any desire ever to leave the ground again." Sally shivered, remembering the Guatemalan jungles spiraling beneath her.

"So you want me to help you look into Champion's stuff? I can do that. You're not the first one to ask about it, but you're the first one I said yes to."

Sally blinked. "Who else asked you?"

"Other clients."

"And you're not going to tell me who they are."

"Nope. Privacy laws."

Sally stared at Vanitha, trying to decide if the hacker was making fun of her. "You're serious."

"Sharing client information is bad for business. What's your plan?"

"Well, I was going to ask if you could hack into his computers, maybe find out what's going on in his private files."

"Sure, I can do that."

"And also research into this church he's created. Somebody at the IRS gave it legitimacy. How did he manage that?"

"So you want me to hack into a private citizen's files as well as those of a government entity?"

Sally winced. It hadn't sounded nearly so illegal to her in her own mind. "You make it sound terrible."

"It is terrible. Hacking is a terrible thing to do. It's the data equivalent of any number of felonies. Kidnapping. Robbery. Even murder. I'm like a digital hitman." Vanitha shrugged inside Jason's voluminous robe. "And like any hitman, I charge a fee."

"A fee? You didn't charge me to help before."

"That was different. That was me wanting to help. What you're asking me to do now with Champion and with the IRS is the kind of thing that forms the cornerstone of my business. I can't let the word get out that I'm doing stuff for free, or else I'm going to run out of paying clients." She folded her arms. "I like you, Sally, and I think what you're doing is noble and just, but I've got bills to pay. I'll give you my best discount. That's all I can do."

Sally sighed. She'd always known, deep down, that it was going to come down to money at some point. It wasn't like she was paying for it out of her own pocket. She could have; with Just Cause paying her a salary, covering her room, board, insurance, and travel expenses, she didn't have much to spend her money on. She was authorized to spend money on private contractors in the course of an investigation, up to a fairly staggering figure, so long as she could justify it in a hearing. Sally didn't doubt that the PRA would approve nearly any expenditure to get to the bottom of Champion and his private superhero team. "All right. Name your price."

"The IRS hack is easy. All I'm doing is investigating a specific case and relevant personnel. That's a straight thousand. The Champion thing is different, because you don't know what you're looking for, and I don't know what kind of tasks I'll have to perform or risks to assume to get it. That one starts at five thousand and goes up from there."

"Done." Sally walked over to her desk, found her wallet, and pulled out her Just Cause Visa. "Do you want it now?"

Vanitha laughed. "The only way I could take information off that card right now would be to hack your account, and that's not the way I work. We'll work out the payment details later. I'm not trying to scam you or anything. It's just that business is business and I have a specific way of working it, and this isn't it."

"So what is this, then?"

"A social call? Giving you a report on the spheres? Two girls hanging out? Call it what you want." Vanitha smiled. "If we're going to do this again here, I'll send over some of my clothes so I don't have to wear your fiancé's robe."

"Maybe. I don't know."

"How's the investigation into Orb's murder going? Did you track down that guy?"

Sally nodded. "We got as far as his rental house and the trail died there. No clues at all. We've got our investigators doing some digging but . . ." She shrugged. "Heinrich Kaiser's been alive a very long time, and he's very good at covering his tracks."

"Look, maybe I can help. That's not part of our business deal. That's still on me. I can try to track his movements after he left ScaleAbility on the last day he was there, and his movements back before he rented the house."

"You'd do that?"

"Yeah. Like I said, that's part of me helping you out from before. Can you give me access to all your reports from your investigation? Maybe I can find a clue your investigators overlooked as unimportant."

"I don't know. They're pretty good."

Vanitha snorted. "They're Feds. They don't have the patience or attention to detail that I do."

Sally bristled. "I'm a Fed too, you know."

"Yeah, but unlike most of them, you've got a real brain instead of a lump of overcooked lentils inside your skull."

Sally snickered. "That's not nice. But thank you anyway." She opened the investigation file folder on the computer. "Here, I guess it's easiest for you to get it on your way out."

Vanitha nodded. "Probably, yeah. Hey, if I don't see you, have a Merry Christmas, Sally."

"You too, Vanitha." Sally realized as she looked at the time on her computer that it was only two hours until Christmas Eve. "Are you going to visit your family or anything?"

Vanitha shook her head. "Nah. We don't keep in touch anymore."

"Friends, then?"

"I guess." Vanitha didn't sound like she'd convinced herself, much less Sally.

"Listen, if you don't have anywhere to be, why don't you come have dinner with me and Jason and Macey? We'd love to have you as our guest. And as our friend."

Vanitha smiled. "I might just do that. Where? Here, I suppose?"

"Yes. Jason's cooking. And et me tell you, that boy can cook." Sally was envious of his ability in the kitchen. She could barely manage mac-and-cheese.

"Okay, maybe I'll come by."

"I'll leave the computer on."

Vanitha grinned. "Like it could stop me if you didn't." She touched the computer. The robe fell to the floor and a low-resolution image of Kali appeared on Sally's screen. It winked at her before vanishing.

Sally texted Jason. *Ok u can come back.*

He came in after only a moment.

"What, were you listening at the door?"

"You bet. I was hoping for some hot girl-on-girl action with my future wife."

"What's wrong with you?" Sally threw the recently-discarded bathrobe at him.

He snagged it out of midair. "Can't a fellow fantasize about threesomes? I mean, it's the future now, right? That's what happens in the future."

"It won't happen in your future anytime soon, mister. I'm not going to share you."

"Awww, man . . ." Jason dragged out the last word like a pouting toddler.

"Listen, I was thinking," said Sally.

"Uh oh."

She smacked him. "No, not like that. Nothing bad. I know it's still not quite Christmas Eve, but this Kaiser thing has me all messed up inside. Every time we run across him, people die. Not just people, Jason, but friends. Glimmer. Forcestar. Trix. Esther from Divine Right. And now Evan. What if one of us is next? What if it's you or me?" Her jovial attitude vanished at the thought of losing Jason forever. "I can't imagine what Macey is going through."

"Nobody else is going to die." Jason squeezed her ever so gently. "This time we're going to catch him before he can do whatever he's going to do."

"And then what? The man has been doing this for sixty years. He plans for long term. He'll probably outlive all of us."

"Then he can do so in jail."

Sally shivered. "I hope you're right. But in the meantime, I want to give you your Christmas gift now."

"You don't have to. You could wait until tomorrow. My family always does the presents on Christmas Eve because Christmas Day is for cooking and eating."

"No. I want to do it now." Sally reached under the bed and pulled out the package she'd wrapped carefully in a few seconds while Jason was showering. "Merry Christmas, babycakes. I hope you like it."

"What is this? You didn't have to get me anything."

"I wanted to. It's what you do on Christmas."

He smiled. "Well, I got you something too. Let me just get it." He sauntered over to his luggage and rummaged through it until he found an envelope. He handed it to Sally with a flourish. "Merry Christmas to you, sweetheart."

"Oooh, what is it?"

"Open it."

"You open yours too."

"Together, then."

They each unwrapped their packages. Jason's eyes widened as he saw the turntable and the three records with it. "Jimi . . . Stevie . . . That's incredible. I've always wanted to hear what they sounded like on analog. Now I can."

"I'm glad." Sally hadn't ever been able to tell the difference, but then she wasn't a musician. She opened the envelope and saw an airline logo. "What is this? Tickets?"

Jason grinned. "A vacation. We haven't taken a proper vacation since you first joined the team, and that's been a long and busy three years. This coming spring, you and me are taking a long trip to do some of the things we've needed to do for awhile. Visiting your mom and grandma in Arizona. Visiting my folks in Georgia. And then down into Florida for sun, fun, and Disney World."

"You're serious?"

"Of course I am. Babe, you need a vacation. You're running yourself ragged. And so am I just trying to keep up with you. Besides, my mom has been calling me almost every day wanting to know when you're going to come visit. So now you know."

"They say that's half the battle." Sally smiled.

"Do they? What's the other half?"

Sally launched herself at the man who was going to marry her, intent upon ravishing him into unconsciousness. "This."

Chapter Sixteen

"Eventually everything connects—people, ideas, objects. The quality of the connections is the key to quality per se."

—*Charles Eames*

Richmond, Virginia
December, 2006

A pounding rhythm in Sally's dream wouldn't go away. It continued, dragging her from the depths of her slumber. The noise repeated and she realized someone was knocking at the door of hers and Jason's room. Beside her, Jason's snores continued unabated. She glanced over at the clock, forcing her eyes to focus from their recent relaxation. It was ten minutes to six in the morning.

Who in the hell . . .

Sally pulled on Jason's hoodie. It hung down to her knees like a fleecy bathrobe. She cinched the hood drawstring tight so the whole thing wouldn't accidentally slip off her shoulders, and went to the door to peek through the peephole.

"Grace?" she whispered when she saw the doctor standing outside in the hallway.

"Sally? Is that you?"

"Yeah, just a minute." Sally dashed into the bathroom and brushed her teeth, splattering the mirror and walls with flecks of toothpaste foam in her vigor. A few seconds later, she returned to the door, opened it, and slipped out into the hallway quickly so as not to wake Jason. She blinked in the overhead lights. "What's up? Why are you here so early?"

"We need to talk."

"At six in the morning?"

"This can't wait. I've got some important information concerning Champion."

"Okay, let me get a little better dressed than I am."

Sally kept the hoodie on; she figured that since Jason had left it on the foot of the bed instead of folding it up or packing it into his dirty laundry bag that it was hers for the taking. She pulled on some yoga pants, thick fluffy socks, and her sneakers. Her hair was a frizzy, kinky mess after she'd slept in it without braiding. She pulled it back into a sloppy ponytail and figured that was good enough for a pre-coffee morning meeting.

"'Sup, babe?" Jason's voice was thick and sleepy.

"Nothing. Go back to sleep, lovely boy. Grace needs to talk to me about something." Sally kissed his forehead.

He said something incomprehensible and was back asleep by the time Sally reached the door.

"Okay, can we go get coffee, at least?" Sally asked.

Grace nodded. "Yes, please. I've been up all night. In fact, I just got back in."

"Back in from where?"

"Newark."

"New Jersey? What were you doing there on Christmas Eve?" They reached the cafeteria. Several Just

Cause employees were there, enjoying their breakfasts before going on duty or a meal at the end of their overnight shift. No other heroes were around. Sally made a beeline for the coffee bar and started doctoring up her cup with hazelnut syrup and whipped cream.

"Beth Israel Medical Center," said Grace, filling a cup with plain black coffee and taking a sip. "An attending physician contacted me there after several patients checked themselves in with unusual symptoms."

Sally felt as if the air in the cafeteria just got colder. "What kind of symptoms? Not more nanotech stuff?"

"No. Vomiting, diarrhea, headache, skin rash. Seven men in all, suffering similar symptoms. All of them were crewmen aboard the oil tanker you helped rescue."

Sally sat down at a table. "Some kind of chemical exposure? Toxic was there. She might have made something that caused side effects while she was helping to fight the fire."

"I thought of that too, and went to examine the men myself. It was a blood test that gave it away. All of them had extremely low blood cell counts. Furthermore, all of them reported that they'd spent the bulk of the incident on deck as opposed to below. That suggested to me one thing in common. All of them were exposed to acute radiation."

Sally stopped with her cup halfway to her lips. "Radiation sickness?" She recalled Champion repeatedly blasting the ocean beside the tanker to try to force the giant ship to turn. "You think that was Champion's doing?"

"It can't be anything else. None of the Young Guns' abilities cause any kind of secondary radiation exposure. Not even Toxic. There were no radioactive materials on board the ship that could have caused the men to grow ill, and even if there had been, the only way they could have been exposed would be if the source were sitting on the deck. Nobody who was under cover of the ship's deck has reported suffering any effects."

"Did you have someone check the ship?"

"Yes. I sent a technician over to sweep it and she reported there is some low level residual radiation, concentrated most strongly along one side of the hull." Grace shook her head. "It has to be Champion."

"God. His powers are radioactive. Oh my God!" Sally set down her cup quickly to avoid dropping it. "His powers are radioactive."

"I've already checked the registry," said Grace. "There's only one parahuman on record with radioactive energy blasts—Isotope. And all his other powers match up to those observed on Champion."

"Isotope," said Sally. "It's him. Heinrich Kaiser is Champion. Oh my God."

"Unless there is a new parahuman with nearly identical abilities, I'd have to say yes."

Sally downed her coffee in several fast gulps. It burned her mouth and tongue, but her rapid healing would take care of that by the time she got to D.C. "I've got to go talk to Juice."

Grace nodded. "Hurry."

Sally stood. "It's about a hundred miles to D.C. from here. I can make that in ten minutes."

Grace looked up at her. "You could just call him."

"And you could have just called me." Sally stared back at Grace.

"You're right," said the doctor after a moment. "Some news just needs to be delivered in person."

"Can you call him, at least? Tell him I'm on my way. It's still early and it's Christmas Eve."

"Yes, of course." Grace reached out to squeeze Sally's hand. "Be careful."

"It's just running. I do that all the time." Sally felt her heart starting to race in anticipation of it.

"That's not what I mean."

"I know." Sally took a shuddering breath, running her burned tongue across the blistered roof of her mouth. The pain helped focus her. Her mind was already racing, coming up with ideas for a plan of attack and just as quickly discarding them as impractical, impossible, or far too dangerous. She fled the cafeteria in a blur and a moment later was back in her room, dressing in her costume.

Jason stirred from his slumber just as Sally finished lacing up her boots. "Babe? What's up? Call-out?"

"Not yet," said Sally. "Maybe soon. I'm going to D.C. to talk to Juice. Heinrich Kaiser is probably Champion. Grace can catch you up. I've got to go. I love you." She pressed a lengthy kiss to his lips, slowing her perception so she could experience every nuance of it.

Jason's "Love you too, babe," echoed in her ears as she raced down the hall to the nearest exit door.

Sally was thankful for her winter costume with its multiple thermal insulation layers, because when she really got going up to speed, the wind chill became an icy, biting hurricane. As she crossed the bridge to the mainland, she tightened her goggles around her eyes and breath mask across her nose and mouth. By the time she hit I-95, a moment later, she'd pulled her cowl up over her head to streamline herself as much as possible. She knew she should have taken a few seconds to braid her hair but instead it flapped behind her like a flag as she accelerated along the breakdown lane. Her vision narrowed to a tunnel as she concentrated on the road ahead. She flashed past cars like they were afterthoughts. Even though she could decelerate instantly, one misstep could still send her careening out of control, likely breaking every bone in her body and shredding her flesh into a mile-long greasy swath.

Wind tore at her as she put one foot in front of the other, dodging around debris or the occasional car in the breakdown lane. She wasn't in any danger of a car colliding with her on the highway at her speed and she occasionally was forced to veer into traffic. At her speed, by the time a driver saw her, she'd already be past and out of view. Minutes ticked by as she sped up the Interstate like a guided missile. She flashed through small towns and bedroom communities as she approached D.C., with a gathering snowstorm building to give people their dreamed-of white Christmas.

One of the benefits when Sally was really cranking out the miles-per-hour was that her ungainly and non-aerodynamic human form didn't slip through the air like a jet or a missile. Instead, she bulled her way through it, creating a wedge of compressed air in front of her and a turbulent wake, like a less-effective version of a villain her mother had battled, called Slipstream. Whereas Slipstream's wedge-and-wake could crack buildings and toss cars like toys, Sally's was effective in keeping herself from being sandblasted by rain, snow, or dust in the air. She skidded to a halt on the slushy sidewalk alongside Pennsylvania Avenue with the Capitol to her back and the White House mostly obscured by falling snow ahead of her. Her phone had a map feature and she needed it to locate Juice's apartment. He and his family had moved there upon his acceptance of the position at the PRA, and she knew they planned to buy a house after the holidays.

"Hey, Mustang Sally! All right!" called a young black man pushing a shovel down the sidewalk.

She smiled and waved. Such was fame. At least he wasn't hurling an insult or worse. Sally had been on the receiving end of that sort of attention as well, as had all Just Cause heroes at some point. Public approval of superheroes tended to wax and wane with the political environment, and the current administration had done a lot to send public opinion in a decidedly negative direction. Sally hoped that upcoming election might see the pendulum swing back positive. It was hard helping people who hated and distrusted your very existence sometimes.

Four blocks left, ten blocks south, and she found herself at the foot of a tall, post-modernist building with decorative brickwork on its façade. She scanned the list of names by the buzzers until she found *Forsythe* and held down the switch.

Juice answered almost immediately. "Sally?"

"Yeah, it's me."

"Come on in. Seventh floor." He buzzed her in.

Sally eschewed the elevators, wound her way up the staircase, and a couple seconds later stood outside the Forsythes' apartment. Juice opened the door as she raised a hand to knock. "Figured you'd come up the quick way," he said. "Merry Christmas, Sally."

Ignoring decorum, Sally embraced the large black man. "I miss having you around, boss."

Juice returned the hug. "I miss you too, kiddo. But I haven't been gone that long. Only a couple of weeks."

"Feels longer."

"Come in, please. I was just making some breakfast. Poached eggs, ham, and toast. Hungry?"

Sally's stomach gurgled and she realized she hadn't eaten anything since awakening. "Yes, please."

Juice held open the door for her and she stepped into the apartment. The lack of decorations definitely gave it a temporary, transitory feel. A large artificial Christmas tree filled one corner of the front room, hung with colorful ornaments and lights and with a handful of wrapped presents beneath it. Sally brought herself up short as she realized that Juice's wife Chantelle and their two daughters, Quinn and Yvette, were perched on barstools around a kitchen island. The girls were respectively five and seven years younger than Sally, but somehow she felt decades older than them. Neither of them had exhibited the slightest bit of parahuman ability, although both carried the genetic marker.

Chantelle gave Sally a radiant smile. "It's lovely to see you again, Sally," she said in her warm contralto. She was an attorney, like Juice, but where he specialized in parahuman law, her focus was on social causes. Sally had tremendous respect for the woman.

"Thanks, Chantelle. I'm sorry to interrupt your family breakfast."

"Nonsense. You're welcome here anytime. Quinn, who in the world are you texting before seven o'clock on Christmas Eve?"

Sixteen-year-old Quinn looked up from her cell phone with shifty eyes and Sally immediately knew she'd been texting a boy. "Just a friend."

"Mm-hmmm," said Chantelle, conveying an entire conversation in one noncommittal noise.

"I bet it's Ja*ron*," teased Yvette.

"Girl, shut up!" Quinn shoved her phone into her Georgetown sweatshirt.

"Yvette," said Chantelle, again making her point with a minimum of dialogue. "Sit down, Sally, please. Would you like coffee or hot chocolate? I'm sure you're half-frozen from your sprint up here."

"Hot chocolate, please." Sally stripped off her gloves and examined her frizzed hair. "I hope I didn't get everyone up."

"Chan and I were already up, but we woke up the girls. They'd be heartbroken if they missed you."

"Yeah, Dad, we weren't asleep or anything." Yvette yawned. "Here, Sally, I'll fix your hair."

Sally sat still while the younger girl worked with girly patience on her tangles.

"Grace wouldn't say why you were coming over, but she suggested that it was very important I listen to you," said Juice. "What's on your mind, Sally?"

"It's, uh, PRA stuff. Is it okay to talk about it in front of the girls?"

"I want to hear," said Yvette immediately.

"That's fine, Sally," said Chantelle. "The girls will not repeat a word of what is spoken in here. Nor will they text about it." She fixed a steady gaze on Quinn.

"Fine, I'm keeping quiet about it. Parahuman stuff is boring, anyway," grumbled Quinn. She slathered butter on her toast and crunched into it with as much teenagery defiance as she could muster in front of her mother.

Sally took a deep breath. "It's Champion. I think that the man under the mask is Heinrich Kaiser."

Juice leaned forward, paying close attention to Sally. Once she might have found his bulk intimidating, but after years spent around him and Jason, she felt just as comfortable around large men as she did anyone else. She noticed a subtle change about him. He was taking her very seriously, and that made her a little more nervous than she expected. Juice had been a superhero and member of Just Cause for twenty years, dwarfing her own three years on the team. And yet, he was treating her with the demeanor of a trusted advisor. "Go on."

Chantelle stood, retrieving her coffee cup as she did so. "Girls, we don't need to be a part of this conversation."

"But Mo-o-om, I want to hear!" Yvette protested.

Chantelle pointed toward the front room. "Out."

Quinn speared another pair of waffles from the stack at the table's center and meandered out of the room. Yvette trudged after her. "It's not fair."

"Sometimes life isn't fair." Chantelle winked at Sally. "Even at Christmastime."

"They could have stayed, couldn't they?" Sally asked Juice after the rest of his family left.

"They could have," he said, "but Chantelle understands when work is *work*. She's smart like that. Now . . . What evidence do you have to support your claim?" He put on his attorney's demeanor.

"It's a combination of things, but the real kicker is that the men on board that tanker, who were out on deck while Champion was blasting the ocean to try to make the ship turn . . . They're all suffering from radiation sickness."

"Were they exposed to any other known sources? Could they have been?"

"I don't know," Sally admitted, "but I don't see how. They were on an oil tanker that had, you know, conventional engines instead of nuclear. The only unusual thing they were exposed to was Champion's energies and Toxy's pollution stuff, but she can't do anything with radiation. It has to have been him."

"I'll accept that hypothesis for now. Continue."

"According to Grace, Heinrich Kaiser, a.k.a. Isotope, is the only parahuman whose abilities include dangerous radiation. That's a historical fact. Combine that with the stuff he did in the Fifties after World War II, when American Justice fought him, and the reactor thing in Guatemala, well, he's kind of got some kind of thing about having his own parahuman army. Isn't that exactly what Champion is doing?"

Juice nodded. "There's a lot more to Kaiser than even you know. I looked through his file when I first got to the PRA."

"Really?"

Juice took a laptop off the kitchen counter. "Come around here and I'll show you." He unfolded the computer screen and logged into the private PRA server. A minute or two of navigation and he brought up the file on Heinrich Kaiser. "It's a large file, but here are the highlights. Kaiser was born in Berlin in 1914. He joined the Nazi party, rose through the ranks, and eventually became part of the S.S. In '42, he volunteered for the Aufstein Experiment, and was the first—and only—apparent success. Observed abilities include flight, radioactive energy blasts, an energy shield of indeterminate function, and he hasn't seemed to age at all since 1942."

Sally's grandfather had written about the Aufstein Experiment, a secret Nazi program to artificially create parahumans like those in Projects Circus and Shetland, which were the forerunners to the American Justice and Just Cause teams. Her grandma Judy, the speedster known as Colt, had even been in Project Shetland and helped fight in the Pacific toward the end of World War II. She'd met her grandfather, Dr. Danger, later after the War. In fact, the first night they met, they wound up battling against Kaiser and his men as they tried to steal uranium.

"Since then, he's turned up either as part of or backing various villain or terrorist groups: The Malice Group, who your mother faced at Woodstock, the Weathermen, the Cult of Destruction, the Contras in Nicaragua. In fact, he's been involved pretty heavily in Central American politics all along. That's probably why he built his own Aufstein reactor in Guatemala."

"Bad memories there." Sally had lost friends in that conflict, as had all American heroes that had participated in the action.

"He's into destabilizing the world through sedition, subversion, terrorism. And he just loves his parahumans," said Juice. "All that adds up to a Nazi who never stopped fighting his war. The difference is that he seems to think parahumans are the master race." He turned away from the laptop. "I think he's setting up a new world war, but to make it us versus them. Parahumans versus non-powered. It certainly seems likely that Champion may in fact be Heinrich Kaiser."

"So what do we do? Can we go arrest him? We have pretty strong evidence that he murdered Evan."

Juice rubbed his hand over his shaved scalp. "We could probably get a warrant and go pick him up, even today. I have a judge that owes me a big favor.

However, that leaves one large question unanswered. Do you know what that is?"

Sally nodded. "What's he up to?"

Juice closed the laptop. "Exactly. I'm afraid that if we move on him now, we may not get the chance to find out, and given his propensity for planning ahead, I suspect that he has contingencies for his plans to continue whether or not he is there to personally supervise them. I find his interest in nanotechnology to be extremely worrisome. We need to find out more about what he's planning before we take him down."

"I'll do it," said Sally before she allowed herself to second-guess her decision.

"You'll do what?"

"I'll infiltrate his team. He's recruiting people from all over. Unknown people. I'll get recruited."

"Sally, he knows you. You're not only famous, but he saw you personally in Guatemala. You can't just walk into his headquarters and announce you're joining his team."

"I'm not going to do it like that. Well, not exactly. I have a plan . . ."

Chapter Seventeen

"If I wasn't an actor, I'd be a secret agent."

—*Thornton Wilder*

Denver, Colorado
January, 2007

Sally presented her plan to Juice; he approved it.

They decided that whatever Champion or Kaiser—if that's who truly hid beneath the featureless mask—was planning wouldn't likely happen before the end of the year. That gave Sally time to work out the details of her plan with those few associates who would know about it.

Jason had been against it from the outset, and it had made for a stressful Christmas and days after. They weren't exactly fighting about it, but they weren't exactly not, either. "Why does it have to be you?" he asked Sally time and time again. "I already almost lost you to the Archmage. And before that, to Destroyer."

He lay sprawled across their bed, his head in her lap, idly plucking at his guitar.

"It's because of those times that it has to be me." Sally stroked his hair. "I'm the most experienced member of Just Cause when it comes to infiltration."

"It ought to be Jack. That's his kind of thing."

"Maybe so, but he doesn't have the mental architecture that I do. Glimmer built it up for me in Guatemala before he died, and then Ment and Switchboard reinforced it when I went into the Archmage's castle. I'm pre-wired to be a mole."

"It's dangerous."

"We're in Just Cause, babycakes. That's what we do."

"I'm worried about you. I should go along."

"I know, but it'll look suspicious then. It needs to just be me. Besides, I'm counting on you to come rescue me when the time is right."

"You know I will."

"I know."

Every day between Christmas and New Year's Day, Sally sat for hours with Ment and Minerva. It took every ounce of her self-control and the occasional dose of melatonin for her to allow the couple to work their magic upon her. Ment worked to strengthen the psionic architecture already in Sally's mind. He built blocks and wards to confound anyone trying to read her mind, traps and blind alleys to catch the unwary, making her into what he claimed would be the most dangerous and secure non-psionic in the entire world. When he worked, it felt to Sally like spiders were crawling across her brain, and the inability to scratch them was infuriating. Except for the constant itching during Ment's sessions, she remained unaware of any of the detailed work he said he was doing. She trusted him; she had to, for Champion could have any number of psionics on his team by the time Sally showed up.

While Ment worked on Sally's mind, Minerva worked upon Sally's body. When the invulnerable Jack had been critically injured by a magical spear during a battle with the Archmage's forces, Minerva had healed him of the seemingly fatal injury over the space of several days where she rebuilt him on a cellular level. Sally had approached her about the possibility of doing something similar to her to change her appearance. Sally knew that going undercover would be hard enough without being so easily recognized. Minerva agreed that such a thing was within her capabilities, but she remained tentative about it. During most of the time she spent with Sally, she was studying Sally's existing face and body. Minerva said that changing Sally to look like someone else would be easy, but returning her to her original appearance would present a great challenge. Sally knew Minerva could over time commit every last detail about Sally to her mind.

While Minerva and Ment worked upon Sally, Jack and Sondra worked on creating her new identity. "We're setting it up in levels," Jack said. "A bad fake ID that leads to a poorly-concealed past that leads to more layers. The whole idea is to make it look like you're an amateur trying to cover your own tracks. Someone with good investigation skills will get past the first few layers easily enough not to arouse their suspicions to go too much further."

"How will I keep it all straight?" Sally asked.

"I'll have Ment feed the data into what he calls a *protected memory core*," said Sondra. "You'll be able to access those false memories as easily as your own, but only you will know they're fake. It'll be like you have your own private Wikipedia."

"Cool."

"What about your powers? There aren't many speedsters out there, and most of them are fairly well known," said Jack when he came to deliver Sally's full identity details to her.

"I thought about that. It could be someone who's been hiding her powers, but even that felt too obvious," said Sally. "So I'm going a different route." She opened a box on her desk and withdrew four colorful spheres. "These are Evan's. I had the costumes department work up rubberized covers for them with hidden vents to allow their sensors and whatever it is that lets them fly keep functioning." She started juggling them, using just enough of her accelerated perceptions to ensure that her hands were always in the right place to catch a ball when it came down. "One of the first known parahumans was *Le Jongleur*. The Juggler was part of the French Resistance in World War II. I could emulate him."

"Super-juggling? That'll strike fear into the hearts of criminals worldwide," said Jack.

"Champion isn't necessarily looking for people with A-list powers," said Sally. "But I can also do this." She hurled the spheres at a wall at an oblique angle. They bounced off one wall, then another, then hit Jack's face. They didn't hurt him, of course, but he jumped back, startled. Sally raised her hands and the spheres dutifully returned to her grasp. "I figure I can treat it like a low-level telekinesis."

Jack grinned. "Nicely done, kiddo." His smile disappeared as his demeanor turned professional. "Now, Jason, Macey, and I are going to be in New York, as near as we can get to Champion's headquarters without compromising you. You're not going to know where we are, because that's safer for all of us. If something happens, and you need to get out, just run. Run as fast as you can until you're somewhere safe, then call in and we'll come get you."

"Running? I can do that," said Sally. "I hear I'm pretty good at it."

"I've noticed." Jack's cheerfulness returned.

Convincing Vanitha to help her took a lot more effort on Sally's part. The young Indian woman had already said she had no interest in being a stooge for Just Cause, but Sally hoped that perhaps she might be willing to help Sally on a personal level. It was important enough to her that she took a special flight out to Boston to talk to the woman in person, even though it would have been just as easy to handle their communication through email or even with Vanitha's ability to transmit herself over the Internet.

"You're asking me to risk a lot," said Vanitha.

"The risk is mostly mine to assume. You'd just be coming along for the ride and when you get a chance, raiding Champion's computer system."

"Look," said Vanitha. "I already know that you want to smuggle me in there inside one of those floating orbs. I get that. It's a good plan. But here's the thing. If I'm on the Internet itself, ranging out into even the most distant system I can find, I'm still connected to all of it. If something happens, I can get out as fast as the speed of a thought. There's no risk of me coming to any kind of actual harm. But if I'm inside one of those orbs, I'm isolated. What if Champion does his radiation thing again? Corrupts the hard drive inside the orb?" Vanitha shuddered. "It would be like I went through a blender."

Sally nodded. She figured that would be the crux of the problem. "I can't guarantee that I can protect you from that," she said. "But we can do everything we can to minimize the risk We've got a sheath that will protect from severe electromagnetic radiation. In the event that Champion fires up his powers, you'll be as protected as we can possibly make you. Plus, you have the benefit of being able to fly away if necessary. Heck, I can even carry you to safety if need be."

"Yeah, that's all well and good, but if push comes to shove, are you Just Cause types going to try to save me? I mean, to you I'm a nobody."

"Vanitha . . ." Sally tried to think of the best way to explain herself without coming across as condescending. "When we take our oaths as members of Just Cause, we swear first and foremost to protect and serve those who need us most. That translates to civilians, whether or not they actually have parahuman abilities or not. I can turn my back on Jack, or even Jason, trusting that they have enough training to handle themselves if I am better suited to help others." She gulped, hoping she wouldn't be put in that position.

"You'd help me over your fiancé?"

"If it came to that, yes."

Vanitha spun around in her spherical chair to stare at the data streams on her various monitors. She was silent while regarding the information flow. "That's a pretty strong argument, but I don't work for free. Not this time. I helped you find your killer. That was the deal I made you. If you want me to risk so much, you've got to offer me something. Something valuable."

Sally nodded. She'd expected that much, and she'd talked to Juice at length about what they might anticipate from her. She pulled an envelope from her coat. Inside it was a check that Juice had signed, with an impressive number of zeroes before the decimal point. "This is what we're willing to pay you for this job. But there's more. The director of the PRA is a close friend of mine. He wants to meet you and make a pitch."

Vanitha's eyes narrowed. "What kind of pitch?"

"He wants you to come work for him."

"A stuffy government job? No thank you."

"I don't think that's what he has in mind. I don't know for sure, but I think it's more along the lines of a civilian contractor. You'd get government pay, benefits, and protection."

"What do you mean, protection?"

"You're a hacker. You break the law. A lot. Sooner or later you're going to run into trouble either of the legal or more personal variety."

"Meaning I'll piss off the wrong person and they'll send legbreakers around."

"Nobody does that anymore. They'll take you out. Anyone can buy a professional hit for as little as ten thousand dollars." Sally had checked that number with Jack. He'd asked if she wanted someone whacked, because he knew some people who knew some people. She'd laughed, but wasn't sure if he was serious or not. "The PRA can shield you from that kind of attention."

"But you don't know the details."

"No, I don't. Will you come to Denver with me? We can talk it over with Juice and work out some details. And we can make sure you're as safe as you can be when we infiltrate Champion's group."

"Isn't the PRA in D.C.?"

"Yes, but Juice flew out to Denver last night. Just Cause is still his baby, and he wanted to talk to us in person. He's waiting for us to come back. Both of us."

Vanitha sighed and looked at the check down in her hands. "There's a lot of money here."

"Yes, there is. More than I've ever seen at once."

"Maybe you should give up superheroing and go freelance. I bet you could make a mint with your abilities, Sally."

Sally shrugged. "I'm not in this business for the money. It's in my blood. It's what I've wanted to do since I was young enough to walk."

"Fair enough. All right, I'll come to Denver with you. Your buddy can make his pitch to me, and maybe I'll even take him up on it. Some new challenges would be nice."

"Pack your bags, then. I've got a jet waiting."

Vanitha laughed. "Seems like you were pretty confident I'd say yes, weren't you?"

"No. I was confident I'd get a firm maybe from you. Guess I outdid myself." Sally smiled.

"Guess so." Vanitha looked at her computer setup with longing in her eyes. "You're really going to make me fly?"

"Yeah, in a plane and everything. With peanuts and warm cola."

The flight back to Denver was quite a bit more comfortable than Sally intimated. The two girls rode on the *Rita*, Just Cause's supersonic transport jet. The cabin was roomy, and Sally made a quick jaunt up the road to the Thai place for food to go. While the *Rita* tore up the miles heading west, the girls ate spicy curry shrimp noodles and pad thai and talked good and bad science fiction movies. When they arrived in Denver, Juice dropped everything to sit down for a long conversation with Vanitha while Sally went to spend some time with Jason out on the town, because the following morning would be when she took on the aspect of her disguise.

Sally and Jason went to some of their favorite places in town. They caught an amateur cover band's performance in the club *Bart's Basement*, where they'd gone on their first date. Then they went to Lazzarino's for pie. Peach for Jason, chocolate silk for Sally. Late night drive through burgers. Making out in a closed park, keeping one eye out for patrolling cops. At last, they returned home, tired but happy, and fell asleep in each others' arms.

Morning came, and Sally was too nervous to eat or drink anything more than a few sips of juice. "I think that's for the best," said Minerva. "I don't know how your body will react to the changes."

"Yeah, that's not making me feel any better," said Sally. "Come on, let's do this before I change my mind."

"If you want to pass, tell me now. Once I start the change, I'll need to finish it. It's like a series of steps. If I don't finish them, I might not remember how to reverse the pattern."

"You're making it sound a lot simpler than it probably is." Sally folded her arms about herself. "No, you better just go through with it. Sooner we get it done, the sooner I can go break open Champion's organization, come home, get changed back, and go on a damn vacation."

Minerva gave her a rare smile. "That's the spirit. Come, Ment and I have prepared a room to work in." She offered Sally her hand.

Sally allowed herself to be led through headquarters. She'd hoped not to cause a fuss, but several of her friends were waiting by the room where Minerva and Ment would be working upon her. Jack hugged her and ruffled her hair in a friendly way. Sondra embraced her, wrapping her great wings around both of them in a feathery cocoon that smelled of baby powder. "Good luck," she whispered.

Doublecharge shook her hand. "You're doing a very brave thing, Sally. I know you'll do a great job."

Juice nodded. "I have every faith in you."

Jason stood off to the side, cracking his knuckles and not looking at anyone.

Sally went over to him. "Hey, it'll be fine," she said.

"I know. It's just . . . you're going to look different. You're going to *be* different."

"I'll still be *me*," she said, touching her heart. "Right here, where it counts. I'll still love you. And when this is all done, I'll be back to the girl you know and love." She took his hand in hers and kissed it. "I promise."

He smiled down at her, a real, tender smile instead of his normal goofy grin. Sally could see the worry in his eyes and it almost made her call things off right then and there. Her sense of duty wouldn't let her back down, though. If Champion was indeed Heinrich Kaiser —and all evidence certainly seemed to point in that direction—she owed so many people justice. Evan. Forcestar, Trix, and Glimmer. Her grandparents. She wouldn't let anyone else assume the risk she was prepared to take. She squeezed Jason's hand and then turned away from him so she wouldn't have to see the fear. "Okay, let's get this show on the road."

Ment opened the door to the room and Sally followed Minerva inside. The room was empty but for a metal-framed cot with a vinyl sheet stretched across it and two padded swivel chairs liberated from the conference room. Sally noted a pair of security cameras mounted in opposite corners. As soon as she spotted them, she just knew that Minerva was going to tell her that she needed to be nude. And a moment later, she wasn't disappointed.

"Really? Naked?" Sally shook her head.

"You can't mold clay while it's still inside its wrapper," said Minerva softly. "I need access to all of you to pull this off."

"Yeah, except I'm the one pulling stuff off." Nevertheless, Sally started peeling off her layers. She spared a glance directly up at one of the cameras. "This better not find its way onto the internet or somebody's going to get a really fast kick in the nutsack."

Ment snickered.

"And that goes double for you, Mr. My-Dad-Was-A-Supervillain."

"It's cool, Sally. I'm going to be way too busy shutting down your pain centers to be ogling you after the first couple minutes." He winked at her.

"Lie down, please," said Minerva. Her pupils dilated until the blackness took over her eyes.

Sally stretched out on the cold vinyl. Goosebumps raised all over her skin. She knew the room wasn't any colder than the rest of headquarters, but it felt like a refrigerator to her. Nervous sweat trickled down from under her arms, making the vinyl beneath her feel cold and slippery. Shivers started somewhere in the center of her chest and kept making her arms and legs twitch at random moments. "I'm sorry," she said through chattering teeth. "I'm r-really cold. And sc-cared."

Ment rolled his chair around until he was sitting above Sally's head. He placed his fingertips lightly against her face, with his pinkies at the bottom of her jaw and thumbs on her temples. "Deep breath, Sally," he said.

She did as he asked and then she was warm, comfortable, and relaxed. The tightness in her chest disappeared and she felt as if she were laying out in the Arizona sunshine. She thought about saying something but her jaw seemed to be frozen in place. Her entire body was paralyzed, although she could still breathe without difficulty. It was as if Ment had disconnected all her voluntary muscles. At a distant, irrational level, she was terrified. The cooler, logical part of her brain that often took charge when she was operating with her perceptions accelerated, understood that the paralysis was completely necessary for the changes Minerva was going to implement.

Minerva's eyes were like pools of obsidian in the depths of her burgundy hood. She stood to one side of Sally and placed her hands upon Sally's legs. A mild, throbbing ache began beneath Minerva's hands, like a muscle that was about to cramp up or shin splints. If anything, Sally would have likened it to growing pains, and perhaps that's what they were. She longed to flex her legs, to stretch them and twist them to try to alleviate the discomfort, but it never grew beyond a slightly irritating level. She imagined that without Ment running interference in her pain receptors, it might very well be the most painful thing she'd ever endured. Sally wondered what Minerva was doing to her. Minerva hadn't discussed any specifics about how she was going to alter Sally's appearance, and Sally had been uncomfortable asking about the details, afraid she would somehow distract or confuse the young woman who was reshaping her flesh.

So she lay there, unmoving, and took it as bravely as she could.

Sally's world seemed to shrink down to the sound of her heartbeat pulsing in her ears and the slow rise and fall of her chest. She couldn't concentrate enough with the aching in her legs to count breaths or anything, so she had no idea how long she'd been lying on the cot.

Eventually, Minerva removed her hands from Sally's legs and she repositioned herself higher up beside Sally's torso. Sally's breath hitched in her chest for a moment as Minerva cupped her breasts in her hands. Even though the touch was far more clinical than intimate, it was still unexpected and made Sally's mind race. What was Minerva doing? Her breasts felt like she was having the worst PMS ever. They became so achey and tender that even Minerva's gentle grasp upon them felt like an iron vise.

"Ment," Minerva whispered.

"Sorry," he replied tersely, and the pain in Sally's breasts lessened to a dull roar.

After another indeterminate time, Minerva moved away from Sally's breasts. Although Sally couldn't move her head, she could see in her peripheral vision that her chest had *changed*. It was hard to tell while she was lying flat, but her breasts seemed to be bigger. Heavier, too, by the way they felt different when she breathed. A random thought that Jason would love her new toys would have made her smile if she could move her face.

Ment chuckled and for a moment pain flooded through Sally's body.

"Ment!" Minerva's voice was sharp.

"Ah, shit. Sorry, Sally. I'm trying to focus here . . ." His voice seemed to come to her from a very long ways off as Minerva moved her hands up to Sally's face.

Her *face*!

Her skin prickled as if she'd gotten a bad sunburn. Her nose stuffed up and her eyes watered like she had a cold. Sally had been hit in the mouth before during training, and her lips felt swollen like she'd caught a fist in the face. She couldn't see Minerva except as a blur thanks to the tears in her eyes.

The pain began to increase, either because Minerva was doing terrible, horrible things to Sally's flesh or because Ment was losing his ability to block it. Or maybe it was both. Sally could feel tears running down her temples to tickle along the back of her neck before soaking into her hair. If only she could have, she would have screamed. It wouldn't have stopped the pain, but it might have helped her tolerate it.

Minerva touched the top of Sally's head and dragged her fingers and palms along Sally's hair, and then she stepped back. "I'm finished," she said. Her voice was ragged and through her tears, Sally could see that the young woman looked gaunt, nearly skeletal. When she used her powers extensively, they seemed to feed on Minerva's own body. She swayed and Ment rushed over to steady her.

When he broke contact with Sally, the pain was like the flash of heat from a furnace, but it dissipated as quickly as it hit her. It was enough to break her paralysis and she gasped in reflex, her hands flying to her face.

Sally sat up, terrified, and looked down upon a body that she had never seen before.

Chapter Eighteen

"Sometimes I wake up and don't even recognize myself. I guess that's why they call me the Man of a Thousand Faces."

—*John Q. Public, American Justice, 1948*

Denver, Colorado
January, 2007

"Oh my God," Sally whispered as she regarded the changes Minerva had wrought upon her flesh.

Her legs.

Her beautiful, shapely legs with muscles that looked like they'd been carved from marble with a razor were gone, replaced by seemingly shapeless masses of soft flesh. Her feet were too far away, and Sally didn't know how she would ever each them. Her legs widened unbelievably at her hips, with curves ranging first outward and then back inward toward her waist. A pad of fat rested over her belly like a slab of clay. It wrinkled and flopped over itself as she sat upright. Unfamiliar weights pulled at her shoulders, neck, and back as her gargantuan breasts swung down. She'd been no more than a B-cup all her life, thanks to constant running, but now she looked like . . .

"A Frazetta girl," she said aloud.

"A what?" asked Ment.

Sally felt her lips, blubbery and thick, start to quiver. "A F-Frazetta girl. He's an artist. He draws c-curvy women."

Minerva smiled weakly as she leaned against Ment. "I love his style. He's a very distant relative. I thought I would make you a tribute to him. I hope you don't mind."

Sally started to cry, and she hated herself for it. She sat there, naked for all the world to see, trapped in a body that wasn't her own.

Ment held out a robe to her. "Here, you don't have to stay naked. That's kind of weird."

Sally sniffled and stuck her arms through the sleeves. Her arms, at least, seemed unchanged, and her hands were still her own. She didn't know how she would have dealt with looking down to see a stranger's hands attached to her arms. As she shrugged her shoulders into the robe, her hair flopped forward. Gone were her cornsilk-yellow tresses, replaced instead by raven colored locks like Sondra's. "Black hair?" She tugged on it, as if it were a wig and she could remove it, but it pulled at her scalp, attached at the roots.

"Frazetta girls should be brunettes," said Minerva. "Are you hungry? I'm starving."

Sally realized that yes, she did have a yawning hole in her belly and a raging thirst to go with it. "Yeah."

"You should be careful," said Ment. "It might be hard to walk on your new legs at first. You're taller now. Like, a good four inches."

True to Ment's prediction, Sally jarred her teeth together when her feet hit the floor before she was ready. She swayed out of balance as she realized her center of gravity had changed. Big hips and a big bosom made it hard for her to move the way she was used to, and her lengthened legs made it feel like she was wearing five-inch platform shoes. She wished she had her running boots on for the lateral support they provided, because she was terrified that she would twist an ankle with every step.

Somehow, her brain was adjusting to the huge changes wrought upon her body, and by the time she tottered over to the room's door, she was already feeling like she wasn't about to topple like a rotten tree in the wind with every step. She asked Ment if he was doing it.

"No," he said. "If I was going to guess, I'd say it's your rapid healing. Your brain is healing itself, kind of, as it creates new structures to handle your new body."

Sally looked at him to see if he was making fun of her. He looked serious. "You don't really know, do you?"

"I really don't. This is all new territory for me."

"Tell me about it." Sally reached down to the door handle and pulled it open.

Juice and Jason were still waiting outside. She didn't know how long the reshaping process had taken, but it seemed like it had been hours. Jason turned at the sound of the door, took one look at her, and it was like all the strength went out of his legs. "Holy shit," he whispered as he leaned against the wall for support. "Sally? Is that you?"

Sally felt tears prick at the corners of her eyes. "Hi."

"God, I never thought . . ." Jason ran out of words and all he could do was stare at her.

"Am I ugly?" Sally rounded on Minerva, managing to call up some vituperative anger.

"No." Minerva didn't back down, but neither did she appear defensive or hurt.

Sally wondered if her raging emotions were a side effect of the changes of her body. Still, she had to see herself. She'd gotten hints from looking down at her nude form, from the way she moved, from Jason's reaction, but she needed to know. She staggered up the hall to the nearest bathroom, not caring that it was a men's room, and pushed her way in, startling a day shift command center employee who was washing his hands.

"Hey, uh, this is the, uh—"

"Get out. *Out!*" Sally screamed at him.

He fled, trailing paper towels and water droplets in his wake.

Sally turned to face herself in the mirror, her eyes cast downward toward her feet. She was terrified to see herself for the first time. But she had to know.

She looked up.

The first thing she noticed was her hair. It was a shiny black, full of body instead of the normal blonde braids. It framed her face like a painted cloud with greens, blues, and purples mixed into the black. The changes to her face were subtle but sufficient in total to make her look thoroughly unfamiliar. Arched black eyebrows replaced her thin, rounded crescents. Her eyes had gone from their light blue to a dark brown that was nearly black. Her eyelashes were thick and full, making her look like she was wearing thick eyeliner. And the eyes were shaped differently. They were subtly slanted just enough to give her an exotic appearance. Her nose looked the same as it always had, but her lips were fuller and redder than before. Her cheeks had filled out, giving her face a more rounded shape, but at the same time her cheekbones were more pronounced.

Sally couldn't believe she was looking at herself. She reached up to touch her cheeks and watched her reflection match her moves. She opened her mouth and moved her head this way and that, looking at how the shape of her face had changed. Every move brought new realizations about the unfamiliarity of Minerva's changes.

She steeled herself and opened the robe to see what else had changed. Her hips were broader, with some extra padding on her ass. The visible six pack she'd had before was obscured by the gentle curve that most women had on their tummies. Her breasts, though, those were positively huge. "God, they're half the size of my head," she said. "I'm not going to fit into any of my clothes." She twisted from side to side, feeling the weights swaying and wondering how she would cope with them when she ran.

Could she even run? She was afraid to try, especially in the confines of the men's room. All she needed was to slip with her bare feet on the tile floor and crash against the far wall. It wouldn't do anyone any good if she hurt herself before going to Champion's base. All of Minerva's work would have gone to waste then and someone else would have to take on the challenge of infiltration.

A knock sounded at the bathroom door. "Sally? You okay in there?" Jason sounded worried.

Sally drew her robe tight across her chest and tied it shut. "I'm fine. I'm coming out." She opened the door and stepped back into the hall. "Sorry I freaked out. This is really weird."

"I can't even imagine what it must feel like to you," said Juice. "I didn't think I could find more respect for you than I already have, but there it is."

"Thanks," said Sally. She reached out to take Jason's hand. He stiffened and hesitated for a moment before clasping it. The hesitation was like a stiletto driven into Sally's heart. She forced herself not to cry. "I'm so hungry. Can we hit the cafeteria?"

"Do you want to change first?"

"I don't have anything I can wear." Sally grimaced. "All my clothes are for a smaller woman."

Juice produced a department store bag. "Minerva already had your measurements in mind before she began. She asked me to bring you something to change into. You'll be able to pick up a more complete wardrobe before you depart for New York, but this should suffice for now."

Sally opened the bag and found a pair of new blue jeans, bra and undershirt, and a thick sweater. There was also a pair of her own fluffy socks and hightop sneakers. Minerva must not have changed the size or shape of her feet at all. That was something at least, she thought. The sweater was burgundy with horses upon it done in yellow and white. She smiled at Juice. "It's perfect. Thank you."

He smiled back. "Thank you, for what you've already done, and what you're going to do."

"I'll be right back, baby," she said to Jason. "I promise it's still me. Try not to . . . to freak out on me."

Jason nodded. "I'm trying. I can still see you inside . . . I mean, I can see the real you. It's like you're wearing stage makeup or something."

"I'm still recognizable?"

He shook his head. "I doubt anybody else would see it. If anybody knows your body and face better than I do, who isn't your mom, they're going to need me to kick their ass."

Sally laughed. "That's fair."

"I've got to take care of some PRA business," said Juice. "I'll be flying back to D.C. in the morning."

"You'll stay for dinner tonight?" asked Sally.

"I wouldn't miss it." Juice turned away and headed up the hall.

"I'll be right back." Sally ducked into the nearby women's room and changed into the new clothes. She probably tightened the new bra too much, but it helped her to feel a little more in control without her new breasts swinging like pendulums with each step.

Sally and Jason went across headquarters to the cafeteria. Minerva and Ment sat by themselves off in a corner of the cafeteria. Minerva had a gigantic bowl of pasta in front of her and tall tumblers of water and iced coffee. She nodded over at Sally as they entered the cafeteria but gave no indication that she and Ment wanted any other company. That was fine with Sally, because she didn't feel particularly social either.

Sally made herself two double cheeseburgers at the burger bar, loaded up with extra pickles, and added a huge basket of fries. It was more food than any reasonable human could eat at a single sitting. Actually, she reflected, it matched Jason's own selection. He grinned at her tray. "You gonna eat all that?"

"I might. May as well treat myself."

Jason stared at her and probably didn't realize how blatant it was. "Sleeping with you's going to be weird tonight, though. It's going to feel like cheating. Kind of. I don't know."

Swallowing her food became more difficult as Sally's throat tightened. "It's not cheating. It's me. I'm still me on the inside."

"You're still you on the outside," said Jason. "Just different. Look, this is really weird for me."

"Weird for *you*?" Sally took another bite. "You have no idea."

"Yeah, I know. I don't. Can I just tell you I love you and we'll get on with our day?"

"I love you too, you big dummy."

After that, Sally felt a little better. Despite his obvious discomfort with the alteration in her appearance, Jason looked like he was trying really hard to reconcile that. She could respect that, and she loved him for it. His acceptance would make it that much easier for her to accept herself.

Sally couldn't believe she'd managed to get outside of all her food, matching Jason bite for bite if not pound for pound. After finishing her last fries, she summoned up a not-very-ladylike belch that made him giggle into his drink. He wiped soda from his chin and grinned at her without guile or reservation, and that made her feel even better.

She went by herself to a couple of discount stores to get some clothes. It was a strange feeling walking around areas where lots of people could see her and not a single one recognized her. Sally was used to being a fairly well-known celebrity, especially in the Denver area, and there was something very refreshing about her new anonymity. She noticed that her new figure was getting a few more appreciative looks from men. She wasn't used to feeling sexy in her runner's body, but the Frazetta-esque look she had now seemed much more of interest to the opposite sex. She shrugged it off; it would make infiltration a lot easier if men saw her first as a sex object instead of as a superhero threat.

Out of a perverse need to prove to herself that she was truly anonymous, she wandered into a bookstore and looked through the magazines until she found one with herself on the cover and bought it. The proprietor didn't even give her a second glance as she bagged up Sally's purchase and handed it back to her.

Sally took her new purchases and returned to Just Cause Headquarters. She was starting to feel nervous about the mission at hand. It would be her last night "at home" for what might be quite some time. She spent some time walking around the facility, visiting some of her favorite off-duty haunts like the Archives, the workout room adjacent to the underground Combat Training Facility, and the lounge where she and her friends and teammates had spent many hours watching movies, playing games, or just talking about the world.

She bundled up against the cold and went outside to the running track. It hadn't snowed for a couple of weeks and the ground was dry. The frigid Arctic wind that blew across the prairie cut right through her layers and raised goosebumps. She didn't care; she had to know. Walking had become second nature for her after only a few minutes on her new, longer legs, but she hadn't yet tried to utilize her super speed powers yet. She didn't have any starting blocks, never having needed them, but she hunched down into a runner's starting crouch anyway. Left leg back with the knee almost touching the ground. Right leg cocked, ready to push off at the imaginary starting gun. Fingertips splayed on the track, supporting her upper body weight. She imagined the race official standing beside her.

On your mark.

She raised her hips up, ready to unleash the power contained within them. At least, she hoped there was still power contained there.

Get set.

Her head came up, the strap of her goggles tugging at the back of her neck. Muscles quivered, aching to move.

Go!

Sally pushed off the track with hands and feet. Her long legs threw off her running rhythm right away and she staggered and tripped by her third step.

She picked herself up, dusted herself off, and crouched down again.

On her second start, she began with a nice, easy lope, slower than an Olympic sprinter. She figured she could do that pace on a pair of broken legs, at least. After all, she'd once run all the way from Central America to Arizona. Her long legs thudded down onto the stiff rubberized track. She worked on finding the rhythm for her steps. The extra inches gave her a much longer stride, and if she pumped her legs too quickly, they'd come down too soon and she'd wind up in the dead grass alongside the track.

As she worked out the pace, she slowly increased it to highway speeds, then runway speeds. Shortly she was whipping around the track at a blistering four hundred miles per hour. At that pace, she was running through a cloud of dust that she whipped up in her previous passing before it could settle back to the ground again. She kept her breath mask tight against her face to keep from aspirating it. The cloud swirled around the inside of the track until it formed a dust devil, rising up into the twilight sky. Her chest ached, not from lack of air but because of the extra weight of her larger breasts. She skidded to a halt and watched the swirling dust whip away on the breeze.

"Looks like you haven't lost a step at all," said a deep voice. Sally turned to see Juice standing off to one side of the track. He was wrapped up in a greatcoat against the cold, with a knit cap over his bald head and a navy blue scarf wrapped around his neck. She'd been so busy paying attention to her own body and the way it had changed in its movement patterns that she hadn't noticed him.

"Hi, Boss." She pulled up the goggles and lowered the breath mask to let the chilly air soothe her sweat. "What's up?"

"Dinner. Also, I thought I'd check to see how you were doing. You've gone through a pretty intense transformation," he said.

Sally smiled. "I think I'm doing okay. I can still run, and that's the most important thing."

"Not quite." He offered her his arm and she took it. It was the sort of thing she'd never have done when he was her direct commander, but now it didn't feel out of place. "The most important thing is that you stay alive. You're going into a potential dragon's den of risk, and I'm worried about you getting out in one piece."

"I'll be fine, Boss. I've been in worse predicaments."

"I know. You're a good soldier, Sally, but you're also special to me. I watched you grow up. It's like you're my oldest daughter."

Sally gasped. She hadn't ever expected to hear such an admission from the rock-solid Juice, whose steadiness had been the cornerstone of Just Cause since 1996 when he'd assumed command of the team upon Sunstorm's retirement. He'd always been a background part of her life. She remembered him showing up for some of her birthdays when she was younger, before his duties precluded such things. When her mom attended Just Cause events as an honored retiree, and Sally got to tag along, Juice had always made a point of talking with her to see how she was doing in school, or with her training. He really had been like a father to her, and she'd been so self-absorbed that she'd never noticed before. She squeezed his arm and looked up at him in the growing darkness. "I'm not going to start calling you *dad*, but yeah, I get it. I'll be careful."

He smiled back. "See that you are."

Chapter Nineteen

"What rights are those that dare not resist for them?"

—*Alfred, Lord Tennyson*

New York City, New York
January, 2007

Sally stepped out of the cab and paid the driver, a Russian who seemed far too happy to peel away from the curb and leave the vicinity of Champions Headquarters at an unsafe rate of speed. She looked at the warehouse where she'd been only a month previously, when it was still the home base for the Young Guns. How much difference a month made. The building seemed generally freshened up, from a new coat of paint to bright lights all around and a large illuminated sign that said *Champions*. Maybe a dozen cars and trucks were parked off to one side of the building underneath a temporary roof of canvas stretched over new girders mounted in fresh concrete.

Construction equipment was parked along one edge, along with pallets of materials. It was evening, and nobody was working, but Sally could tell that a new building was going up alongside the original warehouse. From what she could see, it was going to be three or four times as big.

Leaving Denver that morning had been rough. She and Jason had tried to be intimate the night before, as it would be the last time for a while that they would be together, but it had been difficult. His performance had been half-hearted, and she could tell it was because she didn't look like herself, which had thrown off her own sense of romance as well. In the end, they'd rolled apart, neither one feeling satisfied or happy about the experience. They'd apologized, and Sally tried to joke that she felt more confident than ever that Jason wouldn't cheat on her, but the joke fell flat as soon as she said it. They wound up sleeping as far apart as they ever had since moving in together. It was almost like they'd been fighting, which they didn't do very often because Jason was so easygoing it was hard for her to stay mad at him for long. She'd tossed and turned all night and in the morning when it was time for the car to take her to the airport, she'd only kissed his cheek and stolen away before he awakened. Later, he'd texted her while she awaited her flight, and it was a lot easier to communicate that way when they couldn't actually see each other. He could pretend she was the Sally he knew, loved, and recognized, and she could pretend he wasn't struggling with it.

Ment's implanted data swirled around in her mind like a murky morass. She couldn't recall much of it with clarity, which was by his design. "You won't have most of it right there unless you're prompted to think of it," he said. "Normal people don't think of their names all the time. Really, they hardly ever do at all." She knew her false name was *Lindsay DeMaret* and that she was from Arizona, but beyond that, it was a blur. Jack had designed her fake identity down to details of her high school, and when Ment uploaded it all into Sally's mind, it felt like she'd crammed for the worst final exam ever.

Jack had also created a cover story for why Mustang Sally was out of the public eye. She was being treated for a severe concussion she'd received during a training exercise, and was under the watchful eyes of Just Cause medical personnel. It had been reported on the news and everything. She was going to be out a minimum of three months according to reports. "What if I'm gone longer than three months?" she'd asked him.

"If you're gone that long, something's gone very wrong with your infiltration and we're probably going to have taken down Champion on a more direct level long before then." Jack smiled the same way he did when he was fingering his sniper rifle.

Sally took a deep breath and blew it out in a cloud in the damp cold of New York in January. "Here we go."

Her phone buzzed in her pocket. She pulled it out, wondering if it might be Jason. Instead it was from Vanitha. *I want to see.*

"Somebody might be watching," Sally said. Vanitha was packed inside the duffel bag slung over her shoulder, crammed into the miniaturized databanks she'd rebuilt inside the orb they called Curious. She'd put backup databanks into the other three orbs, but they weren't as complete and she planned to only use them as a last resort. Texting was the only way she could communicate with the outside world, and for security purposes, she could only transmit to Sally's phone through a dedicated wireless connection.

I need some data.

Sally sighed with exasperation and dug into her bag to withdraw Curious. "Just hurry. It's cold out here and I'm afraid somebody might see."

Curious hovered over Sally's hand for a moment, spun around in a complete circle, and then dropped back into her palm. *I'll figure out more later. Be careful.*

After Sally read the message, it vanished.

She walked across the empty street toward the Champions Headquarters entrance. It was brightly lit and clearly identified, but she didn't see any security outside; not even a camera. Was Champion really so convinced of his position that he didn't even need basic protocols? No, that couldn't be it. Sally suspected that his security was so subtle that she might not even notice it when it was staring her in the face. He'd already shown he could make use of nanotechnology. How hard would it be for him to use those tiny robots to be his security net?

She steeled herself and pulled open the door.

A puff of warm air greeted her as she stepped into a comfortable, modern-looking lobby with a muted yellow-and-red color scheme with silver accents. A young blonde woman in a yellow and red jumpsuit modeled after Champion's sat behind a desk, watching a reality TV show on a flatscreen mounted upon one wall. Leaning on the desk beside her was none other than Stefan—Surfboy. Sally swallowed a painful, nervous lump and wondered if she'd get busted before she even barely got in the door.

"Come on in," said Stefan. "Don't be shy."

"I, uh, I wasn't sure if you were open."

"Twenty-four seven," said Stefan. "You never know when we might be needed."

"Can we help you?" asked the young woman behind the desk. She pointed a finger at the television on the wall and it flickered and died. "I'm Dampen. This is Surfboy." Her face looked like one that wasn't accustomed to smiling.

"Uh, I don't know. I mean, I came here because I think I want to join."

"What can you do?" asked Stefan. "We're always accepting new members."

"I can juggle." Sally pulled out three of the spheres, leaving the one with Vanitha in it in her bag for the time being.

Stefan's smile turned pained as Sally began to toss the balls around in some of the patterns she'd taught herself while practicing for the talent show. "Wow, juggling. That's pretty hard to do, right? Maybe you've got some kind of super-dexterity or something? Have you taken a Musashi? We've got them right here if you want."

"Stop it, Stefan. You don't have to be a dick about it," said Dampen. "But, uh, is there anything else you can do? We get a lot of folks coming in here wishing they were parahumans but can't come up with anything."

"I thought you would accept people without powers," said Sally. "That's what the ad said." She narrowed her eyes at Stefan, letting her hands do the work of juggling without focusing on the flying balls. She knew that the orbs wouldn't let her drop them. With Vanitha's help, she'd spent some time training them. They were far smarter than dogs and not only performed specific actions when she ordered, they could anticipate what she wanted based upon her motion and verbal cues. "You said it yourself, Surfer."

"Surfb*boy*," corrected Stefan. "And yes, I did say that, if those unpowered people could meet our stringent requirements. So far, nobody has."

Shit, he was full of himself, Sally thought. He'd always been kind of arrogant, but being in Champion's organization seemed to have taken him past arrogant into full asshole territory. "Well, you don't have to worry," she said. "Because I do have powers. I can do this." She spread her hands wide and the spheres all stopped at the top of their arcs, hovering over her head. "And *this*." She made a throwing motion and all three spheres rocketed across the lobby, narrowly missing

Stefan's head. They deflected off the far wall and sped back to Sally's waiting hands.

Dampen's eyes widened. "Telekinesis. Cool power. We don't have any of those yet."

Stefan cleared his throat, trying to regain his composure after he'd had to duck to avoid being brained. "Yes, well, that's pretty cool. What's your name?"

"I can't be anonymous?" Sally tucked the balls away in her bag once more. She figured that if she kept them mostly out of sight, people would be less likely to associate the spheres with Orb.

Stefan shrugged. "If you'd rather we just call you *hey you*, we can."

"I'm Lindsay," said Sally. "And I was kind of thinking of calling myself The Juggler. You know, after that French guy."

"*Le Jongleur*," said Dampen.

Stefan gaped at her. "How did you know that?"

"There was a special on the History Channel last night. It was quiet." She smiled at Sally. "Most of the people who show up do so during daylight hours. I can project a small electromagnetic pulse. It's enough to shut down unshielded electronics."

Sally's heart started to race. What if Dampen's seemingly innocuous power scrambled Vanitha? She pulled out her phone and glanced at it to see if there was a text message. "It won't screw up my phone, will it? I just bought the stupid thing and I'll be on a contract until I die."

"Your phone should be fine," said Dampen. "It's a pretty narrow focus. Long as I'm not targeting it right at you, no problem."

A brief *I'm fine thanks for asking* message flickered across Sally's phone screen for a moment. She put it away again. "So what all do you do here?"

"I'm second-in-command of the Champions," said Stefan. "Tell you what. The man himself will be giving a welcome speech to the newest recruits in the morning. You have a place to stay or do you want to stay here? We've got some temporary rooms going until the new HQ gets built. You see it next door? It's gonna be huge."

Sally blinked. She couldn't believe Stefan was second in command of his own ass, much less a superhero organization. What did he have on Champion, she wondered. He'd never been all that bright, barely passing many of his classes at the Hero Academy when he'd been her classmate. It hadn't been much of a surprise to anyone that he hadn't been selected for one of the Just Cause teams. And now here he was, large and in charge, as it were. Sally could practically see his chest puffed out in the way he moved. He'd been given a little bit of power and it had gone straight to his head. Maybe that was why Champion had picked him. Being given the gift of command would make him loyal to a fault. "Yeah, I guess I can stay here," she said. "What is it, a cot and a curtain?"

Stefan laughed. "Nothing quite so primitive, I assure you. We have real beds with mattresses and everything. Champion brought 'em in from his private stores. No curtains, just cubicles for now, but they're private enough. Quiet. You're not going to hear your neighbors." He lowered his voice like a conspirator. "Dude is stacked, you know what I mean? Real high roller. He's funding this whole shebang."

"Pretty impressive," said Sally. She yawned, only half acting. "Listen, uh, Surfboy. I'm pretty jetlagged. I don't know what time it is here but in Arizona it's my bedtime. Think Dampen could show me to one of those beds you mentioned?"

Stefan chewed on the inside of his cheek for a moment as his eyes wandered up and down Sally's figure, and she realized that he was *checking her out*. That was a little disturbing. It was one thing to have complete strangers ogling her in a mall, because things like that just happened. This was someone she knew, and even liked as a friend, who was looking at her rather the same way a dog looks at someone eating a steak sandwich. And on the heels of that realization, she knew she could get to Champion a lot faster if she played up the interest with Stefan. It would probably be a short step into Champion's inner circle, and all she had to do was let Stefan sleep with her.

The thought turned her stomach.

Sally had once thought Jason had cheated on her, back when they were still just dating. It had been a misunderstanding, and they'd gotten through it. She couldn't take things a step further here in New York, even though he wouldn't ever know unless she told him. She'd lose all respect for herself if she stooped so low as to use sex as a weapon. Plenty of women spies had done just that, but Sally was better than all of them. She loved Jason far too much to hurt him with infidelity, and there was no way she could keep something like that a secret from him. It would destroy her if she kept it inside, and would destroy him if she admitted it.

Better to put those thoughts aside altogether, for they led down a dark path from which nothing good could arise.

"Yeah, I guess I can watch the front for a few minutes," said Stefan at last. "Just don't take too long, okay? I'm already well past my duty hours."

Dampen smiled at Sally. "This way, Lindsay. I'm Kayla, by the way." She led Sally out of the lobby into the rest of the headquarters. It looked like the entire interior was under construction, with old walls being ripped out and new being erected in different areas. Work lights burned bright even with nobody working. The air was dusty and smelled of drywall, tool lubricant, and glue. "Forgive our dust," said Kayla. "Champion's redesigning this place into an education center. Once the headquarters next door is done, we'll all move over there."

"An education center? Like a school?" asked Sally. She looked around as much as she could, gawking like the newcomer she was without trying to be too obvious.

"You know how Just Cause has their Hero Academy?"

"Yeah. I thought about going, but . . ." Sally shrugged. "Never got around to it."

"Me either. I didn't figure they'd find me very interesting or useful. Anyway, Champion's going to have a lot less stringent entry requirements. He's going to make sure his people are taught to use their powers for the greater good without wasting time on the other stuff."

"Other stuff?"

"You know, like math, science, history . . . All that stuff we can learn in normal schools. Here, we're going to learn how to be superheroes. How to be Champions."

Sally thought Kayla sounded very much like she was spouting recruitment propaganda. All that so-called *other stuff* was taught at the Hero Academy, as it was as much a high school as it was a training center for parahumans. Once Sally had read the *Harry Potter* novels, the Hero Academy became Hogwarts for Heroes in her mind. She'd always recalled that famous quotation by George Santayana: *Those who cannot remember the past are doomed to repeat it.* Sally might not have been exceptional at math or English, but she loved history classes. Her own family had in its own way been instrumental in much of the history of the modern world, from her grandparents' involvement in World War II and afterward in American Justice, to her mother being in Just Cause for almost sixteen years. Sally hoped someday her own children and grandchildren would be able to look back upon her own efforts just as fondly.

"So he's making his own Hero Academy," said Sally.

"Kind of, yeah. But that's something he can talk more about tomorrow when he addresses you and the other new recruits."

"Are there already a lot of us here?"

"Well, besides the original Young Guns, and you and me, there are eleven others. We've had more than two hundred people register on the website. Some of them are already on their way. We're working out the logistics of getting the others here."

"How do you know they're not just faking it? Lying about their powers?"

Kayla stopped outside a door. "Why would anyone do that?"

Sally couldn't detect any sarcasm in the young woman's voice. Maybe she really believed it. "I don't know. Groupies. Wannabes. Do you have a way to weed out anyone who's just pretending?" There was a running joke among the members of Just Cause about a man who kept applying to join the team every six months with a new identity, claiming his powers only manifested when he was naked. They didn't believe for a moment that he was anything except a creep, and sent him on his way. Sally shuddered, wondering if he'd turn up at Champion HQ. This was exactly the sort of thing that would appeal to someone like him.

"Well, we ask for a demonstration. If they can't demonstrate their abilities right away, then I guess they don't belong here. Nobody's come in and been unable to prove themselves, though." Kayla nodded at the door that Sally knew led to the former Just Cause HQ's training floor, and more recently the rave floor for the Young Guns. "The temporary quarters are in here. Try and keep quiet. Some folks are probably sleeping. It's already lights-out for the night."

"No worries," said Sally. "I'm looking forward to getting a good night's sleep. Long trip getting here. What time do we start?"

"Early." Kayla gave her a smile, looking like she wasn't comfortable with the expression. "I'm exempted from it, though. Night watch duty and all that.

Everyone gets nighttime watch. You'll rotate through duties when you're not training."

"Wow, you guys really have a whole paramilitary thing going on, don't you?"

Kayla shrugged. "Seems like a good way to run a superhero team. Otherwise you get lax and the bad guys can take advantage of you."

"You like Champion as a leader? As someone to train you?"

Kayla's smile was much more genuine this time. "Oh yes, he's amazing."

"Does he ever take off his mask?"

"Not as far as I've seen. You think he's good-looking or horribly scarred?"

Sally bit her tongue to keep from uttering what she *really* thought about him. "He's probably just a normal-looking dude."

Kayla nodded. "Yeah, probably. Come on in. We'll find you an empty cubicle." She led Sally into a dimly-lit cubicle farm maze, with rope lights along the lower edges of the cubicle walls showing a path. She could see the flashing blue light of someone watching television or a video from underneath the curtains pulled across the nearest cubicle entrance. Most of the others had no lights showing. There were handwritten name tags beside each entrance, but it was too dark for Sally to read them. "Here we go," said Kayla. She stepped into a cubicle and touched a switch, filling the cubicle with cool lighting from a compact fluorescent lamp.

The cubicle was cramped, and Sally figured that she wouldn't be expected to spend much time in it except for sleeping. It contained a twin-size bed, writing desk, and plastic chest-of-drawers. The lamp was clipped to one wall. The cubicle felt sterile, devoid of any personal touches. Sally wondered if recruits were allowed to decorate or if that would somehow violate Champion's notion of purity. "Looks cozy," she said. "Um, where's the bathrooms?"

"All the way at the far wall. There are showers too, laundry, and locker rooms." Kayla moved to the door of the cubicle. "I'm on duty all night. If you need anything, you come get me. Otherwise, sleep well."

"Thanks." Sally smiled at the unsmiling young woman. Kayla drew the curtain and Sally listened to the sound of her footsteps on the former dance floor as she headed back toward the main lobby. Once she was sure she was alone, she pulled the four orbs from her bag. "Go look around," she told them. "And be very careful. I've only been here a few minutes and met one person and it's already skeeving me out. It's like *Invasion of the Body Snatchers*."

Her phone buzzed with a text from Vanitha. *No computers. No books. Look at your cell service.*

Sally looked and discovered her phone had no bars. "We're cut off from the outside," she muttered.

Brainwashing starts early tomorrow, texted Vanitha.

"I don't doubt it. See what you can find out. Be back before people start moving around in the morning. And don't let anyone see you."

Sally lay back on her bed and watched as the four orbs silently rose out of her cubicle into the darkness of the training floor.

It was a long time before she fell asleep.

Chapter Twenty

"Lots of times you have to pretend to join a parade in which you're not really interested in order to get where you're going."

—Christopher Morley

New York City, New York
January, 2007

An insistent nudging at Sally's shoulder drove away her dreams and made her start to berate Jason for waking her up so early. The poking at her shoulder continued unabated until she opened her eyes to see the gray light filtering into the Champions HQ from the high overhead windows. She remembered then where she was and why she was there and she sat up quickly to see Vanitha seated cross-legged on the desk chair beside her bed, wrapped in Sally's thin coverlet and looking rather like she'd just fallen out of bed herself. That probably wasn't a bad description of what it must be like for Vanitha after spending a lot of time in a computer system. Sally blinked at her. "What are you doing?"

"Filling you in," Vanitha whispered. "Keep your voice down. Some of the others are already awake."

"Why aren't you still in Curious?"

"I can't stay in there forever. I still have to eat and pee and stuff. I snuck outside through a vent and called your fiancé to put a stash of clothes nearby so I can leave when I need to."

"You called Jason? How did you get his number?" asked Sally.

"It's in your phone, smartypants." Vanitha held it up. "Not everything requires super hacker techniques to discover."

"My phone has a lock code."

Vanitha shrugged. "Okay, some things require mundane hacker techniques. Anyway, he said he would and to say hi and he loves you, and I'm done being the middleman between you two already because it makes me want to throw up."

Sally rubbed her face. It felt puffy and unfamiliar, but she couldn't tell whether that was from sleeping on a fairly uncomfortable bed in a cold warehouse on an undercover mission or from the transformation Minerva had performed. "Okay, so what did you find out so far?"

Vanitha ticked off the points on her fingers. "Champion's not here. I found a room that might be his quarters, but it doesn't look like it's been lived-in at all. Three of the Young Guns are here. Toxic and Bombshell are rooming together, and Surfboy had a girl in his room all night that I think goes by the name Statuesque. Besides her and Dampen, who you met last night, there are ten others here. Seven guys and three girls. I put the list of their names and identifying characteristics on your phone."

"What about Johnny Go? Where's he?"

"I don't know. I didn't find him."

Sally frowned. Johnny had been in Champion's commercial. Why wouldn't he be in the training center? Maybe Champion had him on some kind of special recruitment duty. "Okay, we'll follow up on him later. Did you find out anything about Champion's plan or nanotech or anything?"

"No. There's a computer in the front lobby, and I couldn't risk getting into that one. There's another in the room that might be Champion's but it's wiped completely clean. I mean like it doesn't even have an operating system installed. If he's using it, he's plugging an external drive into it and running it from there. And that's it. Not another terminal anywhere I could find."

"That's crazy. Everything runs on computers."

"Maybe he's doing it old school. I can't hack a ledger or a notebook. Or maybe there's areas I couldn't get into. I found several locked rooms and no easy way in. Your little spheres are very cute, but they're horrible at fitting through tight spots. Something long, narrow, and flexible would be better. Like a flying snake or something."

Sally shivered. She'd had an awful experience with a flying snake in Guatemala. Before she could ask anything, Sneaky rolled into her cubicle underneath the curtain.

Vanitha's eyes widened. "Got to go." She vanished into Curious, leaving Sally alone in her cubicle once more, and not a moment too soon, for there was a soft tapping on the outside of the cubicle.

"Lindsay? Are you awake yet? It's Kayla."

"Yeah, I'm up. This bed is pretty uncomfortable." That much was true, at any rate. Sally twisted her back until it popped. It made her feel a little bit better. "Are they all this bad?"

Kayla pushed aside the curtain. Her face was puffy from all-night receptionist duty and she had bags under her eyes. "I don't know. I haven't slept in all of them. Only mine, which is where I'm headed after this. I just wanted to check to see if you needed anything."

"I don't think so. What's the plan for today?"

"After the wakeup call, a group breakfast, then we break up into groups for training. You and the other four newbies will get some one on one time with Champion."

"I'm pretty excited to meet him," said Sally. "I bet he's really impressive in person."

"Yeah, he's pretty awesome." Kayla yawned. "Anyway, I'm going to head off to bed. I should be up by midday. Maybe I'll see you."

"I hope so. Sleep well."

After Kayla left, Sally rummaged through her bag for a change of clothes and some toiletries. She didn't know what all was expected so she figured she'd start with some basic sweatpants and a hoodie. She guessed that she'd be issued a set of the yellow-and-red coveralls like Kayla and Stefan wore.

There was a crackle from the PA system that the Young Guns had used for their last rave, followed by a loud, prolonged boatswain's whistle. "Good morning, Champions." Sally recognized Dannan's voice over the loudspeakers. "All heroes report to breakfast in ten minutes." The boatswain's whistle repeated and the PA shut off.

Ten minutes wasn't much time to get ready. Sally could have done it in less than a minute if she utilized her super-speed, but she was keeping that hidden, so instead she grabbed her things and headed out of her cubicle toward the bathroom. She'd have time to wash her face, brush her hair and teeth, and get dressed, and that was all.

She encountered two other Champion recruits along her way to the bathroom. One was a tall, husky young man with glasses and a scraggly goatee, who introduced himself as Shouty Ed. The other was a woman who looked a few years older than Sally was, with long blonde hair that reached the small of her back, who called herself Statuesque. Sally recalled that she was the one who'd spent the night with Surfboy and made a special effort to be pleasant. She had to do whatever she could to get into Champion's inner circle as quickly as possible, and she figured Surfboy was probably her way in.

"What do you do, Ed?"

"Shout. Like, really loud." Ed's speech patterns seemed more appropriate for a stoner than for a potential superhero, but Sally had to remind herself that these were people that for whatever reason had either been turned down by the Hero Academy or hadn't ever tried to join in the first place.

"I'm a telekinetic," said Sally. "I'm the Juggler."

"Juggalo? You mean like those weirdos with the clown makeup?" asked Statuesque.

"Jugg*ler*," said Sally. "You know, like juggling bowling pins and chainsaws."

"You can juggle chainsaws?"

"No, but you get the idea."

"Sure, I guess," said Statuesque.

"What do you do?" Sally asked her.

"This." Statuesque froze in place and her skin and hair took on the color of charcoal ash. Except for her Champion outfit, she looked like a granite statue. It reminded Sally of John Stone, the Assistant Principal at the Hero Academy, except he was actually animated, whereas Statuesque remained frozen in place.

"Neat," said Sally.

Statuesque unfroze herself and Sally followed her into the bathroom. The only other woman in there was Toxy, brushing out her short hair. "Oh wow," Sally gushed. "You're that one girl, right? Poison?" She hoped that a wildly different approach than she would normally use might help to mask her personality.

"Toxic," said Toxy. "Who're you?"

"They call me the Juggler."

"That's cool. See you around, Juggler." Toxy stuck her brush in her red belt and left the bathroom.

"Hey, when do I get one of those cool jumpsuit thingies?" Sally asked Statuesque.

"Today, sometime. Man of the Cloth will take care of it."

"You have a priest?"

"No. A guy who can control cloth."

"That's a weird power." Sally washed her face.

"So is super-juggling. So is turning into a statue. All of us here have kind of weird powers. We're like the misfits. The second string. The ones who Just Cause didn't want."

"Did you try to get in?"

"No. What's the point? So I can turn into a statue. Big fucking deal."

Sally toweled off her face and squeezed toothpaste onto her brush. "So you came here?"

"Champion is teaching us to be heroes, no matter what we can or can't do. He's teaching us to find ways to use our powers effectively. People are going to look up to us because we're more like them than the big league heroes. And then when they're in trouble, they're going to look to us, not to Just Cause. And we'll be there."

Sally spat a mouthful of foam into the sink. Statuesque was spouting platitudes and propaganda, just like Kayla had before. She had a feeling that Champion's training probably consisted of a lot of that kind of thing. Neurolinguistic programming. As Sally dressed, she realized that this wasn't a hero group, it was a cult. Since she was keeping the assumption that Champion was really Heinrich Kaiser, it was likely that he was using Nazi propaganda techniques to brainwash the members. And when they were trickling in a few at a time, it would be so much more effective. Every new member who joined the Champions would have a bigger and bigger group of pre-existing members spouting off the same lingo.

It was a movement.

Sally followed Statuesque from the bathroom across the training floor and past the cubicle farm where some long tables had been set up with folding chairs. One table had some stainless steel restaurant pans on it with butane heaters keeping the food in them warm. They held the kind of bland fare that was typically found in downscale motels that offered a free breakfast option—powdered eggs, dehydrated potatoes, and some brown wheel things that might have been sausages. There was a vat of plain, watery oatmeal that seemed to be about the least offensive thing on the table. Sally saw watered down pitchers of orange juice and milk, but no coffee. She asked Statuesque about it.

"No, there's no coffee. No tea. Champion doesn't want us polluting our bodies with artificial stimulants."

"I *like* polluting my body that way," muttered Sally. She ladled oatmeal into a styrofoam bowl and poured a glass of juice. At least she wasn't going to starve, she reflected, but on the other hand she wasn't going to stay curvaceous for long if this was the kind of fare Champion was providing his people.

She looked around at the other recruits. They were eating without much interest in their food. The meal was quiet, with almost no conversation going on either. In fact, the only table where anything seemed to be going on at all was where Stefan sat with a couple of recruits Sally didn't recognize. She noticed that they had different food from the rest of the group. Theirs actually looked tasty. She sat down beside Dannan, who had a plate full of the grainy eggs and sausages and was poking at them with a fork without taking many bites. "Hi, can I sit here?"

"Yeah, go ahead."

Sally kept her voice low, as muffled and whispered conversations seemed to be the standard among the other recruits. "What's the story with Surfboy? How come he gets real food?"

"He's an officer," said Dannan. She speared a sausage and ate it with the same expression as a toddler taking cough syrup.

"How come you're not? You're one of the people from that video. Don't you have seniority too?"

"It doesn't work that way."

"How does it work then?"

Dannan looked over at Sally for the first time since she sat down. "You have to prove yourself. Do I know you?"

Sally was taken aback. Dannan had always been friendly and outgoing, and all of a sudden she'd become sullen and bitter. "I'm Lindsay," she said.

Dannan leaned in close. "Lindsay, you want some advice? Pack up your shit and walk away from this place and don't look back."

"Why? What's so bad about it?"

A presence filled the dining area, like a wave breaking against the shoreline. Everyone wearing a yellow and red jumpsuit stood at attention. Sally and the other new recruits still in their civilian attire followed suit. A figure descended from the shadows of the roof.

Champion.

Sally watched as he descended, his cape fluttering as he passed through the breeze from an air vent. He certainly knew how to make an entrance, she thought. He wore the same costume she'd seen him in before, and retained his full-face mask. "At ease, my friends." His voice was soft but carried throughout the entire area, as if he wore a microphone and speakers were placed at every table. "Please finish your meals. I'm looking forward to beginning our work today."

"What work is that?" Sally turned to Dannan, but Dannan had already left her spot. Something was wrong. What had happened to make Dannan so angry? Maybe it was Champion passing her over for his second-in-command in favor of Stefan. She could see how that would make anyone upset. There were some apparent perks in the position, and Stefan was clearly using it to his benefit.

Sally finished her oatmeal as quickly as she could and took her trash to the waste bins at the end of the tables. She hoped to get a little privacy to chat with Vanitha, but before she could leave the dining area, Champion floated up into the air. "My friends, I'd like to get started this morning. We have a lot of work to do to prepare you."

Stefan floated up above the table, at his maximum altitude of six feet. He wasn't as high as Champion, but that would have been inappropriate even if he could have done so. "New recruits will go with Champion. The rest of you, morning training will commence in ten minutes."

Sally and the three other new recruits followed Champion into the conference room. Her companions were a young man of Asian ancestry, a tall, skinny boy with a big nose and acne, and a blonde woman with tattoos and drawn-on eyebrows.

"Please, sit down. Make yourselves comfortable," said Champion. "Do any of you require anything? Water?"

Sally and the other recruits glanced at each other for a moment, but nobody piped up with any needs.

"Excellent. I am Champion, and I want to welcome the four of you to the Champions. With your help, we are going to transform the world for the better. Please tell me a little bit about yourselves. You can share as little or as much as you'd like. We have plenty of time right now." He pointed at the tall boy. "Why don't you begin?"

"Me? Oh, uh, I'm, uh, I'm trying to come up with a good name. I'm Escher, and, uh, I can turn into a talking dog."

"What sort of dog?" asked Champion.

"I'll just show you." Escher hunched his shoulders forward and his body changed. His clothes melded with his skin and became a uniform gray color, like fine velvet. His big nose lengthened while his skull narrowed. A moment later, a large greyhound sat on his haunches on the conference room chair, his forelegs up on the table. "See?" he said, his dog-mouth making the word sound odd and muffled.

Sally had seen a lot of parahuman abilities in her life, having grown up around them, but it was the first time she'd ever seen someone who could actually transform his own body. It made her feel much more self-conscious about her own recent transformation.

"Are you all right, young lady?" asked Champion, and Sally realized he was addressing her.

"Yeah. That just kind of freaked me out." She nodded her head toward the greyhound.

"Transformation abilities are rare," said Champion. "We'll be able to find a lot of uses for you, Escher. Welcome to the Champions. How about you, then?" Again, he nodded at Sally.

"I'm Lindsay. The Juggler." She pulled out three of the orbs, did a few cycles at the table, and then launched the balls to do a quick flight around the table before returning to her hands.

"You're a telekinetic," said Champion.

"Yeah, but I can only move my balls." The young Asian man snorted in amusement. "Sorry, but that's the only way I can really describe it."

"Telekinesis is useful, Lindsay. Welcome to the Champions. How about you, son?" He turned to the smallest one of the newcomers.

The Asian boy smiled. "I'm Ferdinand, but you can call me . . . Particulate." He dissolved into a cloud of dust, flowed across the room in a cloud, and then reformed in another seat.

"That's something I've never seen before," said Champion. "It's not precisely teleportation. I presume you call it *particulation*?"

"Yeah, pretty much."

"Can you travel through solid material?"

"No, but I can move through any crack big enough for my, uh, particles to get through."

"Fascinating. Welcome to the Champions. And last, young lady, tell me about yourself."

"Call me Skimmer," said the last recruit. "I'm a contact mind-reader. If I touch your skin, I can read your surface thoughts."

Sally couldn't tell, but she thought Champion smiled beneath his mask. "Wonderful. That's a tremendously useful ability. I can see the four of you have brought quite an impressive blend of abilities into our growing family. Let me tell you a little about my dream and how the four of you can help it come into being."

Over the next two hours, Champion laid out his plans which were long on propaganda and, as Sally noted, disappointingly short on details. He wanted to create a rival organization to Just Cause. There were other private teams in the United States, but none had formed since the Young Guns had and before that, not since Divine Right in the year 2000. Champion's plan was different. He foresaw his teams and trained heroes spreading across the country instead of being confined to single cities or regions. He wanted to make Champions available to help people wherever they were. Ideally, he wanted Champions to be the first thing people thought of when they needed parahuman assistance.

"The government should not be in the business of controlling parahumans," he said. "Every year, Congress brings forth legislation to require new registration acts. They want to know who you are, where you are, and what you can do. What reason could they have for this if not to control you? And if they can't control you, well, we all know what the government tends to do with those they can't control."

He left it unspoken, but the implication of violence perpetrated against parahumans was unmistakable. Sally glanced at the other recruits. Particulate and Skimmer were nodding. Escher was wagging his tail. She made herself smile a little.

"We are the future of mankind. Parahumans are the next step in the evolution of humanity. We have a duty to help our brothers and sisters here and everywhere in the world, and a duty to see that the non-enhanced see no reason to fear or hunt us."

He had a sneaky way of doing it, but Sally could see that he was subtly aligning the Champions against the rest of the country. He was working on building up his own little jihad, a holy war against the *non-enhanced*, as he called them. She could see why his words were so powerful. Every day in the media, it seemed that someone was railing against parahumans as the product of the devil, or as a danger to mankind. Champion was taking that fear and using it as a psychological tool to bring parahumans to his side. It was classic Heinrich Kaiser, Sally thought. He took the Nazi philosophies of the Master Race and applied them to parahumans.

She wondered how soon he would start his war against the rest of the world.

Chapter Twenty-One

*"Can you imagine if we let just anybody into Just Cause?
It'd be like the world's craziest frat party. It'd be the
Children of the Atom all over again."*

—Kid Crash

**New York City, New York
January, 2007**

The first day of training among the Champions had
been an eye-opening experience for Sally. Following
Champion's lecture on parahumans and their rightful
place at the top of the evolutionary food chain, she
and the other new recruits had gotten fitted for their
new uniforms.

Sally and the others had to strip down to their
underwear and stand nearly naked before the Man of the
Cloth, which was one of the most uncomfortable things
she'd ever done. He was an older man, just on the near
side of fifty, with a paunch and thinning hair, but at least
he had a kind smile that reminded Sally of a mall Santa.

As promised, the Man of the Cloth had let bolts of yellow and red cloth swirl around each of them at his direction as he wrapped them in brand new jumpsuits. It was a very different process than it had been when Just Cause tailors fitted Sally for her updated costume. The Man of the Cloth, who said his name was Ralph, draped the fabric around her as if it were water splashing up onto her. He steered the cloth with his hands, rather like she would have steered her juggling balls if she'd actually been using telekinesis upon them. He drew a line in the air and the fabric split down the front so he could float a zipper into place. Zig zag motions with his fingers made thread stitch itself up and down. Each fitting only took a few minutes of work. It was an unusual power he exhibited, but Sally could see how it could be tremendously useful. She wondered if Just Cause could use him in its organization.

Despite her intention to not let Champion's words affect her, Sally found herself still looking at Just Cause in a new, unfamiliar light. They had such stringent entry requirements, it was no wonder that so many lower-powered parahumans had been denied that role. A lot of people were pretty upset about their treatment by the government, and nearly everyone had some kind of horror story to share about their powers causing problems. There was a lot of disenchantment with the existing superhero organizations, and Sally could see the appeal to a group with an anybody-can-join mindset.

Following the costuming, Champion had passed the new recruits along to Stefan and Statuesque, who conducted some basic training exercises with all of them. Stefan explained that they needed to establish baseline abilities, strengths, and weaknesses before designing custom training programs. Their exercises ranged from tests of physical strength and endurance to mental gymnastics and eventually to examination of their powers.

Partway through the training exercises, Champion stopped by to observe, causing Stefan to puff himself up and work the recruits even harder. After several minutes of Stefan yelling at them to work harder, that they would fail as heroes if they didn't, that they were pathetic, Champion pulled Skimmer out from the training exercises, saying he wanted to examine her abilities in more detail. That made Sally nervous. She knew Ment had built strong psychic defenses into her mind, but surface thoughts were different than those kept safely behind the wall. What if Skimmer managed to catch a stray thought from her that suggested she wasn't who she purported to be? Sally resolved to keep herself as far away from Skimmer as possible.

The midday meal was basically a repeat of breakfast: bland fare and bland, quiet conversation. Sally kept her head down for the most part, but observed the other dozen Champions as she ate her tasteless turkey sandwich. A few of the members exhibited minor injuries that she hadn't noticed in the morning, like bruises and cuts. A few of them looked shell-shocked, like it was maybe the first time any of them had been in any kind of actual conflict. Sally saw unhappiness, and a certain resignation on several faces, like they knew that this was the way their lives would be going forward.

Dannan sat with Toxy and the two of them spoke in muttered tones, growing quiet whenever someone else approached them. Something was bothering the two of them, and Sally was pretty sure it was Stefan's attitude. Johnny Go still wasn't anywhere to be seen. Sally didn't see how she could ask about him without raising suspicions on her. She'd have Vanitha try to figure something out.

She felt guilty about Vanitha, trapped inside the Curious orb. She had to try to resolve the Champion situation as quickly as possible to let the Indian girl get

back to her life. Sally hoped Vanitha could hear her
when she murmured for her to get outside and pass
along what they'd learned from Champion's morning
lecture. And later, when she checked her bag, the
Curious orb was gone, so Sally knew that at least for
the time being, she was on her own.

Afternoon training was markedly different than the
morning abuse as Stefan had conducted it. In charge of
the afternoon session was a heavily-tattooed Hispanic
man. "So you all want to be heroes," he told the group
of four new recruits. "It ain't an easy job. You're going
to find a lot of people who gonna hate you just because
you different. Any of you ever experienced
discrimination? I mean *real* discrimination?"

Sally shook her head, but Particulate nodded. "I
been called names."

The Hispanic man rounded on him. "Names?
Names?" His skin took on a pronounced grayish
metallic sheen. "Names ain't discrimination, slant.
Chink. Jap. Fucker. I been called everything and then
some. That ain't discrimination. That's just bein' an
asshole. If I had a nickel for every time some dickhead
called me a name . . . Well, I already got all the nickel I
ever need." He tapped a metallic finger against a
metallic arm and listened to the dull ring. "You call me
Nickel when we're here. My job is to teach you what it
means to be hated, because those crunchies out there,
they're gonna hate you."

Particulate folded his arms. "Champion said we're
going to be helping people. Why would they hate us?"

Nickel took a step forward. "How you feel when
you're drivin' and you see a cop? You feel guilty. You
hate that. You get a ticket, you hate that cop for givin' it
to you. You get stopped because you wearin' the wrong
clothes or you in the wrong part of town, you hate the
cop who's discriminating against you. You call him
names. You call him a fucking pig. Maybe he's strong

enough to take it and walk away. Or maybe he's the kind who'll break a baton over your knee. Or your head, *pendejo*." He lowered his voice. "Them crunchies? They gonna hate you just like you hate that fucking cop. They're gonna hate your uniform, they're gonna hate whoever's wearing it. They're gonna hate you right up until they need you. Then after you're done, they're gonna hate you again. You ready for that? You ready to be hated because you're different from the crunchies, homes?"

Escher, whom Sally had taken to calling E-Dog, sat up on his haunches. "What are crunchies?" he growled, wrinkling his snout as he pronounced the words.

"People who ain't got powers, Dog. They jealous, and they hate what they can't have. They crunch when you hit 'em hard enough. Just like big damn roaches."

"They're not all like that," said Sally.

Nickel's voice took on a soft, apologetic cast. "They're not? Aw, geez, I'm sorry, *señorita*. I didn't realize I was wrong. I'll just go on back to my goddamn cell and rethink my life." He lunged at her, moving fast for someone made of metal. Sally would have dodged, but she knew deep down that if she moved that fast there would be other questions, so she gritted her teeth and let him come. Nickel grabbed hold of her throat just below her chin, lifting her out of her seat.

"Let her go!" shouted Particulate.

E-Dog barked and snarled.

The ferocity of Nickel's lunge had surprised Sally, and she kicked feebly at him, struggling to draw a breath.

"You think this is just a game, girl? This ain't no playin' dolls in the treehouse. This is real life, and there are fuckers out there who would bust a cap in your sweet ass just because they're scared of you." He set her down, more gently than he'd grabbed her. "And right now, I'm your best bet not to get killed on your first day out wearin' the colors."

Sally rubbed her throat. It was the roughest anyone had ever treated her in a non-combat situation, and it had upset her far more than she'd thought. She knew she had tears in her eyes and chewed on the inside of her lip to try to keep them from spilling down her face.

"You scared of me?" Nickel shouted at her. "You better be scared." He kicked at a table beside him, snapping off a leg. He tossed it into her lap. His metallic sheen disappeared and he became flesh and blood once more. "You seen what I can do to you. And you know what, girl? I'm gonna do it again." He spread his hands wide. "Stop me, whore."

Particulate coalesced between Sally and Nickel. "Cut it out, man."

Nickel backhanded him aside. The Asian boy crashed against a wall and fell, gasping for air. E-Dog snarled at him but backed off with a single glare from the Hispanic man.

Sally didn't know what his game was, but he'd given her a weapon. She raised it as he charged at her. As he reached for her throat, she swung it hard, clocking him right across the face hard enough that the table leg broke with the impact. Nickel staggered to one side, falling to one knee. Blood spurted from his mouth. Sally shrieked and dropped the broken stump. Her arm had gone numb with that blow. Was she going to have to flee right then? Had she just blown her cover?

Nickel, impossibly, began to laugh. He spat blood onto the floor and wiped more from his lips with the back of one tattooed hand. "Still scared of me, girl? If I came after you again, what would you do? What would you do to stop me from doing it again? What if I handed you a gun and did it again? Would you shoot my ass?"

Sally stared back at him, eyes wide in horrific realization. He'd just played her as magnificently as any con artist.

"Because how you feel right now, that's how crunchies are goin' to feel about you. And there are a lot more of them than there are of us." He held out his hand to her. "My job here is to help you understand how they feel so you can watch out for the threats. It's us against them, and I don't intend to be on the losing side. You all right?"

Sally rubbed her arm. "I'll be all right."

Nickel kept his hand extended. "That was a good shot. I'll be feelin' that for days, girl. What's your name, *chica*?"

"L-lindsay." Her shoulder was really throbbing, and she had post-combat shakes. She hadn't suffered from them in years. Somehow this tattooed Hispanic man had gotten right past all her years of training and found the switch deep inside her.

"I'm gonna keep my eye on you. You got potential. But you're soft. All of you are soft." He kept his hand held out to her but addressed Particulate. "You got some balls on you at least, kid, but you're stupid. And you?" He glanced at E-Dog. "You shoulda ripped my throat out. You ain't shit."

E-Dog's tail dropped between his legs and he lowered his chin in a way that made Sally's heart go out to him. *Poor dog*, she thought before she remembered that he was a man.

Nickel returned his attention to Sally. "I'm not askin' you to like me. Hell, I don't even like me very much. But you respect me, and I'll respect you, girl. You got *cojones* most of these assholes don't have. What do you say? Respect?"

Sally looked down at his offered hand. She almost reached out to take it. But there was a gleam in his eye. Instead she nodded. "Respect."

"Good." He dropped the piece of broken table leg he'd been hiding behind his back in his other hand. She hadn't even seen him pick it up. "You're learning."

Over the next couple of hours, Nickel talked to them, berated them, threatened them, and generally acted like some kind of mystical asshole sensei. Sally was getting a sense of the basic idea behind Nickel's—and in turn, Kaiser's—philosophy. Parahumans were the new Master Race, and a war was coming between them and humans. It wouldn't be a war fought along battle lines. It would be more like heroic rebels against the evil empire.

Of course, Sally thought, one man's heroic rebels were another man's terrorists.

By dinner, Sally felt thoroughly drained, physically, mentally, and emotionally. Compared to her first day in the Champions, her first day in Just Cause had been a walk in the park. She wondered if this was the kind of process that people went through who joined the Army. Everything in Champion's organization seemed to be devoted to breaking her down into tiny little pieces, presumably with the intent to build her back up into a real hero.

She shook her head. Why was she even thinking like that? This was all part of the brainwashing methodology. She had to keep that in mind. As long as she was aware of what they were trying to do, it would be like a lifeline to keep her afloat. She couldn't afford to let her guard down even for a moment. She'd found a few minutes of peace hidden in a bathroom stall. She wanted to check her phone for a message from Jason, but knew there wouldn't be one, thanks to the signal interference.

She felt so disconnected from the rest of the world. But how disconnected was she, really? Could she simply walk out of the front door and be free to leave of her own accord? She was tempted to try, but it might have to wait until later in the evening, if the recruits got any kind of free time.

Dinner was as uninspiring as the previous meals had been. She looked down at her plate of bland spaghetti with sauce from a jar. There wasn't any parmesan cheese, or crushed red pepper, or even bread. Sally would have throttled a stranger for a nice, fresh salad with crisp greens and cucumbers. How was anyone supposed to thrive on food like this? She didn't think anything would ever have made her look back fondly upon the school lunches she'd eaten in elementary school, but the Champions' food service managed it.

Sally ran into Kayla by the trash bins as she scooped her half-eaten spaghetti into the can. "Hey, how did your first day go?" asked the young woman, unsmiling as ever.

"It was hard," said Sally. "Are we allowed outside? I need some fresh air."

"Of course you're allowed. You're not a prisoner here," said Kayla.

"Kind of feels like it."

"Ah. You must have met Hector today."

"Hector?"

"Nickel. Here, I'll come outside with you. I'm dying for a smoke anyway."

Sally followed Kayla outside. It was already dark, but there were lots of lights along the docks and across the river, New Jersey sparkled like a carnival. Thick gray clouds reflected the city lights back down and the cold, damp breeze suggested snow was on the way.

"Come around the side of the HQ," said Kayla. "Champion doesn't want us smoking by the door. It looks bad."

"I'm surprised he lets you smoke at all," said Sally. "Doesn't that fall under Champion's category of polluting your body?"

Kayla's laugh was bitter. "Hey, we've all got to go sometime. Might as well be cancer as anything else. You ever try to quit smoking? It's fucking impossible."

"I never started."

"You might, you stay here long enough."

"It doesn't feel like we're being very heroic. It's more like . . . torture." Sally shivered in the breeze, but her new body was a bit better insulated than her old one, and she was loathe to go back inside the headquarters building so quickly.

"Hector takes pleasure in his job."

Sally rubbed her neck. She had bruises where he'd grabbed her. "Does he do that to everyone?"

"Only the ones he thinks are worth anything." Kayla blew out a lungful of smoke and watched it waft away in the breeze. "He did it to me."

"What's his story?"

"He's angry. Discovered his parapower by accident after he'd already messed up his life doing hard time for first degree assault and a handful of other charges. He got turned down by the Hero Academy because of his record. Since then, he's been pissed off."

"I bet he was pissed off before."

Kayla chuckled. "I bet you're right."

"Why are you here?"

"I didn't want to go work at Deep Six. That's where all the low-power parahumans go, isn't it?"

Sally shrugged. She knew that was more or less the case, but not everybody was cut out to work in a prison. "Yeah. Super-juggling. That's not really a high-demand ability either."

"It's nice to have a place to belong, though. Even though the training is hard, eventually we'll be past all that. And then we'll be, you know, heroes. The heroes that the world needs. The ones who can help when Just Cause can't. Or won't."

"Just Cause isn't that bad, is it?"

Kayla shrugged. "They're fine for the big problems. Like the Archmage last year. But what good are they for neighborhood crime? Or domestic abuse? You can't punch poverty in the face, no matter how good a hero you are. Just Cause isn't going to help a little girl whose father likes to drink too much and punch her mother." She took a long drag on her cigarette. "But maybe a Champion can. Maybe *I* can."

"You can't punch poverty in the face," Sally repeated. It made her feel like she'd been punched in the face herself, because it was true. When she was home, she tried hard to help at a local level. She and Jason volunteered their time at a club for underprivileged kids. The whole team had headed to the Gulf Coast to help with relief efforts for Hurricane Katrina. But at the same time, crimes were still committed every day that Just Cause ignored. Maybe Kayla was right. Maybe there really did need to be a second or third tier of superheroes. Perhaps not necessarily *super*heroes, but people who were in a position to make a difference.

Then she remembered Hector's hand around her throat and she knew that Champion's method wasn't the answer. He was the bad guy, and she had to be very careful not to start thinking like him.

Because if she did, she might never leave.

Chapter Twenty-Two

"To the legion of the lost ones, to the cohort of the damned."

—*Rudyard Kipling*

New York City, New York
January, 2007

Sally was exhausted, but she managed to carry on a conversation with Vanitha via her phone in the near darkness of the cubicle farm after lights-out. The Indian girl had managed to find a way out of the building. She'd changed to the clothes that Jason had provided and went to report in and to take care of her human needs like eating and sleeping.

"What did you have? No, don't tell me," said Sally. "God, the food here is terrible. There's no nutrition or anything in it. I feel like I've been in a fog for half the day. I'd kill for some of that Thai seafood curry we had at your place. I'd maim for a cheeseburger. Shout insults for a taco."

Sorry. I can't bring you anything, Vanitha texted.

"I know," said Sally. "Have you gotten into any of the locked rooms yet?"

No. There are baffles in the ventilation far enough back that I can't even look. Who puts security barricades in ventilation shafts?

"Champion does, apparently," said Sally. "He's got a real special kind of paranoia going for him."

How about you? Any news to report?

"Most everyone here has an axe to grind against Just Cause. Lots of folks who got turned down for various reasons. Mostly because they have odd, low-level, and not-very-useful abilities."

So why does Champion want them?

"He thinks parahumans are the Master Race. It's all about the numbers for him. The more he has on his side, the greater his power base becomes."

Maybe he's right.

Sally's eyes widened. "Excuse me?"

We're better than normal people in a lot of ways. You yourself are a third-generation speedster, and you're faster than your mother and grandmother. That's all public knowledge. Musashi proved parahuman powers have genetic origins. Maybe we really are the next phase of human evolution.

"That doesn't make what Champion is doing right."

No, but I can see the validity of his argument. That's what makes it scary. It's simple and easy to understand and the numbers add up. That makes it easier to convince people of lesser mindsets.

"Lesser mindsets?"

Dumbasses. Hey, hush. Someone is coming.

Sally shoved her phone back inside her bra. One of the benefits to being stacked in her new body was that she had a tailor-made spot to hide her phone where nobody was likely to find it without getting fresh with her. She lay back on her bed, feigning sleep as she heard the footsteps approaching. They stopped outside her cubicle and Sally stiffened. Who was out there?

With a soft sound of plastic rings on metal, the curtain was pushed aside and a shadowy figure stole into Sally's cubicle. Sally curled her fingers into fists. Was it Hector, come to torment her some more? Or Surfboy, thinking to act upon his lustful impulses?

The figure reached for Sally's head in the near darkness, and Sally jerked into action. She rolled out of her bed, ducking underneath the grasping hand. She curled her hand around the back of her would-be assailant's neck and delivered a fast right cross to the perpetrator's jaw. Sally fueled the blow with her super-speed, the way she'd been taught in her combat classes. She followed up the first blow with an elbow to the side of the other's head and then brought the back of her hand down across the bridge of her attacker's nose. Warm, sticky blood splattered across Sally's face and hand as the other's nose shattered with the blow. The creep collapsed in a heap at Sally's feet.

Sally lunged for her bedside light. Rules be damned, someone had tried to hassle her in what should have been her sleep!

Crumpled at her feet was Skimmer, unconscious and bleeding profusely from her broken nose. "Oh no," Sally whispered. Her horror at what she'd done quickly vanished in favor of righteous anger. Someone, either Champion or Stefan, had sent her to come read Sally's mind. If Skimmer's abilities only allowed her to read surface thoughts, Sally would have been at her most vulnerable during sleep.

"Hey, what's going on over there?" called a voice.

"Vanitha, go. Now's your chance," Sally hissed as footsteps approached. The Curious orb and its digitized passenger whispered up into the darkness out of sight.

"What did you do? Holy shit!" cried a voice from overhead. Sally glanced up to see Stefan, dressed only in sweatpants, hovering over the cubicles. Sally realized her fist was practically red with gore. She didn't hit hard; as a speedster, that wasn't her thing, but a super-fast punch wasn't much less damaging than a super-strong one.

And nobody could deliver a punch faster than Sally.

It had all gone south so fast the only thing she could think to do was flee. She accelerated her perceptions and ducked through the curtain into the corridor between cubicles. Three recruits barred her way, including Statuesque, Kayla, and a young man whose name Sally couldn't remember.

By her second step, she knew something had gone terribly wrong. Her weight came down on her left leg and it felt completely numb. Her quadricep gave way and she crashed down against another cubicle wall, knocking it askew. She cried out in pain. High-speed collisions were the bane of her existence. The collapse of her leg had sent shooting pains through her knee and she was terrified that she'd blown it out. Still, she tried to pull herself back to her feet, leaving a bloody handprint on the fallen cubicle wall. Then her arm collapsed and she hit her chin so hard she saw stars. Her perceptions grew muddled and snapped back into regular time.

"Good job, Numb," said Stefan. "Where's Dannan?"

"Here," said the tall, muscular blonde. Her arms almost looked grotesque in the dim light.

"Carry our assailant to Conference Room Two and keep her there. If she resists or tries to escape, you have permission to beat her into unconsciousness." Stefan's smile was cold as he gazed down upon Sally with a mixture of disgust and lust on his face.

"Hey," said Statuesque. "I think what's-her-name, Skimmer? I think she needs a doctor. Her face is really messed up."

"Call 9-1-1," said Stefan. "Tell them there's been a training accident. We don't need any crunchy investigators coming through here."

"Shouldn't we call Champion?" asked Kayla. "He's going to want to know about this."

Stefan sniffed in disdain. "There's no need to wake him up for this. I'll report to him in the morning. We can handle this on our own."

"No, call him," said Sally through the pain in her jaw. "I want him to explain himself."

"Dannan, get her out of here," said Stefan. Then he addressed Sally. "One more peep out of you and you get a Bombshell love tap."

Sally couldn't get to her feet. Numb's ability was self-explanatory. She had pins and needles roaring through her leg and arm as the nerves awakened. "I can't walk," she grumbled.

Dannan lifted her up like Sally was a baby. "Don't try anything," she said. "I will knock you out."

"I'm not going to do anything," said Sally. "But I'm really upset. Skimmer came into my cubicle to read me." Dannan said nothing else as she escorted Sally across the training floor toward a conference room that was apparently going to be her temporary cell. "You don't have to do what he says," said Sally in a low voice. "He wasn't always like this, was he?"

"Shut up, Juggler," said Dannan, but Sally could tell she'd struck a nerve. She decided to play it cool and sat down at the table to await whatever judgment was coming her way.

By the time Stefan arrived, Sally's eyes were rolling in her head as she struggled to stay awake. Her fight-or-flight reflex had died out, leaving her exhausted from the day's events and no sleep. Dannan stayed in the conference room door, guarding Sally under direct supervision. Sally hoped Vanitha had found a way into a secure area during all the commotion. It was as good a distraction as anything might have been.

Stefan had taken the time to dress in his Champions uniform. When he came into the room, all spit and polish, Sally felt fat and dumpy all over again. He put his hands behind his back and floated around the room as if he were walking, but his feet never touched the ground. "Well," he said, and that was all he said for what felt to Sally like an eternity.

"Well what?" she asked at last.

"You're in a lot of trouble," he said. "Skimmer's on her way to the hospital for x-rays. The paramedics seem to think you broke her face."

"Well she shouldn't have come into my cubicle!" Sally's ire rose faster than it should have, thanks to her exhaustion. "She startled me."

"I'm sure she had a very good reason for it."

"Did you send her?" Sally challenged him. "Did you tell her to spy on me?"

"If I did, you can be sure it was for the safety of the Champions," said Stefan as he passed behind Sally. "When Champion isn't here, it's my job to make sure everything runs smoothly and everyone behaves themselves. And I do that however I see fit."

"Yeah, you make a great little Nazi," said Sally under her breath.

"Excuse me?" Stefan spun her chair around to face him. "You want to say that to my face?"

Sally got to her feet, wincing at the remnants of numbness still plaguing her left leg. She took her time, stretching out the moment as she composed herself and stared up at Stefan in open defiance. Her new body was taller than before, but he was still several inches higher when floating. "I said, you're a Nazi. Look at you. Blond crew cut. Following your orders blindly, no matter what they are. You think you're a little tin god here, but all you are is Champion's bootlicker." She smiled up at him and raised her middle finger in salute. "How's that? In your face enough, little boy?"

Stefan backhanded her.

Sally was expecting the blow and even though she could have dodged it easily, she steeled herself and let him hit her. She rolled with it enough that it didn't hurt nearly as much as it should have, but she still tumbled across the floor.

"Stefan! What the hell?" shouted Dannan.

Stefan wrung his hand, wincing. "She had it coming."

Sally sniffled, checking her lips for blood. She found some, and wiped it on the back of her hand. "You're so tough," she said. "Beating up a girl. I been hit by professionals, though. You don't even make the minor leagues. That's why you're here, isn't it? Because you're not good enough for Just Cause."

Stefan's face grew dark and he squeezed his hand into a fist.

Sally stood her ground and let him come. "I said, you're a bootlicker."

As Stefan raised his fist to deliver a solid right cross, a hand intercepted his. Dannan had stepped forward and stopped him. "Goddammit, Dannan," began Stefan, but he trailed off when he saw the figure behind her.

Sally had seen Champion enter the room and made sure not to look at him as she goaded Stefan. Champion got a clear picture of Stefan losing control of himself. "Well," said Champion as if he were echoing Stefan. "Perhaps you'd care to explain yourself, Surfboy."

If Stefan's face had been dark before, a crimson flush overtook him and he looked like he was seconds away from exploding into little bits. "She attacked Skimmer. Broke her face. Sent her to the hospital."

"And why would she do such a thing?" Champion's voice was soft and dangerous.

"She came into my cubicle," said Sally before Stefan could answer. "I defended myself."

"Skimmer came into your cubicle," Champion repeated. "How odd. I don't recall asking her to do that. Surfboy, would you please clarify?"

"Okay, look, it's like this. I figured that she's got a useful power and it wouldn't hurt to learn a little more about all our new recruits. You know, taking initiative." If Stefan had been any stiffer, he might have turned to stone like Statuesque.

"Ah yes," said Champion. "I do appreciate initiative. But I can also appreciate defending oneself from an apparent attack. And I notice that Juggler here looks like she's been rather busy defending herself. I see some bruising and swelling around one knee, and a large bruise upon her cheek."

"She wasn't defending herself. That was . . . me . . ." Stefan's eyes widened as he realized what he'd just said. "Oh, shit."

"I see that we have a problem here, Stefan," said Champion. "And it's one that I find disturbing. Certainly there will be . . . incidents . . . as we train and grow as a family, but there are incidents . . . and then there is abuse." His voice grew soft. "It's so hard to tell who will thrive under training and who will grow power-mad. I had hoped you would be the former. It appears I may have been mistaken."

Stefan had been backing away slowly but steadily as Champion spoke and all at once he found his back against a wall, both physically and, Sally thought, metaphorically. "Wh-what are you going to do to me?"

"Do?" Champion crossed his arms. "What do you take me for, an old Republic serials villain? Or a James Bond villain, eager to dispose of his henchmen at the slightest provocation?" He shook his head. "First, I expect you to apologize to this young lady for your unprofessional and unbecoming behavior. Second, you are demoted from your current position. You will now train and dine with the others." He held out his hand. "Your keys, Stefan."

"I, uh, I left them in my room."

"Fetch them."

Stefan left the conference room at speed, not looking back once.

Champion reached down and offered Sally his hand.

Sally recalled Hector's lesson, and got to her feet on her own. If Champion was offended by her rejection of his help, he said nothing about it. "I apologize on behalf of the entire organization," he said. "There are bound to be some growing pains as we solidify our family."

"You keep talking about family and unity and stuff," said Sally, "but all I see is a bunch of second-stringers and scrubs. Nobody here is in any position to be saving peoples' lives. I mean, I can telekinese my juggling balls. How's that going to help anyone?"

"There may be ways yet you can help that you haven't yet considered."

Sally narrowed her eyes. "Like what?"

"You're observant, and quick to react to a perceived threat. You've got a natural resilience about you that can't be trained, and you're sharp. Those are qualities I look for in an officer."

"An officer? What is this now, an army?"

Champion shrugged. "Perhaps."

"An army implies that you have an enemy."

"As I said, you're observant and you're sharp. I'm excusing you from your morning training session, Juggler. Instead, I'd like you to come to my office after breakfast for a more in-depth interview."

"This is more than just name-rank-serial number stuff, right? Because I came here on the understanding that we were allowed a certain level of anonymity." Sally rubbed at her swollen cheekbone where Stefan had struck her. "I don't even know who you are. Nobody does."

"You may call me Enrique," said Champion. He offered his hand once more.

Sally shook it. "Lindsay. Nice to meet you, Enrique." She suspected *Enrique* was a name related to *Heinrich*, and that left only seeing his face as the last piece of the puzzle before she could confirm Champion was Heinrich Kaiser.

Perhaps she'd get to at her interview.

"Any chance there might be coffee at breakfast?" she said. She needed any edge she could get to keep her wits sharp when she stood before him for what was certain to be a grilling session.

"I'm afraid not. But I will have some tea in my office if you wish."

"Thanks, that sounds good, Enrique." Sally already knew she wasn't about to consume anything he handed her. And then the fear of nanotechnology hit her full force. What had he been experimenting with when developing his nanotech? Could he have been doctoring the recruits' food? For that matter, the entire headquarters could be permeated with the microscopic machines. They could be crawling all over and through Sally's body right then. It gave her cold sweats and she tried not to think about it.

"Do you need any treatment for your injuries?"

"No, I think I'll be okay. I just need to get some sleep. I'm more worried about Skimmer. I think I really hurt her."

"She'll receive the very best of care. If you learn one thing from this, it should be that Champions look after their own, because there may come a day when we cannot trust anyone but each other."

Sally didn't ask him to expand upon that. She felt like she'd pushed her luck far enough for the evening. She was exhausted to the point of becoming punchy, and she was terrified that she would say the wrong thing and give herself away. Instead, she thanked Champion for his concern and made a discreet exit.

When Sally returned to the cubicle farm, she found a couple of clusters of recruits huddled together in the near darkness, whispering to each other. She didn't see

Stefan anywhere and wondered if he was still going to get his private room. She was willing to bet that by tomorrow evening, he'd be down in the cubicles like the rest of them, and she was certain he'd be enjoying thin, bland oatmeal in the morning.

"What happened?" asked Particulate as Sally passed by him.

"Champion took care of it," she said. She didn't go into detail. She knew that the word about Stefan's demotion would get around soon enough.

"So what are we supposed to do now?"

"Go back to bed, I guess," said Sally, although she had no idea if that was the case. "We probably have a hectic day tomorrow, and it's already tomorrow. Know what I mean?"

"Yeah," said Particulate. "Good night."

"You too."

Sally returned to her cubicle. She wished she could lock herself in but the curtain provided no security whatsoever. Skimmer's blood still stained the carpeting on the cubicle walls, a grim reminder of how close Sally might have come to killing her. She shuddered, hoping she could get some cleaning supplies to take care of it. Jason wouldn't have been able to sleep knowing the stains were still there.

Sally gasped. Thinking of Jason almost caused her physical pain. She missed him so much. She had no way to reach him short of Vanitha delivering him a message, but she was nowhere to be found. She dug through her bag until she found the other three spheres. She set them up on the desk beside her bed. "Keep an eye on me, guys. I don't want any more surprises."

Then she laid down, squeezed her eyes shut, and sobbed into her pillow until she fell asleep.

Chapter Twenty-Three

"The secrets of slavery are concealed like those of the Inquisition."

—*Harriet Ann Jacobs*

**New York City, New York
January, 2007**

It seemed like Sally had only just fallen asleep when a voice roused her from a dream of Jason. "Good morning, Champions," said Dannan's voice over the PA. "Breakfast is in ten minutes." She sounded just as tired as Sally felt. Sally suspected most of the recruits were running short on sleep, a theory that proved itself as she trudged to and from the bathroom with the other girls.

Sally nearly fell asleep into her bowl of oatmeal. She'd doctored it as much as she could with the limited selection of condiments that were available. Anything to give it some flavor, she figured, even if said flavors didn't really go together. Fake maple syrup and Tabasco sauce? Bring it on. The slight queasiness the competing tastes brought into her stomach helped to bring her to a better semblance of alertness.

"That looks awful," said Kayla as she sat down beside Sally with a plain bagel and some individually-wrapped pieces of margarine.

"It tastes awful," said Sally, resting her elbow on the table and propping her head up on her hand. "But at least *awful* is a flavor."

"Yeah, the food here is pretty nasty. I hear they do that on purpose in the army."

"I thought an army was supposed to march on its stomach. Sun Tzu said that." Jack had made Sally read *The Art of War*. They'd discussed it at length and he'd tried to clarify some of the more esoteric theories within it that Sally didn't think were especially relevant in the modern era.

"Yeah, maybe. But my brother said they give soldiers shitty food so they all have something in common they can unite behind."

"*Give us flavor or give us death*," hissed Sally as if she were a French peasant standing atop the barricades, shouting at Marie Antoinette.

Kayla cracked a smile at that. "So the word came down. I'm running morning training and you're exempted from it. Surfboy's on cleaning duty. Busted all the way back down."

Sally shrugged. "Guess he shouldn't have let it go to his head."

"See that you don't let it go to yours."

"What do you mean?"

Kayla snorted. "Don't be naïve. It's pretty obvious Champion is interviewing you to take over Surfboy's position as his second-in-command."

"Why would he do that? I just got here. You've been here longer than me. Why wouldn't he pick you?"

"I've been here one week longer than you. We're all basically rookies here except for the Young Guns."

"Why not pick another one of them, like Bombshell or the Goth girl or that fast kid. What's his name?"

"Johnny Go. He's sick."

Sally shuddered, wondering if her friend was suffering from radiation sickness. She'd have to try to get word out to Grace. The more she found out during her stay with the Champions, the more she realized just how isolated the group had become. Champion was doing his level best to brainwash the entire group into his own private army. That was textbook Heinrich Kaiser, and Sally was going to do her best to prove it in her interview.

"I'm guessing he sees something in you that he hasn't seen in anyone else. You've made quite a splash in your first twenty-four hours here, and that's got his attention. It's up to you to see what you do with it."

"I guess so." Sally glanced up at the wall clock. "I guess I better go see him. I'm sure he looks down on lateness in a potential second-in-command."

"And everything else that isn't Champion perfection," said Kayla. "Good luck, Lindsay."

Sally scooped her uneaten oatmeal into the garbage and set her bowl in the large plastic tub for dirty dishes. Her appetite had vanished after just a few bites of her overly-flavored gruel. She walked through the headquarters to the front offices where Champion awaited her.

He wasn't in his office, but the door was open, so Sally stepped inside. She was tempted to do a thorough super-speed search, but couldn't be sure the room wasn't under surveillance, so she didn't risk it. Besides, Vanitha had certainly taken the time to do that earlier, and she hadn't reported anything of note. Sally's eye fell on a large ledger leaning up against one side of a mostly empty bookshelf. It called to her like a beacon, and it took all her strength to keep from grabbing and thumbing through it. It occurred to her that Kaiser was a child of the pre-digital era. He might be much more comfortable putting information on paper than into a computer, which might explain why Vanitha hadn't been able to find anything. Maybe she could sneak back in the evening and get a look, when she could have the spheres run interference and security for her. There was a phone on his desktop. She picked up the receiver for a moment and held it to her ear to listen to the dial tone.

Outside Champion's windows, she could see a construction crew hard at work erecting a second floor within the giant cage of steel girders. They were working fast despite the cold. And why wouldn't they work fast? They were most likely being paid very well.

A door along one wall opened and Champion stepped through it. He still wore his basic yellow bodysuit, but had dispensed with his cape and gloves. The omnipresent mask still covered his face, much to Sally's disappointment. "I apologize for my tardiness," he said. "I had a project that wouldn't allow me an early exit."

"It's no problem," said Sally. She gave the construction crew one more look before turning her attention to Champion. What had he been doing back in that other room? She wondered. Watching surveillance videos? Building nanotech? Or maybe it was just a bathroom, she considered.

"Would you like some tea?"

"No thank you, I'm fine. More of a coffee girl, really."

"I can't say I've ever developed the taste for it. But to each of us, our own poisons, yes?"

"I guess so." Sally wondered if she would be able to tell if he began to flood the room with radiation. Would she feel it? Or would she just start to sicken and die without any indication of the reason?

"Now then . . ." Champion pulled off his mask and set it on his desk. "Please, have a seat."

The move was so sudden and deliberate that it caught Sally by surprise. She hadn't really expected him to reveal his face so soon in the conversation, if at all, and it took every ounce of self control she had not to react when she saw Heinrich Kaiser smile. His white-blond hair was cut into a short crew cut, and his eyes were a piercing light blue, making him look like Hitler's wet dream of a perfect Aryan male. His handsome face was unlined, despite being chronologically more than ninety years old. Straight, white teeth sparkled at her, contained in his strong jaw. The way he stared at her made her wonder if he recognized her, or recognized some aspect of her. He'd seen her in Guatemala, and he was by all accounts brilliant and observant. Sally suspected the move with his mask had been calculated. He had hoped to get her to reveal something, some glimmer of recognition. Sally was grateful for the opportunity to sit in the chair facing Kaiser's desk.

He suspected her of something, of that much Sally was certain.

He sat at his desk, leaned forward on his elbows, and touched his fingertips together. "As I said before, I'm Enrique. And you are Lindsay, who calls herself the Juggler."

"I guess that means the introductions are out of the way," said Sally. "You look a lot younger than I expected. You come across like, well, kind of like my grandfather. But you look like you're in your thirties."

"It's not the years, as they say, it's the mileage," said Kaiser. "Tell me about your grandfather."

Sally shrugged. "He died like five years ago."

"My condolences."

"Thanks. It's not really a sore point with me, though. We weren't real close." Sally felt her nerves singing. Her more distant family hadn't been part of the personality architecture that Ment had built her. If Kaiser was going to ask about things like that, she was going to have to make up answers as they went along, and then she'd have to remember everything she said in case he went back to ask again. "But you didn't bring me in here to talk about my dead relatives."

"You're right." Kaiser went to retrieve the teapot as it whistled. "You're surprisingly self-assured for someone so young. How old are you?"

"Twenty-one."

"Perhaps you'd like something stronger than tea? I have a well-stocked liquor cabinet."

Sally crossed her legs and narrowed her eyes. She wasn't sure what game Kaiser was playing, but she could make up her own rules. "I've got a rule about drinking with older men."

"It sounds like that comes from experience."

"Look, uh, Enrique. You said I'm self-assured. Quit being so coy with me here. You brought me here for a reason. Quit wasting both our time and let's get down to it."

Kaiser smiled. It was the same expression he'd shown right before ordering Destroyer to kill Forcestar in Guatemala. "Yes, let's talk. I currently have an opening in my organization for a new lieutenant. I'm considering promoting you to that position."

"Why?"

"You're intelligent. You tell me why."

"Okay. You need someone smart, someone who's observant, someone who can follow orders and issue them when needed. You also need someone who's not going to jump to conclusions and start beating up your other recruits."

Kaiser raised an eyebrow. "Sometimes corporal punishment is the most effective means of control."

"Yeah, but you're trying to make a kinder, gentler version of Just Cause. I'm not saying we're all going to be fluffy bunnies and unicorns, but you want us to be approachable by the general public, as inferior as they might be. You have your command staff issuing beatings, you're going to make an army of skittish heroes who are afraid to act when called upon to do so."

"Very good. Go on."

Sally shrugged. She was afraid she'd already said too much, giving Kaiser something to work with. "I was a manager at a movie theater," she said. That was part of Ment's architecture; it helped her regain her composure. "I'm used to controlling a group of, well, assholes. You ever try to get high school kids to do anything when they couldn't give two shits about it? I know how to do that. I'm not afraid to fire people, and I'm not afraid to train them."

Kaiser laughed. "Very good. It seems you and I have some things in common. I, too, have spent a lot of time controlling assholes. Here's what I'm prepared to offer you. You can have Surfboy's old position of my second-in-command. Your responsibilities will include orientating the new recruits, overseeing training of those already integrated into the system, and ensuring that my philosophies are enforced."

"Yeah, about that. Most of these folks are just kids, really. Maybe not age-wise, but they're not experienced superheroes. Beating them down isn't going to make them into the elite unit you're hoping to achieve," said Sally.

"It's a time-tested military technique." Kaiser took a sip of his tea. "And one that works best on, as you say, kids. You have a different notion in mind?"

Sally shrugged. "You're the boss. I'm just calling it like I see it. You're going to have a lot of people wash out of your program if you're going to give them crap food, lousy accommodations, and brutal training. Is that what you want?"

"The sharpest blades are tempered in the hottest fire," said Kaiser. "I won't have a group of Champions who will fold under the slightest pressure."

"You want them to hate you?"

He smiled. "I don't particularly care if they like me or not. That's not my mission. I've disliked most of my superiors over time. And I'm sure you can say the same."

Sally nodded. She had nothing but admiration and respect—and even love—for those who'd guided her to become the hero she was. And not one of them had beaten her down. At least, not on purpose. Juice had laid her out pretty hard once in training, but that wasn't intentional on his part. She'd once heard her grandmother say that you could catch more flies with honey than with vinegar, although Sally had never understood what would be the good of a having a whole bunch of flies. She understood better now, and she could see that Just Cause and the Hero Academy were using a lot more honey than they were vinegar.

"What's in it for me?" Sally asked, making her voice drip with sarcasm. "Pay raise? Medical and dental? Keys to the executive washroom?" She nodded her head toward the door from which Kaiser had emerged.

He smiled again, this time without much humor in his eyes. "Perhaps later. For now, you'll have access to personnel files and website registrations." He held up a thumbdrive. "You can use the computer in here. I'll expect you to become familiar with my training techniques, the group of recruits, and their abilities. Devise methods that will help each of them maximize their power potential."

"Some of those powers aren't real useful," said Sally. "Even my own are pretty lame."

"I disagree. Telekinesis can be very useful, even at low levels. How would you use Particulate, or E-Dog?"

Sally wasn't aware she'd shared the name E-Dog with anyone. It made her nervous; had Skimmer gotten something from her mind after all and reported it to Kaiser despite her injuries? Or had someone arrived at it independently? She clamped down on her panic. Stay cool, she told herself. This was where she needed to be to bring down Kaiser, and she couldn't give him anything to grow his suspicions. "Well, I think they'd both be good in an infiltration situation. Particulate can sneak through tiny holes, and people tend to look at, say, a lost dog with more pity than suspicion."

Kaiser raised his teacup in salute. "Very good. I can see I've made a good choice." He leaned forward and set the thumbdrive on his desk before her. "I'm looking forward to seeing what you will accomplish as a Champion."

Sally took the thumbdrive and slipped it into the belt of her yellow bodysuit. "Yeah, me too."

"I have some work to complete. My office will be available to you later today. In the meantime, I'd like you to take the recruits who came in with you, plus two others that you pick, and train them."

"Train them to do what?"

"Whatever you feel would be the best. Show me what you can do. Dismissed."

Sally left Kaiser's office feeling both exalted and terrified. She'd managed to wend her way into his graces and been given access to his office and his computer. He'd handed her a thumbdrive that could be full of any amount of useful information. He'd placed a lot of trust on her.

That sudden trust was making her wary, though. What had she really done to earn such trust? She couldn't think of anything she'd done to place herself above reproach. That led her to one conclusion: Kaiser *didn't* trust her, and was giving her enough rope to hang herself if she proved untrustworthy.

It was a terrible spot to be in, and she didn't know what to do. She couldn't keep on taking his orders and training his soldiers and spinning her wheels, wondering when to act or what to do. She felt like she was trying to run on an ice rink, legs blurring at high speed without her making any progress. She'd put Vanitha into an equally untenable situation, expecting the Indian woman to act as her eyes and ears and giving little thought to the discomfort of being trapped inside a tiny sphere without access to the internet that was her home.

Even worse, she had a group of recruits that had suddenly become her responsibility, and she needed to train them not to just be heroes, but to be the *right kind* of heroes. She wasn't going to turn them into the unquestioning Nazis that Kaiser undoubtedly sought. She wanted them to be free thinking, willing and able to challenge orders that they felt were illegal, immoral, or incorrect. She'd received the best training possible first from her mother and grandmother, then from the Hero Academy, and then from the heroes of Just Cause. Her brain was bursting with the knowledge of what it took to be a hero. Surely she could find a way to pass that along to the others on her own terms, not Kaiser's.

"How did it go?" The voice made Sally jump. "Easy, girl," said Kayla. "I'm on your side, remember?"

"Yeah, we're all one big happy family," said Sally. She sighed. "You were right. He gave me Surfboy's job."

"So what are you going to do now?"

Sally's mind raced as she considered and discarded possibilities at high speed. At last, she determined the best course of action was business as usual for the time being, maybe with a bit more friendly twist than Stefan had managed. "Any word on Skimmer from the hospital?"

"I don't know. I haven't heard."

"Go find out how she's doing and report back to me. I feel terrible about the misunderstanding and want to know as soon as she's able to receive visitors or be discharged, whichever comes first."

Kayla looked taken aback, as if she hadn't ever been given orders before. She opened her mouth to say something, and Sally raised an eyebrow as if to say *You want to argue with me?*

"Okay," said Kayla. "I'm on it." She headed up toward the reception lobby.

Off to one side of the training area, Hector was badgering a group of trainees. Sally thought about pulling him aside and telling him to lay off, but she decided that despite his unorthodox technique, he had some valuable lessons to pass along. If he really hurt anyone, though, she was going to bounce his ass all the way to the street, body of nickel or not. She looked around for Dannan and Toxy, but didn't see them anywhere. Were they with Johnny, perhaps? There weren't that many places he could be in the facility that she wouldn't know about, unless it was behind one of the locked doors.

She also hadn't seen Stefan anywhere, and that was a little more bothersome. She knew that if nothing else, she needed to make sure that things were clear between the two of them. She spotted Particulate and called to him.

He flowed over in his trademark cloud and reformed in front of her. "What's up, Juggler?"

"Collect E-Dog and any two other recruits who don't have other duties and wait for me in one of the auxiliary conference rooms."

He saluted her. "You got it. E-Dog, huh? That's clever. I think he'll like it."

At last, Sally found Stefan, sulking in his private room. The bed was rumpled and he had a haggard expression as if he hadn't slept much at all after his run-in with her. She knocked on the open door. He looked up at her, anger sparking in his eyes. "What do you want?"

"I want there to be an understanding between us, Surfboy. I didn't come here to replace you or to make you look like a fool. You managed that all on your own."

"Is that supposed to make me feel better?"

"No, it's supposed to wake you up. Don't obey blindly, and don't let power go to your head. You seem like a nice guy, and you'd do better to treat folks with kindness instead of contempt."

He snorted. "Yeah, that's rich. Nobody ever took me seriously before this."

"Aren't you part of the Young Guns? Didn't you guys help save the world once?"

He shrugged. "We saved New Jersey, for what that's worth. But it was Mustang Sally who did most of it. I'm useless."

"You can fly. I can't fly. That's a neat power, no matter how high you can or can't go. And that's more than ninety-nine percent of the people on this planet will ever do. You're special, and you need to remember that. Champion's not right about everything, but he's right about the fact that people will look up to us. I don't know about you, but I'd rather be loved and respected than feared."

"Yeah, all right. I'll try. Sorry I hit you."

Sally grinned. "That's better. I'll be fine, thanks for asking. Now comes the bad news. I need you to clear out of here. This is now my office."

"You're making me move?"

"Just don't forget your red stapler," said Sally, and then instantly knew it was the wrong thing to say. It was a reference to the movie *Office Space*, which had been one of their favorites to watch in the Hero Academy dorms. Had Stefan made the connection? He picked up his bag and slung it over his shoulder and then turned to look at her. Sally knew what the male gaze felt like; it was like spiders crawling over her skin. What Stefan was doing wasn't appreciating her for her beauty. It was more like he was staring at a puzzle and trying to see the solution. "Surfboy," she said, trying to keep her voice from quavering. "Either ask me out so I can say no or leave, but the staring is creepy."

"Sorry." He floated past her and left the room.

Sally sank onto the desk chair and put her head in her hands. She was pretty sure she'd just been made.

Chapter Twenty-Four

"In dancing with the enemy one follows his steps even if counting under one's breath."

—*Breyten Breytenbach*

New York City, New York
January, 2007

Sally figured the best thing she could do would be to act as if everything was normal and Stefan hadn't actually figured out that she wasn't who she seemed. For all she knew, he hadn't, but she wasn't about to assume that she was safe. Not for a minute. She knew that she would have to try to solve the mystery of Kaiser's nanotech plan that night and call out the troops to take him down in one fell swoop.

In the meantime, she had been given an assignment to train some heroes, and she'd been thinking some on how she was going to do that without turning them into Nazis. She joined Particulate and E-Dog in the auxiliary conference room. They had pulled in two other trainees, a chunky teen who called himself Wire and a woman pushing thirty who introduced herself as Hover.

"Well, here we all are, then," said Sally as brightly as she could manage. "Everyone grab some chairs and tables and things and pull them out into the hallway."

"What for?" asked E-Dog, transforming himself back into his lanky human form.

"Training." Sally winked at him.

It took all five of them to move the heavy conference room table out into the hallway. Particulate discovered that it could split across the middle and that made it much easier to handle. Sally had the recruits place one half of the table right by the conference room door and the other at the far end of the hallway. She scattered chairs and side tables down the hall at random spots, sometimes right next to each other and sometimes with several feet between them. As they worked, the recruits whispered to each other in clear confusion about what this training was supposed to accomplish.

When the trainees had finished, Sally ordered them all to climb onto the table beside the conference room door. It was crowded enough that Hover used her powers, hovering in midair beside the table instead of standing upon it. E-Dog had to transform back into his dog form to make enough room for Particulate and Wire to balance upon it.

"Good," said Sally once everyone was situated. "Okay, this is a simple drill. Any of you ever play *The Floor is Lava* when you were kids?"

Wire and Hover nodded. Particulate looked confused and E-Dog tilted his head to one side in one of the most doggy movements Sally had seen him perform.

"Rules are simple. The floor of this hallway is lava. All four of you have to get to the other table over there. If all four of you don't make it, you lose and have to start over. Anybody touches the floor, you lose and have to start over." Sally stood in the doorway and crossed her arms. "Good luck."

"That's it?" said Wire, incredulous. "We're playing a stupid kids' game? I thought this was going to be some kind of actual training."

"Most kids' games are damn good training for real life," said Sally. "And if you can't win at what you call a *stupid kids' game*, then maybe you're in the wrong business. What's it going to be, Champ?"

Wire frowned. "Yeah, okay, whatever."

At first, the four recruits were unable to work together except at the most rudimentary level. Particulate could have easily traversed the hall from one end to the other with his powers, but the others' abilities weren't nearly as movement-friendly. Hover could fly, but she had no ability to move herself laterally. She could only go up and down. Wire could extrude thin wires from his body, draining his own mass to do so, but they weren't individually strong enough to hold his weight. And E-Dog was able to jump some of the distances between chairs that were too far for the others, but his claws scrabbled helplessly upon landing and often as not dumped him over onto the floor.

After the fourth time Sally sent them back to the start, Particulate said maybe they needed to change their strategy, and then the four trainees began to use their brains first and their powers second. Wire managed to push Hover across empty space with his extrusions. She and Particulate caught a jumping E-Dog. They used their powers to keep from falling to the floor while bracing him on his landing. Hover suggested to Wire that he extrude several wires together, lightening his mass considerably, and then helped him to braid them together to form a cable. She pulled herself along it until she was back beside his gaunt, emaciated figure. She strained and sweated but managed to lift him from the conference table, and then E-Dog and Particulate hauled the two of them over the gap by Wire's cable. They repeated the technique several times, growing more sure with each repetition, until at last Wire set foot on the conference table at the far end of the hall. The four recruits high-fived, excited at their success.

Sally felt elated at her success as a trainer. She thought about some of the training sessions she'd participated in as a member of Just Cause and considered how she might apply some of those techniques to her own group. She wanted to make sure that she was helping them to become *heroes* first and foremost, not *soldiers* like Kaiser seemed to want. To that end, she started presenting them with scenarios and had them talk over how they would resolve each of them. They discussed how to save people from a burning building where the stairs had collapsed, or what they could do if a plane crashed. Then, just to see how they might address things, Sally asked them how they might have stopped the oil tanker from crashing into New Jersey. Since none of them really knew how a ship worked, their ideas ranged from the improbable to the impossible. In the end, though, it got them all thinking about how to solve seemingly insurmountable problems, and by the end of the day, Sally felt proud of her charges. She hoped that by bringing an end to Kaiser's philosophical brainwashing that some of these recruits might actually be able to fulfill the idea of becoming Champions.

She caught Hector watching her train her group a couple of times over the day. When he saw her notice him, he nodded at her before returning to his own training sessions. She wondered if that meant he approved of her techniques or if he was just acknowledging her. She had an irrational urge to please him with her work. He was so angry at the entire world, it seemed, a veritable cauldron of seething rage that threatened to boil over at the slightest provocation. And yet, despite all that fury, he had some poignant ideas and thought processes that made sense to Sally at some level. Maybe she needed more pissed-off people in her life to give her a better sense of balance.

Sally ruminated on that idea as she ate a plate of tasteless pasta for dinner, twirling noodles idly around the tines of her fork. Kaiser may have been a billionaire thanks to his extended lifespan, but he sure wasn't investing any of it in decent food for his people. She felt eyes upon her and looked over to see Stefan staring at her from where he sat alone at a table. All the other recruits had shunned him, and her heart went out to him. He really was a nice guy, if a bit full of himself, and the way Kaiser had played him made her mad enough to spit nails, as her grandmother liked to say.

It was one more thing the long-lived German had to answer for.

Following the evening meal, Sally retired to her new office bedroom. It had a door that shut and locked, which made her feel safe almost for the first time since she'd arrived at Champions headquarters. She found the four orbs sitting patiently on her desk. As soon as she locked the door, Vanitha appeared in the room. Sally tossed her the sweatpants and hoodie she'd kept in her bag for the Indian woman.

"I listened in to your conversation with Champion," said Vanitha.

"Kaiser," said Sally. "His name is Heinrich Kaiser, no matter what he calls himself."

"I don't care if he calls himself Jesus Banzai Mohammed. He's setting you up. Giving you access to his office unsupervised? And a thumbdrive? He's setting you up to fail. He wants you to cheat."

"*It's a trap!*" Vanitha smiled, and Sally smiled back. It was nice that someone got her nerdier movie quotes for a change. "Look, I know it's a trap. That's why this is going to happen tonight."

"I don't get it."

"He's got to suspect me, and so he's expecting me to make a move tonight, because why would I wait?"

"Um, maybe because waiting would be the smartest thing to do?"

"No. Whatever he's working on, the longer we wait, the more chance he has of succeeding. So we move tonight. You raid the computer in his office and I jimmy the lock on that door."

"That computer's a cipher. Nothing on it."

Sally held up the thumbdrive. "There might be something on this. It might only be exactly what he said, but I'm willing to bet you're good enough to suss out digital fingerprints if he left some."

Vanitha nodded. "Everybody does. And if it's web data, I can backtrack a lot of it and maybe find his server. From there, I can find out a lot. It would be a lot easier if I had web access but this place is like a black hole."

Sally grinned. "There's a live phone in his office. That means we can connect you to the outside."

Vanitha's mouth fell open, aghast. "*Dial-up*? Why don't we get a horse and buggy while we're at it? Maybe a nice walking stick?"

"Look, it's the best I can manage, all right? I want you to take all the data on this drive and clear out. Get to a safe location, contact Jason and Jack, and tell them to rouse the troops. I want this place under Just Cause supervision by morning. I'll signal them when they need to move in."

"How are you going to do that?"

"I'll think of something. Jack's smart. He'll recognize it."

"What about Champion—er, Kaiser? If he's set a trap for you, he's going to make sure he's there for you to spring it. He's going to want to question you, and not in a nice job interview kind of way."

"I'm counting on that," said Sally. "I can't arrest him if he's not physically here."

"I'm not sure you can arrest him anyway. He's pretty badass, according to his file."

"Then I'll just have to be more badass than him. I took down the Archmage, and I took down Destroyer before that." Sally folded her arms, trying to sound more confident than she felt.

"And you had lots of help both times. Yes, I read those reports. I have a lot of time to sit around here reading when I'm not spying for you." Vanitha sounded bitter.

Sally squeezed her arm. "Vanitha, I am so grateful for your help. You are my ace in the hole here. They may suspect me, but nobody here could possibly know about you. You're going to bring in my backup, and you're going to work your magic to back me up yourself."

"How'm I supposed to do that with a fucking dial-up connection? This isn't 1995, Sally. The world runs faster than 56.6 kbps."

"My great-great-grandfather was a rider in the Pony Express," said Sally. "They could get mail across the country in ten days before there were telegraphs. They were the fastest thing in the world back then. My grandmother chose the name *Colt* because of them. And my mom was *Pony Girl* and I'm *Mustang Sally*. There are always going to be things faster than us, but nobody runs harder than we do. And we're not going to let something faster than us beat us just on pure speed, because we want it more." Sally folded her arms and fixed Vanitha. "And so should you."

"Damn it," said Vanitha. "You sound like a lame-ass life coach."

"Yeah, but did it work?"

Vanitha shrugged. "I guess we'll find out." She looked down at the four orbs. "*Once more unto the breach, dear friends.*"

"Shakespeare?" asked Sally.

"Yes. *Henry V.* Also a *Deep Space Nine* episode."

"I always liked *Star Wars* better."

Vanitha sniffed. "We can work together, I guess, but we can never be friends now." She winked at Sally and vanished, her empty clothes tumbling to the floor.

Curious and the other three orbs raised off the desk in formation, ready to go to work for Sally. "Stay close, you guys. I'm going to need you all for sure before tonight is done."

The four orbs spun once around her head, reminding her of how they used to encircle Evan's head. Then they dove into her hair, pressing themselves against the back of her neck, hiding beneath her thick raven locks.

"Good enough," said Sally. She gathered up a clipboard that she'd found while training her group. She only had a blank piece of paper to attach to it, but it was better than nothing. Jack had told her once that a clipboard was almost like a free pass into anywhere, if one carried it with confidence and purpose.

Sally squashed down any self-doubts and marched out of her office, heading toward the office where Kaiser had interviewed her that morning. If anyone questioned her, she had the thumbdrive Kaiser had given her to display as evidence when she explained that she was going to review personnel files at Champion's request. Nobody so much as blinked at her.

Particulate was on duty in the front lobby. "Hey, Juggler," he said. "Working late?"

"Yes," she said. For a moment she felt she needed to explain herself further, but realized that saying too much would be more suspicious than not saying enough. "I'll be in Champion's office. Let me know if any new recruits come in tonight, would you? I want to meet them."

"Sure thing." He yawned.

She went on into Champion's office. A moment later, she had the computer powered up and slotted the thumbdrive into a USB port. She lifted the phone receiver to check for a dial tone. The electronic drone reassured her. She returned the receiver to its cradle, unplugged the phone line, and plugged it into the back of the computer tower. "Okay," she whispered, and the four orbs flew out from beneath her hair. Curious set down right beside the tower. For a fraction of a second, Vanitha's nude form appeared beside the desk, and then vanished again as she inserted herself into Champion's computer.

"Okay, guys," said Sally to the other three orbs. "You see that door? I need to get through it. Can you drill out the lock or sever the hinges or something?"

Angry, Thinker, and Sneaky flew to the door and floated around its edge, shining lights along the crack and the handle as they determined the best way to proceed.

While the spheres went to work, Sally took the ledger down from the bookcase. She expected it to be blank, or perhaps to find a note to her inside it saying something like *I am very disappointed*, but instead two words handwritten in the center of the first page struck her.

Aurora aeterna.

She scrunched up her face. That was Latin, wasn't it? She had no idea what it meant. *Aurora* was that light in the sky from charged particles in the Earth's magnetic field. *Aeterna* looked like it might mean *eternal*. Light eternal? She turned the page.

"What the hell are you doing?"

Sally spun around to see Stefan floating in the doorway to the office. He looked angry and confused at the same time. Sally cursed at herself for letting her guard down even for a moment. She should have known he'd be suspicious of her, and by flying, he neatly avoided any footsteps that might give him away. "Surfboy, I can explain."

He floated into the office, his fists cocked. "All this, this is your fault. Things were running fine before you showed up."

Sally raised her hands, careful not to make any sudden moves. The three orbs that had been by the door took up protective positions around her, ready to defend against any moves Stefan might make. "Stefan, it's not my fault. It's not anybody's fault except Champion's. He's the one who made you act this way. It's not who you are, and we both know it."

He pointed at her. "Those are Orb's. I recognize them, even with those colored covers on them. Who are you? Someone from Just Cause?"

"It's me. Sally."

Stefan snorted. "You're too tall. And no offense, but your tits are way too big."

"We used to watch movies on Friday nights in the dorm because we didn't have anywhere else to go. You, me, and Evan liked the science fiction movies the best. Johnny and Dannan liked the action films. Shannon Tokugawa and Toxy liked romances, and we always made fun of them when it was their turn to pick. We used to quote *Star Wars* and *Ghostbusters* lines back and forth during passing periods. And I remember the one time you snuck up on John Stone and he almost knocked you through a wall." Sally took a hesitant step forward. "You've got a scar on your left hip from it." Sally moved in a blur, grabbing hold of Stefan's hands, and spun him around once at high speed. She stepped back as he floated to a halt. "You know me, Stefan. You once told me you couldn't believe I was sixteen because I had the body of a twelve-year-old boy. I hated you for that for months. *Months*, Stefan." She took a deep breath. "But I don't hate you now. I need you. I need your help."

Stefan's hands opened. "Sally? What . . . How . . ."

"Champion's not who you think he is. Stefan, he's almost ninety years old. He gained his parahuman powers in a secret German reactor project in the Forties. He helped build that one we took out in Guatemala three years ago. And now he's trying to build up another parahuman army. Stefan, he's a Nazi."

Stefan shook his head. "No. No, he's not. He's a good man. He's teaching us to be heroes."

"You already know how to be a hero. You're a graduate of the Hero Academy. Champion's real name is Heinrich Kaiser, and he's teaching you to be a Nazi." Sally waved away the floating orbs. She didn't want them between her and Stefan. There couldn't be any barriers between them if she was going to get him to trust her.

"No—"

"Everything he says is calculated to change your mind. He's got you convinced that you're better than anyone without parahuman abilities, right? He wants you to see Just Cause as the enemy. All this here is designed to set up his new Master Race." Sally took another step toward Stefan. He stank of nervous sweat and fear. "I'm here to stop him before he does something drastic. You can help me."

"I don't know." Stefan's hands fluttered around like he didn't know what to do with them. "He trusts me. He put me in charge. Nobody ever did that before."

"He did that because he understands your psychology better than anyone. You always wanted to be better, Stefan. You hate your powers—not because you have them, but because you think they're weak. Everyone here is like you. Low-powered. People who you think are beneath Just Cause's notice. Well, that's a problem, and I'm going to talk to Juice about it after this is done, because I see people here who truly want to help."

Stefan fell into the chair beside Kaiser's desk where Sally had sat that morning for her interview. "It's really you. God. What happened? How did I let this happen?"

"He's a master of psychological warfare. He's had almost a century to perfect it. Don't blame yourself. I certainly don't."

"You should. I hit you."

Sally shrugged. "You hit me in training at the Academy too. It's okay. I forgive you." She glanced down at the ledger on the desk. "You don't know what *Aurora aeterna* means, do you?"

"I think it means *eternal dawn*. I heard him use that phrase once."

"Do you know what it means?"

"No." Stefan put his head in his hands. "But I'll bet it's bad."

"I'd take that bet. We need to find out what it is, and stop it. Whatever it is, it involves nanotechnology, and he murdered Evan to keep it a secret."

Stefan looked up. There were tears in his eyes, and the muscles in his cheeks twitched from him clenching his jaw. "That son of a bitch. How could I have been so stupid? *Stupid!*"

Sally touched his wrist. "Don't beat yourself up, Stefan. Will you help me stop him?"

Stefan floated out of the chair and ran his fingers through his short haircut, the way he used to when it had still been surfer-long. "Yes. Let's make him pay."

Chapter Twenty-Five

"The great majority of parahuman abilities, like so many other genetic mutations, are fated to be evolutionary dead ends . . . But what of those that are not?"

—*Matasuko Musashi*

New York City, New York
January, 2007

"This isn't working," said Sally. She and Stefan were watching as the orbs attempted to bore through the door with miniature tungsten carbide-tipped drills. At first, Sally had thought the door was just heavyweight metal with a solid lock, but after several minutes of sparks flying and no significant progress, she knew that Kaiser had upgraded it far beyond normal security.

Stefan had bitten his nails down to the quick as he paced back and forth, floating a few inches off the floor. He kept looking back toward the door as if he expected Kaiser to come rushing in at any moment. "What are we going to do, uh, Sally?"

"For now, just call me Juggler. That's going to be easier for everyone. We need some help. Can you go get my training team from earlier today? And where's Dannan? We could sure use her muscle."

"She's probably with Johnny. He's been real sick."

"It's probably radiation sickness," said Sally. "The other crewmen who stayed abovedecks on the tanker suffered from it too."

"Then how come I don't have it? I was up there the entire time."

"I don't know. Maybe Kaiser drained any radiation out of you. Or maybe you're immune to radiation. Could be flight isn't your only power after all."

Stefan snorted. "Wow. Immune to radiation is so much better."

"Don't be cynical. You're too much of a goofball to go down that route. Bring Dannan and the others. And you might as well alert Toxy. And Kayla, now that I think about it. Hell, let's just call out all the troops, shall we? I want everyone who'll fit in this office or in the hall right outside as quick as possible. Dannan first, then the others. Sound the alarm."

Surfboy nodded, hesitated, and then saluted. "You got it . . . Boss." The air swirled around the office as he raced away.

"Follow him," Sally said softly to Sneaky. The ball left off its work at the security door and flew after Stefan. It wasn't that she didn't trust him, but she was afraid that Kaiser might have some sort of monitoring device on him and she wanted to know if Stefan might inadvertently compromise her mission.

She pulled out her phone and sent a text to Vanitha. *Where are you?*

Running down an ISP, was Vanitha's reply. *Tracing cell phone records. Alerting Just Cause. Shopping for shoes.*

"Shoes?" muttered Sally.

A whine of feedback came from the headquarters' public address, followed by Stefan's voice. "All Champions, uh, report to Champion's office immediately. This is not a drill. Repeat, this is not a drill."

Dannan appeared in the office doorway. "What's going on? Stefan said Sally was here and needed help."

"It's me, Yogurt. I'm in disguise, okay?"

Dannan squinted at her. "Sally? That's one hell of a good disguise."

"Yeah, tell me about it. Listen, I need you to trust me, okay? You already said you don't like Champion. This is our chance to prove that he's not what he claims. I need you to get this door open. You're the strongest one here. At least get a crack in it."

"For me, right?" A rush of sound like sand pouring through a funnel filled the room as Particulate reformed beside the desk. "What's going on?"

"Bad things," said Sally. "Sit tight."

Champions began to arrive in the office in twos and threes until bodies dressed in yellow and red leaned against all the walls. Hover and Stefan floated up near the ceiling to make more floor space. Dannan spent several minutes trying to shoulder the door open and had given up in favor of breaking the floor apart in front of it to get her fingers underneath it.

"You better have one hell of a good reason for doing this." Nickel pushed through the other recruits, his metallic skin gleaming under the fluorescent lighting.

"Motherfucker," Dannan grunted as she strained against the solid security door to no avail.

"Here, let me," said Particulate. He flowed under the crevice Dannan had created.

Nickel stuck his finger in Sally's face. "Explain yourself, *pendeja*."

Sally stood her ground. "Put that finger away before you lose it, and watch your mouth, *cabrón*. Yeah, I speak Spanish. Now shut up, and I'll explain."

Nickel backed down, muttering things in Spanish that would peel paint off walls.

The group of recruits quieted. "Ladies and gentlemen, you've been brought here to this facility under false pretenses, and I'm here to set the record straight. The man you know as Champion is a wanted international criminal named Heinrich Kaiser. He's been a war criminal and terrorist for seven decades."

"Fucking bullshit," said Nickel. "He ain't no seventy years old. He looks like a goddamn bodybuilder."

"Actually, he's more like ninety," said Sally. "He stopped aging in 1942." She folded her arms. "He was created by a Nazi experiment. He's been living their philosophy all this time, except he doesn't see the Aryans as the master race. He thinks it's parahumans. He's been trying to turn you all into Nazis."

A dozen conversations and arguments broke out amongst the recruits. They seemed to be split roughly half and half, with one group arguing the *I told you so* side, and the other taking the *I knew we were more special than the crunchies* talking point. While the discussion elevated, Sally took a moment to ask Dannan about the door.

"I can't open it," said the muscular blonde girl. "I hope you've got something else in your back pocket, because this is going to be a bust if you have to convince them all without evidence."

"Particulate? Can you open it from the inside?" Sally called.

His reply was muffled and she couldn't hear it over the sound of the escalating arguments. An angry shout made her whirl around. Two recruits had squared off and it looked like they were going to go at it. Tensions ran so high in the room that Sally was afraid the whole group would explode into a brawl. She was losing them.

Stefan and Hover dropped down from where they'd been floating above the group and physically shoved the two would-be combatants apart. "Knock it off," said Stefan. "You think this is a game?"

The security door swung open as Particulate figured out how to unlock it. He looked as if he'd seen a ghost. The arguments around the room died into silence as people saw the fear in his eyes.

"What is it?" asked Kayla into the awkward quiet. "What's in there?"

"I think he's gonna be sick," said Man of the Cloth.

Particulate became a cloud of particles and he flowed out of the room.

Sally pushed past Dannan to see what had freaked out the young Asian man, and then she stopped short, feeling her skin crawling as her accelerated perceptions took in everything in the small room.

A large Nazi flag dominated one wall of the small office, a map of the world on another, and a workbench crammed with equipment on the third. A large chair sat before the workbench, and next to it was a stack of glossy magazines spilling down, showing women in bondage, being abused, violated. A small end table beside the chair held an open jar of petroleum jelly, which made Sally's stomach churn. A rack on the workbench held row after row of small glass jars with rubber stoppers. If the number of empty spots corresponded with the jars, then some twenty jars were missing.

With a lump in her throat, Sally opened a small freezer that sat below the workbench. It looked like it belonged in a dorm room or a garage, and there she found a half dozen jars, rimed with ice and filled with what she knew had to be frozen semen. A handwritten date was scrawled upon each jar, giving mute evidence that despite being over ninety years old, Heinrich Kaiser was virile enough to fill two or three jars per day.

"God . . ." Dannan muttered, sounding like she was choking. "That sick bastard."

Sally shut the freezer door, as if blocking out the sight could help remove the unclean feeling permeating her entire body. She wished she had a hazmat suit to wear, because she didn't think there was enough soap in the world to scrub herself clean from the imagined biological contaminants in the room. Why was Kaiser saving and freezing his sperm?

And then, like when an optical illusion resolved itself into a comprehensible image, the last piece of the puzzle fell into place, and with it went the last of Sally's strength.

The room spun around her and then Dannan was holding her. "Hey, are you all right? What happened?"

"I think . . . I think I know what he's doing," said Sally. She stared at the world map on the wall. When overlaid with her notion of Kaiser's plan, it made sense in a coldly logical way. Major cities were marked with pushpins, either red or black. Lines connected the cities with what Sally figured were air routes. Where cities were given red pushpins, red highlighter overlaid the black lines leading from that city, with handwritten dates noted along them. He was tracking the spread of something, and Sally knew what it had to be.

"Let's get out of here," said Dannan, and she carried Sally out of the awful Nazi masturbation closet like a mother with a sleepy toddler.

E-Dog appeared beside Sally, a plastic water bottle grasped carefully in his jaws. He nudged it against her hand until she took it. "Thanks," he growled in his strange doggy voice. "Plastic tastes weird."

"Get him here," said Sally. "Get him here now."

"Happy to oblige you," said the sickly familiar voice of Heinrich Kaiser. Recruits shrank away from him as he floated into the office. He wore his Champion outfit, but hadn't bothered to mask his face, which meant he no longer cared if he was recognized. Energy limned his hands, and Sally knew he could unleash terrible death and destruction with that power, and there was almost nothing she could do to stop him.

Almost.

She was Just Cause, and she wasn't going to let him hurt anyone. She was faster than him, because she wanted it more.

Sally pushed herself away from Dannan to stand on her own two feet before the Nazi parahuman. "Heinrich Kaiser, you are under arrest for the murder of Evan Roberts. Stand down and cease any parahuman abilities."

Kaiser laughed. "On whose authority?"

"Just Cause." Sally blurted it out before she realized it was exactly what he'd wanted her to say.

"My friends, you see the enemy has come in through our gates here. She's eaten your food, slept in your beds, taken your positions," said Kaiser, eliciting murmurs from some of the recruits. "And what is this? A Nazi flag? Really, you couldn't come up with anything better to frame me? I'm disappointed. I would expect something more unique from what purports to be the greatest superhero team in the world."

"No, it's not like that," said Sally. How had he turned things around on her so quickly. "Stand down, Kaiser. You're under arrest."

"Show me a badge. Prove to me you are who you say you are."

Sally realized that she didn't have anything to back up her claim. She felt her ears get hot as she stood mute, unable to think of anything to say.

"I thought so. You must be new. Why would they send an inexperienced rookie here? Or perhaps you're on your own, trying to make a name for yourself to join Just Cause? Either way, young lady, it appears that you've bitten off quite a bit more than you can chew."

"The sperm, Kaiser. What's it for? Why are you saving it?"

Kaiser smiled. "I have no idea what you're talking about. I think it might be best if you left, young lady. Surfboy, will you please see her out? I'll restore you to your former position. I'm sorry to admit that she misled me."

Stefan looked at Kaiser, then looked at Sally. There was a cast to his jaw that made her wonder if he was considering the idea after all. He floated over to hover before Sally, staring down at her. She met his gaze, silently entreating him to choose the right side. He dropped to the floor and turned to face Kaiser, interposing himself between Sally and the Nazi. "No," he said. "She's right about you. And I trust her."

"So do I," said Dannan, moving to stand beside Sally. E-Dog sat on his haunches next to Surfboy and growled at Kaiser.

A cloud like a sandstorm swirled around to coalesce into Particulate. "Me too, you sick fuck."

Hover nodded her assent, and even Kayla stepped over to add her support.

Other recruits hung back, unwilling to commit to a side, or seemed to be backing Kaiser. "It seems that I was correct in my assessment of your leadership skills," said Kaiser. "What a shame you've wasted them on something like this when you could be commanding the Champions."

"Don't you mean your *master race*?" Sally's voice dripped with acid. "That's what you're all about, right? You're trying to make us better than normal people."

"I don't have to try. We already are better. Even the lowliest parahuman is like a demigod, and should be accorded the respect due to him or her. You Champions, here, now, are the future of the human race. My legacy begins with you."

The power flickered and the lights dimmed in the base. More fearful muttering sounded from the recruits and two of them lit up with their own internal glows.

The radiance from Kaiser's hands lit his face from below like a kid holding a flashlight under his chin to make scary faces. A flatscreen television mounted on one wall of the office lit up to display the familiar image of Kali as she stood upon her nightmare landscape.

"Henry, Henry, Henry," she said, waggling a scolding finger at him. "You have been a very bad boy."

"*Was ist das?*" murmured Kaiser, quiet enough that only Sally could hear him.

"You covered your tracks pretty well, but you can't hide from Kali. I found your workshop. Your *real* workshop. Not your little sperm farm."

Kaiser's demeanor changed. Suddenly he looked far less confident than he had. He glanced to one side as if measuring distance to his windows. Then he came to a decision and held out his hands. "I see. It appears you've outwitted me. I could irradiate this entire room and walk out of here as you all died, vomiting and shitting yourselves, but that's exactly what Just Cause would expect me to do. I don't plan to die a martyr's death. Perhaps someday, but not today." He lowered his head. "I surrender myself to your authority, Juggler."

"Wait," said Nickel, who seemed to be vibrating with barely-suppressed rage. "What's she talkin' about? Why you got a Nazi flag?"

"You needn't concern yourself, Hector," said Kaiser. "You have my trust. You will continue my work while I am a guest of Just Cause."

"I ain't no Nazi," said Nickel, clenching his fists. "Why you keepin' jizz? You some kinda pervert?"

"It's a biological weapon." Sally hoped that she was correct in her deduction. She couldn't afford to look like a fool in front of all the recruits; not if she wanted to sway them away from the spell Kaiser had woven with his oratory. "His legacy is going to be a master race of his own children. He's going to use nanotechnology to impregnate women all over the world."

Dead, horrified silence filled the office.

Statuesque fainted; Shouty Ed caught her before she hit the floor.

Kaiser clapped his hands together, softly, as if he were applauding a good putt at a golf match. "Well done. You're a credit to your species, young lady."

"That's the whole problem with you, Kaiser. You're putting all your emphasis on the *para* part of *parahuman*. We're *humans* first and foremost. All of us." Sally pointed at him. "Except you. You're just a monster."

Kaiser bowed. "My legacy, as I said, is secure. Now I believe you were going to arrest me. Take me away. Lock me up. I have all the time in the world."

"Hey, fucker," said Nickel. He grabbed Kaiser and spun the Nazi around to face him. "I got a little girl." He drove a hard fist into Kaiser's solar plexus, and with a startling wet sound, his fist burst through Kaiser's back in an explosion of blood, tissue, and shattered bones.

Chapter Twenty-Six

"Once you are dancing with the devil, the prettiest capers won't help you."

—*E. T. A. Hoffman*

New York City, New York
January, 2007

Stunned silence filled the air, marred only by the whistle of air racing out of Kaiser's ruined lungs and the patter of his blood pouring onto the carpet. Nickel looked horrified at what he'd done, while Kaiser only looked annoyed. Somebody retched as Kaiser collapsed into a motionless heap on the floor without another word.

Emotions screamed through Sally's mind. She knew she could have stopped Hector from delivering that killing blow. Aided by her accelerated perceptions and super-speed, there were dozens of things she could have done to bring the situation to a different conclusion. And yet, she'd stood by and let Kaiser die in a truly horrific fashion, and the prevailing feeling amid all the others was one of simple relief. Kaiser had been one of the world's true monsters, and she was glad he was dead.

On the heels of that thought came fear like an onrushing locomotive. What if he was emitting radiation now? What if he'd infected all of them with his nanobots? How much of the world had he already spread his tailored plague to? On top of it all, she knew Just Cause was racing in to respond to Vanitha's call for backup, and any minute they would arrive and things could go south very quickly if she didn't get the situation under complete control. She squashed her fear and self-doubt.

"Everyone, listen to me," Sally called out over the rising tide of fear amongst the recruits. "I am Mustang Sally of Just Cause and I am taking full responsibility for this incident. As far as any of you are concerned, I was the one who killed Heinrich Kaiser, and I did so to protect all of you. Stefan, get everyone out of this building in case there's a radiation hazard."

"You got it, *Boss*," said Stefan. He emphasized *boss* and Sally knew that he was accepting her command without question. His tacit endorsement would lend weight to her orders and she was grateful for it. "Come on, people, let's move."

"Just Cause is on their way," said Sally. "Wait for them. Tell them I want full medical examinations of the entire group, especially checking for radiation and nanotech infestation. Make sure nobody leaves before they've been cleared."

"We're on it, Sally," said Dannan. "Outside, everyone. Nobody leave. Your lives might depend on it."

"Not you, Hector," said Sally as Nickel made for the exit. "Go clean yourself up, first. Try to remove any evidence of . . . you know."

"Why? I ain't ashamed to have killed that son of a bitch." Nickel stood in defiance, drops of Kaiser's blood falling from his clenched fist.

"If you step out of this building looking like you committed a murder, Just Cause will have no choice but to arrest you. Using parahuman abilities to commit a crime is a federal offense. With the overwhelming evidence against you, you're going to go back to prison. And as you say, you've got a little girl."

"So what, you're going to take the rap for me? That ain't right, *chica*."

"Hector, I'm an officer of the law. I might get suspended and investigated, but Heinrich Kaiser was a very bad man, a known felon, and wanted for crimes all over the world. I'll be cleared." She pointed at him. "You won't be. You don't want this much heat. Let me take it. Wash your hands and go home to your little girl."

Nickel looked down at his gore-streaked hand. "I ain't no Nazi," he said, "but that fucker was right about you. I told you before, you got *cojones*. Respect." He nodded at her and then ran in the direction of the nearest bathroom.

A nude Vanitha appeared beside Kaiser's desktop computer. "Ah, shit," she gasped, and gagged at the reek of death.

"Thanks for your help, Vanitha," said Sally. "I couldn't have done this without you."

"Does it always end up this gross?" Vanitha dressed herself, grimacing every few seconds.

"Sometimes," Sally admitted. "Sometimes it's a lot worse, though." Her heart raced as she looked down at Kaiser's corpse. She'd seen death before, but it still frightened her. Even worse was her admission that it was growing easier for her to deal with it. Heinrich Kaiser had spent almost seven decades fighting his own war against the human race. Her grandparents had fought him after World War II, and she'd faced him herself before in Guatemala. It felt almost like vindication to stare at his body, but she knew what she had to do to make sure her story stuck. "Angry, come here."

The orb floated over to her.

"What are you going to do?" Vanitha spat to one side.

"Provide evidence." Sally took hold of Angry. "Sorry about this. Just remember this is the guy who killed Evan." She forced herself to overcome her revulsion and she pushed the orb into the gaping wound in Kaiser's chest. "Oh God . . ." Nausea threatened to overwhelm her as she pushed her hand into the hole, making sure the orb was well-covered in gore.

"Girl . . ." Vanitha turned green beneath her normal skin tone.

"Don't you dare puke." Sally gasped as she pulled her hand free. "Or I'm going to."

The office windows rattled as Sally heard the familiar whine of the *Rita*'s engines. Just Cause had arrived at last. She felt faint and wondered if she'd received a lethal dose of radiation herself, or if nanites were swarming through her uterus, seeking an egg to impregnate. She wanted to pass out but couldn't let herself stop yet. "You said you found Kaiser's lab. What was in it?"

"Machines to make nanites," said Vanitha. "He wasn't quite as nontechnical as he made himself out to be here. He had detailed files on his computer. He's, um, he made two different kinds of 'bots. One for men and one for women." Vanitha hugged herself. "He's going to sterilize men and impregnate women."

"The perfect genocide," said Sally. "Hitler would have been proud. Th-that map in his, uh, in there, it looks like he's spread stuff halfway around the world already. How do we shut them down?"

Tears rolled down Vanitha's cheeks. "I don't know. He didn't have any details about that. Why would he? This was his plan."

Panic hammered in Sally's head. How could they stop a nanotechnology plague? How could they fight a worldwide, microscopic menace? It would be like trying to shut down a virus like smallpox or AIDS, except that this plague wouldn't have any indicating symptoms. Every pregnancy that began after Kaiser began spreading his nanotech would be suspect. Even hers and Jason's future children might be Kaiser's instead.

Sally's legs gave out at last and she burst into tears. "I don't know what to do," she cried.

Then fucking give up, puta! It was almost as if Hector was standing over her, screaming at her face. No, she couldn't give up. She was in Just Cause, dammit. She was one of the world's greatest superheroes. They'd faced plenty of dire threats before and this one was no different. There had to be someone in the PRA files who could do something, someone who could heal the entire world.

And then it came to her, and it was like a knife twisting in her gut.

Sally wiped her eyes. "Vanitha . . . I need you to do one more thing for me, and then I'll never bother you again. I'm s-sorry I involved you in the first place."

Vanitha sniffled. "It'd be worse for everyone if you hadn't. Name it and I'll do it."

"Get onto the PRA servers. The private ones. I want you to get everything you can about one man and find him. Set up a meeting with him for me."

"Okay. Who is it?"

Sally spoke through clenched teeth. It hurt to even utter his name after the atrocities he'd perpetrated against her friends and family. "Harlan Washington. Also known as *Destroyer.*"

Harlan Washington had fought his one-man war against Just Cause since before Sally was born. He'd killed her father when her mother was seven months pregnant with her. He'd helped Kaiser build the

Guatemalan reactor, and he'd killed several of her friends and teammates when Just Cause took it down. He hated Just Cause with psychopathic passion, and every time he turned up, he added more names to the already-lengthy body count.

Only by making a deal with the devil could she hope to save mankind.

"Okay, I'll get back to you." Vanitha looked profoundly grateful to have an excuse to leave. She vanished into the computer, leaving her clothes in a pile on the floor.

"Sally? Are you in here?" Jason's voice was like a lighthouse beacon in a storm. And then he rushed into the room at no less than a dead run, and all she could think of was how badly she wanted him to hold her. He skidded to a halt as he saw the huge swath of blood across the office carpet and Heinrich Kaiser lying amid it, his chest a ruin. "Jesus."

"Jason?" Sally's lips quivered and she knew she was going to break down.

"Babe, what . . . What happened?" He hesitated instead of hurrying over to her and sweeping her up in his arms. That hesitation felt like she'd had her own heart ripped out.

She swallowed the painful lump in her throat. "He's dead, Jason. Heinrich Kaiser. I k-killed him."

Jason opened his mouth to say something but no words came out.

"I'm sorry. I'm sorry." Sally felt like she was miles distant from him.

Jack slipped past Jason with a Geiger counter. He gave Kaiser's body a cursory glance and nodded his satisfaction at a job well done. "Sally, you okay?"

"I'm . . . Oh, Jack, I'm so sorry."

"She's in shock," said Jack. "And no wonder. Jason, get her out of here and to triage. The room's clean. No radiation threat."

Then Jason really did sweep up Sally in his arms and she buried her face against his shoulder and sobbed. She was so relieved to have survived the ordeal, and yet she was terrified at the lasting legacy Kaiser had left behind.

It seemed like there were hundreds of people outside the Champions' headquarters building. Just Cause and the Second Team were both present, coordinating rescue and recovery efforts, assisting medical personnel as they examined the recruits. New York emergency responders swarmed all over the area. Sally caught a glimpse of Stefan and Dannan directing recruits into various examination tents.

Shortly, Sally found herself in a tent being examined by none other than Grace Devereaux. "Sally, please tell me none of this blood is yours," said the doctor.

"It's not m-mine."

"Thank God for that, anyway." Grace swept an instrument over Sally and regarded the results. "And you're not irradiated either. You're lucky. Your friend hasn't been quite so fortunate." She nodded to the next cot over, and Sally saw a thin boy with burns and pockmarks on the skin of his face and hairless scalp.

With a start, she recognized him. "Johnny. Oh no!"

"He's very sick," said Grace, "but I think I can pull him through."

Fresh tears washed down Sally's face. "I'm sorry."

"You need rest, my dear, and a familiar body. Minerva is waiting for you." Grace raised a hypodermic, squirted a few droplets into the air, and then without fanfare stuck it into Sally's shoulder.

The last thing Sally saw was Jason's face, before her surroundings blurred and darkened and she slept.

Some time later, she awakened in her own body, in the medical wing of the Second Team. She ached all over, as if she'd suffered a bad case of the flu. But the legs that felt like she'd run an eighteen-hundred mile marathon were hers. Gone were the gigantic breasts, leaving her with her much more sensibly-sized B-cups. Her unbraided hair spread around her shoulders like a blonde haystack. It was such a relief to be back to herself that she cried soft, thankful tears.

Grace bustled in from another room and smiled at Sally. "I thought you might be awake. It's uncanny how Minerva can pinpoint things like that."

Sally wiped her eyes. "She's amazing, that's for sure."

"You're pretty amazing yourself. You took a horrible risk going into that situation."

"I wasn't going to make anyone else take it. How long have I been out?"

"About sixteen hours."

"Was there any radiation from Kaiser? How about his body?" Sally kicked off the thin sheet over her and fingered the cotton nightgown she wore with distaste.

"No, Sally. You need to take it easy. You've had some terrible stresses upon you, both physically and psychologically, and I can't let you go dashing off." Grace put a gentle but firm hand upon her shoulder.

"Am I . . . am I . . ." Sally couldn't bring herself to say the word *pregnant*. The thought of that was horrifying.

"You're not pregnant. None of the women in Champion's organization were. In fact, aside from being scared about what comes next, every one of those recruits is unharmed. The Young Guns have been very helpful in keeping everyone settled down and figuring out what to do next."

"How's Johnny?" Sally could still see his emaciated face and skin covered with sores when she closed her eyes.

"He's very sick, but Minerva is helping me to treat him. I'm not sure how she does it, but after her fixing Jack and transforming you, I'm willing to let her try her own abilities in addition to what medical treatment I can provide."

Sally nodded. "Good. But you haven't said. Am I full of nanites?"

Grace's smile disappeared. "Not full, no. But we found some in a scan. They're in your uterus. I'm not sure how to remove them without a full hysterectomy."

Sally's heart began a rapid tattoo against her rib cage. "If they're in me, they're in everyone. And they're spreading around the world. Oh God, Grace, what do we do?"

"I've got a team of engineers, doctors, and a few parahumans that might have useful abilities working together to develop a cure."

"How long is that going to take? You said I'm not pregnant, but what if they're just waiting for me to, you know, ovulate?"

"Sally, we're doing the best we can. If you become pregnant, and it becomes apparent the fetus was conceived through Kaiser's nanotech, there are . . . other options."

Sally swallowed a lump. "You mean an abortion."

"Yes."

Sally felt lost, like her mind was fragmenting in a thousand directions. "Is Jason here? Can I see him?"

"I'm sorry, dear. He's still in New York helping to sort things out. He promised he'd come back with the Second Team as soon as they return. However, if you feel up to it, you have a visitor." Grace adjusted Sally's IV drip.

Gentle warmth started to spread through Sally's body and she knew Grace had given her a mild sedative. "Yeah, all right. Where else am I going to go?"

"You can come in for a few minutes," Grace said to someone out of Sally's field of view.

Heavy footsteps on the floor sounded and then Juice pulled up a chair and sat down beside Sally's bed. "Hi, kiddo."

"Hi, Boss."

"I wanted to come here to commend you personally. You solved the murder of one of our own, you broke open a mystery that nobody else could crack, and the only body I have to write up belongs to the culprit." He smiled. "These things usually end up with a lot more dead and injured people, and anytime they don't, I call that a successful mission."

"What's going to happen to the Champions?" asked Sally. She found that she was already missing the earnest trainees like E-Dog and Particulate. She wondered if there was a place in Just Cause for them.

"Well, that's something that will take some time to figure out. Despite being brought to New York under false pretenses, most of them seem to be of the mindset that they really *do* want to be heroes."

"But not part of Just Cause."

"I'm not going to say no out of hand, because my world is bigger than Just Cause alone. There's room for private teams, like Divine Right, the New Guard, and the Lucky Seven. I don't see why the Champions couldn't find a way to move forward with their big dreams. It seems like Surfboy and Bombshell especially are optimistic about building a team in New York. Maybe we could set up some sort of minor-league arrangement for superheroes, like they have in baseball and hockey. Give people who want to use their powers a support system that allows it. Give Just Cause the ability to call them up for specific purposes." He rubbed his chin and Sally could see the wheels turning beneath his bald scalp.

Sally yawned. Her feet and hands seemed like they were tremendously far away from the rest of her. "That's a good idea."

"I'm considering making a fairly large change in the organization of Just Cause as well. The world is changing and I'm not sure we can afford to be quite so exclusive in our membership. There are perhaps hundreds more parahumans across the country that should really be part of the organization, so we can best utilize their abilities."

"Sounds like . . . you've . . ." Sally yawned again. "I'm sorry. Sleepy."

Juice smiled and brushed her hair away from her face. He bent over and kissed her forehead. "I'm proud of you, Sally."

Sally slept.

Chapter Twenty-Seven

"The problem with parahumans is that we can't always solve every problem with our fists."

—*Dr. Danger*

Richmond, Virginia
January, 2007

The next time Sally awakened, it was dark outside and the lights were dimmed in the medical wing. At first she wasn't sure why she was awake, but then she saw the blue glow of a laptop reflecting off Vanitha's face. The young woman sat hunched over the computer, a blue ethernet cable running from it to a wall jack. "Hey," she said.

"Hey." Sally sat up in her bed. She felt much better than she had when Grace had given her the sedative. She'd always healed quickly, thanks to her parahuman metabolism. Even the shock of Kaiser's death seemed more of a distant memory than fresh wound. Vanitha was dressed, so she'd been there long enough to find clothing. Why did she have a laptop? She couldn't have brought it with her. It would have already needed to be present for her to materialize. Someone had aided her in her arrival. "Let me guess. Minerva?"

"No. Your friend Macey. And your fiancé is waiting outside to make sure that doctor doesn't interrupt."

"Jason's here? Baby?" Sally whisper-called.

Jason stuck his head in the room just long enough to grin at Sally. "Hey, babe. Take care of your business." He disappeared back out into the hall beyond.

Sally looked at Vanitha. "What business?"

Vanitha turned around the laptop to show the screen to Sally. It displayed a map with an address highlighted in Philadelphia. "I found your guy Washington. It wasn't easy. He's good."

"Is that where he lives?"

"No. At least, I don't think so. But that's a coffee shop where he's going to meet you."

Sally swung her legs down to the floor. Cold air flowed down her bare back as the nightgown threatened to open. She didn't care. She yanked the IV out of her arm, wincing at the sharp pain. Not wanting to take the time to look for bandages, she pressed the sleeve of her nightgown against her elbow to stanch the flow of blood. Her fast healing would take care of it in short order. "When?"

"Jeez, you don't fool around, do you? Good thing, too. He said he'll be there five hours from now, and he'll wait for you for five minutes before he leaves."

"You only gave me a five minute window?"

"You're Mustang Sally. The Fastest Girl in the World. If you can't make a five minute window five hours from now, you don't deserve the title."

"Who else knows?"

"Nobody. Not anyone in Just Cause. Not your doctor. Not even Juice."

"Good. I'm going so far out on a limb here with a big saw that I don't want to risk anyone else."

Vanitha grinned. "And on that note, I'm out of here. See that this laptop gets back to me. I hate loose ends. Let me know if you cure the nanotech plague. I'm not ready to bring anyone's bastard into this world. Not now, not ever." She vanished into the laptop. The Kali image obscured the map for a moment before it, too, disappeared.

Sally took a deep breath and steeled herself. She didn't want to tell Jason the whole truth at first because he might try to stop her, and she couldn't let anyone interfere with her meeting Harlan Washington. He might be the only one who could save her and possibly every other woman on the planet from bearing Heinrich Kaiser's children.

She peeked out the door. Jason was lounging in an overstuffed chair he must have brought from the Second Team's rec room, playing a handheld video game. It looked comically small in the giant paws of his hands. Sally couldn't believe he could press all those buttons accurately with his thick fingers, but he seemed to be doing well. "Hey," she said softly.

He looked at her and gave her one of his grins that made her weak in the knees. "Well, if it isn't the future Mrs. Tibbets. What are you doing out of bed, babe?"

"You know how you said for me to take care of my business? I still have some left to finish." Sally felt her ears burning.

"And you can't finish it in your hospital bed? I get it. Anything I can do to help?"

His easygoing manner was like soothing balm on the burn of her heart. "Jase . . . I have to go do something kind of . . . well, I think you'd disapprove. But it's something that could make a difference or the better in our lives. Really, in everyone's lives."

"It's about the nanotech, isn't it?"

"Yes." Sally felt like she was dangerously close to breaking down in tears once again, and she gritted her teeth against them. "I can't tell you, though. Not yet. If someone asks you, you can't tell them what you don't know."

He stood and put his arms around her. "Babe, I trust you, no matter what. Just be careful, okay? I just got you back."

She wanted to disappear in them forever, and only pulled away with extreme reluctance. "I promise I'll come back. The entire population of Deep Six couldn't keep me away from you longer than I have to be gone."

Jason bent down and kissed her. "I love you."

"I love you too." She turned away before she talked herself out of going after all. "Cover for me. I'll be back as soon as I can." She trotted down the hall and by the time she reached the corner, she was already warming up for a sprint.

She'd packed her cold-weather costume when she came out to Virginia, and she slipped into it in a half-dozen seconds. As she laced up her boots tight in front and in back, the thermal underlayer was already growing warm. She'd need every erg of that warmth for the wind chill, because Philadelphia was two hundred and fifty miles away, and she wasn't planning to get there by any other method besides her own two feet. She pulled up her cowl and strapped the goggles and rebreather over her face. Her overcoat got rolled up into as tight a ball as she could manage and shoved into a reinforced backpack which had been designed to survive her high-speed travel. Gloves completed her ensemble and she took a moment to look at herself in the mirror.

Crap. She'd forgotten to braid her hair. She'd have a nightmare of frizzed split ends by the time she arrived in Philly. To hell with it, she decided. Maybe she'd cut her hair to a shorter, more sensible length for a speedster.

The last thing she did before leaving was to shut off the GPS locator in the collar of her suit and to set her phone on top of her suitcase. She'd made a promise to meet Washington under a flag of truce, and she couldn't honor that promise if Just Cause tracked her down and turned up in full force to try to apprehend Destroyer.

She left the Second Team's headquarters at a sensible ninety miles per hour, well ahead of anyone who might want to ask questions. Once she got to the highway, she really opened things up and poured on the speed. Even at the late hour, traffic was still heavy, and she could imagine people freaking out as the crimson-and-yellow blur flashed past in the breakdown lane. Reports would be made, and eventually someone in Just Cause would figure out where she'd gone. By that time, she hoped to be done with her meeting.

Rate of speed was something Sally understood very well, and she could tell when she passed two hundred, then three hundred miles-per-hour. She held her speed down below four hundred. After all, she'd just been in a hospital bed a few minutes ago. As much as Sally had trained in sprinting, which was often the best use of her abilities in deployment situations, she'd spent equally as much time working on endurance running. At the most extreme, she'd once run all the way across Mexico from Guatemala to wind up in her hometown of Phoenix. She and Jason had looked it up on a map and they figured that she'd covered somewhere between twenty-three and twenty-five hundred miles. It had taken her about ten hours and she'd been beyond exhaustion when she crawled up onto her mother's front porch.

During normal training, she was able to run between three and four hours at a stretch at a comfortable pace of two hundred miles-per-hour. That was a good time for a marathon runner, and could just about take her into an adjacent time zone. On her trip to Philly, she was traveling twice as fast, but didn't think she'd tire herself out. Besides, she'd be early enough to have a cup of hot chocolate to drive away the chill from her bones. The wind of her passing tore at her, threatening to shred any unprotected seams in her costume. Only the thermal lining of her suit kept her from freezing solid at that speed.

It felt good just to run. She hadn't for such a long time. Her muscles ached from the welcome exertion.

She'd never been to Philadelphia, and had to slow down to highway speeds so she wouldn't get lost. The joke in her family was that they might be lost, but they were always making excellent time.

At last she came to a halt outside the coffee shop that Vanitha had identified for her. It was barely six in the morning and they had just opened. Sally ducked around the side of the building, removed her overcoat, and put it on over her costume, buttoning it up high enough to cover the horse-head insignia over her chest. Her yellow boots clashed with the cranberry-colored coat, but it couldn't be helped. She stripped off her gloves, goggles, and rebreather, and stuck them into her backpack. Her hair, as she feared, was a frizzed-out mess. She looked like she'd used an entire bottle of hairspray to give it volume as she checked her reflection in the shop window. Again, it couldn't be helped. She went inside. Having a good ninety minutes to kill before her five-minute window to meet Washington arrived.

Her perceptions shifted into high gear as she stepped into the coffee shop, and it wasn't until she saw the middle-aged black man with short graying curls sitting in a corner booth with his back against the wall that she realized why she'd gone into a defensive mode. His gaze bored into her like he was shooting lasers from his eyes. With glacial slowness, he raised a cup of coffee to his lips, never once looking away from her.

Sally's heart raced as she looked upon the man who'd killed her father and so many of her friends; the man who'd tried to kill her. He didn't look like the vicious, evil killer that had plagued Sally's nightmares for the past couple of years. He looked . . .

He looked *old*.

Sally knew he was in his mid-forties. His face was starting to develop age lines, his hair was graying, and he had a paunch that she'd never imagined. He almost looked like somebody's kindly grandfather instead of one of the most hunted criminals in the entire world. Except for that gaze, Sally thought, which looked like it belonged to a psychopathic serial killer.

Nevertheless, she'd made the overture to him and she knew she had to follow through. She sped her perceptions back up so she could interact with him better. She walked across the coffee shop and sat down in the booth opposite him, not waiting for him to invite her to join him.

"You're early," he said evenly.

"So are you," she retorted.

"Salena, Salena . . . This was your idea. The least you could do is be civil with me. You look cold. Might I suggest a mocha latte? They're quite good here."

"Thanks." Sally ordered one from the waitress who flounced over to take her order and then flounced back to the barista bar to make it.

"I've spent many years making myself very difficult to find. You can imagine my surprise at being contacted by your friend Kali. She was very insistent, and I'll admit you've piqued my curiosity. You wouldn't go to all this trouble simply to entrap me. So why are we here together?"

"What do you know about nanotechnology?" Sally's nerves sang as she sat across from her enemy.

"Quite a bit, actually. I spent a couple of months working on the Combat Training Facility crew so I could reverse-engineer some of the Just Cause nanotech. Fascinating place. I see why you train there. And were I looking for long-term work, the salary and benefits are top-notch."

Sally's mouth dropped open in shock. "You were *working* there?"

"Your security could stand to be overhauled. Really, you should be embarrassed at how easily I infiltrated there. I had ample opportunity to take my revenge upon you and yours."

Sally's latte arrived. It smelled delicious but unlike Jason, Sally couldn't drink super-hot things and had to wait for them to cool off like mundane people did. "Why didn't you? Hasn't that been your thing since you were a kid?"

Washington sipped his coffee. "Priorities change. I decided to focus my attention elsewhere, and so far it has been a good decision."

"I'm grateful for that, anyway."

"Which isn't to say that I may not take up my war against Just Cause again in the future. But for now, I have other projects. I suggest you plan accordingly."

Sally ignored the not-so-veiled threat. "Did Heinrich Kaiser ever consult with you about nanotech?"

"Interesting. Yes, as a matter of fact, he did. He became quite enamored with it after Guatemala. We spoke several times about it. I take it you've had some recent contact with him? How is the dear old Nazi?"

Sally crossed her arms. "He's dead."

"Not by your hand? No, I can see that much on your face. You're far too heroic to be a killer, Salena."

"I can see you've got me all figured out." Sally touched her hot chocolate to her lips. It was still too hot to drink. She felt like she had snipers training their sights on her from all directions. Everything she knew about Washington told her that he'd have no compunctions about attacking her right there in the middle of an innocuous Philadephia coffee shop. Something about his demeanor made her feel like she was in terrible danger. He'd had three years since she'd destroyed his last set of powered armor in Guatemala. That was plenty of time for him to have upgraded, and she trembled to imagine what new devastating technologies would be incorporated into his next suit. "But let me tell you something about your friend. He's loosed a plague on the world. A nanotech plague. I've seen the map. The spread has already begun. We can't stop it."

"And what is so terrible about this plague that you've swallowed the last vestiges of your pride to come crawling to me for help?"

"The nanites are carrying his genetic material. He's going to impregnate women all over the globe. Imagine a world populated with Heinrich Kaiser's children. All of them will be dominant carriers of the MK gene. A lot of them will have parahuman abilities." She leaned forward, trying somehow to convey to the psychopath in front of her that he should give a shit. "And they'll probably all live for a very long time. Imagine a world where those children come to power. You think it'll be a very nice place? Because I think it's everything that Hitler ever dreamed of, and now it's coming to pass."

Washington sighed. "That's a lovely story, but I fear I have other pressing engagements and I'm not going to waste my time any further with your nonsense." He stood, pulling a knit cap over his head. "I came here under a flag of truce, but the next time I see you, I'm going to make you pay for destroying my suit." He turned to leave.

"You don't have anyone you care about, Washington? No wife? No children? What about your sister? She's probably still young enough to be fertile. How'd you like to be an uncle to one of the Nazi Youth?"

Washington froze. Sally didn't know what part of what she'd said had gotten to him, but he sat back down. "You want me to stop this plague? What makes you think I could do it, even if I cared to?"

"You're smart. Smart with machines. You're a parahuman like me. Your gift is with machinery, like mine is with speed. If anyone can counter this contagion, it's you."

"And what's in it for me?" He smiled.

Sally shivered. His smile was even more frightening than the normal dead-eyed expression he wore. "Name your price. If it's at all in my power to grant it . . ." She swallowed painfully, her mouth suddenly gone dry. "I will."

Washington rested his elbows on the table and touched his fingertips together. "I'd need to see samples of Kaiser's work before I answer. After all, it wouldn't be fair for me to exact a price from you and then be unable to fulfill my end of the bargain." He smiled again. "That would be wrong."

"They're in me. I'm infected with them." She swallowed her fear. "You can take samples."

He sniffed in disdain. "I suppose. Come outside."

Sally narrowed her eyes. "Why?"

"If you'd rather me examine your nanotech here on the table, we can do that too. I don't particularly care."

"Oh." Sally left a twenty dollar bill on the table and followed Washington out of the coffee shop. He sauntered out like he didn't have a care in the world. And why would he? *He* wasn't risking an unwanted pregnancy. He didn't even seem like he was worried about a double cross. He *knew* something that Sally didn't, and that made her very nervous.

It had begun to snow, but the shiver in Sally's bones didn't come from the cold as she and Washington walked around the side of the coffee shop to the alley access. She knew she could outrun him if needed, but he'd doubtless thought of ways to get around that. All she could hope for was that his personal sense of honor or whatever would keep him from lashing out.

"Open your coat," said Washington.

Sally shivered. "Right here?"

"I'm not going to ogle you, child. You're not my type. I'm old enough to be your father. Heh." He smiled suddenly. "In a way, I guess I am."

"What?!" Sally couldn't believe what she'd just heard come out of his mouth.

"Who's had more of an effect on your life than I have? Everything you are today is because of me. If that doesn't make me a role model, I don't know what does."

The very thought made the hot chocolate in Sally's stomach roil and threaten to come back up to decorate the coffee house's brick wall. "No. Just . . . no."

He shrugged. "Suit yourself. You'll see it that way someday, I'm sure. Now open your coat."

Sally choked back her fear and unbuttoned her overcoat. Even though she was wearing her costume beneath it with its built-in armor, she felt horribly exposed. When she'd been in her altered body, with those ridiculously giant breasts, nobody stared at her with the same intensity that she saw in Harlan Washington's face. He touched his hands together and then pulled them apart with something between them. A round transparent membrane of some kind stretched between his forefingers and thumbs, as if he were holding a lens frame on the edges. Sally gasped as she realized the membrane seemed to be emerging directly from his skin. "Wh-what is that?"

He lowered the membrane to hold it over her lower abdomen. Images appeared upon it. "I've been dabbling in some nanotech myself. That's why Kaiser consulted with me, I'm sure. Hmmm . . ." He moved the membrane across Sally's belly, examining the images that appeared upon it. "There they are, the little lovelies. They're all spread throughout your uterus, waiting for their opportunity."

Sally felt queasy. She knew they were there, but she felt like Washington was gazing into more than just her body, but into her soul. "C-can you stop them? Can you make them go away?"

Washington raised his hands away from Sally and spread them further apart. The membrane grew, as did the image on it. A wry grin crossed his face. "Ha. Yes, I recognize this design. That sly old bastard stole my work."

"You were going to unleash a plague?"

He snapped his hands back together. When he separated them, the membrane was gone. "Nothing so petty, I assure you. I have greater aspirations than that old fucker ever could imagine." He stuck his hands in his pockets. "The problem with wanting the world is what the hell do you do with it once you've got it? I don't need the headache."

Sally buttoned up her overcoat as quickly as she could. Anything to put one more layer of protection between her and one of the world's most dangerous men. "You've seen the nanotech. Can you stop it or not?"

Washington smiled. "Of course. I'll need a week to culture the batches and then I'll send them to Just Cause to distribute them. You'll get to be the heroes for the entire world once more. At least, you will be for this week." His voice dripped with sarcasm. "And as for my fee?"

"Yeah? What do you want?"

He told her.

Chapter Twenty-Eight

"Be careful what you wish for, you may receive it."

—W.W. Jacobs

Denver, Colorado
February, 2007

Vanitha delivered the vial from Harlan Washington in person. Sally held it up to the light, looking at the gleaming, swirling particles that flowed through the vial like graphite and glitter. "So this is it, huh?"

"That's what he said."

"Why you?" asked Sally.

Vanitha looked at the ground as if she could slip into it and disappear. Sally knew that she could have vanished into the workstation near them without answering the question, but she chose to remain. "He's, um, I impressed him. When I found him."

"He hired you." Sally didn't make it a question.

Vanitha nodded. "Just to set up his systems. It's a good gig. Worth more than anything else I've done in five years. Plus it's challenging, you know?"

"No, I don't know. But it's your life and your career. You have to do what you think is best for it."

"Look, I'm sorry. I know he killed your dad, okay? But this has nothing to do with you, Sally. I'm not doing it to hurt you."

"Maybe you shouldn't have told me at all, then." Sally stalked away to stare out the window at the bleak, brown winter Colorado landscape outside headquarters. It would be another month and a half before it turned green, briefly, and then dried out as summer set in.

"You deserved to know. You went way out on a limb for everyone. The whole world owes you a debt. And so do I. I don't want to be pregnant with a fucking Nazi baby." Vanitha moved to stand beside Sally.

Sally looked at Vanitha. "You're welcome."

"If it makes you feel any better, I'm leaving a handful of backdoors into his system. He'll find three of them, but I'd stake my reputation that he won't find the other two."

"You're not risking your reputation with Destroyer, you're risking your life," said Sally.

"Somebody has to. You're going to need to find him again someday for something. Even if it's for something just as petty as revenge."

"Petty?" Sally felt her temper spike. She forced herself to take a deep breath. Vanitha was not her enemy, and she needed to remember that. As she calmed down, she saw something in the Indian woman's face. "God, you *like* him."

"What? No. Not like that. I . . . *admire* him. What he can do with machinery. I understand it. It's like what I do with computers."

"Just make sure that admiration doesn't get you into trouble. He's a devious son of a bitch who's killed a lot of my friends and family in a temper tantrum that's lasted thirty years."

"What did it cost you, to get him to work for you?" Vanitha asked in a soft voice, barely above a whisper.

"I don't want to talk about it." Sally looked away from her.

"Suit yourself."

After a moment, Sally turned back to Vanitha, but all that she saw was a pile of discarded clothing.

Sally delivered the vial of nanites to Grace Devereaux, who had been working day and night with a brain trust of nanotech engineers to try to develop a cure for the plague. The Just Cause command center had been monitoring media from around the world, watching carefully for any indications of mysterious pregnancies, but so far no news had developed. Grace theorized that the Champion Plague, as it had become known amongst Just Cause, was only targeting parahuman women. "It makes sense, given his obsession with parahumans as the Master Race," said the doctor. "The MK gene is dominant. By mixing his own DNA with those of female parahumans, he's ensuring all his offspring will be carriers, and likely have active abilities. He could increase the percentages of parahumans in the general population by a thousand percent or more."

The fear of that unintended pregnancy had made Sally had resist sex with Jason. She was terrified that the act would somehow trigger the nanites in her womb, even though Grace had assured her the two were mutually exclusive. It was straining their relationship, which was making Sally's daily duty on the team that much harder to maintain.

"What is this?" Grace asked Sally when she handed over the vial.

"The cure."

"It is? Where did you get this?"

"A . . . friend."

Grace folded her arms. "And this so-called friend happens to be an expert on nanotechnology? And he or she isn't already here?"

"Yes. And no. I believe him, though."

"How do you know it's the right design? We've run simulation after simulation and can't find a surefire method to knock out the Champion Plague."

Sally touched her own belly. "Try it on me."

"Sally, I'm not going to just inject you with strange nanites that we haven't tested or even examined yet. We don't know what kind of effects there will be. We have to test—"

"Grace!" Sally grabbed onto the doctor's arm. "Please! Test them on me. I know they'll work. What's the worst that can happen? I'll die. It's better than carrying a mongrel Nazi baby instead of Jason's."

"Sally, there are always other options," said Grace.

"Not for everyone. What if you're wrong and the Plague is infecting all fertile women in the world? You can't perform enough abortions for that. Nobody can." She raised Grace's hand and unfolded the doctor's fingers from around the vial. "But this can. This can stop it all before it starts. Please, Grace. Do it for me. Do it for everyone."

Grace reached up and wiped tears from Sally's face. "All right."

Under Grace's careful monitoring, Sally learned that Washington's nanites located, latched onto, and broke apart all the Champion nanites, and then dissolved themselves into their harmless, component molecules. "You're clean," Grace announced three days later after she'd run an exhaustive series of tests on Sally. "Not a single bug in your body. I hope you're right about this stuff."

"I know I am." Sally dressed herself and left the room in the medical wing as Grace issued orders for the cure to be duplicated and distributed according to the map Kaiser had left in his office. Sally stopped off by Johnny Go's room. Grace had brought him to Just Cause herself so she could better monitor his recovery while she worked on the Champion Plague cure.

Johnny smiled as Sally stepped into his room. He looked much better than he had a month previously. The sores the radiation had left upon him were healing, and although he was going to bear scars from them for the rest of his life, it was, as he said, far better than the alternative. Fine dark peach fuzz covered his scalp as his hair was starting to come back. "Hey, Sally," he said as he thumbed his cell phone. "Doc says I'm doing great and should be out of here in a week or so."

Sally sat down beside his bed. "I'm really glad to hear that. I was so worried about you."

"You and everyone else. But I'm a superhero. That means I'm going to live forever." He grinned. "Besides, I wouldn't want to give that bastard the satisfaction. I'll die someday, but it'll be with my boots on, saving the world."

"Better than being shot by a jealous lover at age eighty," said Sally.

Johnny chuckled. "Dannan, Toxy, and Stefan all say hello."

"Are you texting while you're talking to me? That's so rude."

"I'm multitasking."

"How are things going with them in New York?"

"It's a rough go. They've still got people showing up expecting to become Champions, even though they took down the website. Stefan is doing his best to run things. He's got that girl Kayla helping him out." Johnny grinned. "He hasn't said, but I think they hooked up. The PRA is getting them some funding to operate but it's taking time to get there."

"I'll talk to Juice. Maybe he can expedite things."

"I doubt it. Government isn't known for moving at the speed of anything faster than stalled."

Sally strained her voice to do her best James Earl Jones impression. "*Perhaps I can find new ways to motivate them.*" She finished with a credible Darth Vader breath.

Johnny giggled. "Darth Sally. That's awesome."

Sally sobered. "Any word from Hector?"

"Nobody's seen or heard from him."

"Maybe that's for the best. If he turns up, though, make sure he knows that I'm grateful to him and that I think there's a place for him in the Just Cause organization somewhere."

"He's a killer, Sally. And from what I heard from the others, a real asshole."

"I think Just Cause needs more killers. And more assholes. We can't be so far elevated above everyone else. We're supposed to be protecting the world, but we can't get so wrapped up in that task that we lose sight of everyone we're protecting. And if that means we open up our ranks, or make ourselves more accessible, or whatever, we need to do it. Juice said a minor league. Like in baseball or hockey."

"Maybe that's the niche the Champions can fill," said Johnnny. "I hope so. There are a lot of them who really do want to help, and it's better than them never using their powers for good, or turning to crime."

Sally squeezed Johnny's hand. "Get better soon. I'll check in with you later. Tell the others I said hi."

"Will do. And when I get out of here, first thing I'm doing is racing you."

Sally snorted. "*You* might be racing, but *I'll* only be jogging." She left and went to find Jason.

He was in the gym beside the Combat Training Facility, straining against a machine that was giving him enough resistance to feel like he was bench pressing five tons. He must have been exercising for a long time, for the entire room smelled of his musky sweat and the equipment was damp with humidity. Sally watched the way his arms quivered as he raised the reinforced titanium bar back up to its fully extended position. He sat up, pulled a towel from the rack beside the weight machine, and wrapped it around his neck.

"Hi," said Sally.

He stiffened. "Hi. Uh, how are you?"

She smiled. "Cured."

His discomfort disappeared and his sweet lopsided grin returned. "Yeah?"

She didn't care that he was slick with sweat. "Yeah." She pulled off her top and launched herself at her fiancé.

His arms went around her. "I missed you."

She didn't care that they could be walked in upon at any moment. "I missed you too."

"I love you, babe."

"I love you too."

And for the moment, Sally didn't care that she owed Destroyer a favor of his choosing, to be called in at any time.

ABOUT THE AUTHOR

Ian Thomas Healy dabbles in many different genres. He's a ten-time participant and winner of National Novel Writing Month and is also the creator of the *Writing Better Action Through Cinematic Techniques* workshop, which helps writers to improve their action scenes.

When not writing, which is rare, he enjoys watching hockey, reading comic books (and serious books, too), and living in the great state of Colorado, which he shares with his wife, children, house-pets, and approximately five million other people.

Visit www.ianthealy.com for more information.

ABOUT THE COVER ARTIST

Irshad Karim is a digital illustrator based out of Ottawa, Canada. While largely self-taught, he has reinforced his knowledge with courses at Concept Design Academy in Los Angeles, and studied under entertainment industry professionals such as Kevin Chen, James Paick, John Park and Peter Han. More of his work can be seen on his online portfolio, www.irshadkarim.com.